CLASSIC SCIENCE FICTION

The First Golden Age

Classic

SCIENCE

FICTION

THE FIRST GOLDEN AGE

Edited by Terry Carr

HARPER & ROW, PUBLISHERS

New York, Hagerstown, San Francisco, London

Grateful acknowledgment is made for permission to reprint:

"The Smallest God" by Lester del Rey. Copyright 1940 by Street & Smith Publications, Inc. Copyright renewed 1968 by Lester del Rey. From *Astounding Science-Fiction,* January 1940. Reprinted by permission of the author and his agents, Scott Meredith Literary Agency, Inc., 845 Third Avenue, New York, New York 10022.

"Into the Darkness" by Ross Rocklynne. Copyright 1940 by Fictioneers, Inc. From *Astonishing Stories,* June 1940, by permission of the author and his agent, Forrest J. Ackerman, 2495 Glendower Avenue, Hollywood, California 90027.

"Vault of the Beast" by A. E. van Vogt. Copyright 1940 by Street & Smith Publications, Inc. Copyright renewed 1968 by A. E. van Vogt. From *Astounding Science-Fiction,* August 1940, by permission of the author and his agent,

continued on next page

Designed by C. Linda Dingler

Library of Congress Cataloging in Publication Data
Main entry under title:

Classic science fiction.

    CONTENTS: Del Ray, L. The smallest god.—Rocklynne, R.   Into the darkness.—Van Vogt, A. E.   Vault of the beast. [etc.]

    1. Science fiction, American.   I. Carr, Terry.

PZ1.C5645   [PS648.S3]   813'.0876   74–1798
ISBN 0–06–010634–4

78 79 80 81 82 10 9 8 7 6 5 4 3 2 1

CONTENTS

For Lynn Hickman, Alva Rogers and Bob Silverberg,
with gratitude

CLASSIC SCIENCE FICTION
The First Golden Age

INTRODUCTION

by Terry Carr

In the fifty-plus years since science fiction became a discrete literary genre, many changes have marked its history. We've had periods of economic boom and bust, of innovation and consolidation, of emphasis on magazines or books. Writers, editors, artists have come and gone; dominant themes changed from space travel and robots to atomic power or genetic engineering, ad infinitum. The changes usually came gradually, so that they could be seen clearly only in retrospect; and even now, different readers come up with varying interpretations of the many periods through which science fiction has passed.

The one era of sf's history about which all readers agree is that of the early 1940s: it was such a remarkable time for science fiction that even the most critical admit that it was a "Golden Age." Those few years between the end of the Great Depression of the 1930s and the chaos of World War II produced an explosion of new science fiction magazines, new writers, ideas and techniques; the results were sensational then and they remain so today.

Simply citing a few names is enough to identify this period in science fiction: Robert A. Heinlein, Theodore Sturgeon, L. Ron Hubbard, Clifford D. Simak, A. E. van Vogt, Henry Kuttner, Lester del Rey, Fritz Leiber, C. L. Moore, L. Sprague de Camp, Isaac Asimov . . . Actually, it's difficult to confine such a list to only a *few* names, for there were so many writers then who were either new to the field or just beginning to show the full range of their abilities.

Usually the sf historian who wants to sum up the Golden Age of the early 1940s resorts to just one name: John W. Campbell, Jr.

Campbell took over the editorial reins of *Astounding Stories* in 1938 and immediately began making changes that established the magazine as pre-eminent in the field. He had already been *two* of the most popular science fiction writers of the 1930s. Under his own name he had written a series of galaxy-spanning space opera novels after the manner of E. E. Smith, and as "Don A. Stuart" he'd published a number of moody, atmospheric stories of the far future that showed he was interested in exploring new science fictional territory. He stopped writing shortly after becoming *Astounding*'s editor, but his belief that "even the youngest of our readers are mentally older than has been believed" was implemented even more broadly in his editorial work. He changed the title of *Astounding Stories* to *Astounding Science-Fiction* with the March 1938 issue and, by means of thoughtful letters and long discussions with authors, he induced a revolutionary maturation in science fiction. Beginning writers such as Heinlein and Asimov were guided by his ideas and criticisms, and established writers like Clifford Simak and Jack Williamson were inspired to new heights. (Indeed, Simak had entirely lost interest in science fiction for four years, till Campbell's policy brought him back to sf writing.)

Having quit writing himself, Campbell fed ideas for stories to many of his writers. The details of how he suggested the idea for Asimov's "Nightfall" will be told later in this book, and it's already well known that Heinlein's "Sixth Column" was based on a story Campbell had actually written but had never published. Lester del Rey has said that "nobody has any idea of how many of the stories in [Campbell's] magazine came from ideas he suggested, but a group of us once determined that the figure must be greater than half." Cleve Cartmill, who lived in California, relates that Campbell "wrote his writers at great length and in detail. I have letters from him about story ideas that add up to wordage equal to the wordage of the finished stories."

Campbell was clearly the single most important influence in this Golden Age, but we're left as always with the question: Did the leader produce the era, or did the era call forth the leader? Donald A. Wollheim has some interesting thoughts on this; he says of the sf writers of the early 1940s that "they were actually the first generation of writers who had grown up on science fiction, had been grounded and, as it were, schooled in science fiction and hence were able to utilize this in advancing further. . . . this generation of writers reached their twenties in time to write for Campbell when he . . . was waiting and looking for better stuff. Campbell became an editor when the field itself came of age."

There's a lot of truth here. The first all–science fiction magazine, *Amazing Stories*, had been launched in 1926, just fourteen years before the start of this Golden Age. Virtually all of the major writers of the early 1940s had begun reading science fiction when they were ten or twelve years old, so by 1940 they were well into maturity; they had grown up reading Weinbaum, Keller, Smith (E. E. and Clark Ashton), Williamson, Hamilton, Breuer and, yes, Campbell—so now they were ready to add their own contributions to the field.

In addition to the new writers, there were the editors. Raymond A. Palmer at *Amazing Stories* and *Fantastic Adventures;* Frederik Pohl at *Astonishing Stories* and *Super Science Stories;* Mort Weisinger at *Startling Stories, Thrilling Wonder Stories* and *Captain Future;* Donald Wollheim editing *Cosmic* and *Stirring Science Stories;* Robert Lowndes with *Future* and *Science Fiction Quarterly;* and more. They had all been fans before they became editors. John Campbell too had been a fan as much as a writer in his early days, sending letters of criticism and praise to the magazines.

It was the second generation in science fiction, and there were now people writing and buying science fiction stories who were determined to fulfill the dreams they'd had as teenaged readers.

The time was right. The United States was finally lifting itself

out of the economic disasters of the 1930s, industries were flour-
ishing and science was the wave of the future. The New York
World's Fair of 1939, avowedly intended by Big Business to
"show off the marvels of its industrial technology," featured
General Motors's *Futurama,* which drew crowds of thousands
every day to view the "world of 1960," with emphasis on super
express highways. Visitors received buttons reading, "I have
seen the future." (This exhibit, by the way, included a movie
puppet named Pete Roleum, an oildrop-headed fellow who
gave an alarming demonstration of the desolation that would
soon reign in a world deprived of oil.)

But there were more ominous signs for the future: World War
II had already begun in Asia and Europe. Japan had invaded
China and was enjoying increasing victory there; the Axis pow-
ers of Europe, principally Germany and Italy, were conquering
nation after nation. In 1940, they overran Denmark, Norway,
Belgium, Luxembourg, the Netherlands, Greece, Yugoslavia,
Hungary, Bulgaria and Rumania. All British forces were driven
from the continent, and France sued for armistice in June.

The United States had been following a policy of "isolation-
ism," hoping to stay out of the war, but by August this officially
ended when Congress enacted a law requiring alien residents
to register with the government, and approved this country's
first peacetime draft.

On December 7, 1941, Japanese air forces attacked the U.S.
naval base at Pearl Harbor, Hawaii; a declaration of war against
Japan came the next day, and within a week Germany and Italy
declared war on the U.S., which responded in kind. 1942 saw
Japan capture the Philippine Islands, after which the U.S. government began its "internment" of Japanese-American citizens. United States counterattacks began in the Pacific and in
North Africa, and in November 1942 Congress voted to lower
the draft age from twenty-one to eighteen.

This was a grim background for science fiction's first Golden
Age, and the war's effects on sf will be seen throughout this
book. The war affected all the arts. Popular songs of the period

included "The Last Time I Saw Paris," "This Is the Army, Mr. Jones," "When the Lights Go On Again," "Praise the Lord and Pass the Ammunition!" and "We're Going to Find the Fellow Who Is Yellow and Beat Him till He's Red, White and Blue." Major books included *For Whom the Bell Tolls* and *See Here, Private Hargrove;* in the movies, *The Great Dictator* and *Mrs. Miniver* were important full-length productions, while documentaries such as *Battle of Midway* and *Prelude to War* won Academy Awards, as did a Walt Disney cartoon, *Der Fuehrer's Face.*

The effect of the war on science fiction pervaded every aspect of publishing. Frederic Arnold Kummer, Jr., published a story as early as the beginning of 1940 in which he felt it necessary to change a German scientist named Schmidt to a Dutch one named Tromp. Robert Bloch recalls that the publishers of *Amazing Stories,* fearful of charges of anti-Semitism as a result of Nazi persecution of the Jews, changed a character named "Gorilla Goldfarb" to "Gorilla Gabface."

There were a great many science fiction stories whose plots grew directly from the war: Nazi scientists inventing machines to aid the Axis, time travelers from the future returning to 1942 to aid the Allied cause, German agents allying with alien invaders of Earth to help them destroy all but the "super race." There were also stories that attempted to comment on warfare from a future and saner viewpoint:

. . . that strange, horrible practice men had engaged in for centuries . . . What was it—this practice which ran through all the dealings of the dawn men, right up through the 20th Century? Oh yes, that was it— a little word: war.

I knew that it was not the common people of Jupiter's moons who wanted war—the rank and file never want war until their leaders wave the hot red flag of Jovian, or Venerian, or Aryan superiority.

Typically, it was John Campbell who came to a pragmatic conclusion about the stories in his magazine; in a 1942 editorial he wrote, "There is . . . a pretty good probability that a large portion of the material to be published in the near future will be laid in the far future. The devices of 7000 A.D. can reasonably be presumed to be based on principles so far extended from our known data that good guessing won't be interference with National Defense."

(However, this consideration didn't prevent Campbell from publishing, two years later, a story by Cleve Cartmill whose speculations about atomic bombs were so close to the work then being done at the Manhattan Project that Campbell was visited by U.S. military agents demanding to be told how he or Cartmill had obtained this information. Campbell was able to show them papers in scientific journals available to all that had made the guesswork easy; he also convinced them that if science fiction magazines were prohibited from publishing stories about atomic research, that could tip off the enemy to our government's serious involvement in the subject.)

World War II had much more influence on this period of sf history than simply suggesting plots for writers; in truth, the war was as much a cause of the Golden Age as was Campbell, or second-generation writers and editors. The United States had suffered through a decade of economic depression until U.S. manufacturers realized that the outbreak of war overseas offered a burgeoning market for war materiel; as a result, war-connected industries and even those that were only secondarily involved in armaments, shipping, food supplies, communications and military clothing were able to gain significant profits years before the United States itself was officially involved in warfare. Jobs were becoming available again even in the late 1930s, and wages were beginning to go up.

The publishing industry quickly benefited from increasing prosperity in the U.S. In 1939, ten U.S. science fiction magazines produced fifty-three issues; by 1941 there were fifteen magazines totaling eighty-seven issues. But the numbers began to decrease as soon as the U.S. entered the war: by 1943 we were back to eleven magazines and fifty-seven issues.

The decline didn't occur because of poor sales. On the contrary, Robert Lowndes remembers that "war conditions made every pulp magazine that could get paper a profit-making proposition." But paper had been rationed, so publishers cut editorial and typesetting costs by stopping production of their less popular magazines and concentrating all of their paper allotments on their top sellers. For some publishers, Western, detective or other genre pulps sold more than did their sf magazines, so marginally profitable magazines such as *Future* and *Science Fiction Quarterly* were suspended. Other publishers had strong entries in the sf field, and these were retained. Though Ziff-Davis ceased three-quarters of their pulp-magazine production, they continued to publish *Amazing Stories* and *Fantastic Adventures*.

The war also brought rationing of gasoline and rubber, so travel became difficult. This had the effect of preventing writers in other parts of the country from visiting New York editorial offices, so Raymond A. Palmer was able to gather a group of steady contributors for his Chicago-based *Amazing* and *Fantastic Adventures*. Robert Bloch says, "From where I stood (Milwaukee, in those days) it seemed to me that sf writers could be roughly divided into two groups—the Eastern-based majority, who contributed the bulk of material published in New York, and the second-class citizens like myself who found it more convenient to sell to Ziff-Davis in Chicago. . . . Of course there were exceptions . . . but those of us who lacked contact with an idea-dispenser like Campbell were at a distinct disadvantage." C. L. Moore, who lived in New Jersey then, remembers that she never wrote for *Amazing* because "It was way out yonder in Chicago, and that was too far, that was beyond the bounds of human thought."

Palmer tried to lure some of the New York authors to his magazines by employing David Vern as a New York–based associate editor, but Vern—a teenager who wrote sf under the pen name "David V. Reed"—wasn't noticeably successful, perhaps because he too had difficulties communicating with the home offices in Chicago. Once, in fact, he tried to send a tele-

gram stating "SHIPPING CORPSE WHO WALKS AT NIGHT TO RE-
PLACE LABORATORY MONSTERS," but Western Union refused to
transmit such an ominous message until he convinced them
that he was an editor and the telegram referred to titles of
manuscripts.

This fragmentation of the science fiction community led to
the formation of a number of informal groups of writers in
various cities. New York City, the hub of the industry, had at
least three writers' circles, with some overlapping. The authors
who wrote for *Astounding* constituted one such group, running
into each other at Campbell's office or being invited to his
home; science-fictional ideas were discussed at length and very
critically. One such gathering included John Campbell, L. Ron
Hubbard and R. D. Swisher. Hubbard, a prolific pulp writer and
later the founder of Dianetics and Scientology, was then estab-
lishing himself as one of *Astounding*'s star writers; Swisher was
a knowledgeable fan who had been on the faculty of M.I.T. for
over a decade.

F. Towner Laney, who wrote about the meeting a decade
later, said, "It seems that Hubbard had gotten some story idea
involving a city suspended in the sky, and was discussing the
pseudo-science he would use to suspend it there. Campbell and
Swisher were having a field day showing L. Ron why his theories were untenable. As fast as they'd demolish a Hubbardian
idea, he'd come back with another one. At the end of four or
five hours, Hubbard's city was still in the sky with its colors
flying merrily."

Another group met every Friday at Steuben's Tavern in mid-
Manhattan. These were mostly the writers whose stories appeared in *Startling* and *Thrilling Wonder Stories:* Manly Wade
Wellman, Henry Kuttner, Edmond Hamilton, Otto ("Eando")
Binder, Malcolm Jameson, science fiction's premier agent Julius
Schwartz, and of course the *Startling* and *Thrilling Wonder*
editors Mort Weisinger and Oscar J. Friend. Discussions covered every conceivable subject, but the talk most frequently
turned to science fiction, and many of the stories of the authors
present were plotted and discussed at the table.

Alfred Bester, who joined this group when he was a fledgling writer, remembers that "Once I broke Kuttner up quite unintentionally. I said to Weisinger, 'I've just finished a wild story. ... It's awfully long, 20,000 words, but I can cut the first 5,000.' Kuttner burst out laughing." (Then as now, sf magazine writers were paid by the word, so for one to volunteer to shorten a story by 25 per cent must have seemed truly silly to a working author such as Kuttner.)

A third New York City group was the Futurians, which had begun as a fan club a few years before but quickly became a group of writers when three members became editors of sf magazines: Frederik Pohl, Donald A. Wollheim and Robert W. Lowndes. They bought many stories from each other and from their friends in the Futurians. C. M. Kornbluth, James Blish, Richard Wilson, John B. Michel and Damon Knight made their first sales to these magazines. Even the illustrations were often done by people in the Futurians's wide circle of friends; Damon Knight did much of his early professional work as an artist, and Hannes Bok's drawings and paintings were featured in all the Futurian magazines.

This seeming favoritism was largely a result of financial limitations. Pohl, for instance, had been hired by Popular Publications, one of the biggest publishers of pulp magazines. Popular paid at least one cent per word, which was comparatively high in those days, but they decided to launch a "bargain basement" line of pulps that would pay half a cent per word. They invented a supposedly separate company called Fictioneers, Inc., with a different address, and it was for this company that Pohl worked. Most pulps then sold for fifteen or twenty cents a copy, but *Astonishing Stories* went onto the newsstands selling for only a dime. (*"10 STORIES 10¢,"* they advertised.) Pohl's total budget per issue was $405 when he began—for stories, covers and interior art.

(Compare this with the budget for *Amazing Stories* the same year: $825 per issue for stories and artwork. *Amazing* sold for twenty cents.)

When he assumed the editorship of *Future,* Robert Lowndes

too was able to pay just half a cent per word—but the payments from *his* publisher weren't made when the stories were accepted, only after they were published. Even then the authors sometimes had to wait for their money. Fritz Leiber remembers that he was paid a hundred dollars for a 20,000-word story in *Future*, in four monthly installments of twenty-five dollars each, after publication.

Donald A. Wollheim's budget made these editors seem like plutocrats. He was allotted no money whatsoever to pay authors and thus had to get stories from friends and writers who were unable to sell them elsewhere. (By the third issue of *Cosmic*, Wollheim was able to make token payments of five or ten dollars per story, but this can't have helped very much.) Wollheim did a remarkable job anyway, and several of the fantasy stories he published are still being reprinted today.

The Futurians as a group were talented but young. Pohl, for instance, was only nineteen when he became an editor, and C. M. Kornbluth was just seventeen when he published his first story; James Blish and Damon Knight were still in their teens. Most of them were eccentric and iconoclastic. Knight tells the story of Kornbluth in 1941, then eighteen years old, buying a drawing by Edd Cartier at a convention auction, then tearing it in half because he didn't like it.

But the most determined individualist of all those around the Futurians was Hannes Bok, who sold a number of stories—to John Campbell as well as to Futurian editors—in addition to his artwork. Wollheim remembers that Bok "would work for anyone who would not edit or make changes . . . money was never an objective of his." Lowndes confirms this judgment of Bok's attitude with an anecdote about an illustration Bok did for one of Lowndes's own stories. Lowndes loved the drawing but was disturbed by "two characters looking very much like pretty young men lying in each other's arms." He asked Bok to cover them up in some way, and Bok complied; but Lowndes didn't notice till after his magazine had been published that there were four legs in one corner that could belong only to two people who were copulating.

It was just as well that Bok wasn't overly concerned with money, for he was working in a field where most artists were paid five dollars per drawing, and cover paintings might bring fifty or seventy-five. Much pulp-magazine artwork was churned out by artists who could devote little time or talent to it, but the sf magazines attracted a surprising number of excellent artists who were willing to work cheaply because they loved science fiction. Besides Bok, they included Virgil Finlay, Hubert Rogers, J. Allen St. John, Charles Schneeman, Frank R. Paul and Edd Cartier. (Campbell lured Cartier away from *The Shadow* by giving him comparatively lucrative cover assignments in addition to interior illustration.)

Science fiction writers in the Midwest gathered around *Amazing*'s editor Raymond A. Palmer, who organized frequent poker games and even gathered a team of authors to play in a bowling league. The latter was surprising, for Palmer had been hit by a truck when he was seven; his back had been broken and he'd been left with a pronounced spinal curvature that made him very short and limited his physical mobility. "He was, I think you could say, a hunchback. He only stood about four feet tall, but it was all guts," says Theodore Sturgeon. Palmer's determination led him to a remarkable career as an author, editor and publisher. Between 1930 and 1938, when he took over the reins of *Amazing,* Palmer sold half a dozen stories to sf magazines, including Campbell's *Astounding;* but he made his living primarily by writing more than three million words for such publications as *True Gang Life* and *Scarlet Adventures.*

People who knew him in the early 1940s remember him as mercurial and devious, a "little Napoleon" to his staff authors, from whom he'd commission ten or twenty thousand words each month. Writers such as William P. McGivern, Don Wilcox, Robert Moore Williams, Leroy Yerxa and David Wright O'Brien (who had fifty-seven stories in *Amazing* and *Fantastic Adventures* between January 1941 and August 1942) were dependent on him for their livelihoods, so even though they suspected that he cheated at poker, they didn't dare call him on it.

In California the sf writers gathered in Los Angeles, sometimes attending meetings of the local fan club, or getting together to entertain visitors from far-off money-dispensing New York City. One of these was the agent Julius Schwartz, whose visits to Los Angeles brought about the meeting of Leigh Brackett and Edmond Hamilton, and who read and offered helpful criticism of stories by "the kid who sold newspapers on our corner": twenty-year-old Ray Bradbury.

Brackett has told of the "ping-penny" incident of 1941, when "Ed was doing a Captain Future or something, and he was pounding his typewriter and Schwartz was lying there looking at the ceiling, listening to the bell going 'Ping, ping, ping.'" Schwartz, who was Hamilton's agent, received 10 per cent of his earnings—therefore, since Hamilton's rate was one cent per word, and every line he wrote included about ten words, each time the bell went off Schwartz was richer by a penny.

There was a somewhat more formal meeting place for sf writers in Los Angeles: the Mañana Literary Society, hosted by Robert A. Heinlein and including from time to time such members as Anthony Boucher, Arthur K. Barnes, Edmond Hamilton, L. Ron Hubbard, Henry Kuttner, C. L. Moore, L. Sprague de Camp, Cleve Cartmill, Leigh Brackett and Jack Williamson. Heinlein's house was atop Lookout Mountain, and Schwartz recalls that "driving down that winding road at night was a harrowing experience. For that reason, Bob never served hard liquor. Looking back on it, Heinlein was more than a considerate, generous host. He could have wiped out half his sf competition with a few bottles of Scotch!"

The science fiction field in these years was simply a branch of the pulp-magazine industry, which supplied millions of readers with inexpensive fiction much as the paperback industry does today. (Paperbacks began to be published as early as 1939, when Pocket Books, Inc., was founded, but they weren't yet a major field of publishing.) Most pulp publishing was done by giant corporations that produced "chains" of magazines in every imaginable genre: *Jungle Stories, Dime Mystery Maga-*

zine, Western Story, South Sea Stories, R.A.F. Aces, Navy Stories, Spicy Mystery, Railroad Stories, Doc Savage, Popular Love, Sport Story Magazine, Far East Adventures, etc., etc. Popular Publications, Inc., published fifty or more magazines; Better Publications, Inc., had nearly forty.

These high-volume publishers required large editorial staffs and standardized office procedures. Editors often had to work in several different fields at once. Wollheim was once an editor for *Ten Detective Aces, Ace Detective, Ace Sports, 12 Sports Aces, Western Trails* and *Western Aces;* Lowndes simultaneously edited science fiction, Westerns, detective, love and sports magazines. Interoffice memos were made in triplicate, and editors had a variety of printed rejection letters to use, each explaining a common story error. H. L. Gold, who was an assistant editor for Better Publications, Inc., says the job was "so mechanical that two years of it destroyed the pleasure of editing."

Some idea of just how mechanical pulp-magazine editing could be can be gained from Frederik Pohl's description of life in the offices where Gold worked: "Each day's work by an editor was checked over by the boss. He didn't bother to read the stories. He did carefully assess the quantity of pencil markings on each page. If there wasn't a lot, the editor was called on the carpet."

Nor was the pay enough to make these conditions worthwhile. A top editor such as Leo Margulies, editor-in-chief of Better Publications, Inc., might make $25,000 or more a year, but lowly junior editors like Pohl were hired at ten dollars a week. ("That wasn't so bad," says Pohl. "They hired another editor at the same time, and he had to work three months for nothing before they *raised* him to $10 a week.") Gold, hired to work on more magazines than Pohl, made thirty dollars a week.

Many editors coped with low salaries by writing stories and selling them to themselves under pen names. Pohl was one of these; and even Raymond A. Palmer, who had contrived to make a decent living by working for a percentage of the profits from *Amazing* and *Fantastic Adventures* and then raising their circulations so much that he was soon making more than the vice president of the company, wrote stories for himself under pen names in order to make more money. He said in 1975 that his publishers had been aware of it but had looked the other way; pulp-magazine publishers were accustomed to such tactics.

The editors of *Startling* and *Thrilling Wonder Stories,* however, were expected to write stories for their magazines as part of their editorial duties. Leo Margulies, interviewed in 1974, remembered showing a visitor around the offices one day. His guest asked him why Oscar J. Friend, one of the assistant editors, had been sitting at his desk staring blankly at a painting. Margulies explained that Friend had been plotting a story he was assigned to write around that painting.

John W. Campbell had no such problems; he worked for perhaps the most prestigious of the pulp publishers, Street and Smith Publications, Inc., which paid him a living wage and didn't require him to write stories in addition to his editorial duties. Moreover, his work was focused strictly on *Astounding* and its companion fantasy magazine, *Unknown.* Donald Wollheim has suggested this may have been the reason Campbell was so successful as an editor: "He had the time to do a better job than usual, to give more attention to each story."

Nonetheless, Campbell's work surroundings were far from plush. Street and Smith's headquarters were in an old building whose elevator had seen better days. To get to Campbell's office, one went through a gloomy barnlike space piled high with enormous bales of pulp paper, down a series of tiny hallways, and finally, behind a door obscured by more rolls of paper, there was the office: small, cluttered with magazines, manuscripts and illustrations, and vibrating with the sound of nearby printing presses.

Campbell dominated the room. He was a large man, barrel-chested and sharp-nosed; his eyes were piercing and he talked

"as if each idea were a move in some absorbing mental game"
—but when he smiled, "he suddenly looked like some over-grown pixie."

It was here, in this office and from this man, for whatever reasons we may care to postulate, that the First Golden Age of Science Fiction came into being. It didn't seem so golden to the writers and artists who worked hard for pittances (even Jack Williamson, already a top author for more than a decade, had never made as much as $2000 a year), nor to most of the editors, who worked for just as little in noisy word factories. The threat and then the actuality of global war was a frightening background. Yet science fiction suddenly began to grow up in these years, gaining ideas and writing techniques whose influences can be seen in even the best stories written today.

It was an era that's worth revisiting in an anthology of many of its finest stories; you'll find such a selection here. In addition, because of the importance of this period in science fiction it's worth our study and understanding. My notes throughout are intended to show not only *what* happened, but also *how* . . . and to evoke the flavor of the entire science fiction experience in the First Golden Age.

REFERENCES:

(In the interest of readability, I've decided against using numbered footnotes. The references that follow this Introduction and the introductions to each story are given in the order in which they were used; I believe interested readers will be able to correlate them with the text rather easily.)

"John W. Campbell" by Walter Gillings. *Science Fiction Monthly,* Vol. 2, No. 1, 1974.

The Encyclopedia of Science Fiction and Fantasy, Vol. 1 by Donald H. Tuck. Advent:Publishers, 1974.

"MFS Members" by "Squanchfoot." *The Fantasite,* November-December 1941.

"Big, Big, Big" by Isaac Asimov. Introduction to *The Space Beyond* by John W. Campbell, Jr. Pyramid Books, 1976.

Early del Rey by Lester del Rey. Doubleday, 1975.

"A Rose Is a Rose Is a File Folder" by Cleve Cartmill. *Bixel,* December 1962.

The Universe Makers by Donald A. Wollheim. Harper & Row, 1971.

"World's Fair." *Life,* March 13, 1939.

"At the New York World's Fair" by Dick Wilson. *Super Science Stories,* September 1940.

Variety Music Cavalcade by Julius Mattfeld. Prentice-Hall, 1952.

The Academy Awards: A Pictorial History by Paul Michael. Bobbs-Merrill, 1964.

Frederic Arnold Kummer, Jr., in "The Reader Speaks." *Thrilling Wonder Stories,* July 1940.

Letter from Robert Bloch, February 20, 1975.

"Silence Is—Deadly" by Bertrand L. Shurtleff. *Astounding Science-Fiction,* April 1942.

"The Flight That Failed" by E. Mayne Hull. *Astounding Science-Fiction,* December 1942.

"The Whispering Spheres" by R. R. Winterbotham. *Comet Stories,* July 1941.

"Passage to Sharanee" by "Carol Grey" (Robert W. Lowndes). *Future combined with Science Fiction,* April 1942.

"Factory in the Sky" by Basil E. Wells. *Astonishing Stories,* September 1941.

"Too Good at Guessing" by John W. Campbell, Jr. *Astounding Science-Fiction,* April 1942.

Explorers of the Infinite by Sam Moskowitz. World Publishing, 1963.

The Complete Checklist of Science-Fiction Magazines by Bradford M. Day. Science-Fiction and Fantasy Publication, 1961.

"The Columbia Pulps" by Robert A. W. Lowndes. *The Pulp Era,* May-June 1967.

"Down to Earth" by Robert W. Lowndes. *Future Science Fiction,* January 1954.

Letter from Raymond A. Palmer, August 1975.

Interview with C. L. Moore, October 23, 1977.

Fantasy News, March 24, 1940.

The Encyclopedia of Science Fiction and Fantasy, Vol. 2 by Donald H. Tuck. Advent:Publishers, 1978.

Fantasy News, March 10, 1940.

"Dianuts and Dianetics" by F. Towner Laney. *The Unspeakable Thing,* April 1952.

"Fifty Years of Heroes" by Edmond Hamilton. *Weird Heroes,* Vol. 6. Pyramid Books, 1977.

"The Campbell Era" by Jack Williamson. *Algol,* Summer 1975.

Fantasy News, April 21, 1940.

"My Affair with Science Fiction" by Alfred Bester. *Hell's Cartographers.* Weidenfeld and Nicolson, 1975.

The Early Pohl by Frederik Pohl. Doubleday, 1976.

Letter from Frederik Pohl, March 12, 1974.

"The Sky's No Limit" by Jerry K. Westerfield. *Writer's Digest,* January 1940.

Interview with Fritz Leiber, September 20, 1974.

Letter from Donald A. Wollheim, April 11, 1975.

"Knight Piece" by Damon Knight. *Hell's Cartographers.* Weidenfeld and Nicolson, 1975.

Letter from Robert A. W. Lowndes, January 22, 1977.

Letter from Damon Knight, April 7, 1976.

"Hannes Bok: Artist and Man" by Ben Indick. *Chacal,* Winter 1976.

Fantasy News, April 28, 1940.

Interview with Frank M. Robinson, July 10, 1976.

The History of the Science Fiction Magazine, Part 2 by Michael Ashley. New English Library, 1975.

Interview with Theodore Sturgeon, October 23, 1977.

Interview with Leigh Brackett, October 23, 1977.

Afterword by Julius Schwartz. *Weird Heroes,* Vol. 6. Pyramid Books, 1977.

The Early Asimov by Isaac Asimov. Doubleday, 1972.

The Early Williamson by Jack Williamson. Doubleday, 1975.

THE SMALLEST GOD

Lester del Rey

We begin with a story from the January 1940 issue of *Astounding Science-Fiction,* which is an appropriate starting point even though the magazine actually appeared on the newsstands in December 1939. Lester del Rey—whose full name is Ramón Felipe San Juan Mario Silvio Enrico Smith Heathcourt-Brace Sierray Alvarez-del Rey y de los Uerdes—had been writing science fiction for less than two years; he had produced fourteen previous stories, nine of which he'd sold, most to *Astounding* and *Unknown.*

Just twenty-four years old, del Rey didn't regard himself as a professional writer, despite the fact that he'd made over $1000 from his fiction in 1939—more than he was to make for many years to come. He had begun writing on a dare; as he recalled nearly forty years later, he was reading a story in the January 1938 *Astounding* when "my girl friend dropped by to see me . . . she appeared just as I was throwing the magazine rather forcibly onto the floor." When she asked what the fuss was about, del Rey responded with "a long and overly impassioned diatribe against the story. In return, I got the most irritating question a critic can receive: 'What makes you think you have the right to judge writers when you can't write a story yourself?'

" 'So what makes you think I can't write?' I wanted to know.

" 'Prove it,' she answered."

He did; in three hours (the next night) he wrote a 4000-word story titled "The Faithful," which he sent to John Campbell. He didn't expect to sell it, but he did hope Campbell would say something sufficiently nice in his rejection to enable him to win his bet. Instead, two weeks later he received a check for forty dollars.

His point was proven, but as he stared at the check he thought, How long has all this been going on? So he wrote a second story, which Campbell rejected, and a third . . . also rejected. He nearly quit then, fearing that he was a one-story writer, but when "The Faithful" was published Campbell wrote him a note: "Your story was darned well received, del Rey, and it's been moving up steadily in the readers' choice. But as I look through my inventory, I don't find anything more by you. I hope you'll remedy this."

So del Rey wrote a short story called "Helen O'Loy," about a female robot who fell in love with her owner and convinced him to accept her as his wife. It was saccharine and male chauvinistic, but it was just the sort of story that would appeal to the teenaged-boy bookworms who made up most of the science fiction readership then, and it was an enormous hit. It made del Rey's reputation as a writer, and to this day it's often referred to by (male) critics as a science fiction classic.

Del Rey followed with many other popular stories during this Golden Age, such as "The Day Is Done," "The Wings of Night" and "Nerves," a suspenseful novella that would have been included in this book if it weren't so long (30,000 words). But John Campbell insisted that his writers keep on their toes, so even with his mounting list of successes, del Rey still suffered an occasional rejection. One that he remembers in particular came when he delivered to Campbell a story called "The Milksop":

"When I came back that evening, there was a strange look on [Campbell's] face, half puckish, half troubled. When I was seated, he reached over to his manuscript pile and extracted my story. Holding it gingerly at the corner between thumb and one finger, he moved it over above the wastebasket. 'Do you really want this back?' he asked. 'Or should I just drop it in the permanent file?'

"I suppose I gulped, 'Really that bad?'

"He nodded sadly and dropped it into the wastebasket."

Del Rey later reread his carbon copy of the story and found that he agreed with Campbell. The story has never been published.

Campbell was much kinder when someone sent him a story he particularly liked: he paid bonuses for them, usually a quarter of a cent a word. "The Smallest God" is one of the stories for which del Rey received a bonus; running to about 15,000 words, it earned a check from Campbell for $187.50. It's easy to see why Campbell liked it so much: not only is it original and amusing, but it fulfilled Campbell's wish to publish stories showing how scientists *really* worked.

Prior to John Campbell's tenure at *Astounding,* the typical inventor in science fiction was an eccentric recluse who built spaceships in his back yard or smashed atoms in his basement laboratory. Campbell knew better, and so did del Rey: laboratory equipment is expensive, and researchers need incomes with which to buy food, no matter how eccentric they may be. This means they work for corporations or universities, where they have to justify their expenditures in advance. Interdepartmental battles for funding are common.

So del Rey built his story around such a rivalry between the chemist Arlington Brugh and the biochemist Hiram Hodges, and the result was that for all its playfulness, the tale had a ring of authenticity that had been rare in science fiction till then.

Del Rey didn't manage to avoid every cliché endemic to 1940s science fiction, however: on the very first page we meet Dr. Ernst Meyer, a stereotyped German scientist complete with vaudevillian accent; later in the story comes a drunk who sees snakes, then a gruff Irish cop and a superstitious Irish woman, both of whom seem to have taken elocution lessons from Barry Fitzgerald.

Such ethnic stereotypes were as common in pulp science fiction as in other forms of pulp fiction (and in the movies of the time, and on radio). Fredric Brown, in his famous story "The Star-Mouse," featured a German inventor whose accent was indistinguishable from that of del Rey's Dr. Ernst Meyer: "Und now, ve vill see vether this eggshaust tube vas broperly machined. It should fidt vithin vun vun-hundreth thousandth uf an indtch. Ahhh, it is berfect. Und now . . ."

Manly Wade Wellman had a Brooklyn cop in one story who said things like "So ya trun de goil down. Moider, huh? . . . Dat means de electric chair. . . . T'ousan's of volts all troo ya body, boin ya tuh deat'."

Lester del Rey himself, in another 1940 story, used a Chinese cook who spoke like this: "Mebbeso you fella catchee plenty man. You fella catchee li'l planet, fin' allee same time catchee time makee free."

Such dialects, rendered painstakingly not to say painfully, were supposed to lend "colorful characterization" to stories—and, of course, a bit of humor. They were *not* meant as racist slurs. (Del Rey later chided himself for the way he presented the Chinese cook: "I knew better, since a couple of my friends in college were Chinese.")

Still, it's upsetting to see the stereotype of the black man as presented in some of these early-1940s stories. Mary Elizabeth Counselman, in a rare science fiction story in *Weird Tales,* wrote this:

". . . the Negro delivery boy shambled in . . . then shuffled over to the table . . .

" 'Aw,' he grinned. 'You's jest funnin' me, ain't you, Cap'n?' "

And one of her characters, discounting the fact that the delivery boy had witnessed a scientific apparition, said, "Why, that nig seeing it doesn't prove a thing! . . . A darky is very sensitive, like dogs."

Even Clifford D. Simak, one of the most compassionate writers in science fiction, wrote one story that included a black man named Rastus who was always stealing whiskey and "feeling lonesome because no one would shoot a game of craps with him." At one point in the story he bellowed, "Good Lawd, where is I?" Later, confronted with strange Mercurian natives who resembled whirlwinds, he exulted, "Just give me a razor. I'se a powerful dangerous man with a razor blade."

But even here the intention was clearly nothing more dire than to provide humorous leavening for an adventure story, for Simak's other characters included a white man named Old Creepy, a hillbilly who played "hoedown music" on his "fiddle."

The world seemed much less complex to most people in the early forties: there was less mingling of races and nationalities, so people's assumptions about other groups were less frequently challenged by experience. We'll see some more startling examples of this when we consider the effects of World War II propaganda. (Nor will we miss noticing the attitude of science fiction writers toward that most numerous of all underprivileged groups, women.)

But for now, here's one of the stories that helped make Lester del Rey a giant among the writers of science fiction's first Golden Age: "The Smallest God," a tale of a rubber doll who came to life in a laboratory and set about finding how to grow up.

REFERENCES:

"Lester del Rey: An Appreciation" by Robert Silverberg. *NyCon3 Program & Memory Book,* 1967.

Early del Rey by Lester del Rey. Doubleday, 1975.

"The Star-Mouse" by Fredric Brown. *Planet Stories,* Spring 1942.

"There Was No Paradise" by Manly Wade Wellman. *Thrilling Wonder Stories,* August 1940.

"The Stars Look Down" by Lester del Rey. *Astounding Science-Fiction,* August 1940.

"Drifting Atoms" by Mary Elizabeth Counselman. *Weird Tales,* May 1941.

"Masquerade" by Clifford D. Simak. *Astounding Science-Fiction,* March 1941.

*　　*　　*

I

Dr. Arlington Brugh led his visitor around a jumble of machinery that made sense only to himself, and through a maze of tables and junk that occupied most of his laboratory.

"It's a little disordered just now," he apologized, glad that his assistant had been able to clear up the worst of the mess. "Sort of gets that way after a long experiment."

Herr Dr. Ernst Meyer nodded heavy agreement. "Ja, so. Und mit all dis matchinery, no vunder. It gives yet no goot place v'ere I can mit comfort vork, also in mine own laboradory. Und v'at haff ve here?"

THE SMALLEST GOD · 23

"That's Hermes—my mascot." Brugh picked up the little, hollow rubber figure of the god Hermes; Mercury, the Romans called him. "The day I bought him for my daughter, the funds for my cyclotron were voted on favorably, so I've kept him in here. Just a little superstition."

Meyer shook his head. "Nein. I mean here." He tapped a heavy lead chest bearing a large "Keep Out" label. "Is maybe v'at you make?"

"That's right." The physical chemist pulled up the heavy cover and displayed a few dirty crystals in a small compartment and a thick, tarry goo that filled a half-liter beaker. "Those are my latest success and my first failure. By the way, have you seen Dr. Hodges over in the biochemistry department?"

"Ja. Vunderful vork he makes yet, nicht wahr?"

"Um-m—opinions differ. I'll admit he did a good job in growing that synthetic amoeba, and the worm he made in his chemical bath wasn't so bad, though I never did know whether it was really alive or not. Maybe you read about it? But he didn't stick to the simple things until he mastered his technique. He had to go rambling off trying to create a synthetic man."

Meyer's rough face gleamed. "Ja, so. Dot is hübsch—nice. Mit veins und muschles. Only it is not mit der life upfilled."

Brugh sifted a few of the crystals in the chest out onto a watch glass where they could be inspected more carefully. Then he put them into an opened drawer and closed it until the crystals were in a much dimmer light. In the semidarkness, a faint gleam was visible, hovering over the watch glass.

"Radioactive," he explained. "There is the reason Hodges' man isn't filled with life. If there had been some of this in his chemical bath when he was growing Anthropos—that's what he calls the thing—it would be walking around today. But you can't expect a biochemist to know that, of course. They don't keep up with the latest developments the way the physical chemists do. Most of them aren't aware of the fact that the atom can be cracked up into a different kind of atom by using Bertha."

"Bert'a? Maybe she is die daughter?"

Brugh grinned. "Bertha's the cyclotron over there. The boys started calling her Big Bertha, and then we just named her Bertha for short." He swung around to indicate the great mass of metal that filled one end of the room. "That's a lot of material to make so few crystals of radioactive potassium chloride, though."

"Ach, so. Den it is der radioagdivated salt dot vould give life to der synt'etic man, eh?"

"Right. We're beginning to believe that life is a combination of electricity and radioactivity, and the basis of the last seems to be this active potassium we've produced by bombarding the ordinary form with neutrons. Put that in Anthropos and he'd be bouncing around for his meals in a week."

Meyer succeeded in guessing the meaning of the last and cocked up a bushy eyebrow. "Den v'y not der salt to der man give?"

"And have Hodges hog all the glory again? Not a chance." He banged his hand on the chest for emphasis, and the six-inch figure of Hermes bounced from its precarious perch and took off for the watch glass. Brugh grabbed frantically and caught it just before it hit. "Someday I'll stuff this thing with something heavy enough to hold it down."

The German looked at the statue with faint interest, then pointed to the gummy mess in the beaker. "Und dis?"

"That's a failure. Someday I might analyze a little of it, but it's too hard to get the stuff out of that tar, and probably not worth a quarter of the energy. Seems to be a little of everything in it, including potassium, and it's fairly radioactive, but all it's good for is—well, to stuff Hermes so he can't go bouncing around."

Brugh propped the little white figure against a ring stand and drew out the beaker, gouging out a chunk of the varicolored tar. He plopped it into a container and poured methyl alcohol over it, working with a glass rod until it was reasonably plastic. "Darned stuff gets soft, but it won't dissolve," he grumbled.

Meyer stood back looking on, shaking his head gently. Americans were naturally crazy, but he hadn't expected such foolishness from so distinguished a research man as Dr. Brugh. In his own laboratory, he'd have spent the next two years, if necessary, in finding out what the tar was, instead of wasting it to stuff a cheap rubber cast of a statue.

"Dis Herr Dr. Hodges, you don't like him, I t'ink. Warum?"

Brugh was spooning the dough into his statue, forcing it into the tiny mouth, and packing it in loosely. "Hodges wanted a new tank for his life-culture experiments when I was trying to get the cyclotron and the cloud chamber. I had to dig up the old antivivisection howl among the students' parents to keep him from getting it, and he thought that was a dirty trick. Maybe it was. Anyway, he's been trying ever since to get me kicked out, and switch the appropriations over to his department. By the way, I'd hate to have word of this get around."

"Aber—andivifisegtion!" Meyer was faintly horrified at such an unscientific thing.

Brugh nodded. "I know. But I wanted that cyclotron, and I got it; I'd do worse. There, Hermes won't go flying around again. Anything else I can show you, Dr. Meyer?"

"T'ank you, no. Der clock is late now, and I must cadge my train by der hour. It has a bleasure been, Dr. Brugh."

"Not at all." Brugh set the statue on a table and went out with the German, leaving Hermes in sole possession of the laboratory, except for the cat.

II

The clock in the laboratory said four o'clock in the morning. Its hum and the gentle breathing of the cat, that exercised its special privileges by sleeping on the cyclotron, were the only noises to be heard. Up on the table Hermes stood quietly, just as Dr. Brugh had left him, a little white rubber figure outlined in the light that shone through from the outside. A very ordinary little statue he looked.

But inside, where the tar had been placed, something was

stirring gently. Faintly and low at first, life began to quiver. Consciousness began to come slowly, and then a dim and hazy feeling of individuality. He was different in being a unit not directly connected in consciousness with the dim outlines of the laboratory.

What, where, when; who, why, and how? Hermes knew none of the answers, and the questions were only vague and hazy in his mind, but the desire to know and to understand was growing. He took in the laboratory slowly through the hole that formed his partly open mouth and let the light stream in against the resinous matter inside. At first, only a blur was visible, but as his "eyes" grew more proficient from experience, he made out separate shapes. He had no names for them, but he recognized the difference between a round tube and a square table top.

The motion of the second hand caught his attention, and he studied the clock carefully, but could make no sense of it. Apparently some things moved and others didn't. What little he could see of himself didn't, even when he made a clumsy attempt at forcing motion into his outthrust arm. It took longer to notice the faint breathing of the cat; then he noticed it not only moved, but did so in an irregular fashion. He strained toward it, and something clicked in his mind.

Tabby was dreaming, but Hermes couldn't know that, nor understand from whence came the pictures that seemed to flash across his gummy brain; Tabby didn't understand dreams, either. But the little god could see some tiny creature that went scurrying rapidly across the floor, and a much-distorted picture of Tabby was following it. Tabby had a definitely exaggerated idea of herself. Now the little running figure began to grow until it was twice the size of the cat, and its appearance altered. It made harsh explosive noises and beat a thick tail stiffly. Tabby's picture made a noise and fled, but the other followed quickly and a wide mouth opened. Tabby woke up, and the pictures disappeared. Hermes could make no sense of them, though it was plain in Tabby's mind that such things often happened when her head turned black inside.

But the cat awake was even more interesting than she was sleeping. There were the largest groups of loosely classified odor, sights, and sensations to be absorbed, the nicest memories of moving about and exploring the laboratory. Through Tabby's eyes he saw the part of the laboratory that was concealed from him, and much of the outside in the near neighborhood. He also drew a hazy picture of himself being filled, but it made no sense to him, though he gathered from the cat's mind that the huge monster holding him was both to be despised and respected, and was, all in all, a very powerful person.

By now his intelligence was great enough to recognize that the world seen through the cat's eyes was in many ways wrong. For one thing, everything was in shades of white and black, with medial grays, while he had already seen that there were several colors. Hermes decided that he needed another point of view, though the cat had served admirably to start his mind on the way to some understanding of the world about him.

A low howling sound came from outside the laboratory, and Hermes recoiled mentally, drawing a picture of a huge and ferocious beast from his secondhand cat's memory. Then curiosity urged him to explore. If the cat's color sense was faulty, perhaps her ideas on the subject of dogs were also wrong. He thrust his mind out toward the source of the sound, and again there was the little click that indicated a bridge between two minds.

He liked the dog much better than the cat. There was more to be learned here, and the animal had some faint understanding of a great many mysteries which had never interested Tabby. Hermes also found that hard, selfish emotions were not the only kind. On the whole, the mind of Shep seemed warm and glowing after the frigid self-interest of Tabby.

First in the dog's mind as in all others, was the thought of self, but close behind was mistress and master, the same person whom the cat's mind had pictured filling the god. And there were the two little missies. Something about the dog's mental image of one of them aroused an odd sensation in the little god, but it was too confused to be of any definite interest.

But the dog retained hazy ideas of words as a means of thought, and Hermes seized on them gratefully. He gathered that men used them as a medium of thought conveyance, and filed the sixty partly understood words of Shep's vocabulary carefully away. There were others with tantalizing possibilities, but they were vague.

Shep's world was much wider than that of Tabby, and his general impression of color—for dogs do see colors—was much better. The world became a fascinating place as he pictured it, and Hermes longed for the mysterious power of mobility that made wide explorations possible. He tried to glean the secret, but all that Shep knew on the subject was that movement followed desire, and sometimes came without any wish.

The god came to the conclusion that in all the world the only animals that could satisfy his curiosity were men. His mind was still too young to be bothered with such trifles as modesty, and he was quite sure there could be no animal with a better intelligence than he had. The dog couldn't even read thoughts, and Hermes had doubts about man's ability to do the same; otherwise, why should the master have punished Shep for fighting, when the other dog had clearly started it?

And if he hadn't, Shep would have been home, instead of skulking around this place, where he sometimes came to meet the master after work.

Hermes tried to locate a man's mind, but there was none near. He caught a vague eddy of jumbled thought waves from someone who was evidently located there to guard the building, but there was a definite limit to the space that thought could span.

The cat's brain had gone black inside again, with only fitful images flickering on and off, and the dog was drifting into a similar state. Hermes studied the action with keen interest and decided that sleep might be a very fine way of passing the time until a man came back to the laboratory, as he gathered they did every time some big light shone from somewhere high up above.

But as he concentrated on the matter of turning off his mind, he wondered again what he was. Certainly neither a dog nor a cat, he had no real belief that he was a man; the dog didn't know about him, but the cat regarded him as a stone. Maybe he was one, if stones ever came to life. Anyway, he'd find out in the morning when the master came in. Until then he forced thoughts from his mind and succeeded in simulating sleep.

III

A strange noise wakened Hermes in the morning. From what he had seen in Shep's mind, he knew it was the sound of human speech, and listened intently. The people were talking at a point behind him, but he was sure it was the master and one of the little missies. He tuned his mind in on that of the master and began soaking up impressions.

"I wish you'd stay away from young Thomas," Dr. Brugh was saying. "I think he's the nephew of Hodges, though he won't admit it. Your mother doesn't like him, either, Tanya."

Tanya laughed softly at her father's suspicions, and Hermes felt a glow all over. It was a lovely sound. "You never like my boy friends," she said. "I think you want me to grow up into an old-maid schoolmarm. Johnny's a nice boy. To hear you talk, a person would think Hodges and his whole family were ogres."

"Maybe they are." But Brugh knew better than to argue with his older daughter; she always won, just as her mother always did. "Hodges tried to swindle me out of my appropriations again at the meeting last night. He'd like to see me ruined."

"And you swindled him out of his tanks. Suppose I proved to the president who sent those anonymous vivisection letters to all the parents?"

Brugh looked around hastily, but there was no one listening. "Are you trying to blackmail me, Tanya?"

She laughed again at his attempt at anger. "You know I won't tell a soul. 'By, dad. I'm going swimming with Johnny." Hermes felt a light kiss through Brugh's senses, and saw her start around the table to pass in front of him. He snapped the connection with the master's mind and prepared his own eyes for confirmation of what he had seen by telepathy.

Tanya was a vision of life and loveliness. In the fleeting second it took her to cross the little god's range of sight, he took in the soft, waving brown hair, the dark, sparkling eyes, and the dimple that lurked in the corner of her mouth, and something happened to Hermes. As yet he had no word for it, but it was pure sensation that sped through every atom of his synthetic soul. He began to appreciate that life was something more than the satisfaction of curiosity.

A sound from Brugh, who was puttering around with a cloudy precipitate, snapped him back to reality. The questions in his mind still needed answering, and the physicist was the logical one to answer them. Again he made contact with the other's mind.

This was infinitely richer than the dog's and cat's combined. For one thing, there was a seemingly inexhaustible supply of word thoughts to be gleaned. As he absorbed them, thinking became easier, and the words provided a framework for abstractions, something utterly beyond the bounds of the animal minds. For half an hour he studied them, and absorbed the details of human life gradually.

Then he set about finding the reasons for his own life; that necessitated learning the whole field of physical chemistry, which occupied another half-hour, and when he had finished, he began putting the knowledge he had gleaned together, until it made sense.

All life, he had found, was probably electricity and radioactivity, the latter supplied by means of a tiny amount of potassium in the human body. But life was really more than that. There were actions and interactions between the two things that had thus far baffled all students. Some of them baffled the rubber god, but he puzzled the general picture out to his own satisfaction.

When the experiment had gone wrong and created the tarry lump that formed the real life of Hermes, there had been a myriad of compounds and odd arrangements of atoms formed in it, and the tarry gum around them had acted as a medium for their operations. Then, when they were slightly softened by the addition of alcohol, they had begun to work, arranging and rearranging themselves into an interacting pattern that was roughly parallel to human life and thought.

But there were differences. For one thing, he could read thoughts accurately, and for another he had a sense of perception which could analyze matter directly from its vibrations. For another, what he called sight and sound were merely other vibrations, acting directly on his life substance instead of by means of local sensory organs. He realized suddenly that he could see with his mouth instead of his eyes, and hear all over. Only the rubber casing prevented him from a full three-hundred-and-sixty-degree vision. But, because of the minds he had tapped, he had learned to interpret those vibrations in a more or less conventional pattern.

Hermes analyzed the amount of radioactive potassium in Brugh's body carefully and compared it with his own. There was a great difference, which probably accounted for his more fully developed powers. Something ached vaguely inside him, and he felt giddy. He turned away from his carefully ordered thoughts to inspect this new sensation.

The alcohol inside him was drying out—almost gone, in fact, and his tarry interior was growing thicker. He'd have to do something about it.

"Dr. Brugh," he thought, fixing his attention on the other, "could I have some alcohol, please? My thoughts will be slowed even below human level if I can't have some soon."

Arlington Brugh shook his head to clear it of a sudden buzz, but he had not understood. Hermes tried again, using all the remaining thought power he could muster.

"This is Hermes, Dr. Brugh. You brought me to life, and I want some alcohol, please!"

Brugh heard this time, and swung suspiciously toward the end of the room, where his assistant was working. But the young man was engaged in his work, and showed no sign of having spoken or heard. Hermes repeated his request, squeezing out his fast failing energy, and the master jerked quickly, turning his eyes slowly around the room. Again Hermes tried, and the other twitched.

Brugh grabbed for his hat and addressed the assistant. "Bill, I'm going for a little walk to clear my head. That session last night seems to have put funny ideas in it." He paused. "Oh, better toss that little rubber statue into the can for the junkman. It's beginning to get on my nerves."

He turned sharply and walked out of the room. Hermes felt the rough hands of the assistant, and felt himself falling. But his senses were leaving him, drained by the loss of alcohol and the strain of forcing his mind on the master. He sank heavily into the trash can and his mind grew blank.

IV

A splatter of wetness against Hermes' mouth brought him back to consciousness, and he saw a few drops fall near him from a broken bottle that was tipped sidewise. Occasionally one found its way through his mouth, and he soaked it up greedily. Little as he got, the alcohol still had been enough to start his dormant life into renewed activity.

There was a pitch and sway to the rubbish on which he lay, and a rumbling noise came from in front of him. Out of the corner of his "eye" he saw a line of poles running by, and knew he was on something that moved. Momentarily he tapped the mind of the driver and found he was on a truck bound for the city dump, where all garbage was disposed of. But he felt no desire to use the little energy he had in mind reading, so he fell back to studying the small supply of liquid left in the bottle.

There was an irregular trickle now, running down only a few inches from him. He studied the situation carefully, noting that the bottle was well anchored to its spot, while he was poised precariously on a little mound of rubbish. One of Newton's laws of momentum flashed through his mind from the mass of information he had learned through Brugh; if the truck were to speed up, he would be thrown backward, directly under the stream trickling down from the bottle—and with luck he might land face up.

Hermes summoned his energy and directed a wordless desire for speed toward the driver. The man's foot came down slowly on the accelerator, but too slowly. Hermes tried again, and suddenly felt himself pitched backward—to land face down! Then a squeal of brakes reached his ears, as the driver counteracted his sudden speed, and the smallest god found himself rolling over, directly under the stream.

There were only a few teaspoons left, splashing out irregularly as the bouncing of the truck threw the liquid back and forth in the fragment of glass, but most of them reached his mouth. The truck braked to a halt and began reversing, and the last drops fell against his lips. It was highly impure alcohol, filled with raw chemicals from the laboratory, but Hermes had no complaints. He could feel the tar inside him soften, and he lay quietly enjoying the sensation until new outside stimuli caught his attention.

The truck had ceased backing and was parked on a slope leading down toward the rear. There was a rattle of chains and the gate dropped down to let the load go spinning out down the bank into the rubbish-filled gulley. Hermes bounced from a heavy can and went caroming off sidewise, then struck against a rock with force enough to send white sparks of pain running through him.

But the rock had changed his course and thrown him clear of the other trash. When he finally stopped, his entire head and one arm were clear, and the rest was buried under only a loose litter of papers and dirt. No permanent damage had been done; his tarry core was readjusting itself to the normal shape of the rubber coating, and he was in no immediate danger.

But being left here was the equivalent of a death sentence. His only hope was to contact some human mind and establish friendly communications, and the dump heap was the last place to find men. Added to that, the need for further alcohol was a serious complication. Again he wished for the mysterious power of motion.

He concentrated his mental energy on moving the free arm, but there was no change; the arm stayed at the same awkward angle. With little hope he tried again, watching for the slightest movement. This time a finger bent slightly! Feverishly he tried to move the others, and they twisted slowly until his whole hand lay stretched out flat. Then his arm began to move sluggishly. He was learning.

It was growing dark when he finally drew himself completely free of the trash and lay back to rest, exulting over his newfound ability. The alcohol was responsible, of course; it had softened the tar slightly more than it had been when he made his first efforts in the laboratory, and permitted motion of a sort through a change of surface tension. The answer to further motion was more alcohol.

There were bottles of all kinds strewn about, and he stared at those within his range of vision, testing their vibrations in the hope of finding a few more drops. The nearer ones were empty, except for a few that contained brackish rain water. But below him, a few feet away, was a small-sized one whose label indicated that it had contained hair tonic. The cork was in tightly, and it was still half full of a liquid. That liquid was largely ethyl alcohol.

Hermes forced himself forward on his stomach, drawing along inch by inch. Without the help of gravity, he could never have made it, but the distance shortened. He gave a final labored hitch, clutched the bottle in his tiny hands, and tried to force the cork out. It was wedged in too firmly!

Despair clutched at him, but he threw it off. There must be some way. Glass was brittle, could be broken easily, and there were stones and rocks about with which to strike it. The little god propped the neck of the bottle up against one and drew himself up to a sitting position, one of the stones in his hands. He could not strike rapidly enough to break the glass, but had to rely on raising the rock and letting it fall.

Fortunately for his purpose, the bottle had been cracked by its fall, and the fourth stone shattered the neck. Hermes forced it up on a broken box and tipped it gingerly toward his mouth. The smell of it was sickening, but he had no time to be choosy about his drinks! There was room inside him to hold a dozen teaspoonfuls, and he meant to fill those spaces.

The warm sensation of softening tar went through him gratefully as the liquid was absorbed. According to what he had read in Brugh's mind, he should have been drunk, but it didn't feel that way. It more nearly approximated the sensation of a man who had eaten more than he should and hadn't time to be sorry yet.

Hermes wriggled his toes comfortably and nodded his approval at the ease with which they worked. Another idea came to him, and he put it to the test. Where his ear channels were, the rubber was almost paper-thin; he put out a pseudopod of tar from the lumps inside his head and wriggled it against the membrane; a squeaky sound was produced like a radio speaker gone bad. He varied the speed of the feeler, alternating it until he discovered the variation of tones and overtones necessary, and tried a human word.

"Tanya!" It wasn't perfect, but there could be no question as to what it was. Now he could talk with men directly, even with Tanya Brugh if fate was particularly kind. He conjured up an ecstatic vision of her face and attempted a conventional sighing sound. Men in love evidently were supposed to sigh, and Hermes was in love!

But if he wanted to see her, he'd have to leave the dump. It was dark now, but ultraviolet and infrared light were as useful to him as the so-called visible beams, and the amount of light needed to set off his sight was less than that for a cat. With soiled hands he began pulling his way up the bank, burrowing through the surface rubbish. Then he reached the top and spied the main path leading away.

His little feet twinkled brightly in the starlight, and the evening dew washed the stains from his body. A weasel, prowling for food, spied him and debated attack, but decided to flee when the little god pictured himself as a dog. Animals accepted such startling apparent changes without doubting their sanity. He chuckled at the tricks he could play on Tabby when he got back, and sped down the lane at a good two miles an hour.

V

Brugh worked late in the laboratory, making up for the time he had taken off to clear his head. All thoughts of his trouble with Hermes had vanished. He cleared up the worst of the day's litter of dirty apparatus, arranged things for the night, and locked up.

Dixon, head of the organic-chemistry department, was coming down the hall as the physicist left. He stopped, his pudgy face beaming, and greeted the other. "Hi, there, Brugh. Working late again, eh?"

"A little. How's the specific for tuberculosis going?"

Dixon patted his paunch amiably. "Not bad. We're able to get the metal poison into the dye, and the dye into the bug. We still can't get much of the poison out of the dye after that to kill our friend, the bacillus, but we've been able to weaken him a little. By the way, I saw your daughter today, out with Hodges' nephew, and she told me—"

"You mean Johnny Thomas?" Brugh's eyebrows furrowed tightly and met at the corners. "So Hodges is his uncle! Hm-m-m."

"Still fighting the biochemistry department?" By a miracle of tact and good nature, Dixon had managed to keep on friendly terms with both men. "I wish you two would get together; Hodges is really a pretty decent sort. . . . Well, I didn't think so; you're both too stubborn for your own good. That nephew of his isn't so good, though. Came up here to pump money out of his uncle and get away from some scandal in New York. His reputation isn't any too savory. Wouldn't want my daughter going with him."

"Don't worry; Tanya won't be going with Hodges' nephew any longer. Thanks for the tip." They reached the main door, and Brugh halted suddenly. "Darn!"

"What is it?"

"I left my auto keys on the worktable upstairs. Don't bother waiting for me, Dixon. I'll see you in the morning."

Dixon smiled. "Absent-minded professor, eh? All right, good night." He went out and down the steps while Brugh climbed back to his laboratory, where he found the keys without further trouble. Fortunately he carried a spare door key to the lab in his pocket; it wasn't the first time he'd done this fool trick.

As he passed down the hall again, a faint sound of movement caught his ear and he turned toward Hodges' laboratory. There was no one there, and the door was locked, the lights all out. Brugh started for the stairs, then turned back.

"Might as well take advantage of an opportunity when I get it," he muttered. "I'd like to see that creation of Hodges, as long as he won't know about it." He slipped quietly to the door, unlocked it, and pulled it shut after him. The one key unlocked every door in the building and the main entrance; he had too much trouble losing keys to carry more than needed with him.

There was no mistaking the heavy tank on the low table, and Brugh moved quietly to it, lifted the cover, and stared inside. There was a light in the tank that went on automatically when the cover was raised, and the details of the body inside were clearly defined. Brugh was disappointed; he had been hoping for physical defects, but the figure was that of a young man, almost too classically perfect in body, and with an intelligent, handsome face. There was even a healthy pink glow to the skin.

But there was no real life, no faintest spark of animation or breathing. Anthropos lay in his nutritive bath, eyes open, staring blankly at the ceiling and seeing nothing. "No properly radioactive potassium," Brugh gloated. "In a way, it's a pity, too. I'd like to work on you."

He put the cover down and crept out again, making sure that the night watchman was not around. The man seldom left the first floor, anyway; who'd steal laboratory equipment? Brugh reached for his keys and fumbled with them, trying to find the proper one. It wasn't on the key ring. "Damn!" he said softly. "I suppose it fell off back on the table."

But he still had the spare, and the other could stay on the table. With the duplicate, he opened and relocked the door, then slipped down the hall to leave the building. Again a faint sound reached him, but he decided it was the cat or a rat moving around. He had other worries. Mrs. Brugh would give him what-for for being late again, he supposed. And Tanya probably wouldn't be home yet from the beach. That was another thing to be attended to; there'd be no more running with that young Thomas!

In the latter supposition he was wrong; Tanya was there, fooling with her hair and gushing to her mother about a date she had that night with Will Young. She usually had seven dates a week with at least four different men serving as escorts. Brugh thoroughly approved of Young, however, since he was completing his Ph.D. work and acting as lab assistant. Mrs. Brugh approved of him because the young man came from a good family and had independent means, without the need of the long grind up to a full professorship. Tanya was chiefly interested in his six-foot-two, his football reputation, and a new Dodge he owned.

Margaret Brugh spied her husband coming through the door, and began her usual worried harangue about his health and overwork. He muttered something about a lost key, and Tanya changed the subject for him. Brugh threw her a grateful smile and went in to wash up. He decided to postpone the lecture on Thomas until after supper; then she was in too much of a hurry to be bothered, and he put it off until morning.

The old Morris chair was soothing after a full meal—so soothing that the paper fell from his lap and scattered itself over the floor unnoticed, until the jangling of the telephone brought him back with a jerk. "It's for you," his wife announced.

The voice was that of Hodges, his nasal Vermont twang unmistakable. "Brugh? Your latest brainstorm backfired on you! I've got evidence against you this time, so you'd better bring it back." The pitch of the voice indicated fury that was only partly controlled.

The back hairs on Brugh's neck bristled up hotly, and his voice snapped back harshly: "You're drunk or crazy, like all biochemists! I haven't done anything to you. Anyway, what is it you want back?"

"You wouldn't know? How touching, such innocence! I want Anthropos, my synthetic man. I suppose you weren't in the laboratory this evening?"

Brugh gulped, remembering the faint noises he had heard. So it had been a trap! "I never—"

"Of course. But we had trouble before—someone trying to force their way in—and we set up a photoelectric eye and camera with film for u. v. light. Didn't expect to catch you, but there's a nice picture of your face on it, and your key is in the lock—the number shows it's yours. I didn't think even you would stoop to stealing!"

Brugh made strangling sounds. "I didn't steal your phony man; wouldn't touch the thing! Furthermore, I didn't leave a key. Go sleep your insanity off!"

"Are you going to return Anthropos?"

"I don't have him." Brugh slammed the receiver down in disgust, snorting. If Hodges thought that he could put such a trick over, he'd find out better. With all the trumped-up evidence in the world, they'd still have to prove a few things. He'd see the president in the morning before Hodges could get to him.

But he wasn't prepared for the doorbell a half-hour later, nor for the blue-coated figures that stood outside. They wasted no time.

"Dr. Arlington Brugh? We have a warrant for your arrest, charge being larceny. If you'll just come along quietly—"

They were purposeful individuals, and words did no good. Brugh went along—but not quietly.

VI

Hermes spied the public highway below him, and began puzzling about which direction to take back to town. Brugh had never been out this way, and he had failed to absorb the necessary information from the garbage man, so he had no idea of the location of Corton. But there was a man leaning against a signpost, and he might know.

The little god approached him confidently, now that he could both move and talk. He wanted to try his new power instead of telepathy, and did not trouble with the man's thoughts, though a faint impression indicated they were highly disordered.

"Good evening, sir," he said pleasantly, with only a faint blur to the words. "Can you direct me to Corton University?"

The man clutched the signpost and gazed down solemnly, blinking his eyes. "Got 'em again," he said dispassionately. "And after cutting down on the stuff, too. 'Sfunny, they never talked before. Wonder if the snakes'll talk, too, when I begin seeing them?"

It made no sense to Hermes, but he nodded wisely and repeated his question. From the vibrations, the man was not unacquainted with the virtues of alcohol.

The drunk pursed his lips and examined the little figure calmly. "Never had one like you before. What are you?"

"I suppose I'm a god," Hermes answered. "Can you direct me to Corton, please."

"So it's gods this time, eh? That's what I get for changing brands. Go away and let me drink in peace." He thought it over slowly as he drew out the bottle. "Want a drink?"

"Thank you, yes." The little god stretched up and succeeded in reaching the bottle. This time he filled himself to capacity before handing it back. It was worse than the hair tonic, but there was no question of its tar-softening properties. "Could you—"

"I know. Corton. To your right and follow the road." The man paused and made gurgling noises. "Whyn't you stick around? I like you; snakes never would drink with me."

Hermes made it quite clear he couldn't stay, and the drunk nodded gravely. "Always women. I know about that; it's a woman that drove me to this—seeing you. 'Stoo bad. Well, so long!"

Filled with the last drink, the god stepped his speed up to almost five miles an hour. There was no danger of fatigue, since the radioactive energy within him poured out as rapidly as he could use it, and there were no waste products to poison his system. His tiny legs flickered along the road, and the little feet made faint tapping sounds on the smooth asphalt surface.

He came over a hill and spied the yellow lights of Corton, still an hour's trot away. It might have been worse. The swishing of the water inside him bothered him, and he decided that he'd stick to straight alcohol hereafter; whiskey contained too many useless impurities. Hermes flopped over beside the road, and let the water and some of the oil from the hair tonic trickle out; the alcohol was already well inside his gummy interior where there was no danger of losing it. For some reason, it seemed to be drying out more slowly than the first had, and that was all to the good.

The few cars on the road aroused a faint desire for some easier means of locomotion, but otherwise they caused him no trouble. He clipped off the miles at a steady gait, keeping on the edge of the paving, until the outskirts of the town had been reached. Then he took to the sidewalk.

A blue-coated figure, ornamented with brass buttons, was pacing down the street toward him, and Hermes welcomed the presence of the policeman. One of the duties of an officer was directing people, he had gathered, and a little direction would be handy. The smallest god stopped and waited for the other to reach him.

"Could you direct me to the home of Dr. Arlington Brugh, please?"

The cop looked about carefully for the speaker. Hermes raised his voice again. "I'm here, sir."

Officer O'Callahan dropped his eyes slowly, expecting a drunk, and spied the god. He let out a startled bellow. "So it's tricks, is it now? Confound that Bergen, after drivin' the brats wild about ventriloquence. Come out o' there, you spalpeen. Tryin' your tricks on an honest police, like as if I didn't have worries o' me own."

Hermes watched the officer hunting around in the doorways for what he believed must be the source of the voice, and decided that there was no use lingering. He put one foot in front of the other and left the cop.

"Pssst!" The sound came from an alley a couple of houses below, and Hermes paused. In the shadows, he made out a dirty old woman, her frowsy hair blowing about her face, her finger crooked enticingly. Evidently she wanted something, and he turned in hesitantly.

"That dumb Irish mick," she grunted, and from her breath Hermes recognized another kindred spirit; apparently humans were much easier to get along with when thoroughly steeped in alcohol, as he was himself. "Sure, now, a body might think it's never a word he'd heard o' the Little Folks, and you speaking politely, too. Ventriloquence, indeed! Was you wanting to know what I might be telling you?"

Hermes stretched his rubber face into a passable smile. "Do you know where Dr. Arlington Brugh lives? He's a research director at Corton University."

She shook her head, blinking bleary eyes. "That I don't, but maybe you'd take the university? It's well I knew where that may be."

Dr. Brugh lived but a short distance from the campus he knew, and once on the university grounds, Hermes would have

THE SMALLEST GOD · 43

no trouble in finding the house. He nodded eagerly. She reached down a filthy hand and caught him up, wrapping a fold of her tattered dress about him.

"Come along, then. I'll be taking you there myself." She paused to let the few last drops trickle from a bottle into her wide mouth, and stuck her head out cautiously; the policeman had gone. With a grunt of satisfaction, she struck across the street to a streetcar stop. "'Tis the last dime I have, but a sorry day it'll be when Molly McCann can't do a favor for a Little Folk."

She propped herself against the car-stop post and waited patiently, while Hermes pondered the mellowing effects of alcohol again. When the noisy car stopped, she climbed on, clutching him firmly, and he heard only the bumping of a flat wheel and her heavy breathing. But she managed to keep half awake, and carried him off the car at the proper place.

She set him down as gently as unsteady nerves would permit and pointed a wavering finger at the buildings on the campus. "There you be, and it's the best of luck I'm wishing you. Maybe, now that I've helped a Little Man, good luck'll be coming to me. A very good night to you."

Hermes bowed gravely as he guessed she expected. "My thanks, Molly McCann, for your kindness, and a very good night to you." He watched her totter away, and turned toward the laboratory building, where he could secure a few more drops of straight alcohol. After that, he could attend to his other business.

VII

Tanya Brugh was completely unaware of the smallest god's presence as he stood on a chair looking across at her. A stray beam of moonlight struck her face caressingly, and made her seem a creature of velvet and silver, withdrawn in sleep from all that was mundane. Hermes probed her mind gently, a little fearfully.

Across her mind, a flickering pageant of tall men, strong men, lithe and athletic men, ran in disordered array, and none of them were less than six feet tall. Hermes gazed at his own small body, barely six inches high; it would never do. Now the face of John Thomas fitted itself on one of the men, and Tanya held the image for a few seconds. The god growled muttered oaths; he had no love for the Thomas image. Then it flickered into the face of Will Young, Brugh's assistant.

Hermes had probed her thoughts to confirm his own ideas of the wonderful delight that Tanya must be, and he was faintly disappointed. In her mind were innocence and emptiness— except for men of tall stature. He sighed softly, and reverted to purely human rationalization until he had convinced himself of the rightness of her thoughts.

But the question of height bothered him. Children, he knew, grew up, but he was no child, though his age was measured in hours. Some way, he must gain a new body, or grow taller, and that meant that Dr. Brugh would be needed for advice on the riddle of height increase.

He dropped quietly from the chair and trotted toward the master's bedroom, pushing against the door in the hope that it might be open. It wasn't, but he made a leap for the doorknob and caught it, throwing his slight weight into the job of twisting it. Finally the knob turned, and he kicked out against the door jamb with one foot until the door began to swing. Then he dropped down and pushed until he could slide through the opening. For his size, he carried a goodly portion of strength in his gum-and-rubber body.

But the master was not in the bed, and the mistress was making slow strangling sounds that indicated emotional upset. From Brugh's mind, Hermes had picked up a hatred of the sound of a woman crying, and he swung hastily out, wondering what the fuss was about. There was only one person left, and he headed toward the little Missie Katherine's room.

She was asleep when he entered, but he called softly: "Miss Kitty." Her head popped up suddenly from the pillow and she groped for the light. For an eight-year-old child, she was lovely with the sleep still in her eyes. She gazed at the little white figure in faint astonishment.

Hermes shinnied up the leg of a chair and made a leap over onto the bed where he could watch her. "What happened to your father?" he asked.

She blinked at him with round eyes. "It talks—a little doll that talks! How cute!"

"I'm not a doll, Kitty; I'm Hermes."

"Not a doll? Oh, goody, you're an elf then?"

"Maybe." It was no time to bicker about a question that had no satisfactory answer. But his heart warmed toward the girl. She wasn't drunk, yet she could still believe in his existence. "I don't know just what I am, but I think I'm the smallest of the gods. Where's your father?"

Memory overwhelmed Kitty in a rush, and her brown eyes brimmed with tears. "He's in jail!" she answered through a puckered mouth. "A nasty man came and took him away, and mamma feels awful. Just 'cause Mr. Hodges hates him."

"Where's jail? Never mind, I'll find out." It would save time by taking the information directly from her head, since she knew where it was. "Now go back to sleep and I'll go find your father."

"And bring him home to mamma?"

"And bring him home to mamma." Hermes knew practically nothing of jails, but the feeling of power was surging hotly through him. So far, everything he had attempted had been accomplished. Kitty smiled uncertainly at him and dropped her head back on the pillow. Then the little god's sense of vibration perception led him toward the cellar in search of certain vital bottles.

A child's toy truck, overburdened with a large bottle and a small god, drew up in front of the dirty white building that served as jail. Hermes had discovered the toy in the yard and used it as a boy does a wagon to facilitate travel. Now he stepped off, lifted the bottle, and parked the truck in a small shrub where he could find it again. Then he began the laborious job of hitching himself up the steps and into the building.

It was in the early morning hours, and there were few men about, but he stayed carefully in the shadow and moved only when their backs were turned. From his observation, men saw only what they expected, and the unusual attracted attention only when accompanied by some sudden sound or movement. Hermes searched one of the men's minds for the location of Brugh, then headed toward the cell, dragging the half-pint bottle behind him as noiselessly as he could.

Dr. Brugh sat on the hard iron cot with his head in his hands, somewhat after the fashion of Rodin's "Thinker"; but his face bore rather less of calm reflection. An occasional muttered invective reached the little god, who grinned. Arlington Brugh was a man of wide attainments, and he had not neglected the development of his vocabulary.

Hermes waited patiently until the guard was out of sight and slipped rapidly toward the cell, mounting over the bottom brace and through the bars. The scientist did not see him as he trotted under the bunk and found a convenient hiding place near the man's legs. At the moment, Brugh was considering the pleasant prospect of attaching all police to Bertha and bombarding them with neutrons until their flesh turned to anything but protoplasm.

Hermes tapped a relatively huge leg and spoke softly. "Dr. Brugh, if you'll look down here, please—" He held up the bottle, the cap already unscrewed.

Brugh lowered his eyes and blinked; from the angle of his sight, only a half-pint bottle of whiskey, raising itself from the floor, could be seen. But he was in a mood to accept miracles without question, and he reached instinctively. Ordinarily he wasn't a drinking man, but the person who won't drink on occasion has a special place reserved for him in heaven—well removed from all other saints.

As the bottle was lowered again, Hermes reached for it and drained the few remaining drops, while Brugh stared at him. "Well?" the god asked finally.

The alcohol was leaving the scientist's stomach rapidly, as it does when no food interferes, and making for his head; the mellowing effect Hermes had hoped for was beginning. "That's my voice you're using," Brugh observed mildly.

"It should be; I learned the language from you. You made me, you know." He waited for a second. "Well, do you believe in me now?"

Brugh grunted. "Hermes, eh? So I wasn't imagining things back in the lab. What happened to you?" A suspicious look crossed his face. "Has Hodges been tinkering again?"

As briefly as he could, the little god summarized events and explained himself, climbing up on the cot as he did so, and squatting down against the physicist's side, out of sight from the door. The other chuckled sourly as he finished.

"So while Hodges was fooling around with amoebas and flesh, I made superlife; only I didn't know it, eh?" There was no longer doubt in his mind, but that might have been due to the whiskey. The reason for more than one conversion to a new religious belief lies hidden in the mysterious soothing effect of ethanol in the form of whiskey and rum. "Well, glad to know you. What happens now?"

"I promised your daughter I'd take you home to the mistress." But now that he was here, he wasn't so sure. There were more men around than he liked. "We'll have to make plans."

Brugh reflected thoughtfully. "That might not be so good. They'd come after me again, and I'd have less chance to prove my innocence."

Hermes was surprised. "You're innocent? I thought you'd murdered Hodges." After all, it was a reasonable supposition, based on the state of the physicist's mind the day before. "What happened?"

"No, I haven't murdered him—yet." Brugh's smile promised unpleasant things at the first chance. "It's still a nice idea, after this trick, though. It all started with the key."

"Maybe I better take it from your head," Hermes decided. "That way I'll be less apt to miss things, and more sure to get things straight."

Brugh nodded and relaxed, thinking back over the last few hours. He lifted the bottle and tried to extract another drop, but the only dampness in it was such as condensed from his breath. Hermes followed the mental pictures and memory until the story was complete in his head.

"So that's the way it was," he grunted, finished. "Some of it doesn't make sense."

"None of it does. All I know is that I'm here and Hodges has enough trumped-up evidence to convict me. He wanted to make the charge kidnaping, but they suggested corpse stealing, and compromised on larceny—grand larceny, I guess."

"I still might be able to swipe the guard's keys, and attract their attention—"

Brugh gathered his somewhat pickled senses. "No. Your biggest value to me is in your ability to get in places where a man couldn't, and find out things without anyone knowing it. If I get out, I can do no more than I can here—I'm not a detective when it comes to human reactions; just physical or chemical puzzles."

There was something in that, Hermes had to concede. "Then I'm to work outside?"

"If you want to. You're a free agent, not bound to me. Slaves have gone out of fashion, and you're hardly a robot." The physicist shook his head. "Why should you help me, come to think of it?"

"Because I want to grow up, and you might help me; and because in a sense we both have the same memories and thought actions—I started out with a mixture of dog, cat and you." He climbed off the bunk and scuttled across the floor. "I'll give Hodges your love if I see him."

Brugh grinned crookedly. "Do."

VIII

Professor Hiram Hodges stirred and turned over in his bed, a sense of something that wasn't as it should be troubling his mind. He grunted softly and tried to sleep again, but the premonition still bothered him. And then he realized that there was a rustling sound going on in his study and that it was still too early for his housekeeper.

He kicked off the sheet and rummaged under the bed for his slippers, drawing on the tattered old robe he'd worn for the last six years. As quietly as he could, he slipped across to the study door, threw it open, and snapped on the light switch, just as the rustling sound stopped. Probably his nephew up to some trick—

But the room contained neither a nephew nor any other man. Hodges blinked, adjusting his eyes to the light, and stared at his desk. It had been closed when he went to bed, he was sure of that. Now it was open, and a litter of papers was strewn across it in haphazard fashion. Someone must have been there and disappeared in the split second it took to snap on the lights.

Hodges moved over to the desk, stopping to pick up a few scraps of paper that had fallen on the floor, then reached up to close the roll top. As he did so, something small and white made a sudden frantic lunge from among the papers and hit the floor to go scuttling across the room. With startlingly quick reactions for his age, the professor spun his lank frame and scooped up the scurrying object.

Apparently it was an animated rubber doll that lay twisting in his grasp. Words came spilling out, though the tiny mouth did not move. "All right, you've caught me. Do you have to squeeze me to death?"

Some men, when faced with the impossible, go insane; others refuse to believe. But Hodges' life had been spent in proving the impossible to be possible, and he faced the situation calmly. A robot wouldn't have spoken that way, and obviously this wasn't flesh and blood; equally obviously, it was some form of life. He lifted the figure onto the desk and clamped the wire wastebasket down over it.

"Now," he said, "what are you, where from, and what do you want?"

Hermes devoted full energy to picturing himself as a charging lion, but the professor was not impressed.

"It's a nice illusion," he granted, smiling. "Come to think of it, maybe your other shape isn't real. Which is it—my nephew or Brugh?"

Hermes gave up and went over the story of his creation again, point by point, while dawn crept up over the roofs of the adjacent houses and urged him to hurry. Hodges' first incredulity turned to doubt, and doubt gave place to half belief.

"So that's the way it is? All right, I'll believe you, provided you can explain how you see without the aid of a lens to direct the light against your sensory surface."

Hermes had overlooked that detail, and took time off to investigate himself. "Apparently the surface is sensitive only to light that strikes it at a certain angle," he decided. "And my mouth opening acts as a very rough lens—something on the order of the old pinhole camera. The tar below is curved, and if I want clearer vision, I can put out a think bubble of fairly transparent surface material to rectify the light more fully, as a lens would. I don't need an iris."

"Um-m-m. So Brugh decided he'd made life and wanted to make a fool of me by bringing my man to consciousness, eh? Is that why he kidnaped Anthropos?"

Hermes grunted sourly. His mind was incapable of the sudden rages and dull hates that seemed to fill men's thoughts, but it was colored by the dislike Brugh cultivated for the biochemist. "It's a nice way of lying, professor, but I know Dr. Brugh had nothing to do with your creation."

The other grinned skeptically. "How do you know?"

"I read his mind, where he had to reveal the truth." In proof, the little god transferred part of the picture he had drawn from Brugh's mind to that of Hodges.

"Hm-m-m." The biochemist lifted the wastebasket off and picked up the little figure. "That would account for the exposed film. Suppose you come with me while I get dressed and try reading my mind. You might be surprised."

Hermes was surprised, definitely. In the professor's mind there had been complete conviction of Brugh's guilt, shaken somewhat now by the story transferred by Hermes. Instead of being a cooked-up scheme to ruin his rival, the theft of the synthetic man was unquestionably genuine. The god fixed on one detail, trying to solve the riddle.

A note received the night before had first apprised the biochemist of the disappearance of his pet creation and sent him to the laboratory to investigate. "What happened to that ransom note?" Hermes asked.

Hodges was struggling with man's symbol of slavery to the law of fashion, his necktie. "It's still in my pocket—here." He flipped it across the room, where the other could study the crude scrawl. The words were crude and direct:

Perffeser, we got yur artifishul man itll cost you 1000$ to get him back leave the dough in a papre sak in the garbaj can bak of yur hows noon tomorer an dont cawl the bulls.

"Obviously the work of a well-educated man," Hodges grunted, succeeding finally with the tie. "They always try to appear too illiterate when writing those notes. That's why I thought Dr. Brugh wrote it to throw me off the trail."

"Hatred had nothing to do with it, I suppose?"

"I don't hate Brugh, and if his conscience didn't bother him, he wouldn't hate me. We used to be fairly good friends. We could still be if we weren't so darned stubborn." The professor grinned as he picked up the small figure and moved toward the kitchen. "You don't eat, do you? Well, I do. Brugh played a dirty trick on me, but I've put over a few of them myself to get money for my department. At Corton, it's always been dog eat dog when appropriations were under debate."

"But did you think he'd leave his key lying around for evidence?"

"People do funny things, and only the department heads are permitted master keys. It had his number." Hodges swallowed the last of a bun and washed it down with milk. "It is funny, though. Let's see, now. Brugh left the keys on the table, and sometime yesterday he lost one of them. Tanya was in the laboratory in the morning, just before a date with that confounded nephew of mine. Hm-m-m."

"But Tanya wouldn't—" Hermes felt duty bound to protect Tanya's reputation.

Hodges cut in on his protest. "It's plain you don't know Tanya Brugh. For herself, she wouldn't take it. But give her a fairly handsome young man with a smooth line, and she'd sell her own father down the river. That ransom note might be some of Johnny's pleasant work."

"Then you think it's your nephew?"

"I don't think anything, but it might be. He's the type. Tell you what I'll do; you try to get some of that potassium salt—oh, yes, I knew about it long ago—from your patron, and I'll help you investigate Johnny."

"If you'll help increase my size." That question was still a major one in the god's mind. "How'll we find out whether Thomas has the thing?"

"That's your worry, son. I'll carry you there, but from then on it's in your hands." Hodges pocketed Hermes and turned out of the kitchen.

IX

Johnny Thomas looked reasonably pleasant as he stuck his head out of the door, though the circles under his eyes were a little too prominent in the early morning hours. He grinned with evident self-satisfaction.

"Ah, my dear maternal uncle. Do come in." He kicked aside a newspaper that was scattered across the floor and flipped the cigarette ashes off the one comfortable chair in the room, seating himself on the bed. "What can I do for you this morning?"

Hodges coughed to cover the noise of Hermes slipping across the room to a dark place under the table. With that attended to, he faced his nephew. "You know Anthropos—that synthetic man I grew in a culture bath? Somebody stole him last night, tank and all, and slipped a note under my door demanding a thousand dollars for his return."

"Too bad. But surely, uncle, you don't think I had anything to do with it?"

"Of course not; how could you get into the laboratory? But I thought you might help me contact the men and make arrangements to pay. Of course, I'd be willing to let you have a few dollars for your work."

Thomas smiled, and looked across the room while apparently making up his mind. As he looked, a cat came out from where no cat should be, gravely lifted a bottle of whiskey and drank deeply. "Excellent, my dear Thomas," the cat remarked. "I suppose when you collect that grand from your uncle, we'll have ever better drinks. Smart trick, stealing that thing."

The cat licked its chops, sprouted wings and turned into a fairy. "Naughty, naughty," said the fairy. "Little boys shouldn't steal." It fluttered over to Thomas' shoulder and perched there, tinkling reproachfully.

The young man swatted at it, felt his hand pass through it, and jumped for the chair. Now the room was empty, though his eyes darted into every corner. His uncle coughed again. "If you're done playing, John—" he suggested.

"Didn't you see it?"

"See what? Oh, you mean that fly? Yes, it was a big one. But about this business I have—"

"I think he'd make a nice meal," said a grizzly bear, materializing suddenly. "So young and succulent."

A shining halo of light quivered violently. "You'd poison your system, Bruin. Go back home." The bear obediently trotted to the window and passed through the glass; the halo of light struck a commanding note, and a face of wrath appeared in it. "Young man, repent of your ways and learn that your sins have found you out. Time is but short on this mortal sphere, and the bad that we do must follow us through all eternity. Repent, for the hour has come!"

Thomas quivered down onto the bed again, wiping his forehead. The idea of getting nervous at a time like this! The things couldn't be real. He turned back to Hodges, who was waiting patiently. "Just a little nervous this morning; not used to getting up so early. Now, as we were saying—"

Click! The sound was in the young man's head, and a soft purring voice followed it. "I know a secret, I know a secret, and I'm going to tell! Johnny, old kid, tell the old fossil what a smart guy you are, putting over a trick like that on him. Go ahead and tell!" There was a hot flicker of pain that stabbed up the backbone, then ran around the ribs and began doing something on the order of a toe dance in Thomas' stomach.

He gritted his teeth and groaned. Hodges became all solicitation. "Something you ate?" asked the professor. "Just lie down on the bed and relax."

There was a whole den of rattlesnakes curled up on the bed, making clicking sounds that seemed to say: "Come ahead, young fellow, it's breakfast time and we're hungry!" Thomas had no desire to relax among even imaginary snakes.

"Gulp—ugh!" he said, and an angel unscrewed its head from the light socket and dropped near him. *"Gulp—ouch!"* The angel sprouted horns and tail, and carried a red-hot fork that felt most unpleasant when rubbed tenderly along his shins.

Click! Again the voice was in his head. "Remember that girl at Casey's? Well, when she committed suicide, it wasn't so nice. But that was gas, and she didn't feel any pains. When you commit suicide—"

"I won't commit suicide!" The bellow was involuntary, forced out just as the little devil decided his fork would feel worse in the stomach. "Take 'em away!"

Hodges clucked sympathetically. "Dear, dear! Do you have a dizzy feeling, Johnny?"

Johnny did, just as the words were out. His head gave an unpleasant twang and leaped from his body, then went whirling around the room. A gnome picked it up, whittled the neck quickly to a point, and drew a whip. "Hi, fellows!" called the gnome. "Come, see the top I made." He drew the whip smartly across Thomas' head and sent it spinning as a horde of other little hobgoblins jumped out of odd places to watch. That was a little too much for Johnny, with the addition of two worms that were eating his eyes.

Hodges chuckled. "All right, Hermes, let him alone. The boy's fainted. It's a pity I couldn't see the things you were forcing on his mind. Must have been right interesting."

Hermes came out of the corner, smiling. "They were very nice. I think he'll talk when he comes to. He persuaded Tanya to get him the key by pretending an interest in cyclotrons—said he was writing a story. She wouldn't have done it, except that the key was lying so temptingly within reach. He worked on her innocence."

"O. K., Hermes," Hodges grunted. "She's washed whiter than snow, if you want it that way. Better get back in my pocket; Johnny's coming around again."

It was noon when Hodges came to the cell where Brugh sat. The biochemist dropped the little god on the floor and grinned. "You're free now, Arlington," he informed the other. "Sorry I got you in here, but I've tried to make up for that."

Brugh looked up at the professor's voice, and his face wasn't pretty. *"Arrughh!"* he said.

The smile on Hodges' face remained unchanged. "I expected that. But Hermes here can tell you I honestly thought you'd stolen Anthropos. We just finished putting him back where he belongs, and seeing that young nephew of mine leave town. If you'll avoid committing homicide on me, the warden will unlock the door."

"What about my reputation?"

"Quite untouched," Hermes assured him. "Professor Hodges succeeded in keeping everything hushed up, and it's Sunday, so your absence from the university won't mean anything."

The physicist came out of the cell, and his shoulders lifted with the touch of freedom. The scowl on his face was gone, but uncertainty still remained in the look he gave Hodges.

The biochemist put out a hand. "I've been thinking you might help me on Anthropos," he said. "You know, Arlington, we might make something out of that yet if we worked together."

Brugh grinned suddenly. "We might at that, Hiram. Come on home to lunch, and we'll talk it over while Hermes tells me what happened."

Hermes squirmed as a hand lifted him back into the pocket. "How about helping me grow up?"

But the two men were busy discussing other things. The height increase would have to wait.

X

Hermes sat on the edge of Anthropos' tank, kicking his small legs against it and thinking of the last two days. To live in the same house, breathe the same air as Tanya Brugh! He dug up another sigh of ecstasy and followed it with one of despair.

For Tanya regarded him as some new form of bug, to be tolerated since he was useful, but not to be liked—an attitude shared by her mother. Dr. Brugh had the greatest respect for the little god, and Kitty was fond of him. Of them all, Kitty treated him best, and Tanya worst.

Of course, that was due to his height. John Thomas was gone, but there were still Will Young and her other escorts, none less than six feet in height. And Hermes was far from being tall. The consultation held with Brugh and Hodges had resulted in nothing; when all was said and done, there was no hope for him.

He sighed again, and Dixon, who was helping Hodges and Brugh with Anthropos, noticed him. "What's the matter, son?" he asked good-naturedly. "Alcohol drying out again? Why not try carbon tetrachloride this time?"

Hermes shook his head. "I don't need anything. The alcohol seems to have permanently combined with the tar, something like water with a crystal to form a hydrate. I'm softened thoroughly for all time."

Hodges looked up and then turned back to the tank where the synthetic man lay, and Hermes turned his attention to it. As far as outward appearance went, Anthropos was nearly perfect, and a tinge of envy filled the little god's thoughts.

Dixon wiped his forehead. "I give up. When three separate divisions of chemistry can't bring life to him, there's no hope. Hodges, your man is doomed to failure."

"He's breathing, though," the biochemist muttered. "Ever since we injected the potassium into him and put it in his nutritive bath, he's been living, but not conscious. See, his heartbeat is as regular as clockwork." He indicated the meter that flickered regularly on the tank.

Brugh refused to look. "To anyone but a biochemist," he informed the room, "the answer would be obvious. Hiram's created life, yes; but he can't give it a good brain. That's too complex for his electric cell formation determiner. What Anthropos needs is a new brain."

"I suppose you'd like to stick his head full of that gummy tar of yours?" Old habit made the words tart, though good fellowship had been restored between them.

"Why not?" It was Hermes' voice this time. Inspiration had flashed suddenly through his small mind, opening a mighty vista of marvels to his imagination. "Why wouldn't that solve it?"

"I'll bite. Why?" Dixon grinned, sweat rolling from his chubby face. "That's the best suggestion we've had today."

"But he wouldn't be real life then, not organic life. Besides, we can't be sure that another batch of the tar would live—it might be an accident that Hermes contained just the right ingredients. The rest of the tar probably isn't the same."

Hermes wriggled in his excitement. "Organic life is merely a chemicoelectrical reaction, with radioactivity thrown in; and I'm all of that. What difference does it make?" He stretched out a small leg. "Dr. Brugh, will you examine my feet?"

With a puzzled frown, Brugh complied. "They're wearing out," he said. "The rubber is almost paper-thin. You'll need a new body soon, Hermes."

"Precisely. That's what I'm talking about. Why couldn't I be put in Anthropos' brainpan?"

Hodges let out a startled wail that died out and left his mouth hanging open. Finally he remembered to close it. "I wonder—" he muttered. "Would it work?"

Dixon demurred. "It'd be a delicate operation, removing the useless higher part of the brain and leaving the essential vital areas that control the heart and organs. Besides, could Hermes control the nerves?"

"Why not? He can control your nerves at a distance if he tries hard enough. But the operation would need a doctor's skill."

Hermes had that all figured out by now, and he voiced his plan while the others listened carefully. Hodges finally nodded. "It might work, son, and Anthropos isn't much good as is. I promised to help you grow up, and if you can use this body, it's yours. The university doesn't seem to value it much."

The borrowed dissecting equipment from the zoölogy department was in readiness and the men stood looking on as Hermes prepared for his work. He paused at the brink of the tank. "You know what you're to do?"

"We do. After you open it, we'll lower your temperature until you harden up to unconsciousness, remove your casing, pack you in the brainpan, so there's no danger of nerve pressure, and cover the opening with the removed section of the skull."

"Right. In that nutrient fluid, it should heal completely in a few hours." Hermes dropped into the tank and was immersed by the liquid; his ability to work in any medium facilitated the operation.

And his sense of perception made him capable of performing the work with almost uncanny skill. As the others watched, he cut briskly around the skull, removed a section, and went into the brain, analyzing it almost cell by cell and suturing, cutting, and scraping away the useless tissue.

Blood oozed out slowly, but the liquid's restorative power began functioning, healing the soft nerve tissue almost as rapidly as it was cut. Hermes nodded approval and continued until only the vital centers that functioned properly were left. Then he indicated that he was finished and Hodges pulled him out.

The dry ice was numbing as they packed it around him, and his thoughts began moving more sluggishly. But as consciousness left him, a heady exultation was singing its song through every atom of his being. He would be tall and handsome, and Tanya would love him.

Consciousness faded as Hodges began the relatively simple job of removing his casing and inserting him into the vacancy in Anthropos' head.

XI

Darkness. That was the first thought Hermes felt on regaining consciousness. He was in a cave with no entrance, and light could not stream through. Around him was a warm shell that held him away from direct contact with the world. He started to struggle against it, and the uneasy sense of closeness increased.

Then he remembered he was in the head of the synthetic man. He must open his eyes and look out. But his eyes refused to open. Again he concentrated, and nothing seemed to happen.

Brugh's voice, muffled as from a great distance, reached him. "Well, he's awake. His big toe twitched then." There was another sensation, the feeling of a faint current pouring in from one of the nerve endings, and Hermes realized that must be his ears sending their message to his brain.

This time he tried to talk, and Hodges spoke. "That was his leg moving. I wonder if he can control his body." Hermes was learning; the sound and nerve messages co-ordinated this time. Learning to use Anthropos' auditory system would not be too difficult.

But he was having trouble. He had tried to open his eyes, and a toe had twitched; an effort to use his tongue resulted in a leg moving. There was only one thing to do, and that was to try everything until the desired result was obtained.

It was several minutes later when Dixon's voice registered on his nerves: "See, his eyes are open. Can you see, Hermes—or Anthropos?"

Hermes couldn't. There was a wild chaos of sensation pouring in through the optic nerve, which must be the effect of light, but it made little sense to him. He concentrated on one part that seemed to register less strongly, and succeeded in making out the distorted figure of a man. It was enough to begin with, but learning to use his eyes took more time than the ears had.

He gave up trying to speak and sent his thought out directly to Brugh. "Lift me out and move me around so I can study which sensations are related to my various parts."

Brugh obeyed promptly with the help of the others, enthusiasm running high. Hermes had the entire job of learning to make his body behave before him, but he brought a highly developed mind to bear on the problem. Bit by bit, the sensation sent up by the nerves registered on his brain, were catalogued and analyzed, and became familiar things to him. He tried touching a table with his finger, and made it in two attempts.

"You'll be better than any man when we're done with you," Hodges gloated. "If I'd brought consciousness into Anthropos, I'd still have had to educate him as a child is taught. You can learn by yourself."

Hermes was learning to talk again, in the clumsy system of breathing, throat contraction, and oral adaptation that produces human words. He tried it now. "Let me walk alone."

Another half-hour saw a stalwart young figure striding about the laboratory, examining this and that, trying out implements, using his body in every way that he could. It answered his commands with a smooth co-ordination that pleased them all.

Brugh was elated. "With a brain like that, Hermes, and the body you have now, we could make the world's greatest physical chemist out of you. A little wire pulling and a few tricks, examinations, and things, and you'd have your degrees in no time. I could use you here."

"He'd be a wonderful biochemist," Hodges cut in. "Think of what that sense of perception would mean to us in trying to determine the effect of drugs on an organism."

Dixon added his opinion. "As an organic chemist, think what it would mean in analyzing and synthesizing new compounds. But why not all three? What we really need is someone to co-ordinate the various fields, and Hermes is ideal." He held out an old pair of trousers, acid stained, but whole, and Hermes began climbing into them. That was a complication he hadn't thought of, and one which was not entirely pleasant. He saw no reason to conceal the new body of which he was so proud.

Brugh had accepted Dixon's idea. "How about getting yourself added to our staff in a few years? It would mean a lot to science, and the board of directors couldn't refuse the appointment if you'd force a little thought into their empty heads."

Hermes had been considering it, and the prospect appealed to him. But Tanya wouldn't like it, probably. He'd have to see her before he could make any decision. Of course, now that he was a real man instead of a rubber statue, she couldn't refuse him.

There was an interruption from the door, a small child's voice. "Daddy, daddy, are you there?" The door swung open and Kitty Brugh came tripping in.

"Kitty, you don't belong here." Brugh faced her with a scowl of annoyance. "I'm busy."

"But mamma sent me." Her voice was plaintive. "She gave me this telegram to bring you."

Brugh took it and read it through, his face lighting up. "Great luck," he told Hermes, handing it over. "I never thought Tanya would choose so well."

The telegram was as simple as most telegrams are:

HAVE MARRIED WILL YOUNG AND ON HONEYMOON IN MILLSBURG
STOP EVER SO HAPPY STOP LOVE

TANYA

And with it, the newly created man's hopes went flying out into nothingness.

But somehow he felt much better than he should. He handed it back to Brugh, and the sigh he achieved was halfhearted. Kitty's eyes noticed him for the first time.

She squeaked delightedly. "Oh, what a pretty man! What's your name?"

Hermes' heart went out to her. He stooped and picked her up in his strong young arms, stroking her hair. "I'm the little god, Kitty. I'm your Hermes in a new body. Do you like it?"

She snuggled up. "Um-hmm. It's nice." There was no surprise for her in anything Hermes might do. He turned back to the three men then.

"Dr. Brugh, I've decided to accept your offer. I'd like nothing better than working with all of you here at Corton."

"Splendid, my boy. Splendid. Eh, Hiram?"

They crowded around him, shaking his hand, and he thoroughly enjoyed the flattery of their respect. But most of his thoughts were centered on Kitty. After all, she was the only woman—or girl—who had treated him with any consideration, and her little mind was open and honest. She'd make a wonderful woman in ten more years.

Ten more years; and he wasn't so very old himself. There might be hope here yet.

INTO THE DARKNESS

Ross Rocklynne

About the time "The Smallest God" appeared in *Astounding,* Ross Rocklynne heard that a new market had opened for science fiction: Frederik Pohl was starting a new magazine called *Astonishing Stories.* Rocklynne, not quite twenty-seven years old, was already a veteran science fiction writer, having published more than a dozen stories in the preceding five years in magazines as diverse as *Astounding* and *Fantastic Adventures.* But he had one favorite manuscript that he'd never managed to get into print; originally written in 1934, when F. Orlin Tremaine had been featuring imaginative "Thought Variant" stories in *Astounding,* it was a kaleidoscope of cosmic wonders that was evidently beyond even Tremaine's grasp, for he had rejected it.

Charles Hornig had accepted the tale for *Wonder Stories,* but that magazine had foundered in 1936 and passed on to new management; the manuscript had been returned to Rocklynne. (He hadn't been paid for it: *Wonder* paid on publication, not acceptance.) He'd tried it with every other science fiction editor around, but no one had been willing to take a chance on a story that didn't even have human characters. Its title was "Into the Darkness," and he sent it to Pohl's new magazine.

Then he went back to his typewriter to write new stories, for then as now the livelihood of a free-lance writer depended on continuous production. He soon ran into a fallow period for ideas, though, so he resorted to a stratagem he'd employed before: he rolled a sheet of paper into his typewriter and began to type his thoughts as rapidly as he could, hoping to turn up an idea. Here's what he wrote:

Should I lay this story in modern times on Earth or on another planet, or should I put it in the future when the imagination can be used more. . . . Now in the canals of Mars the water flows toward the equator doubtless and so what lord I can type faster when I ignor punctuations oh the hell with it all no I cant take that attitude. Monday morning I will go up to the mail box with a manuscript I wonder if there will be a mail box chock full of checks I don't think so into the darkness has already been rejected by pohl, undoubtedly, and the only place would be strange stories or maybe science-fiction tapping on this typer may so drive me into a stupor that a story will simply come popping out of this thing that I must call a brain what a hell of a brain no it is a very good brain so it is . . .

Everybody has days like that, but Rocklynne needn't have worried about Pohl rejecting "Into the Darkness." He loved it, and bought it immediately. His readers loved it too; the next issue's letter column was filled with reactions like "the most refreshing story to appear anywhere in science fiction in at least a year!", "one of the best science fiction stories I have ever had the pleasure of reading," and "I particularly liked Ross Rocklynne's 'Into the Darkness.' It surely was unusual and unexpected." The latter comment was from a nineteen-year-old named Ray Bradbury, then only a year away from selling his first story.

Rocklynne received just sixty dollars, half a cent a word, for "Into the Darkness," but its popularity induced Pohl to break his budget and pay a full cent a word for a sequel in 1941. This too was popular with the readers, so Rocklynne did another in 1942. *Astonishing* died during the war, but Rocklynne published a fourth novelette in the series in a 1951 issue of *Imagination*. In 1973, Ace Books collected the four stories for publication as half of an "Ace Double." (Frederik Pohl was then the editor at Ace.)

So Rocklynne's faith in the story that had gone unpublished for six years was obviously justified. Written in a time when science fiction was dominated by the cosmic concepts of authors like E. E. Smith and the early Jack Williamson, "Into the Darkness" was so daring a story that it went without a market till Pohl, young and willing to experiment, took a chance on it. In fact, Harlan Ellison remembers that when the *fourth* story of the series appeared in 1951 it was "well beyond the terms and intents of what was being written in the field" even then.

I don't mean to suggest that "Into the Darkness" is the ultimate science fiction story, of course. It's written in pulp style and, for all its alienness, it indulges in anthropomorphism at times. Not only that, I realized with amusement at one point, but the main character knew of only ninety-eight elements. He could travel between galaxies in seconds, create and destroy whole solar systems, but he thought there were only ninety-eight elements—whereas today we know of over a hundred, with the number still climbing.

I decided it was a good example of how even the most imaginative science fiction stories can become dated within a few years. After all, hadn't I seen many worse examples in the stories of the early forties? Not only stories whose scientific backgrounds soon became embarrassingly inaccurate—such as the 1942 Henry Kuttner story that referred twice to Piltdown man—but also those in which everyday aspects of life c. 1940 were so taken for granted that they were carried forward into the future:

Bob Olsen had a story in which a married couple of the future replaced their icebox with a refrigerator, and simultaneously bought a robot maid. The maid eloped with the refrigerator.

One of Alfred Bester's early stories of the future included the line "The acceleration tumbled his attackers from the running board."

Don Wilcox wrote a story set in the thirtieth century that included an invisible Venusian car; one of its remarkable features was "built-in headlights."

I have to wonder how many readers of this book have ever heard of iceboxes or running boards, and if anyone considers built-in headlights to be futuristic. I also wonder how understandable today are the following lines from stories by Robert Moore Williams and William P. McGivern:

"All the weight of his body was behind that blow. He drove it straight at Sharp's chin. It would have made Joe Louis bat his expressionless eyes."

"I popped out of the cab and did a Jessie Owens into the place."

(You probably know that Louis was the heavyweight boxing champion of the world for many years, but maybe his characteristic implacability in the ring is less well remembered. Owens was a famous Olympics sprinter.)

Some of the stories from this period fairly begged to become dated, such as C. M. Kornbluth's "The Rocket of 1955" (about the first trip to the moon, of course). But these stories were written in a time when sf authors had no markets beyond the pulp magazines, which would be on sale for a month or so; science fiction anthologies simply did not exist then, so the idea of "writing for the ages" was unknown even to the authors of a genre devoted to the future.

But it turns out that there's no need to pardon Ross Rocklynne for his ninety-eight elements. Contrary to my initial assumption that Rocklynne had simply listed the number of elements known to science when he wrote the story—or that Pohl might have updated the number when he published the story in 1940—with a little checking I found that in 1940 only ninety-*two* elements were known. Rocklynne *had* extrapolated the number forward; he had simply fallen a bit short.

He didn't fall short with the story itself, though. "Into the Darkness" remains to this day one of the most unusual stories ever written, wondrous in its concepts and thematically resonant. The term "far out" hadn't entered the language in 1940, but it fits.

REFERENCES:

"Meet the Authors" by Ross Rocklynne. *Amazing Stories,* June 1940.
Index to the Science-Fiction Magazines by Donald B. Day. Perri Press, 1952.
"Introducing the Author" by Ross Rocklynne. *Imagination,* January 1954.
"The Time Stream" by Sam Moskowitz. *Fantasy News,* February 25, 1940.
Letter from Julius Schwartz, January 17, 1977.
"Gostacus: Discii: Destimabat" by Ross Rocklynne. *The Fantasite,* May-June 1943.
Conversation with Ross Rocklynne, April 26, 1974.
"Viewpoints." *Astonishing Stories,* August 1940.
Letter from Frederik Pohl, March 12, 1974.
Introduction by Harlan Ellison to "Ching Witch!" by Ross Rocklynne. *Again, Dangerous Visions.* Doubleday, 1972.
"False Dawn" by Henry Kuttner. *Thrilling Wonder Stories,* June 1942.
"Our Robot Maid" by Bob Olsen. *Future Fiction,* November 1940.
"Slaves of the Life Ray" by Alfred Bester. *Thrilling Wonder Stories,* February 1941.
"Invisible Raiders of Venus" by Don Wilcox. *Amazing Stories,* April 1941.

INTO THE DARKNESS · 67

"Lord of the Silent Death" by Robert Moore Williams. *Comet,* December 1940.

"The Dynamouse" by William P. McGivern. *Fantastic Adventures,* January 1941.

"The Rocket of 1955" by "Cecil Corwin" (C. M. Kornbluth). *Stirring Science Stories,* April 1941.

* * *

I. Birth of "Darkness"

Out in space, on the lip of the farthest galaxy, and betwixt two star clusters, there came into being a luminiferous globe that radiated for light-years around. A life had been born!

It became aware of light; one of its visions had become activated. First it saw the innumerable suns and nebulae whose radiated energy now fed it. Beyond that it saw a dense, impenetrable darkness.

The darkness intrigued it. It could understand the stars, but the darkness it could not. The babe probed outward several light-years and met only lightlessness. It probed further, and further, but there was no light. Only after its visions could not delve deeper did it give up, but a strange seed had been sown; that there was light on the far edge of the darkness became its innate conviction.

Wonders never seemed to cease parading themselves before this newly-born. It became aware of another personality hovering near, an energy creature thirty millions of miles across. At its core hung a globe of subtly glowing green light one million miles in diameter.

He explored this being with his vision, and it remained still during his inspection. He felt strange forces plucking at him, forces that filled him to overflowing with peacefulness. At once, he discovered a system of energy waves having marvelous possibilities.

"Who are you?" these waves were able to inquire of that other life.

Softly soothing, he received answer.

"I am your mother."

"You mean—?"

"You are my son—my creation. I shall call you—Darkness. Lie here and grow, Darkness, and when you are many times larger, I will come again."

She had vanished, swallowed untraceably by a vast spiral nebula—a cloud of swiftly twisting stardust.

He lay motionless, strange thoughts flowing. Mostly he wondered about the sea of lightlessness lapping the shore of this galaxy in which he had been born. Sometime later, he wondered about life, what life was, and its purpose.

"When *she* comes again, I shall ask her," he mused. "Darkness, she called me—Darkness!"

His thoughts swung back to the darkness.

For five million years he bathed himself in the rays that permeate space. He grew. He was ten million miles in diameter.

His mother came; he saw her hurtling toward him from a far distance. She stopped close.

"You are much larger, Darkness. You grow faster than the other newly-born." He detected pride in her transmitted thoughts.

"I have been lying here, thinking," he said. "I have been wondering, and I have come to guess at many things. There are others, like you and myself."

"There are thousands of others. I am going to take you to them. Have you tried propellents?"

"I have not tried, but I shall." There was a silence. "I have discovered the propellents," said Darkness, puzzled, "but they will not move me."

She seemed amused. "That is one thing you do not know, Darkness. You are inhabiting the seventeenth band of hyperspace; propellents will not work there. See if you can expand."

All these were new things, but instinctively he felt himself expand to twice his original size.

"Good. I am going to snap you into the first band. . . . There. Try your propellents."

He tried them, and, to his intense delight, the flaring lights that were the stars fled past. So great was his exhilaration that he worked up a speed that placed him several light-years from his Mother.

She drew up beside him. "For one so young, you have speed. I shall be proud of you. I feel, Darkness," and there was wistfulness in her tone, "that you will be different from the others."

She searched his memory swirls. "But try not to be too different."

Puzzled at this, he gazed at her, but she turned away. "Come."

He followed her down the aisles formed by the stars, as she accommodated her pace to his.

They stopped at the sixth galaxy from the abyss of lightlessness. He discerned thousands of shapes that were his kind moving swiftly past and around him. These, then, were his people.

She pointed them out to him. "You will know them by their vibrations, and the varying shades of the colored globes of light at their centers."

She ran off a great list of names which he had no trouble in impressing on his memory swirls.

"Radiant, Vibrant, Swift, Milky, Incandescent, Great Power, Sun-eater, Light-year . . ."

"Come, I am going to present you to Oldster."

They whirled off to a space seven light-years distant. They stopped, just outside the galaxy. There was a peculiar snap in his consciousness.

"Oldster has isolated himself in the sixth band of hyperspace," said his Mother.

Where before he had seen nothing save inky space, dotted with masses of flaming, tortured matter, he now saw an energy creature whose aura fairly radiated old age. And the immense purple globe which hung at his core lacked a certain vital luster which Darkness had instinctively linked with his own youth and boundless energy.

His Mother caught the old being's attention, and Darkness felt his thought-rays contact them.

"Oh, it's you, Sparkle," the old being's kindly thoughts said. "And who is it with you?"

Darkness saw his Mother, Sparkle, shoot off streams of crystalline light.

"This is my first son."

The newly-born felt Oldster's thought-rays going through his memory swirls.

"And you have named him Darkness," said Oldster slowly. "Because he has wondered about it." His visions withdrew, half-absently. "He is so young, and yet he is a thinker; already he thinks about life."

For long and long Oldster bent a penetrating gaze upon him. Abruptly, his vision rays swung away and centered on a tiny, isolated group of stars. There was a heavy, dragging silence.

"Darkness," Oldster said finally, "your thoughts are useless." The thoughts now seemed to come from an immeasurable distance, or an infinitely tired mind. "You are young, Darkness. Do not think so much—so much that the happiness of life is destroyed in the over-estimation of it. When you wish, you may come to see me. I shall be in the sixth band for many millions of years."

Abruptly, Oldster vanished. He had snapped both Mother and son back in the first band.

She fixed her vision on him. "Darkness, what he says is true —every word. Play for a while—there are innumerable things to do. And once in great intervals, if you wish, go to see Oldster; but for a long time do not bother him with your questions."

"I will try," answered Darkness, in sudden decision.

II. Cosmic Children

Darkness played. He played for many millions of years. With playmates of his own age, he roamed through and through the endless numbers of galaxies that composed the universe. From one end to another he dashed in a reckless obedience to Old-ster's command.

He explored the surfaces of stars, often disrupting them into fragments, sending scalding geysers of belching flame millions of miles into space. He followed his companions into the swirling depths of the green-hued nebulae that hung in intergalactic space. But to disturb these mighty creations of nature was impossible. Majestically they rolled around and around, or coiled into spirals, or at times condensed into matter that formed beautiful, hot suns.

Energy to feed on was rampant here, but so densely and widely was it distributed that he and his comrades could not even dream of absorbing more than a trillionth part of it in all their lives.

He learned the mysteries of the forty-seven bands of hyper-space. He learned to snap into them or out again into the first or true band at will. He knew the delights of blackness impenetrable in the fifteenth band, of a queerly illusory multiple existence in the twenty-third, and an equally strange sensation of speeding away from himself in an opposite direction in the thirty-first, and of the forty-seventh, where all space turned into a nightmarish concoction of cubistic suns and galaxies.

Incomprehensible were those forty-seven bands. They were coexistent in space, yet they were separated from each other by a means which no one had ever discovered. In each band were unmistakable signs that it was the same universe. Darkness only knew that each band was one of forty-seven subtly differing faces which the universe possessed, and the powers of his mind experienced no difficulty in allowing him to cross the unseen bridges which spanned the gulfs between them.

And he made no attempts toward finding the solution—he was determined to cease thinking, for the time being at least. He was content to play, and to draw as much pleasure and excitement as he could from every new possibility of amusement.

But the end of all *that* came, as he had suspected it would. He played, and loved all this, until . . .

He had come to his fifty-millionth year, still a youth. The purple globe at his core could have swallowed a sun a million miles in diameter, and his whole body could have displaced fifty suns of that size. For a period of a hundred thousand years he lay asleep in the seventh band, where a soft, colorless light pervaded the universe.

He awoke, and was about to transfer himself to the first band and rejoin the children of Radiant, Light-year, Great Power and all those others.

He stopped, almost dumbfounded, for a sudden, overwhelming antipathy for companionship had come over him. He discovered, indeed, that he never wanted to join his friends again. While he had slept, a metamorphosis had come about, and he was as alienated from his playmates as if he had never known them.

What had caused it? Something. Perhaps, long before his years, he had passed into the adult stage of mind. Now he was rebelling against the friendships which meant nothing more than futile play.

Play! Bouncing huge suns around like rubber balls, and then tearing them up into solar systems; chasing one another up the scale through the forty-seven bands, and back again; darting about in the immense spaces between galaxies, rendering themselves invisible by expanding to ten times normal size.

He did not want to play, and he never wanted to see his friends again. He did not hate them, but he was intolerant of the characteristics which bade them to disport amongst the stars for eternity.

He was not mature in size, but he felt he had become an adult, while they were still children—tossing suns the length of a galaxy, and then hurling small bits of materialized energy around them to form planets; then just as likely to hurl huger masses to disrupt the planetary systems they so painstakingly made.

He had felt it all along—this superiority. He had manifested it by besting them in every form of play they conceived. They generally bungled everything, more apt to explode a star into small fragments than to whirl it until centrifugal force threw off planets.

"I have become an adult in mind, if not in body; I am at the point where I must accumulate wisdom, and perhaps sorrow," he thought whimsically. "I will see Oldster, and ask him my questions—the questions I have thus far kept in the background of my thoughts. But," he added thoughtfully, "I have a feeling that even his wisdom will fail to enlighten me. Nevertheless, there must be answers. What is life? Why is it? And there must be—another universe beyond the darkness that hems this one in."

Darkness reluctantly turned and made a slow trail across that galaxy and into the next, where he discovered those young energy creatures with whom it would be impossible to enjoy himself again.

He drew up, and absently translated his time standard to one corresponding with theirs, a rate of consciousness at which they could observe the six planets whirling around a small, white-hot sun as separate bodies, and not mere rings of light.

They were gathered in numbers of some hundreds around this sun, and Darkness hovered on the outskirts of the crowd, watching them moodily.

One of the young purple lights, Cosmic by name, threw a mass of matter a short distance into space, reached out with a tractor ray and drew it in. He swung it 'round and 'round on the tip of that ray, gradually forming ever-decreasing circles. To endow the planet with a velocity that would hurl it unerringly between the two outermost planetary orbits required a delicate sense of compensatory adjustment between the factors of mass, velocity, and solar attraction.

When Cosmic had got the lump of matter down to an angular velocity that was uniform, Darkness knew an irritation he had never succeeded in suppressing. An intuition, which had unfail-

ingly proved itself accurate, told him that anything but creating
an orbit for that planet was likely to ensue.

"Cosmic." He contacted the planet-maker's thought-rays.
"Cosmic, the velocity you have generated is too great. The
whole system will break up."

"Oh, Darkness." Cosmic threw a vision on him. "Come on,
join us. You say the speed is wrong? Never; you are! I've cal-
culated everything to a fine point."

"To the wrong point," insisted Darkness stubbornly. "Undoubtedly, your estimation of the planet's mass is the factor
which makes your equation incorrect. Lower the velocity.
You'll see.

Cosmic continued to swing his lump of matter, but stared
curiously at Darkness.

"What's the matter with you?" he inquired. "You don't sound
just right. What does it matter if I do calculate wrong, and
disturb the system's equilibrium? We'll very probably break up
the whole thing later, anyway."

A flash of passion came over Darkness. "That's the trouble,"
he said fiercely. "It doesn't matter to any of you. You will always
be children. You will always be playing. Careful construction,
joyous destruction—that is the creed on which you base your
lives. Don't you feel as if you'd like, sometime, to quit playing,
and do something—worthwhile?"

As if they had discovered a strangely different set of laws
governing an alien galaxy, the hundreds of youths, greens and
purples, stared at Darkness.

Cosmic continued swinging the planet he had made through
space, but he was plainly puzzled. "What's wrong with you,
Darkness? What else is there to do except to roam the galaxies,
and make suns? I can't think of a single living thing that might
be called more worthwhile."

"What good is playing?" answered Darkness. "What good is
making a solar system? If you made one, and then, perhaps,
vitalized it with life, that would be worthwhile! Or think, think!
About yourself, about life, why it is, and what it means in the
scheme of things! Or," and he trembled a little, "try discovering

what lies beyond the veil of lightlessness which surrounds the universe."

The hundreds of youths looked at the darkness.

Cosmic stared anxiously at him. "Are you crazy? We all know there's nothing beyond. Everything that is is right here in the universe. That blackness is just empty, and it stretches away from here forever."

"Where did you get that information?" Darkness inquired scornfully. "You don't know that. Nobody does. But I am going to know! I awoke from sleep a short while ago, and I couldn't bear the thought of play. I wanted to do something substantial. So I am going into the darkness."

He turned his gaze hungrily on the deep abyss hemming in the stars. There were thousands of years, even under its lower time-standard, in which awe dominated the gathering. In his astonishment at such an unheard-of intention, Cosmic entirely forgot his circling planet. It lessened in velocity, and then tore loose from the tractor ray that had become weak, in a tangent to the circle it had been performing.

It sped toward that solar system, and entered between the orbits of the outmost planets. Solar gravitation seized it, the lone planet took up an erratic orbit, and then the whole system had settled into complete stability, with seven planets where there had been six.

"You see," said Darkness, with a note of unsteady mirth, "if you had used your intended speed, the system would have coalesced. The speed of the planet dropped, and then escaped you. Some blind chance sent it in the right direction. It was purely an accident. Now throw in a second sun, and watch the system break up. That has always amused you." His aura quivered. "Goodbye, friends."

III. Oldster

He was gone from their sight forever. He had snapped into the sixth band.

He ranged back to the spot where Oldster should have been. He was not.

"Probably in some other band," thought Darkness, and went through all the others, excepting the fifteenth, where resided a complete lack of light. With a feeling akin to awe, since Oldster was apparently in none of them, he went into the fifteenth, and called out.

There was a period of silence. Then Oldster answered, in his thoughts a cadence of infinite weariness.

"Yes, my son; who calls me?"

"It is I, Darkness, whom Sparkle presented to you nearly fifty million years ago." Hesitating, an unexplainable feeling, as of sadness unquenchable, came to him.

"I looked for you in the sixth," he went on in a rush of words, "but did not expect to find you here, isolated, with no light to see by."

"I am tired of seeing, my son. I have lived too long. I have tired of thinking and of seeing. I am sad."

Darkness hung motionless, hardly daring to interrupt the strange thought of this incredible ancient. He ventured timidly, "It is just that I am tired of playing, Oldster, tired of doing nothing. I should like to accomplish something of some use. Therefore, I have come to you, to ask you three questions, the answers to which I must know."

Oldster stirred restlessly. "Ask your questions."

"I am curious about life." Oldster's visitor hesitated nervously, and then went on. "It has a purpose, I know, and I want to know that purpose. That is my first question."

"But why, Darkness? What makes you think life *has* a purpose, an ultimate purpose?"

"I don't know," came the answer, and for the first time Darkness was startled with the knowledge that he really didn't! "But there must be some purpose!" he cried.

"How can you say 'must'? Oh, Darkness, you have clothed life in garments far too rich for its ordinary character! You have given it the sacred aspect of meaning! There is no meaning to it. Once upon a time the spark of life fired a blob of common energy with consciousness of its existence. From that, by some obscure evolutionary process, we came. That is all. We are born. We live, and grow, and then we die! After that, there is nothing! Nothing!"

Something in Darkness shuddered violently, and then rebelliously. But his thoughts were quiet and tense. "I won't believe that! You are telling me that life is only meant for death, then. Why—why, if that were so, why should there be life? No, Oldster! I feel that there must be something which justifies my existence."

Was it pity that came flowing along with Oldster's thoughts? "You will never believe me. I knew it. All my ancient wisdom could not change you, and perhaps it is just as well. Yet you may spend a lifetime in learning what I have told you."

His thoughts withdrew, absently, and then returned.

"Your other questions, Darkness."

For a long time Darkness did not answer. He was of half a mind to leave Oldster, and leave it to his own experiences to solve his other problems. His resentment was hotter than a dwarf sun, for a moment. But it cooled and though he was beginning to doubt the wisdom to which Oldster laid claim, he continued with his questioning.

"What is the use of the globe of purple light which forever remains at my center, and even returns, no matter how far I hurl it from me?"

Such a wave of mingled agitation and sadness passed from the old being that Darkness shuddered. Oldster turned on him with extraordinary fierceness. "Do not learn *that* secret! I will not tell you! What might I not have spared myself had I not sought and found the answer to that riddle! I was a thinker, Darkness, like you! Darkness, if you value— Come, Darkness," he went on in a singularly broken manner, "your remaining question." His thought-rays switched back and forth with an uncommon sign of utter chaos of mind.

Then they centered on Darkness again. "I know your other

query, Darkness. I know, knew when first Sparkle brought you to me, eons ago.

"What is beyond the darkness? That has occupied your mind since your creation. What lies on the fringe of the lightless section by which this universe is bounded?"

"I do not know, Darkness. Nor does anyone know."

"But you *must* believe there is something beyond," cried Darkness.

"Darkness, in the dim past of our race, beings of your caliber have tried—five of them I remember in my time, billions of years ago. But, they never came back. They left the universe, hurling themselves into that awful void, and they never came back."

"How do you know they didn't reach that foreign universe?" asked Darkness breathlessly.

"Because they didn't come back," answered Oldster, simply. "If they could have gotten across, at least one or two of them would have returned. They never reached that universe. Why? All the energy they were able to accumulate for that staggering voyage was exhausted. And they dissipated—died—in the energiless emptiness of the darkness."

"There must be a way to cross!" said Darkness violently. "There must be a way to gather energy for the crossing! Oldster, you are destroying my life-dream! I have wanted to cross. I want to find the edge of the darkness. I want to find life there —perhaps then I will find the meaning of all life!"

"Find the—" began Oldster pityingly, then stopped, realizing the futility of completing the sentence.

"It is a pity you are not like the others, Darkness. Perhaps they understand that it is as purposeful to lie sleeping in the seventh band as to discover the riddle of the darkness. They are truly happy, you are not. Always, my son, you over-estimate the worth of life."

"Am I wrong in doing so?"

"No. Think as you will, and think that life is high. There is no harm. Dream your dream of great life, and dream your dream of another universe. There is joy even in the sadness of unattainment."

Again that long silence, and again the smoldering flame of resentment in Darkness' mind. This time there was no quenching of that flame. It burned fiercely.

"I will not dream!" said Darkness furiously. "When first my visions became activated, they rested on the darkness, and my new-born thought-swirls wondered about the darkness, and knew that something lay beyond it!

"And whether or not I die in that void, I am going into it!"

Abruptly, irately, he snapped from the fifteenth band into the first, but before he had time to use his propellents, he saw Oldster, a giant body of intense, swirling energies of pure light, materialize before him.

"Darkness, stop!" and Oldster's thoughts were unsteady. "Darkness," he went on, as the younger energy creature stared spellbound, "I had vowed to myself never to leave the band of lightlessness. I have come from it, a moment, for—you!

"You will die. You will dissipate in the void! You will never cross it, if it can be crossed, with the limited energy your body contains!"

He seized Darkness' thought-swirls in tight bands of energy.

"Darkness, there is knowledge that I possess. Receive it!"

With new-born wonder, Darkness erased consciousness. The mighty accumulated knowledge of Oldster sped into him in a swift flow, a great tide of space-lore no other being had ever possessed.

The inflow ceased, and as from an immeasurably distant space came Oldster's parting words:

"Darkness, farewell! Use your knowledge, use it to further your dream. Use it to cross the darkness."

Again fully conscious, Darkness knew that Oldster had gone again into the fifteenth band of utter lightlessness, in his vain attempt at peace.

He hung tensely motionless in the first band, exploring the

knowledge that now was his. At the portent of one particular portion of it, he trembled.

In wildest exhilaration, he thrust out his propellents, dashing at full speed to his Mother.

He hung before her.

"Mother, I am going into the darkness!"

There was a silence, pregnant with her sorrow. "Yes, I know. It was destined when first you were born. For that I named you Darkness." A restless quiver of sparks left her. Her gaze sad and loving. She said, "Farewell, Darkness, my son."

She wrenched herself from true space, and he was alone. The thought stabbed him. He was alone—alone as Oldster.

Struggling against the vast depression that overwhelmed him, he slowly started on his way to the very furthest edge of the universe, for there lay the Great Energy.

Absently he drifted across the galaxies, the brilliant denizens of the cosmos, lying quiescent on their eternal black beds. He drew a small sun into him, and converted it into energy for the long flight.

And suddenly afar off he saw his innumerable former companions. A cold mirth seized him. Playing! The folly of children, the aimlessness of stars!

He sped away from them, and slowly increased his velocity, the thousands of galaxies flashing away behind. His speed mounted, a frightful acceleration carrying him toward his goal.

IV. Beyond Light

It took him seven millions of years to cross the universe, going at the tremendous velocity he had attained. And he was in a galaxy whose far flung suns hung out into the darkness, were themselves traveling into the darkness at the comparatively slow pace of several thousand miles a second.

Instantaneously, his vision rested on an immense star, a star so immense that he felt himself unconsciously expand in an effort to rival it. So titanic was its mass that it drew all light rays save the short ultra-violet back into it.

It was hot, an inconceivable mass of matter a billion miles across. Like an evil, sentient monster of the skies it hung, dominating the tiny suns of this galaxy that were perhaps its children, to Darkness flooding the heavens with ultra-violet light from its great expanse of writhing, coiling, belching surface; and mingled with that light was a radiation of energy so virulent that it ate its way painfully into his very brain.

Still another radiation impinged on him, an energy which, were he to possess its source, would activate his propellents to such an extent that his velocity would pale any to which his race had attained in all its long history!—would hurl him into the darkness at such an unthinkable rate that the universe would be gone in the infinitesimal part of a second!

But how hopeless seemed the task of rending it from that giant of the universe! The source of that energy, he knew with knowledge that was sure, was matter, matter so incomparably dense, its electrons crowding each other till they touched, that even that furiously molten star could not destroy it!

He spurred back several million of miles, and stared at it. Suddenly he knew fear, a cold fear. He felt that the sun was animate, that it knew he was waiting there, that it was prepared to resist his pitiable onslaughts. And as if in support of his fears, he felt rays of such intense repelling power, such alive, painful malignancy that he almost threw away his mad intentions of splitting it.

"I have eaten suns before," he told himself, with the air of one arguing against himself. "I can at least split that one open, and extract the morsel that lies in its interior."

He drew into him as many of the surrounding suns as he was able, converting them into pure energy. He ceased at last, for no longer could his body, a giant complexity of swarming intense fields sixty millions of miles across, assimilate more.

Then, with all the acceleration he could muster, he dashed headlong at the celestial monster.

It grew and expanded, filling all the skies until he could no longer see anything but it. He drew near its surface. Rays of fearful potency smote him until he convulsed in the whiplash agony of it. At frightful velocity, he contacted the heaving surface, and—made a tiny dent some millions of miles in depth.

He strove to push forward, but streams of energy repelled him, energy that flung him away from the star in acceleration.

He stopped his backward flight, fighting his torment, and threw himself upon the star again. It repulsed him with an uncanny likeness to a living thing. Again and again he went through the agonizing process, to be as often thrust back.

He could not account for those repelling rays, which seemed to operate in direct contrariness to the star's obviously great gravitational field, nor did he try to account for them. There were mysteries in space which even Oldster had never been able to solve.

But there was a new awe in him. He hung in space, spent and quivering.

"It is *almost* alive," he thought, and then adopted new tactics. Rushing at the giant, he skimmed over and through its surface in titanic spirals, until he had swept it entirely free of raging, incandescent gases. Before the star could replenish its surface, he spiraled it again, clinging to it until he could no longer resist the repelling forces, or the burning rays which impinged upon him.

The star now lay in the heavens diminished by a tenth of its former bulk. Darkness, hardly able to keep himself together, retired a distance from it and discarded excess energy.

He went back to the star.

Churning seas of pure light flickered fitfully across. Now and then there were belchings of matter bursting within itself.

Darkness began again. He charged, head on. He contacted, bored millions of miles, and was thrown back with mounting velocity. Hurtling back into space, Darkness finally knew that all these tactics would in the last analysis prove useless. His glance roving, it came to rest on a dense, redly glowing sun. For a moment it meant nothing, and then he knew, knew that here at last lay the solution.

He plucked that dying star from its place, and swinging it in huge circles on the tip of a tractor ray, flung it with the utmost of his savage force at the gargantuan star.

Fiercely, he watched the smaller sun approach its parent. Closer, closer, and then—they collided! A titanic explosion ripped space, sending out wave after wave of cosmic rays, causing an inferno of venomous, raging flames that extended far into the skies, licking it in a fury of utter abandon. The mighty sun split wide open, exhibiting a violet hot, gaping maw more than a billion miles wide.

Darkness activated his propellents, and dropped into the awful cavity until he was far beneath its rim, and had approached the center of the star where lay that mass of matter which was the source of the Great Energy. To his sight, it was invisible, save as a blank area of nothingness, since light rays of no wave-length whatsoever could leave it.

Darkness wrapped himself exotically around the sphere, and at the same time the two halves of the giant star fell together, imprisoning him at its core.

This possibility he had not overlooked. With concentrated knots of force, he ate away the merest portion of the surface of the sphere, and absorbed it in him. He was amazed at the metamorphosis. He became aware of a vigor so infinite that he felt nothing could withstand him.

Slowly, he began to expand. He was inexorable. The star could not stop him; it gave. It cracked, great gaping cracks which parted with displays of blinding light and pure heat. He continued to grow, pushing outward.

With the sphere of Great Energy, which was no more than ten million miles across, in his grasp, he continued inflation. A terrific blast of malignant energy ripped at him; cracks millions of miles in length appeared, cosmic displays of pure energy flared. After that, the gargantua gave way before Darkness so readily that he had split it up into separate parts before he ever knew it.

He then became aware that he was in the center of thousands of large and small pieces of the star that were shooting away from him in all directions, forming new suns that would chart individual orbits for themselves.

He had conquered. He hung motionless, grasping the sphere of Great Energy at his center, along with the mystic globe of purple light.

He swung his vision on the darkness, and looked at it in fascination for a long time. Then, without a last look at the universe of his birth, he activated his propellents with the nameless Great Energy, and plunged into that dark well.

All light, save that he created, vanished. He was hemmed in on all sides by the vastness of empty space. Exaltation, coupled with an awareness of the infinite power in his grasp, took hold of his thoughts and made them soar. His acceleration was minimum rather than maximum, yet in a brief space of his time standard he traversed uncountable billions of light-years.

Darkness ahead, and darkness behind, and darkness all around—that had been his dream. It had been his dream all through his life, even during those formless years in which he had played, in obedience to Oldster's admonishment. Always there had been the thought—what lies at the other end of the darkness? Now he was in the darkness, and a joy such as he had never known claimed him. He was on the way! Would he find another universe, a universe which had bred the same kind of life as he had known? He could not think otherwise.

His acceleration was incredible! Yet he knew that he was using a minimum of power. He began to step it up, swiftly increasing even the vast velocity which he had attained. Where lay that other universe? He could not know, and he had chosen no single direction in which to leave his own universe. There had been no choice of direction. Any line stretching into the vault of the darkness might have ended in that alien universe. . . .

Not until a million years had elapsed did his emotions subside. Then there were other thoughts. He began to feel a dreadful fright, a fright that grew on him as he left his universe farther behind. He was hurtling into the darkness that none before him had crossed, and few had dared to try crossing, at a velocity which he finally realized he could attain, but not comprehend. Mind could not think it, thoughts could not say it!

And—he was alone! *Alone!* An icy hand clutched at him. He had never known the true meaning of that word. There were none of his friends near, nor his Mother, nor great-brained Oldster—there was no living thing within innumerable light-centuries. *He* was the only life in the void!

Thus, for almost exactly ninety millions of years he wondered and thought, first about life, then the edge of the darkness, and lastly the mysterious energy field eternally at his core. He found the answer to two, and perhaps, in the end, the other.

Ever, each infinitesimal second that elapsed, his visions were probing hundreds of light-years ahead, seeking the first sign of that universe he believed in; but no, all was darkness so dense it seemed to possess mass.

The monotony became agony. A colossal loneliness began to tear at him. He wanted to do anything, even play, or slice huge stars up into planets. But there was only one escape from the phantasmal horror of the unending ebon path. Now and anon he seized the globe of light with a tractor ray and hurled it into the curtain of darkness behind him at terrific velocity.

It sped away under the momentum imparted to it until sight of it was lost. But always, though millions of years might elapse, it returned, attached to him by invisible strings of energy. It was part of him, it defied penetration of its secret, and it would never leave him, until, perhaps, of itself it revealed its true purpose.

Infinite numbers of light-years, so infinite that if written a sheet as broad as the universe would have been required, reeled behind.

Eighty millions of years passed. Darkness had not been as old as that when he had gone into the void for which he had been named. Fear that he had been wrong took a stronger foothold in his thoughts. But now he knew that he would never go back.

Long before the eighty-nine-millionth year came, he had exhausted all sources of amusement. Sometimes he expanded or contracted to incredible sizes. Sometimes he automatically went through the motions of traversing the forty-seven bands. He felt the click in his consciousness which told him that if there had been hyper-space in the darkness, he would have been transported into it. But how could there be different kinds of darkness? He strongly doubted the existence of hyper-space here, for only matter could occasion the dimensional disturbances which obtained in his universe.

But with the eighty-nine-millionth year came the end of his pilgrimage. It came abruptly. For one tiny space of time, his visions contacted a stream of light, light that was left as the outward trail of a celestial body. Darkness' body, fifty millions of miles in girth, involuntarily contracted to half its size. Energy streamed together and formed molten blobs of flaring matter that sped from him in the chaotic emotions of the moment.

A wave of shuddering thankfulness shook him, and his thoughts rioted sobbingly in his memory swirls.

"Oldster, Oldster, if only your great brain could know this . . ."

Uncontrollably inflating and deflating, he tore onward, shearing vast quantities of energy from the tight matter at his core, converting it into propellent power that drove him at a velocity that was more than unthinkable, toward the universe from whence had come that light-giving body.

V. The Colored Globes

In the ninety-millionth year a dim spot of light rushed at him, and, as he hurtled onward, the spot of light grew, and expanded, and broke up into tinier lights, tinier lights that in turn broke up into their components—until the darkness was blotted out, giving way to the dazzling, beautiful radiance of an egg-shaped universe.

He was out of the darkness; he had discovered its edge. Instinctively, he lessened his velocity to a fraction of its former self, and then, as if some mightier will than his had overcome him, he lost consciousness, and sped unknowingly, at steady speed, through the outlying fringe of the outer galaxy, through it, through its brothers, until, unconscious, he was in the midst of that alien galactic system.

First he made a rigid tour of inspection, flying about from star to star, tearing them wantonly apart, as if each and every atom belonged solely to him. The galaxies, the suns, the very elements of construction, all were the same as he knew them. All nature, he decided, was probably alike, in this universe, or in that one.

But was there life?

An abrupt wave of restlessness, of unease, passed over him. He felt unhappy, and unsated. He looked about on the stars, great giants, dwarfs fiercely burning, other hulks of matter cooled to black, forbidding cinders, intergalactic nebulae wreathing unpurposefully about, assuming weird and beautiful formations over periods of thousands of years. He, Darkness, had come to them, had crossed the great gap of nothing, but they were unaffected by this unbelievable feat, went swinging on their courses knowing nothing of him. He felt small, without meaning. Such thoughts seemed the very apostasy of sense, but there they were—he could not shake them off. It was with a growing feeling of disillusionment that he drifted through the countless galaxies and nebulae that unrolled before him, in search of life.

And his quest was rewarded. From afar off, the beating flow of the life-energy came. He drove toward its source, thirty or forty light-years, and hung in its presence.

The being was a green-light, that one of the two classes in which Darkness had divided the life he knew. He himself was a purple-light, containing at his core a globe of pure light, the purpose of which had been one of the major problems of his existence.

The green-light, when she saw him, came to a stop. They stared at each other.

Finally she spoke, and there was wonder and doubt in her thoughts.

"Who are you? You seem—alien."

"You will hardly believe me," Darkness replied, now trembling with a sensation which, inexplicably, could not be defined by the fact that he was in converse with a being of another universe. "But I am alien. I do not belong to this universe."

"But that seems quite impossible. Perhaps you are from another space, beyond the forty-seventh. But that is more impossible!" She eyed him with growing puzzlement and awe.

"I am from no other space," said Darkness somberly. "I am from another universe beyond the darkness."

"From beyond the darkness?" she said faintly, and then she involuntarily contracted. Abruptly she turned her visions on the darkness. For a long, long time she stared at it, and then she returned her vision rays to Darkness.

"So you have crossed the darkness," she whispered. "They used to tell me that that was the most impossible thing it was possible to dream of—to cross that terrible section of lightlessness. No one could cross, they said, because there was nothing on the other side. But I never believed, purple-light, I never believed them. And there have been times when I have desperately wanted to traverse it myself. But there were tales of beings who had gone into it, and never returned. . . . And you have crossed it!"

A shower of crystalline sparks fled from her. So evident was the sudden hero worship carried on her thought waves, that Darkness felt a wild rise in spirits. And suddenly he was able to define the never before experienced emotions which had enwrapped him when first this green-light spoke.

"Green-light, I have journeyed a distance the length of which I cannot think to you, seeking the riddle of the darkness. But perhaps there was something else I was seeking, something to fill a vacant part of me. I know now what it was. A mate, green-light, a thinker. And you are that thinker, that friend with whom I can journey, voyaging from universe to universe, finding the secrets of all that is. Look! The Great Energy which alone made it possible for me to cross the darkness, has been barely tapped!"

Imperceptibly she drew away. There was an unexplainable wariness that seemed half sorrow in her thoughts.

"You are a thinker," he exclaimed. "Will you come with me?"

She stared at him, and he felt she possessed a natural wisdom he could never hope to accumulate. There was a strange shrinkage of his spirits. What was that she was saying?

"Darkness," she said gently, "you would do well to turn and leave me, a green-light, forever. You are a purple-light, I a green. Green-light and purple-light—is that all you have thought about the two types of life? Then you must know that beyond the difference in color, there is another: the greens have a knowledge not vouchsafed the purples, until it is . . . too late. For your own sake, then, I ask you to leave me forever."

He looked at her puzzled. Then slowly, "That is an impossible request, now that I have found you. You are what I need," he insisted.

"But don't you understand?" she cried. "I know something you have not even guessed at! Darkness—leave me!"

He became bewildered. What was she driving at? What was it she knew that he could not know? For a moment he hesitated. Far down in him a voice was bidding him to do as she asked, and quickly. But another voice, that of a growing emotion he could not name, bid him stay; for she was the complement of himself, the half of him that would make him complete. And the second voice was stronger.

"I am not going," he said firmly, and the force of his thoughts left no doubt as to the unshakable quality of his decision.

She spoke faintly, as if some outside will had overcome her. "No, Darkness, now you are not going; it is too late! Learn the secret of the purple globe!"

Abruptly, she wrenched herself into a hyper-space, and all his doubts and fears were erased as she disappeared. He followed her delightedly up the scale, catching sight of her in one band just as she vanished into the next.

And so they came to the forty-seventh, where all matter, its largest and smallest components, assumed the shapes of unchangeable cubes; even he and the green-light appeared as cubes, gigantic cubes millions of miles in extent, a geometric figure they could never hope to distort.

Darkness watched her expectantly. Perhaps she would now start a game of chopping chunks off these cubed suns, and swing them around as planets. Well, he would be willing to do that for a while, in her curious mood of playfulness, but after that they must settle down to discovering possible galactic systems beyond this one.

As he looked at her she vanished.

"Hmm, probably gone down the scale," thought Darkness, and he dropped through the lower bands. He found her in none.

"Darkness . . . try the . . . forty-eighth. . . ." Her thought came faintly.

"The forty-eighth!" he cried in astonishment. At the same time, there was a seething of his memory-swirls as if the knowledge of his life were being arranged to fit some new fact, a strange alchemy of the mind by which he came to know that there *was* a forty-eighth.

Now he knew, as he had always known, that there was a forty-eighth. He snapped himself into it.

Energy became rampant in a ceaseless shifting about him. A strange energy, reminding him of nothing so much as the beating flow of an energy creature approaching him from a near distance. His vision sought out the green-light.

She was facing him somberly, yet with a queerly detached arrogance. His mind was suddenly choked with the freezing sensation that he was face to face with horror.

"I have never been here before," he whispered faintly.

He thought he detected pity in her, but it was overwhelmed by the feeling that she was under the influence of an outside will that could not know pity.

Yet she said, "I am sadder than ever before. But too late. You are my mate, and this is the band of—life!"

Abruptly while he stared, she receded, and he could not follow, save with his visions. Presently, as if an hypnotist had clamped his mind, she herself disappeared, all that he saw of her being the green globe of light she carried. He saw nothing else, knew nothing else. It became his whole universe, his whole life. A peacefulness, complete and uncorroded by vain striving, settled on him like stardust.

The green globe of light dimmed, became smaller, until it was less than a pinpoint, surrounded by an infinity of colorless white energy.

Then, so abruptly it was in the nature of a shock, he came from his torpor, and was conscious. Far off he still saw the green globe of light, but it was growing in size, approaching—approaching a purple globe of light that in turn raced toward it at high velocity.

"It is my own light," he thought, startled. "I must have unwittingly hurled it forth when she settled that hypnotic influence over me. No matter. It will come back."

But would it come back? Green globe of light was expanding in apparent size, approaching purple which, in turn, dwindled toward it at increasing speed.

"At that rate," he thought in panic, "they will collide. Then how will my light come back to me?"

He watched intently, a poignantly cold feeling clutching at him. Closer . . . closer. He quivered. Green globe and purple globe had crashed.

They met in a blinding crescendo of light that brightened space for light-years around. A huge mistiness of light formed into a sphere, in the center of which hung a brilliant ball. The misty light slowly subsided until it had been absorbed into the brighter light that remained as motionless as Darkness himself.

Then it commenced pulsating with a strange, rhythmic regularity.

Something about that pulsing stirred ancient memories, something that said, "You, too, were once no more than that pulsing ball."

Thoughts immense in scope, to him, tumbled in his mind.

"That globe is life," he thought starkly. "The green-light and I have created life. That was her meaning, when she said this was the band of life. Its activating energy flows rampant here.

"That is the secret of the purple globe; with the green globe it creates life. And I had never know the forty-eighth band until she made it known to me!

"The purpose of life—to create life." The thought of that took fire in his brain. For one brief, intoxicating moment he thought that he had solved the last and most baffling of his mighty problems.

As with all other moments of exaltation he had known, disillusionment followed swiftly after. To what end was that? The process continued on and on, and what came of it? Was creation of life the only use of life? A meaningless circle! He recalled Oldster's words of the past, and horror claimed him.

"Life, my life," he whispered dully. "A dead sun and life—one of equal importance with the other. That is unbelievable!" he burst out.

He was aware of the green-light hovering near; yes, she possessed a central light, while his was gone!

She looked at him sorrowfully. "Darkness, if only you had listened to me!"

Blankly, he returned her gaze. "Why is it that you have a light, while I have none?"

"A provision of whatever it was that created us, endows the green-lights with the ability to replace their lights three times. Each merging of a purple and green light may result in the creation of one or several newly-born. Thus the number born over-balances the number of deaths. When my fourth light has gone, as it will some day, I know, I too, will die."

"You mean, I will—die?"

"Soon."

Darkness shuddered, caught half-way between an emotion of blind anger and mental agony. "There is death everywhere," he whispered, "and everything is futile!"

"Perhaps," she said softly, her grief carrying poignantly to him. "Darkness, do not be sad. Darkness, death does indeed come to all, but that does not say that life is of no significance.

"Far past in the gone ages of our race, we were pitiful, tiny blobs of energy which crept along at less than light speed. An energy creature of that time knew nothing of any but the first and forty-eighth band of hyper-space. The rest he could not conceive of as being existent. He was ignorant, possessing elementary means of absorbing energy for life. For countless billions of years he never knew there was an edge to the universe. He could not conceive an edge.

"He was weak, but he gained in strength. Slowly, he evolved, and intelligence entered his mind.

"Always, he discovered things he had been formerly unable to conceive in his mind, and even now there are things that lie beyond the mind; one of them is the end of all space. And the greatest is, why life exists. Both are something we cannot conceive, but in time evolution of mental powers will allow us to conceive them, even as we conceived the existence of hyper-space, and those other things. Dimly, so dimly, even now I can see some reason, but it slips the mind. But Darkness! All of matter is destined to break down to an unchanging state of maximum entropy; it is life, and life alone, that builds in an upward direction. So . . . faith!"

She was gone. She had sown what comfort she could.

Her words shot Darkness full of the wild fire of hope. That was the answer! Vague and promissory it was, but no one could arrive nearer to the solution than that. For a moment he was suffused with the blissful thought that the last of his problems was disposed of.

Then, in one awful space of time, the green-light's philosophy was gone from his memory as if it had never been uttered. He felt the pangs of an unassailable weariness, as if life energies were seeping away.

Haggardly, he put into effect one driving thought. With lagging power, he shot from the fatal band of life . . . and death . . . down the scale. Something unnameable, perhaps some natal memory, made him pause for the merest second in the seventeenth band. Afar off, he saw the green-light and her newly-born. They had left the highest band, come to the band where propellents became useless. So it had been at his own birth.

He paused no more and dropped to the true band, pursuing a slow course across the star-beds of this universe, until he at last emerged on its ragged shore. He went on into the darkness, until hundreds of light-years separated him from the universe his people had never known existed.

VI. Dissipation

He stopped and looked back at the lens of misty radiance. "I have not even discovered the edge of the darkness," he thought. "It stretches out and around. That galactic system and my own are just pinpoints of light, sticking up, vast distances apart, through an unlimited ebon cloth. They are so small in the darkness they barely have the one dimension of existence!"

He went on his way, slowly, wearily, as if the power to activate his propellents were diminishing. There came a time, in his slow, desperate striving after the great velocity he had known in crossing the lightless section, when that universe, that pinpoint sticking up, became as a pinpoint to his sight.

He stopped, took one longing look at it, and accelerated until it was lost to view.

"I am alone again," he thought vaguely. "I am more alone than Oldster ever was. How did he escape death from the green-lights? Perhaps he discovered their terrible secret, and fled before they could wreak their havoc on him. He was a lover of wisdom, and he did not want to die. Now he is living, and he is alone, marooning himself in the lightless band, striving not to think. He could make himself die, but he is afraid to, even though he is so tired of life, and of thinking his endless thoughts.

"I will die. But no . . . ! Ah, yes, I will."

He grew bewildered. He thought, or tried to think, of what came after death. Why, there would be nothing! He would not be there, and without him nothing else could exist!

"I would not be there, and therefore there would be nothing," he thought starkly. "Oh, that is inconceivable. Death! Why, forever after I died, I would be—dead!"

He strove to alleviate the awfulness of the eternal unconsciousness. "I was nothing once, that is true; why cannot that time come again? But it is unthinkable. I feel as if I am the center of everything, the cause, the focal point, and even the foundation."

For some time this thought gave him a kind of gloating satisfaction. Death was indeed not so bad, when one could thus drag to oblivion the very things which had sponsored his life. But at length reason supplanted dreams. He sighed. "And that is vanity!"

Again he felt the ineffably horrible sensation of an incapacity to activate his propellents the full measure, and an inability to keep himself down to normal size. His memory swirls were pulsating, and striving, sometimes, to obliterate themselves.

Everything seemed meaningless. His very drop into the darkness, at slow acceleration, was without purpose.

"I could not reach either universe now," he commented to himself, "because I am dying. Poor Mother! Poor Oldster! They will not even know I crossed. That seems the greatest sorrow —to do a great thing, and not be able to tell of it. Why did they not tell me of the central lights? With Oldster, it was fear that I should come to the same deathless end as he. With Mother— she obeyed an instinct as deeply rooted as space. There must be perpetuation of life.

"Why? Was the green-light right? Is there some tangible purpose to life which we are unable to perceive? But where is my

gain, if I have to die to bring to ultimate fruition that purpose?
I suppose Oldster knew the truth. Life just is, had an accidental
birth, and exists haphazardly, like a star, or an electron.

"But, knowing these things, why do I not immediately give
way to the expanding forces within me? Ah, I do not know!"

Convulsively he applied his mind to the continuance of life
within his insistently expanding body. For a while he gloried in
the small increase of his fading vigor.

"Making solar systems!" his mind took up the thread of a lost
thought. "Happy sons of Radiant, Incandescent, Great Power,
and all the others!"

He concentrated on the sudden thought that struck him. He
was dying, of that he was well aware, but he was dying without
doing anything. What had he actually done, in this life of his?

"But what can I do? I am alone," he thought vaguely. Then,
"I could make a planet, and I could put the life germ on it.
Oldster taught me that."

Suddenly he was afraid he would die before he created this
planet. He set his mind to it, and began to strip from the sphere
of tight matter vast quantities of energy, then condensed it to
form matter more attenuated. With lagging power, he formed
mass after mass of matter, ranging all through the ninety-eight
elements that he knew.

Fifty-thousand years saw the planet's first stage of completion. It had become a tiny sphere some fifteen-thousand miles
in diameter. With a heat ray he then boiled it, and with another
ray cooled its crust, at the same time forming oceans and conti-
nents on its surface. Both water and land, he knew, were necessary to life which was bound by nature of its construction to the
surface of a planet.

Then came the final, completing touch. No other being had
ever deliberately done what Darkness did then. Carefully, he
created an infinitesimal splash of life-perpetuating protoplasm;
he dropped it aimlessly into a tiny wrinkle on the planet's surface.

He looked at the finished work, the most perfect planet he or his playmates had ever created, with satisfaction, notwithstanding the dull pain of weariness that throbbed through the complex energy fields of his body.

Then he took the planet up in a tractor ray, and swung it around and around, as he now so vividly recalled doing in his childhood. He gave it a swift angular velocity, and then shot it off at a tangent, in a direction along the line of which he was reasonably sure lay his own universe. He watched it with dulling visions. It receded into the darkness that would surround it for ages, and then it was a pinpoint, and then nothing.

"It is gone," he said, somehow wretchedly lonely because of that, "but it will reach the universe; perhaps for millions of years it will traverse the galaxies unmolested. Then a sun will reach out and claim it. There will be life upon it, life that will grow until it is intelligent, and will say it has a soul, and purpose in existing."

Nor did the ironic humor of the ultimate swift and speedy death of even that type of life, once it had begun existence, escape him. Perhaps for one or ten million years it would flourish, and then even it would be gone—once upon a time nothing and then nothing again.

He felt a sensation that brought blankness nearer, a sensation of expansion, but now he made no further attempts to prolong a life which was, in effect, already dead. There was a heave within him, as if some subconscious force were deliberately attempting to tear him apart.

He told himself that he was no longer afraid. "I am simply going into another darkness—but it will be a much longer journey than the other."

Like a protecting cloak, he drew in his vision rays about him, away from the ebon emptiness. He drifted, expanding through the vast, interuniversal space.

The last expansion came, the expansion that dissipated his memory-swirls. A vast compact sphere of living drew itself out until Darkness was only free energy distributed over light-years of space.

And death, in that last moment, seemed suddenly to be a far greater and more astounding occurrence than birth had ever seemed.

VAULT OF THE BEAST

A. E. van Vogt

Alfred Elton van Vogt was one of the most important writers discovered by John Campbell. His first published science fiction story, "Black Destroyer," appeared in the July 1939 *Astounding* and was voted the best story in the issue (ahead of stories by C. L. Moore and Isaac Asimov, among others). He followed with "Discord in Scarlet" and other popular stories in *Astounding* and *Unknown,* so van Vogt's reputation was firmly established by the time the following story appeared in August 1940. He had proven himself a master of adventure stories that were both fast-moving and eerie.

Who was this man who seemed to burst into science fiction with his talents already at full strength? He was a Canadian, twenty-six years old when he began writing science fiction—but he'd been writing professionally in other fields since the early 1930s, when he'd begun writing confessions for *True Story.* He remembers spending his first acceptance check immediately, so that when the story appeared on the newsstands he had to borrow money from his mother to buy the magazine. He continued to write confessions for a couple of years, but despite the fact that he won $1000 for one of them in a prize contest, he lost interest in 1934 and turned instead to fifteen-minute radio plays for a Canadian station. He sold about fifty of them, but earned no more than $600 total.

He turned to science fiction writing almost by accident. He'd read *Amazing Stories* in his teens, but when T. O'Conor Sloane took over the editorship, van Vogt lost interest. (Sloane was in his eighties, a man of conservative tastes who admitted in the pages of *Amazing* that he didn't believe in the possibility of space flight.) Van Vogt had never bothered to look at any other science fiction magazine, but one day in 1938, in McKnight's Drug Store in Winnipeg, he casually picked up a copy of *Astounding* and began to read a story called "Who Goes There?"

He was hooked: "I read about half of it while standing there; then I decided that I'd better buy the magazine." He did, and was so impressed that he wrote a one-paragraph outline of "a story that was suggested to me, not exactly by this story, but by the mood and feeling of it." He sent the outline to Campbell, unaware that it was Campbell himself who had written "Who Goes There?" (It had appeared under the pen name "Don A. Stuart.")

Campbell wrote back to say he was interested, and he cautioned, "In writing this story, be sure to concentrate on the mood and atmosphere. Don't just make it an action story." Despite this, van Vogt found when he'd finished it that he *had* written it as an action story, so he rewrote it; the second time through he was satisfied with it. He titled it "Vault of the Beast."

So this story is actually van Vogt's first venture into science fiction writing. Immediately after it he wrote "Black Destroyer," and then, on May 9, 1939, he married Edna Mayne Hull, a writer of free-lance articles for the *Winnipeg Free Press.* She helped him with much of his work, typing final drafts from his handwriting or two-finger typing. Her help became particularly valuable after *Astounding* serialized van Vogt's first novel, "Slan!"

Campbell was so delighted with it that he wrote to him, "I would like to contract you to write for *Astounding.* I'm willing to buy two or three hundred dollars worth of stories a month from you. In other words, it's wide open."

Van Vogt responded with seven stories in 1942, totaling 115,000 words; they included "Recruiting Station," "Asylum" and "The Weapon Shop." By the end of the year his wife had decided to take up science fiction herself, and the first E. Mayne Hull story, "The Flight That Failed," appeared in the December 1942 *Astounding,* beginning her own successful career in science fiction.

But van Vogt was more than successful; he was a superstar in science fiction, his popularity rivaled only by that of Robert A. Heinlein. (In 1943 van Vogt more than doubled his 1942 production, selling all his stories to *Astounding* and *Unknown*.) In part this was a result of the beginning of World War II, which commandeered the time and talents of most of the other major writers in the field; but van Vogt, who had been turned down by his draft board because of poor eyesight, couldn't have filled the gap if he hadn't had the ability to write gripping and imaginative stories.

In a 1947 symposium on "The Science of Science Fiction Writing," van Vogt explained his writing method. He visualized every story in terms of scenes of about 800 words, each scene introducing a new idea to the story. "Every scene has a purpose, which is stated near the beginning, usually by the third paragraph, and that purpose is either accomplished or not accomplished by the end of the scene." It seems a difficult formula, one that could easily straitjacket a writer, but van Vogt had already mastered it when he wrote "Vault of the Beast" and as a result the story fairly leaped along from one event to another. The readers loved it.

Van Vogt did come in for some criticism of the science in his story, however. A letter in the "Science Discussions" section of *Astounding's* letter column pointed out:

In the first place, there is no such thing as the "ultimate prime number." This was first proved by Euclid centuries ago. . . . In the second place, Mr. van Vogt speaks of infinity as though it were some single huge number. This is a common misconception. The term "infinity" actually does not denote a numerical quantity, but simply the absence of a limit. . . . Mr. van Vogt speaks of "infinity minus one" being a number divisible by two. There is really no such number as that. In fact it can be shown that if any finite number is subtracted from an infinite quantity, the remainder is still infinite. Now if infinity minus one—which is still infinity—is "divisible by two," and infinity is a prime as Mr. van Vogt proclaims—whoa! How's that again? Remember that $\infty - \infty$ is an indeterminate form and may even be infinite.

Such arguments from readers were much more common in the early 1940s than they are now: magazine science fiction had, after all, developed just fourteen years before out of Hugo Gernsback's science magazines *Radio News* and *Science and Invention.* Gernsback's belief that the purpose of science fiction was to teach science by dramatizing its future applications was no longer taken seriously by most readers, but they did resent stories containing what they considered to be flagrant scientific errors.

Nor was this feeling confined to *Astounding,* the most scientifically oriented of the magazines. *Thrilling Wonder Stories* was purely a future-adventures pulp, but a letter in a 1942 issue complained that

in "Land of the Burning Sea" [by Malcolm Jameson] the hero is carried off in an interstellar liner which quickly accelerates to almost the speed of light, but the only effect on our hero is to knock him cold for a few days. Anyone with a half ounce of relativity in his head would know he'd have been reduced to a grease spot—even with benefit of anti-traumatic serum!

Why in the name of common sense couldn't the author have used an electrocosmic gravitator or some such gadget to change the value of the gravitational constant enough to keep Prescott's body from being disintegrated by his own inertia? I'm not asking authors to cramp their style by a too rigid adherence to physical laws, but their stories would be a lot better if they'd invent a plausible line of "baloney" to account for their departures from the straight and narrow.

Authors of this period usually did make at least a pretense of scientific accuracy, and many of them constructed their stories by setting up climactic scenes in which the heroes saved the day by applying a few bits of knowledge which they would explain to their companions in the fadeouts. Among the writers who specialized in this were Nelson S. Bond and Alfred Bester.

Bond had one of his heroes escape captivity on Venus by dumping the capsules from his heat-gun into a stream that flowed through the underground domain of the vampiric Harpies, after which he and his companions simply walked out unmolested. He explained:

Bats are hibernating creatures . . . automatically forced into slumber when the temperature drops below 46°F. . . . Our apparatus was, perforce, crude, but we had all the elements of a refrigerating unit. Ammoniated water, running in a constant stream, capsules of condensed and concentrated heat from our needle-guns—a small room which was connected, by ventilating ducts, with the rest of the underground city. The principle of the absorption process depends on the fact that vapors of low boiling point are readily absorbed in water and can be separated again by the application of heat. At 60°F., water will absorb about 760 times its own volume of ammonia vapor, and this produces evaporation, which, in turn, gives off vapor at a low temperature, thereby becoming a refrigerator abstracting heat from any surrounding body. In this case—the rooms above!

Bester told of a scientist who created a creature of pure protons; it began to grow menacingly as it fed on the protons in everything around it. Bester's hero surrounded it with Coolidge tubes and destroyed it in their radiation. "Look, stupid," he told the scientist-creator. "Your pal ate protons and the waste product of his metabolism was electrons. We surrounded him with nothing but free electrons so he had nothing to ingest but his own waste. Get it? He died from auto-intoxication. They call it constipation in the ads."

Perhaps the most amusing of these lessons in applied science was dreamed up by Ross Rocklynne in a story about a spaceship carrying much-needed water to Mars; four enemy ships were in close pursuit and accelerating, about to destroy the unarmed cargo spaceship. The hero shut off his ship's rockets and ordered, "Give the stern valve of the water tank a five-inch aperture—no more. Leave it that way and start your pumps at top speed. Turn them off every three seconds, then on again with a one-second interval."

Then he explained to his friends: "It's simple. Water will freeze in empty space. It evaporates quickly. The energy of evaporation freezes the rest of the water. If it's in small quantities such as we're shooting out every four seconds, it'll freeze quick."

Thus the enemy spaceships were destroyed by "cannon balls of ice" as they accelerated in pursuit. Gernsback would have been proud.

These stories were frequently ingenious, but peopled by spaceship captains and their beautiful daughters, mad scientists, space pirates and other cardboard characters. Van Vogt's stories didn't depend on this kind of gimmick, and his characters usually had unexpected aspects—such as the robot-monster in "Vault of the Beast," which engages our sympathy even as it cuts a murderous swath through the humans it encounters. Van Vogt was full of surprises even at the start of his career, and this story remains one of his own favorites to this day. Reading it will show you why.

REFERENCES:

"The Worlds of A. E. van Vogt" by Sam Moskowitz. *Amazing Stories,* August 1961.

Reflections of A. E. van Vogt by A. E. van Vogt. Fictioneer Books Ltd., 1975.

"Complication in the Science Fiction Story" by A. E. van Vogt. *Of Worlds Beyond,* Fantasy Press, 1947.

Glen Taylor in "Science Discussions." *Astounding Science-Fiction,* November 1940.

D. E. Allen in "The Reader Speaks." *Thrilling Wonder Stories,* December 1942.

"Beyond Light" by Nelson S. Bond. *Planet Stories,* Winter 1940.

"The Pet Nebula" by Alfred Bester. *Astonishing Stories,* February 1941.

"Storm in Space" by Ross Rocklynne. *Thrilling Wonder Stories,* December 1942.

Introduction by A. E. van Vogt. *The Best of A. E. van Vogt,* Sphere Books, 1974.

*　　*　　*

The creature crept. It whimpered from fear and pain, a thin, slobbering sound horrible to hear. Shapeless, formless thing yet changing shape and form with every jerky movement.

It crept along the corridor of the space freighter, fighting the terrible urge of its elements to take the shape of its surroundings. A gray blob of disintegrating stuff, it crept, it cascaded, it rolled, flowed, dissolved, every movement an agony of struggle against the abnormal need to become a stable shape.

Any shape! The hard, chilled-blue metal wall of the Earth-bound freighter, the thick, rubbery floor. The floor was easy to fight. It wasn't like the metal that pulled and pulled. It would be easy to become metal for all eternity.

But something prevented. An implanted purpose. A purpose

that drummed from electron to electron, vibrated from atom to atom with an unvarying intensity that was like a special pain: *Find the greatest mathematical mind in the Solar System, and bring it to the vault of the Martian ultimate metal. The Great One must be freed! The prime number time lock must be opened!*

That was the purpose that hummed with unrelenting agony through its elements. That was the thought that had been seared into its fundamental consciousness by the great and evil minds that had created it.

There was movement at the far end of the corridor. A door opened. Footsteps sounded. A man whistling to himself. With a metallic hiss, almost a sigh, the creature dissolved, looking momentarily like diluted mercury. Then it turned brown like the floor. It became the floor, a slightly thicker stretch of dark-brown rubber spread out for yards.

It was ecstasy just to lie there, to be flat and to have shape, and to be so nearly dead that there was no pain. Death was so sweet, so utterly desirable. And life such an unbearable torment of agony, such a throbbing, piercing nightmare of anguished convulsion. If only the life that was approaching would pass swiftly. If the life stopped, it would pull it into shape. Life could do that. Life was stronger than metal, stronger than anything. The approaching life meant torture, struggle, pain.

The creature tensed its now flat, grotesque body—the body that could develop muscles of steel—and waited in terror for the death struggle.

Spacecraftsman Parelli whistled happily as he strode along the gleaming corridor that led from the engine room. He had just received a wireless from the hospital. His wife was doing well, and it was a boy. Eight pounds, the radiogram had said. He suppressed a desire to whoop and dance. A boy. Life sure was good.

Pain came to the thing on the floor. Primeval pain that sucked through its elements like acid burning, burning. The brown floor shuddered in every atom as Parelli strode over it. The aching urge to pull toward him, to take his shape. The thing fought its horrible desire, fought with anguish and shivering dread, more consciously now that it could think with Parelli's brain. A ripple of floor rolled after the man.

Fighting didn't help. The ripple grew into a blob that momentarily seemed to become a human head. Gray, hellish nightmare of demoniac shape. The creature hissed metallically in terror, then collapsed palpitating, slobbering with fear and pain and hate as Parelli strode on rapidly—too rapidly for its creeping pace.

The thin, horrible sound died; the thing dissolved into brown floor, and lay quiescent yet quivering in every atom from its unquenchable, uncontrollable urge to live—live in spite of pain, in spite of abysmal terror and primordial longing for stable shape. To live and fulfill the purpose of its lusting and malignant creators.

Thirty feet up the corridor, Parelli stopped. He jerked his mind from its thoughts of child and wife. He spun on his heels, and stared uncertainly along the passageway from the engine room.

"Now, what the devil was that?" he pondered aloud.

A sound—a queer, faint yet unmistakably horrid sound was echoing and re-echoing through his consciousness. A shiver ran the length of his spine. That sound—that devilish sound.

He stood there, a tall, magnificently muscled man, stripped to the waist, sweating from the heat generated by the rockets that were decelerating the craft after its meteoric flight from Mars. Shuddering, he clenched his fists, and walked slowly back the way he had come.

The creature throbbed with the pull of him, a gnawing, writhing, tormenting struggle that pierced into the deeps of every restless, agitated cell, stabbing agonizingly along the alien nervous system; and then became terrifyingly aware of the inevitable, the irresistible need to take the shape of the life.

Parelli stopped uncertainly. The floor moved under him, a

visible wave that reared brown and horrible before his incredulous eyes and grew into a bulbous, slobbering, hissing mass. A venomous demon head reared on twisted, half-human shoulders. Gnarled hands on apelike, malformed arms clawed at his face with insensate rage—and changed even as they tore at him.

"Good God!" Parelli bellowed.

The hands, the arms that clutched him grew more normal, more human, brown, muscular. The face assumed familiar lines, sprouted a nose, eyes, a red gash of mouth. The body was suddenly his own, trousers and all, sweat and all.

"—God!" his image echoed; and pawed at him with letching fingers and an impossible strength.

Gasping, Parelli fought free, then launched one crushing blow straight into the distorted face. A drooling scream of agony came from the thing. It turned and ran, dissolving as it ran, fighting dissolution, uttering strange half-human cries.

And, struggling against horror, Parelli chased it, his knees weak and trembling from sheer funk and incredulity. His arm reached out, and plucked at the disintegrating trousers. A piece came away in his hand, a cold, slimy, writhing lump like wet clay.

The feel of it was too much. His gorge rising in disgust, he faltered in his stride. He heard the pilot shouting ahead:

"What's the matter?"

Parelli saw the open door of the storeroom. With a gasp, he dived in, came out a moment later, wild-eyed, an ato-gun in his fingers. He saw the pilot, standing with staring, horrified brown eyes, white face and rigid body, facing one of the great windows.

"There it is!" the man cried.

A gray blob was dissolving into the edge of the glass, becoming glass. Parelli rushed forward, ato-gun poised. A ripple went through the glass, darkening it; and then, briefly, he caught a glimpse of a blob emerging on the other side of the glass into the cold of space.

The officer stood gaping beside him; the two of them watched the gray, shapeless mass creep out of sight along the side of the rushing freight liner.

Parelli sprang to life. "I got a piece of it!" he gasped. "Flung it down on the floor of the storeroom."

It was Lieutenant Morton who found it. A tiny section of floor reared up, and then grew amazingly large as it tried to expand into human shape. Parelli with distorted, crazy eyes scooped it up in a shovel. It hissed; it nearly became a part of the metal shovel, but couldn't because Parelli was so close. Changing, fighting for shape, it slobbered and hissed as Parelli staggered with it behind his superior officer. He was laughing hysterically. "I touched it," he kept saying. "I touched it."

A large blister of metal on the outside of the space freighter stirred into sluggish life, as the ship tore into the Earth's atmosphere. The metal walls of the freighter grew red, then white-hot, but the creature, unaffected, continued its slow transformation into gray mass. Vague thought came to the thing, realization that it was time to act.

Suddenly, it was floating free of the ship, falling slowly, heavily, as if somehow the gravitation of Earth had no serious effect upon it. A minute distortion in its electrons started it falling faster, as in some alien way it suddenly became more allergic to gravity.

The Earth was green below; and in the dim distance a gorgeous and tremendous city of spires and massive buildings glittered in the sinking Sun. The thing slowed, and drifted like a falling leaf in a breeze toward the still-distant Earth. It landed in an arroyo beside a bridge at the outskirts of the city.

A man walked over the bridge with quick, nervous steps. He would have been amazed, if he had looked back, to see a replica of himself climb from the ditch to the road, and start walking briskly after him.

Find the—greatest mathematician!

It was an hour later; and the pain of that throbbing thought was a dull, continuous ache in the creature's brain, as it walked along the crowded street. There were other pains, too. The pain of fighting the pull of the pushing, hurrying mass of humanity that swarmed by with unseeing eyes. But it was easier to think, easier to hold form now that it had the brain and body of a man.

Find—mathematician!

"Why?" asked the man's brain of the thing; and the whole body shook with startled shock at such heretical questioning. The brown eyes darted in fright from side to side, as if expecting instant and terrible doom. The face dissolved a little in that brief moment of mental chaos, became successively the man with the hooked nose who swung by, the tanned face of the tall woman who was looking into the shop window, the—

With a second gasp, the creature pulled its mind back from fear, and fought to readjust its face to that of the smooth-shaven young man who sauntered idly in from a side street. The young man glanced at him, looked away, then glanced back again startled. The creature echoed the thought in the man's brain: "Who the devil is that? Where have I seen that fellow before?"

Half a dozen women in a group approached. The creature shrank aside as they passed, its face twisted with the agony of the urge to become woman. Its brown suit turned just the faintest shade of blue, the color of the nearest dress, as it momentarily lost control of its outer atoms. Its mind hummed with the chatter of clothes and "My dear, didn't she look dreadful in that awful hat?"

There was a solid cluster of giant buildings ahead. The thing shook its human head consciously. So many buildings meant metal; and the forces that held metal together would pull and pull at its human shape. The creature comprehended the reason for this with the understanding of the slight man in a dark suit who wandered by dully. The slight man was a clerk; the thing caught his thought. He was thinking enviously of his boss who was Jim Brender, of the financial firm of J. P. Brender & Co.

The overtones of that thought struck along the vibrating elements of the creature. It turned abruptly and followed Lawrence Pearson, bookkeeper. If people ever paid attention to other people on the street, they would have been amazed after a moment to see two Lawrence Pearsons proceeding down the street, one some fifty feet behind the other. The second Lawrence Pearson had learned from the mind of the first that Jim Brender was a Harvard graduate in mathematics, finance and political economy, the latest of a long line of financial geniuses, thirty years old, and the head of the tremendously wealthy J. P. Brender & Co. Jim Brender had just married the most beautiful girl in the world; and this was the reason for Lawrence Pearson's discontent with life.

"Here I'm thirty, too," his thoughts echoed in the creature's mind, "and I've got nothing. He's got everything—everything while all I've got to look forward to is the same old boarding-house till the end of time."

It was getting dark as the two crossed the river. The creature quickened its pace, striding forward with aggressive alertness that Lawrence Pearson in the flesh could never have managed. Some glimmering of its terrible purpose communicated itself in that last instant to the victim. The slight man turned; and let out a faint squawk as those steel-muscled fingers jerked at his throat, a single, fearful snap.

The creature's brain went black with dizziness as the brain of Lawrence Pearson crashed into the night of death. Gasping, whimpering, fighting dissolution, it finally gained control of itself. With one sweeping movement, it caught the dead body and flung it over the cement railing. There was a splash below, then a sound of gurgling water.

The thing that was now Lawrence Pearson walked on hurriedly, then more slowly till it came to a large, rambling brick house. It looked anxiously at the number, suddenly uncertain if it had remembered rightly. Hesitantly, it opened the door.

A streamer of yellow light splashed out, and laughter vibrated in the thing's sensitive ears. There was the same hum of many thoughts and many brains, as there had been in the street. The creature fought against the inflow of thought that threatened to crowd out the mind of Lawrence Pearson. A little dazed by the struggle, it found itself in a large, bright hall, which looked through a door into a room where a dozen people were sitting around a dining table.

"Oh, it's you, Mr. Pearson," said the landlady from the head of the table. She was a sharp-nosed, thin-mouthed woman at whom the creature stared with brief intentness. From her mind, a thought had come. She had a son who was a mathematics teacher in a high school. The creature shrugged. In one penetrating glance, the truth throbbed along the intricate atomic structure of its body. This woman's son was as much of an intellectual lightweight as his mother.

"You're just in time," she said incuriously. "Sarah, bring Mr. Pearson's plate."

"Thank you, but I'm not feeling hungry," the creature replied; and its human brain vibrated to the first silent, ironic laughter that it had ever known. "I think I'll just lie down."

All night long it lay on the bed of Lawrence Pearson, bright-eyed, alert, becoming more and more aware of itself. It thought:

"I'm a machine, without a brain of my own. I use the brains of other people, but somehow my creators made it possible for me to be more than just an echo. I use people's brains to carry out my purpose."

It pondered about those creators, and felt a surge of panic sweeping along its alien system, darkening its human mind. There was a vague physiological memory of pain unutterable, and of tearing chemical action that was frightening.

The creature rose at dawn, and walked the streets till half past nine. At that hour, it approached the imposing marble entrance of J. P. Brender & Co. Inside, it sank down in the comfortable chair initialed L. P.; and began painstakingly to work at the books Lawrence Pearson had put away the night before.

At ten o'clock, a tall young man in a dark suit entered the

arched hallway and walked briskly through the row after row of offices. He smiled with easy confidence to every side. The thing did not need the chorus of "Good morning, Mr. Brender" to know that its prey had arrived.

Terrible in its slow-won self-confidence, it rose with a lithe, graceful movement that would have been impossible to the real Lawrence Pearson, and walked briskly to the washroom. A moment later, the very image of Jim Brender emerged from the door and walked with easy confidence to the door of the private office which Jim Brender had entered a few minutes before.

The thing knocked and walked in—and simultaneously became aware of three things: The first was that it had found the mind after which it had been sent. The second was that its image mind was incapable of imitating the finer subtleties of the razor-sharp brain of the young man who was staring up from dark-gray eyes that were a little startled. And the third was the large metal bas-relief that hung on the wall.

With a shock that almost brought chaos, it felt the overpowering tug of that metal. And in one flash it knew that this was ultimate metal, product of the fine craft of the ancient Martians, whose metal cities, loaded with treasures of furniture, art and machinery were slowly being dug up by enterprising human beings from the sands under which they had been buried for thirty or fifty million years.

The ultimate metal! The metal that no heat would even warm, that no diamond or other cutting device could scratch, never duplicated by human beings, as mysterious as the *ieis* force which the Martians made from apparent nothingness.

All these thoughts crowded the creature's brain, as it explored the memory cells of Jim Brender. With an effort that was a special pain, the thing wrenched its mind from the metal, and fastened its eyes on Jim Brender. It caught the full flood of the wonder in his mind, as he stood up.

"Good lord," said Jim Brender, "who are you?"

"My name's Jim Brender," said the thing, conscious of grim amusement, conscious, too, that it was progress for it to be able to feel such an emotion.

The real Jim Brender had recovered himself. "Sit down, sit down," he said heartily. "This is the most amazing coincidence I've ever seen."

He went over to the mirror that made one panel of the left wall. He stared, first at himself, then at the creature. "Amazing," he said. "Absolutely amazing."

"Mr. Brender," said the creature, "I saw your picture in the paper, and I thought our astounding resemblance would make you listen, where otherwise you might pay no attention. I have recently returned from Mars, and I am here to persuade you to come back to Mars with me."

"That," said Jim Brender, "is impossible."

"Wait," the creature said, "until I have told you why. Have you ever heard of the Tower of the Beast?"

"The Tower of the Beast!" Jim Brender repeated slowly. He went around his desk and pushed a button.

A voice from an ornamental box said: "Yes, Mr. Brender?"

"Dave, get me all the data on the Tower of the Beast and the legendary city of Li in which it is supposed to exist."

"Don't need to look it up," came the crisp reply. "Most Martian histories refer to it as the beast that fell from the sky when Mars was young—some terrible warning connected with it— the beast was unconscious when found—said to be the result of its falling out of sub-space. Martians read its mind; and were so horrified by its subconscious intentions they tried to kill it, but couldn't. So they built a huge vault, about fifteen hundred feet in diameter and a mile high—and the beast, apparently of these dimensions, was locked in. Several attempts have been made to find the city of Li, but without success. Generally believed to be a myth. That's all, Jim."

"Thank you!" Jim Brender clicked off the connection, and turned to his visitor. "Well?"

"It is not a myth. I know where the Tower of the Beast is; and I also know that the beast is still alive."

"Now, see here," said Brender good-humoredly, "I'm intrigued by your resemblance to me; and as a matter of fact I'd like Pamela—my wife—to see you. How about coming over to dinner? But don't, for Heaven's sake, expect me to believe such a story. The beast, if there is such a thing, fell from the sky when Mars was young. There are some authorities who maintain that the Martian race died out a hundred million years ago, though twenty-five million is the conservative estimate. The only things remaining of their civilization are their constructions of ultimate metal. Fortunately, toward the end they built almost everything from that indestructible metal."

"Let me tell you about the Tower of the Beast," said the thing quietly. "It is a tower of gigantic size, but only a hundred feet or so projected above the sand when I saw it. The whole top is a door, and that door is geared to a time lock, which in turn has been integrated along a line of ieis to the ultimate prime number."

Jim Brender stared; and the thing caught his startled thought, the first uncertainty, and the beginning of belief.

"Ultimate prime number!" Brender ejaculated. "What do you mean?" He caught himself. "I know of course that a prime number is a number divisible only by itself and by one."

He snatched at a book from the little wall library beside his desk, and rippled through it. "The largest known prime is— ah, here it is—is 230584300921393951. Some others, according to this authority, are 77843839397, 182521213001, and 78875943472201."

He frowned. "That makes the whole thing ridiculous. The ultimate prime would be an indefinite number." He smiled at the thing. "If there is a beast, and it is locked up in a vault of ultimate metal, the door of which is geared to a time lock, integrated along a line of ieis to the ultimate prime number— then the beast is caught. Nothing in the world can free it."

"To the contrary," said the creature. "I have been assured by the beast that it is within the scope of human mathematics to solve the problem, but that what is required is a born mathematical mind, equipped with all the mathematical training that Earth science can afford. You are that man."

"You expect me to release this evil creature—even if I could perform this miracle of mathematics."

"Evil nothing!" snapped the thing. "That ridiculous fear of the unknown which made the Martians imprison it has resulted in a very grave wrong. The beast is a scientist from another space, accidentally caught in one of his experiments. I say 'his' when of course I do not know whether this race has a sexual differentiation."

"You actually talked with the beast?"

"It communicated with me by mental telepathy."

"It has been proven that thoughts cannot penetrate ultimate metal."

"What do humans know about telepathy? They cannot even communicate with each other except under special conditions." The creature spoke contemptuously.

"That's right. And if your story is true, then this is a matter for the Council."

"This is a matter for two men, you and I. Have you forgotten that the vault of the beast is the central tower of the great city of Li—billions of dollars' worth of treasure in furniture, art and machinery? The beast demands release from its prison before it will permit anyone to mine that treasure. You can release it. We can share the treasure."

"Let me ask you a question," said Jim Brender. "What is your real name?"

"P-Pierce Lawrence!" the creature stammered. For the moment, it could think of no greater variation of the name of its first victim than reversing the two words, with a slight change on "Pearson." Its thoughts darkened with confusion as the voice of Brender pounded:

"On what ship did you come from Mars?"

"O-on *F4961,*" the thing stammered chaotically, fury adding to the confused state of its mind. It fought for control, felt itself slipping, suddenly felt the pull of the ultimate metal that made up the bas-relief on the wall, and knew by that tug that it was dangerously near dissolution.

"That would be a freighter," said Jim Brender. He pressed a button. "Carltons, find out if the *F4961* had a passenger or person aboard, named Pierce Lawrence. How long will it take?"

"About a minute, sir."

"You see," said Jim Brender, leaning back, "this is mere formality. If you were on that ship, then I shall be compelled to give serious attention to your statements. You can understand, of course, that I could not possibly go into a thing like this blindly. I—"

The buzzer rang. "Yes?" said Jim Brender.

"Only the crew of two was on the *F4961* when it landed yesterday. No such person as Pierce Lawrence was aboard."

"Thank you." Jim Brender stood up. He said coldly, "Goodby, Mr. Lawrence. I cannot imagine what you hoped to gain by this ridiculous story. However, it has been most intriguing, and the problem you presented was very ingenious indeed—"

The buzzer was ringing. "What is it?"

"Mr. Gorson to see you, sir."

"Very well, send him right in."

The thing had greater control of its brain now, and it saw in Brender's mind that Gorson was a financial magnate, whose business ranked with the Brender firm. It saw other things, too; things that made it walk out of the private office, out of the building, and wait patiently until Mr. Gorson emerged from the imposing entrance. A few minutes later, there were two Mr. Gorsons walking down the street.

Mr. Gorson was a vigorous man in his early fifties. He had lived a clean, active life; and the hard memories of many climates and several planets were stored away in his brain. The thing caught the alertness of this man on its sensitive elements, and followed him warily, respectfully, not quite decided whether it would act.

It thought: "I've come a long way from the primitive life that couldn't hold its shape. My creators, in designing me, gave to me powers of learning, developing. It is easier to fight dissolution, easier to be human. In handling this man, I must remember that my strength is invincible when properly used."

With minute care, it explored in the mind of its intended victim the exact route of his walk to his office. There was the entrance to a large building clearly etched on his mind. Then a long, marble corridor, into an automatic elevator up to the eighth floor, along a short corridor with two doors. One door led to the private entrance of the man's private office. The other to a storeroom used by the janitor. Gorson had looked into the place on various occasions; and there was in his mind, among other things, the memory of a large chest—

The thing waited in the storeroom till the unsuspecting Gorson was past the door. The door creaked. Gorson turned, his eyes widening. He didn't have a chance. A fist of solid steel smashed his face to a pulp, knocking the bones back into his brain.

This time, the creature did not make the mistake of keeping its mind tuned to that of its victim. It caught him viciously as he fell, forcing its steel fist back to a semblance of human flesh. With furious speed, it stuffed the bulky and athletic form into the large chest, and clamped the lid down tight.

Alertly, it emerged from the storeroom, entered the private office of Mr. Gorson, and sat down before the gleaming desk of oak. The man who responded to the pressing of a button saw John Gorson sitting there, and heard John Gorson say:

"Crispins, I want you to start selling these stocks through the secret channels right away. Sell until I tell you to stop, even if you think it's crazy. I have information of something big on."

Crispins glanced down the row after row of stock names; and his eyes grew wider and wider. "Good lord, man!" he gasped finally, with that familiarity which is the right of a trusted adviser, "these are all the gilt-edged stocks. Your whole fortune can't swing a deal like this."

"I told you I'm not in this alone."

"But it's against the law to break the market," the man protested.

"Crispins, you heard what I said. I'm leaving the office. Don't try to get in touch with me. I'll call you."

The thing that was John Gorson stood up, paying no attention to the bewildered thoughts that flowed from Crispins. It went out of the door by which it had entered. As it emerged from the building, it was thinking: "All I've got to do is kill half a dozen financial giants, start their stocks selling, and then—"

By one o'clock it was over. The exchange didn't close till three, but at one o'clock, the news was flashed on the New York tickers. In London, where it was getting dark, the papers brought out an extra. In Hankow and Shanghai, a dazzling new day was breaking as the newsboys ran along the streets in the shadows of skyscrapers, and shouted that J. P. Brender & Co. had assigned; and that there was to be an investigation—

"We are facing," said the chairman of the investigation committee, in his opening address the following morning, "one of the most astounding coincidences in all history. An ancient and respected firm, with world-wide affiliations and branches, with investments in more than a thousand companies of every description, is struck bankrupt by an unexpected crash in every stock in which the firm was interested. It will require months to take evidence on the responsibility for the short-selling which brought about this disaster. In the meantime, I see no reason, regrettable as the action must be to all the old friends of the late J. P. Brender, and of his son, why the demands of the creditors should not be met, and the properties liquidated through auction sales and such other methods as may be deemed proper and legal—"

"Really, I don't blame her," said the first woman, as they wandered through the spacious rooms of the Brenders' Chinese palace. "I have no doubt she does love Jim Brender, but no one could seriously expect her to remain married to him *now*. She's a woman of the world, and it's utterly impossible to expect her to live with a man who's going to be a mere pilot or space hand or something on a Martian spaceship—"

Commander Hughes of Interplanetary Spaceways entered the office of his employer truculently. He was a small man, but extremely wiry; and the thing that was Louis Dyer gazed at him tensely, conscious of the force and power of this man.

Hughes began: "You have my report on this Brender case?"

The thing twirled the mustache of Louis Dyer nervously; then picked up a small folder, and read out loud:

"Dangerous for psychological reasons . . . to employ Brender. . . . So many blows in succession. Loss of wealth, position and wife. . . . No normal man could remain normal under . . . circumstances. Take him into office . . . befriend him . . . give him a sinecure, or position where his undoubted great ability . . . but not on a spaceship, where the utmost hardiness, both mental, moral, spiritual and physical is required—"

Hughes interrupted: "Those are exactly the points which I am stressing. I knew you would see what I meant, Louis."

"Of course, I see," said the creature, smiling in grim amusement, for it was feeling very superior these days. "Your thoughts, your ideas, your code and your methods are stamped irrevocably on your brain and"—it added hastily—"you have never left me in doubt as to where you stand. However, in this case, I must insist. Jim Brender will not take an ordinary position offered by his friends. And it is ridiculous to ask him to subordinate himself to men to whom he is in every way superior. He has commanded his own space yacht; he knows more about the mathematical end of the work than our whole staff put together; and that is no reflection on our staff. He knows the hardships connected with space flying, and believes that it is exactly what he needs. I, therefore, command you, for the first time in our long association, Peter, to put him on space freighter *F4961* in the place of Spacecraftsman Parelli who collapsed into a nervous breakdown after that curious affair with the creature from space, as Lieutenant Morton described it—By the way, did you find the . . . er . . . sample of that creature yet?"

"No, sir, it vanished the day you came in to look at it. We've searched the place high and low—queerest stuff you ever saw. Goes through glass as easy as light; you'd think it was some form of light-stuff—scares me, too. A pure sympodial development—

actually more adaptable to environment than anything hitherto discovered; and that's putting it mildly. I tell you, sir—But see here, you can't steer me off the Brender case like that."

"Peter, I don't understand your attitude. This is the first time I've interfered with your end of the work and—"

"I'll resign," groaned that sorely beset man.

The thing stifled a smile. "Peter, you've built up the staff of Spaceways. It's your child, your creation; you can't give it up, you know you can't—"

The words hissed softly into alarm; for into Hughes' brain had flashed the first real intention of resigning. Just hearing of his accomplishments and the story of his beloved job brought such a rush of memories, such a realization of how tremendous an outrage was this threatened interference. In one mental leap, the creature saw what this man's resignation would mean: The discontent of the men; the swift perception of the situation by Jim Brender; and his refusal to accept the job. There was only one way out—that Brender would get to the ship without finding out what had happened. Once on it, he must carry through with one trip to Mars; and that was all that was needed.

The thing pondered the possibility of imitating Hughes' body; then agonizingly realized that it was hopeless. Both Louis Dyer and Hughes must be around until the last minute.

"But, Peter, listen!" the creature began chaotically. Then it said, "Damn!" for it was very human in its mentality; and the realization that Hughes took its words as a sign of weakness was maddening. Uncertainty descended like a black cloud over its brain.

"I'll tell Brender when he arrives in five minutes how I feel about all this!" Hughes snapped; and the creature knew that the worst had happened. "If you forbid me to tell him, then I resign. I—Good God, man, your face!"

Confusion and horror came to the creature simultaneously. It knew abruptly that its face had dissolved before the threatened ruin of its plans. It fought for control, leaped to its feet, seeing the incredible danger. The large office just beyond the frosted glass door—Hughes' first outcry would bring help—

With a half sob, it sought to force its arm into an imitation of a metal fist, but there was no metal in the room to pull it into shape. There was only the solid maple desk. With a harsh cry, the creature leaped completely over the desk, and sought to bury a pointed shaft of stick into Hughes' throat.

Hughes cursed in amazement, and caught at the stick with furious strength. There was sudden commotion in the outer office, raised voices, running feet—

It was quite accidental the way it happened. The surface cars swayed to a stop, drawing up side by side as the red light blinked on ahead. Jim Brender glanced at the next car.

A girl and a man sat in the rear of the long, shiny, streamlined affair, and the girl was desperately striving to crouch down out of his sight, striving with equal desperation not to be too obvious in her intention. Realizing that she was seen, she smiled brilliantly, and leaned out of the window.

"Hello, Jim, how's everything?"

"Hello, Pamela!" Jim Brender's fingers tightened on the steering wheel till the knuckles showed white, as he tried to keep his voice steady. He couldn't help adding: "When does the divorce become final?"

"I get my papers tomorrow," she said, "but I suppose you won't get yours till you return from your first trip. Leaving today, aren't you?"

"In about fifteen minutes." He hesitated. "When is the wedding?"

The rather plump, white-faced man who had not participated in the conversation so far, leaned forward.

"Next week," he said. He put his fingers possessively over Pamela's hand. "I wanted it tomorrow but Pamela wouldn't—er, good-by."

His last words were hastily spoken, as the traffic lights switched, and the cars rolled on, separating at the first corner.

The rest of the drive to the spaceport was a blur. He hadn't expected the wedding to take place so soon. Hadn't, when he came right down to it, expected it to take place at all. Like a fool, he had hoped blindly—

Not that it was Pamela's fault. Her training, her very life made this the only possible course of action for her. But—*one week!* The spaceship would be one fourth of the long trip to Mars—

He parked his car. As he paused beside the runway that led to the open door of *F4961*—a huge globe of shining metal, three hundred feet in diameter—he saw a man running toward him. Then he recognized Hughes.

The thing that was Hughes approached, fighting for calmness. The whole world was a flame of cross-pulling forces. It shrank from the thoughts of the people milling about in the office it had just left. Everything had gone wrong. It had never intended to do what it now had to do. It had intended to spend most of the trip to Mars as a blister of metal on the outer shield of the ship. With an effort, it controlled its funk, its terror, its brain.

"We're leaving right away," it said.

Brender looked amazed. "But that means I'll have to figure out a new orbit under the most difficult—"

"Exactly," the creature interrupted. "I've been hearing a lot about your marvelous mathematical ability. It's time the words were proved by deeds."

Jim Brender shrugged. "I have no objection. But how is it that you're coming along?"

"I always go with a new man."

It sounded reasonable. Brender climbed the runway, closely followed by Hughes. The powerful pull of the metal was the first real pain the creature had known for days. For a long month, it would now have to fight the metal, fight to retain the shape of Hughes—and carry on a thousand duties at the same time.

That first stabbing pain tore along its elements, and smashed the confidence that days of being human had built up. And then, as it followed Brender through the door, it heard a shout behind it. It looked back hastily. People were streaming out of several doors, running toward the ship.

Brender was several yards along the corridor. With a hiss that was almost a sob, the creature leaped inside, and pulled the lever that clicked the great door shut.

There was an emergency lever that controlled the anti-gravity plates. With one jerk, the creature pulled the heavy lever hard over. There was a sensation of lightness and a sense of falling.

Through the great plate window, the creature caught a flashing glimpse of the field below, swarming with people. White faces turning upward, arms waving. Then the scene grew remote, as a thunder of rockets vibrated through the ship.

"I hope," said Brender, as Hughes entered the control room, "you wanted me to start the rockets."

"Yes," the thing replied, and felt brief panic at the chaos in its brain, the tendency of its tongue to blur. "I'm leaving the mathematical end entirely in your hands."

It didn't dare stay so near the heavy metal engines, even with Brender's body there to help it keep its human shape. Hurriedly, it started up the corridor. The best place would be the insulated bedroom—

Abruptly, it stopped in its headlong walk, teetered for an instant on tiptoes. From the control room it had just left, a thought was trickling—a thought from Brender's brain. The creature almost dissolved in terror as it realized that Brender was sitting at the radio, answering an insistent call from Earth—

It burst into the control room, and braked to a halt, its eyes widening with humanlike dismay. Brender whirled from before the radio with a single twisting step. In his fingers, he held a revolver. In his mind, the creature read a dawning comprehension of the whole truth. Brender cried:

"You're the ... thing that came to my office, and talked about prime numbers and the vault of the beast."

He took a step to one side to cover an open doorway that led down another corridor. The movement brought the telescreen into the vision of the creature. In the screen was the image of the real Hughes. Simultaneously, Hughes saw the thing.

"Brender," he bellowed, "it's the monster that Morton and Parelli saw on their trip from Mars. It doesn't react to heat or any chemicals, but we never tried bullets. Shoot, you fool!"

It was too much, there was too much metal, too much confusion. With a whimpering cry, the creature dissolved. The pull of the metal twisted it horribly into thick half metal; the struggle to be human left it a malignant structure of bulbous head, with one eye half gone, and two snakelike arms attached to the half metal of the body.

Instinctively, it fought closer to Brender, letting the pull of his body make it more human. The half metal became fleshlike stuff that sought to return to its human shape.

"Listen, Brender!" Hughes' voice came urgently. "The fuel vats in the engine room are made of ultimate metal. One of them is empty. We caught a part of this thing once before, and it couldn't get out of the small jar of ultimate metal. If you could drive it into the vat while it's lost control of itself, as it seems to do very easily—"

"I'll see what lead can do!" Brender rapped in a brittle voice.

Bang! The half-human creature screamed from its half-formed slit of mouth, and retreated, its legs dissolving into gray dough.

"It hurts, doesn't it?" Brender ground out. "Get over into the engine room, you damned thing, into the vat!"

"Go on, go on!" Hughes was screaming from the telescreen.

Brender fired again. The creature made a horrible slobbering sound, and retreated once more. But it was bigger again, more human; and in one caricature hand a caricature of Brender's revolver was growing.

It raised the unfinished, unformed gun. There was an explosion, and a shriek from the thing. The revolver fell, a shapeless, tattered blob, to the floor. The little gray mass of it scrambled frantically toward the parent body, and attached itself like some monstrous canker to the right foot.

And then, for the first time, the mighty and evil brains that had created the thing, sought to dominate their robot. Furious, yet conscious that the game must be carefully played, the Controller forced the terrified and utterly beaten thing to its will. Scream after agonized scream rent the air, as the change was forced upon the unstable elements. In an instant, the thing stood in the shape of Brender, but instead of a revolver, there grew from one browned, powerful hand a pencil of shining metal. Mirror bright, it glittered in every facet like some incredible gem.

The metal glowed ever so faintly, an unearthly radiance. And where the radio had been, and the screen with Hughes' face on it, there was a gaping hole. Desperately, Brender pumped bullets into the body before him, but though the shape trembled, it stared at him now, unaffected. The shining weapon swung toward him.

"When you are quite finished," it said, "perhaps we can talk."

It spoke so mildly that Brender, tensing to meet death, lowered his gun in amazement. The thing went on:

"Do not be alarmed. This which you hear and see is a robot, designed by us to cope with your space and number world. Several of us are working here under the most difficult conditions to maintain this connection, so I must be brief.

"We exist in a time world immeasurably more slow than your own. By a system of synchronization, we have geared a number of these spaces in such fashion that, though one of our days is millions of your years, we can communicate. Our purpose is to free our colleague, Kalorn, from the Martian vault. Kalorn was caught accidentally in a time warp of his own making and precipitated onto the planet you know as Mars. The Martians, needlessly fearing his great size, constructed a most diabolical prison, and we need your knowledge of the mathematics peculiar to your space and number world—and to it alone—in order to free him."

The calm voice continued, earnest but not offensively so,

insistent but friendly. He regretted that their robot had killed human beings. In greater detail, he explained that every space was constructed on a different numbers system, some all negative, some all positive, some a mixture of the two, the whole an infinite variety, and every mathematic interwoven into the very fabric of the space it ruled.

Ieis force was not really mysterious. It was simply a flow from one space to another, the result of a difference in potential. This flow, however, was one of the universal forces, which only one other force could affect, the one he had used a few minutes before. Ultimate metal was *actually* ultimate.

In their space they had a similar metal, built up from negative atoms. He could see from Brender's mind that the Martians had known nothing about minus numbers, so that they must have built it up from ordinary atoms. It could be done that way, too, though not so easily. He finished:

"The problem narrows down to this: Your mathematic must tell us how, with our universal force, we can short-circuit the ultimate prime number—that is, factor it—so that the door will open any time. You may ask how a prime can be factored when it is divisible only by itself and by one. That problem is, for your system, solvable only by your mathematic. Will you do it?"

Brender realized with a start that he was still holding his revolver. He tossed it aside. His nerves were calm as he said:

"Everything you have said sounds reasonable and honest. If you were desirous of making trouble, it would be the simplest thing in the world to send as many of your kind as you wished. Of course, the whole affair must be placed before the Council—"

"Then it is hopeless—the Council could not possible accede—"

"And you expect me to do what you do not believe the highest governmental authority in the System would do?" Brender exclaimed.

"It is inherent in the nature of a democracy that it cannot gamble with the lives of its citizens. We have such a government here; and its members have already informed us that, in a similar condition, they would not consider releasing an unknown beast upon their people. Individuals, however, can gamble where governments must not. You have agreed that our argument is logical. What system do men follow if not that of logic?"

The Controller, through its robot, watched Brender's thoughts alertly. It saw doubt and uncertainty, opposed by a very human desire to help, based upon the logical conviction that it was safe. Probing his mind, it saw swiftly that it was unwise, in dealing with men, to trust too much to logic. It pressed on:

"To an individual we can offer—everything. In a minute, with your permission, we shall transfer this ship to Mars; not in thirty days, but in thirty seconds. The knowledge of how this is done will remain with you. Arrived at Mars, you will find yourself the only living person who knows the whereabouts of the ancient city of Li, of which the vault of the beast is the central tower. In this city will be found literally billions of dollars' worth of treasure made of ultimate metal; and according to the laws of Earth, fifty percent will be yours. Your fortune re-established, you will be able to return to Earth this very day, and reclaim your former wife, and your position. Poor silly child, she loves you still, but the iron conventions and training of her youth leave her no alternative. If she were older, she would have the character to defy those conventions. You must save her from herself. Will you do it?"

Brender was as white as a sheet, his hands clenching and unclenching. Malevolently, the thing watched the flaming thought sweeping through his brain—the memory of a pudgy white hand closing over Pamela's fingers, watched the reaction of Brender to its words, those words that expressed exactly what he had always thought. Brender looked up with tortured eyes.

"Yes," he said, "I'll do what I can."

A bleak range of mountains fell away into a valley of reddish gray sand. The thin winds of Mars blew a mist of sand against the building.

Such a building! At a distance, it had looked merely big. A bare hundred feet projected above the desert, a hundred feet of length and *fifteen hundred feet of diameter*. Literally thousands of feet must extend beneath the restless ocean of sand to make the perfect balance of form, the graceful flow, the fairy-like beauty, which the long-dead Martians demanded of all their constructions, however massive. Brender felt suddenly small and insignificant as the rockets of his spacesuit pounded him along a few feet above the sand toward that incredible building.

At close range the ugliness of sheer size was miraculously lost in the wealth of the decoration. Columns and pilasters assembled in groups and clusters, broke up the façades, gathered and dispersed again restlessly. The flat surfaces of wall and roof melted into a wealth of ornaments and imitation stucco work, vanished and broke into a play of light and shade.

The creature floated beside Brender; and its Controller said: "I see that you have been giving considerable thought to the problem, but this robot seems incapable of following abstract thoughts, so I have no means of knowing the course of your speculations. I see however that you seem to be satisfied."

"I think I've got the answer," said Brender, "but first I wish to see the time lock. Let's climb."

They rose into the sky, dipping over the lip of the building. Brender saw a vast flat expanse; and in the center—He caught his breath!

The meager light from the distant sun of Mars shone down on a structure located at what seemed the exact center of the great door. The structure was about fifty feet high, and seemed nothing less than a series of quadrants coming together at the center, which was a metal arrow pointing straight up.

The arrow head was not solid metal. Rather it was as if the metal had divided in two parts, then curved together again. But not quite together. About a foot separated the two sections of metal. But that foot was bridged by a vague, thin, green flame of ieis force.

"The time lock!" Brender nodded. "I thought it would be

something like that, though I expected it would be bigger, more substantial."

"Do not be deceived by its fragile appearance," answered the thing. "Theoretically, the strength of ultimate metal is infinite; and the ieis force can only be affected by the universal I have mentioned. Exactly what the effect will be, it is impossible to say as it involves the temporary derangement of the whole number system upon which that particular area of space is built. But now tell us what to do."

"Very well." Brender eased himself onto a bank of sand, and cut off his antigravity plates. He lay on his back, and stared thoughtfully into the blue-black sky. For the time being all doubts, worries and fears were gone from him, forced out by sheer will power. He began to explain:

"The Martian mathematic, like that of Euclid and Pythagoras, was based on endless magnitude. Minus numbers were beyond their philosophy. On Earth, however, beginning with Descartes, an analytical mathematic was evolved. Magnitude and perceivable dimensions were replaced by that of variable relation-values between positions in space.

"For the Martians, there was only one number between 1 and 3. Actually, the totality of such numbers is an infinite aggregate. And with the introduction of the idea of the square root of minus one—or i—and the complex numbers, mathematics definitely ceased to be a simple thing of magnitude, perceivable in pictures. Only the intellectual step from the infinitely small quantity to the lower limit of every possible finite magnitude brought out the conception of a variable number which oscillated beneath any assignable number that was not zero.

"The prime number, being a conception of pure magnitude, had no reality in *real* mathematics, but in this case was rigidly bound up with the reality of the ieis force. The Martians knew ieis as a pale-green flow about a foot in length and developing say a thousand horsepower. (It was actually 12.171 inches and 1021.23 horsepower, but that was unimportant.) The power produced never varied, the length never varied, from year end to year end, for tens of thousands of years. The Martians took the length as their basis of measurement, and called it one 'el'; they took the power as their basis of power and called it one 'rb.' And because of the absolute invariability of the flow they knew it was eternal.

"They knew furthermore that nothing could be eternal without being prime; their whole mathematic was based on numbers which could be factored, that is, disintegrated, destroyed, rendered less than they had been; and numbers which could not be factored, disintegrated or divided into smaller groups.

"Any number which could be factored was incapable of being infinite. Contrariwise, the infinite number must be prime.

"Therefore, they built a lock and integrated it along a line of ieis, to operate when the ieis ceased to flow—which would be at the end of Time, provided it was not interfered with. To prevent interference, they buried the motivating mechanism of the flow in ultimate metal, which could not be destroyed or corroded in any way. According to their mathematic, that settled it."

"But you have the answer," said the voice of the thing eagerly.

"Simply this: The Martians set a value on the flow of one 'rb.' If you interfere with that flow to no matter what small degree, you no longer have an 'rb.' You have something less. The flow, which is a universal, becomes automatically less than a universal, less than infinite. The prime number ceases to be prime. Let us suppose that you interfere with it to the extent of *infinity minus one*. You will then have a number divisible by two. As a matter of fact, the number, like most large numbers, will immediately break into thousands of pieces, i.e., it will be divisible by tens of thousands of smaller numbers. If the present time falls anywhere near one of those breaks, the door would open then. In other words, the door will open immediately if you can so interfere with the flow that one of the factors occurs in immediate time."

"That is very clear," said the Controller with satisfaction and the image of Brender was smiling triumphantly. "We shall now use this robot to manufacture a universal; and Kalorn shall be free very shortly." He laughed aloud. "The poor robot is protesting violently at the thought of being destroyed, but after all it is only a machine, and not a very good one at that. Besides, it is interfering with my proper reception of your thoughts. Listen to it scream, as I twist it into shape."

The cold-blooded words chilled Brender, pulled him from the heights of his abstract thought. Because of the prolonged intensity of his thinking, he saw with sharp clarity something that had escaped him before.

"Just a minute," he said. "How is it that the robot, introduced from your world, is living at the same time rate as I am, whereas Kalorn continues to live at your time rate?"

"A very good question." The face of the robot was twisted into a triumphant sneer, as the Controller continued. "Because, my dear Brender, you have been duped. It is true that Kalorn is living in our time rate, but that was due to a shortcoming in our machine. The machine which Kalorn built, while large enough to transport him, was not large enough in its adaptive mechanism to adapt him to each new space as he entered it. With the result that he was transported but not adapted. It was possible of course for us, his helpers, to transport such a small thing as the robot, though we have no more idea of the machine's construction than you have.

"In short, we can use what there is of the machine, but the secret of its construction is locked in the insides of our own particular ultimate metal, and in the brain of Kalorn. Its invention by Kalorn was one of those accidents which, by the law of averages, will not be repeated in millions of our years. Now that you have provided us with the method of bringing Kalorn back, we shall be able to build innumerable interspace machines. Our purpose is to control all spaces, all worlds—particularly those which are inhabited. We intend to be absolute rulers of the entire Universe."

The ironic voice ended; and Brender lay in his prone position the prey of horror. The horror was twofold, partly due to the Controller's monstrous plan, and partly due to the thought that was pulsing in his brain. He groaned, as he realized that warning thought must be ticking away on the automatic receiving brain of the robot. "Wait," his thought was saying, "that adds a new factor. Time—"

There was a scream from the creature as it was forcibly dissolved. The scream choked to a sob, then silence. An intricate machine of shining metal lay there on that great gray-brown expanse of sand and ultimate metal.

The metal glowed; and then the machine was floating in the air. It rose to the top of the arrow, and settled over the green flame of ieis.

Brender jerked on his antigravity screen, and leaped to his feet. The violent action carried him some hundred feet into the air. His rockets sputtered into staccato fire, and he clamped his teeth against the pain of acceleration.

Below him, the great door began to turn, to unscrew, faster and faster, till it was like a flywheel. Sand flew in all directions in a miniature storm.

At top acceleration, Brender darted to one side.

Just in time. First, the robot machine was flung off that tremendous wheel by sheer centrifugal power. Then the door came off, and, spinning now at an incredible rate, hurtled straight into the air, and vanished into space.

A puff of black dust came floating up out of the blackness of the vault. Suppressing his horror, yet perspiring from awful relief, he rocketed to where the robot had fallen into the sand.

Instead of glistening metal, a time-dulled piece of junk lay there. The dull metal flowed sluggishly and assumed a quasi-human shape. The flesh remained gray and in little rolls as if it were ready to fall apart from old age. The thing tried to stand up on wrinkled, horrible legs, but finally lay still. Its lips moved, mumbled:

"I caught your warning thought, but I didn't let them know. Now, Kalorn is dead. They realized the truth as it was happening. End of Time came—"

It faltered into silence; and Brender went on: "Yes, end of Time came when the flow became momentarily less than eternal—came at the factor point which occurred a few minutes ago."

"I was . . . only partly . . . within its . . . influence, Kalorn all the way. . . . Even if they're lucky . . . will be years before . . . they invent another machine . . . and one of their years is billions . . . of yours. . . . I didn't tell them. . . . I caught your thought . . . and kept it . . . from them—"

"But why did you do it? Why?"

"Because they were hurting me. They were going to destroy me. Because . . . I liked . . . being human. I was . . . somebody!"

The flesh dissolved. It flowed slowly into a pool of lavalike gray. The lava crinkled, split into dry, brittle pieces. Brender touched one of the pieces. It crumbled into a fine powder of gray dust. He gazed out across that grim, deserted valley of sand, and said aloud, pityingly:

"Poor Frankenstein."

He turned toward the distant spaceship, toward the swift trip to Earth. As he climbed out of the ship a few minutes later, one of the first persons he saw was Pamela.

She flew into his arms. "Oh, Jim, Jim," she sobbed. "What a fool I've been. When I heard what had happened, and realized you were in danger, I—Oh, Jim!"

Later, he would tell her about their new fortune.

THE MECHANICAL MICE

Eric Frank Russell

Science fiction's first Golden Age was almost entirely an American phenomenon, which seems odd, considering that it was an Englishman, H. G. Wells, who virtually invented the genre of adult science fiction forty years earlier. In novels like *The War of the Worlds, The Time Machine* and *The First Men in the Moon,* and in dozens of short stories, Wells explored most of the basic ideas of science fiction with more intelligence and craft than any American writer before Campbell's editorship of *Astounding.* In the early 1930s another Englishman, Olaf Stapledon, began a brilliant series of millennia-spanning novels with *Last and First Men* and *Last Men in London.*

But England went without a science fiction magazine until 1934, when a twopenny weekly named *Scoops* appeared, intended for schoolboys and relying heavily on serials about the Secret Service with only slight speculative content. *Scoops* aimed too low and after twenty issues it folded because of poor sales.

Thereafter, despite the success in U.S. sf magazines of English writers like John Russell Fearn and John Beynon Harris (who was later to become famous under his pen name "John Wyndham"), British magazine stalls were devoid of science fiction until June 1937, when the first issue of *Tales of Wonder* appeared. This magazine was aimed at adults, but it too followed a very conservative policy; a memorandum to authors from its editor, Walter H. Gillings, cautioned that "new ideas and 'thought variant' plots such as are required by the leading American magazines are not necessary. . . . On the contrary, it is the more simple straightforward theme that is required (however 'hackneyed' it might be for America), in order that the story shall be acceptable to a reading public unused to the many fantastic notions that have been developed by American science fiction in the course of eleven years."

Tales of Wonder was successful enough to achieve regular quarterly publication by its second year; it featured British sf writers with a liberal sprinkling of reprinted stories by U.S. authors as examples of the sort of material Gillings was seeking.

A second British sf magazine, *Fantasy,* appeared in 1938 under the editorship of a man who rejoiced (presumably) in the name T. Stanhope Sprigg. *Fantasy* was backed by a richer publisher than *Tales of Wonder*'s, but Sprigg was the only editor there interested in science fiction, so when Great Britain declared war on the Axis in September 1939 and Sprigg was mobilized by the RAF, *Fantasy* was allowed to die after just three issues. It had made little impact on the sf scene.

Tales of Wonder struggled on for several years, but paper rationing forced the page-count down from 128 in the Fall 1939 issue to 72 in the Spring 1942 issue, its last. Gillings, a longtime sf fan, had made a brave attempt, in the face of insuperable odds, to establish a "home-grown" science fiction product; he had published the first stories by William F. Temple, and Arthur C. Clarke's first science articles. But the war forced British sf publishing to cease.

(Science fiction in France suffered a similar blow: Georges H. Gallet had prepared the first two issues of *Conquêtes* before the declaration of war, but he was immediately mobilized and no further issues appeared.)

Nevertheless, English sf writers continued to write when they could, whether or not there were magazine markets at home. Olaf Stapledon published *Darkness and the Light* in book form in 1942, a far-reaching history of alternate futures branching from the contemporary battle between the forces of humanity's base and nobler natures. C. S. Lewis was working on *Perelandra* and reading selections from it to his friends at Oxford, who included Charles Williams and J. R. R. Tolkien. Arthur C. Clarke, young and not yet successful at fiction, was writing a novel called *Raymond.* "He'd burn the midnight oil working on it," remembers William F. Temple, who shared a flat with him, "then burst into our bedroom in the small hours to declaim to us some passage of pure genius he'd just penned. Later it became *Against the Fall of Night.*"

The first money Clarke earned from science fiction had come through one of England's few established sf writers, Eric Frank Russell. Clarke had supplied the idea of blending sound and color simultaneously into a new type of music, and Russell had included the notion in "The Prr-r-eet" (*Tales of Wonder,* Winter 1937). Russell paid Clarke 10 per cent of the proceeds from the story—less than three dollars.

Russell had begun writing science fiction in 1934, at the comparatively advanced age of twenty-nine. By 1940 he had published eleven stories; his unusual "Sinister Barrier" led off the first issue of *Unknown* in 1939 and caused such a sensation that it made him the most popular English sf writer in America. This was no accident, for Russell had made a close study of the hardboiled-detective magazine *Black Mask* and particularly the works of Raymond Chandler: his writing style was surprisingly "American."

But he sometimes had trouble, in those days, coming up with plots; his purchase of an idea from Clarke hadn't been so unusual for him. His first story had been strongly influenced by the work of Stanley G. Weinbaum; another of his tales had been based on an unsold manuscript by John Russell Fearn and Leslie J. Johnson; the idea for "Sinister Barrier" had come from the works of Charles Fort. So when Maurice G. Hugi, a close friend but a dreadful writer, showed him a story that had been rejected twenty times, Russell noticed that it did have one incidental idea that could serve as the basis for an interesting story, and he offered Hugi fifty dollars for it. Hugi jumped at the offer.

Hugi's idea, concerning a self-perpetuating robot, served as the initial inspiration for "The Mechanical Mice," which Russell wrote during a German bombing raid on Liverpool. There were many moments when Russell paused at the typewriter seriously doubting that he would survive the next five minutes. He was so distracted that he wrote the story in the first person, a technique he usually avoided.

But he was able to finish the story, and he sent it to Campbell, who replied in his customary fashion with no letter, just a check. ("It was his feeling that the check was eloquent enough," Isaac Asimov remembers.) The check was for eighty-five dollars, so Russell had netted less money on the story than had Hugi.

"The Mechanical Mice" appeared in the January 1941 *Astounding* under Hugi's name, at Russell's request. Hugi had never sold to an American magazine and Russell wanted to give his morale a boost. Hugi was a chronic diabetic, kept alive by frequent doses of insulin. "His days were numbered and he knew it," Russell recalled; getting into *Astounding,* if only by proxy, made him happy. Hugi died a few years later.

This evidence of Russell's compassion was characteristic. An individualist and iconoclast, he often expressed himself in strong terms (he lived in Egypt for a while as a child, and learned Arabic, but later forgot all of it except for profanity); yet he could make a point by indirection too. In 1941, he published a remarkably anti-racist sf story, "Jay Score," in which a robot earned the friendship of his human crewmates on a spaceship. The ship's doctor was a black man, and no comment was made or implied about this. He didn't even speak in dialect.

Russell went on to an outstanding career in science fiction; his later stories include "Dreadful Sanctuary," "Dear Devil" and the Hugo-winning "Allamagoosa." But he was already an accomplished writer in 1940 when he crouched over his typewriter with bombs exploding outside and wrote "The Mechanical Mice," an intriguing story of a man who built a machine from the future . . . then tried to find out what it *did.*

REFERENCES:

"The Impatient Dreamers" by Walter Gillings. *Vision of Tomorrow,* January 1970 and April 1970.

"SF Bandwaggon" by Michael Ashley. *The History of the Science Fiction Magazine, Part 2, 1936–1945.* New English Library, 1975.

"War Stops Publication of First French Magazine" by Jack Speer. *Fantasy News,* October 29, 1939.

A Pictorial History of Science Fiction by David Kyle. Hamlyn Publishing Group, 1976.

Imaginary Worlds by Lin Carter. Ballantine Books, 1973.

"The Saga of the Flat" by William F. Temple. *Vision of Tomorrow,* June 1970.

The Encyclopedia of Science Fiction and Fantasy, Vol. 1 by Donald H. Tuck. Advent:Publishers, 1974.

"Eric Frank Russell: Death of a Doubter" by Sam Moskowitz. *Amazing Stories,* June 1963.

Index to the Science-Fiction Magazines by Donald B. Day. Perri Press, 1952.

Letter from Eric Frank Russell, August 31, 1975.

The Early Asimov by Isaac Asimov. Doubleday, 1972.

"In Search of Justice" by Eric Frank Russell. *Hyphen,* March 1960.

* * *

It's asking for trouble to fool around with the unknown. Burman did it! Now there are quite a lot of people who hate like the very devil anything that clicks, ticks, emits whirring sounds, or generally behaves like an asthmatic alarm clock. They've got mechanophobia. Dan Burman gave it to them.

Who hasn't heard of the Burman Bullfrog Battery? The same chap! He puzzled it out from first to last and topped it with his now world-famous slogan: "Power In Your Pocket." It was no mean feat to concoct a thing the size of a cigarette packet that would pour out a hundred times as much energy as its most efficient competitor. Burman differed from everyone else in thinking it a mean feat.

Burman looked me over very carefully, then said, "When that technical journal sent you around to see me twelve years ago, you listened sympathetically. You didn't treat me as if I were an idle dreamer or a congenital idiot. You gave me a decent write-up, and started all the publicity that eventually made me much money."

"Not because I loved you," I assured him, "but because I was honestly convinced that your battery was good."

"Maybe." He studied me in a way that conveyed he was anxious to get something off his chest. "We've been pretty pally since that time. We've filled in some idle hours together, and

I feel that you're the one of my few friends to whom I can make a seemingly silly confession."

"Go ahead," I encouraged. We had been pretty pally, as he'd said. It was merely that we liked each other, found each other congenial. He was a clever chap, Burman, but there was nothing of the pedantic professor about him. Fortyish, normal, neat, he might have been a fashionable dentist to judge by appearances.

"Bill," he said, very seriously, "I didn't invent that damn battery."

"No?"

"No!" he confirmed. "I pinched the idea. What makes it madder is that I wasn't quite sure of what I was stealing and, crazier still, I don't know from whence I stole it."

"Which is as plain as a pikestaff," I commented.

"That's nothing. After twelve years of careful, exacting work I've built something else. It must be the most complicated thing in creation." He banged a fist on his knee, and his voice rose complainingly. "And now that I've done it, I don't know what I've done."

"Surely when an inventor experiments he knows what he's doing?"

"Not me!" Burman was amusingly lugubrious. "I've invented only one thing in my life, and that was more by accident than by good judgment." He perked up. "But that one thing was the key to a million notions. It gave me the battery. It has nearly given me things of greater importance. On several occasions it has nearly, but not quite, placed within my inadequate hands and half-understanding mind plans that would alter this world far beyond your conception." Leaning forward to lend emphasis to his speech, he said, "Now it has given me a mystery that has cost me twelve years of work and a nice sum of money. I finished it last night. I don't know what the devil it is."

"Perhaps if I had a look at it—"

"Just what I'd like you to do." He switched rapidly to mounting enthusiasm. "It's a beautiful job of work, even though I say so myself. Bet you that you can't say what it is, or what it's supposed to do."

"Assuming it can do something," I put in.

"Yes," he agreed. "But I'm positive it has a function of some sort." Getting up, he opened a door. "Come along."

It was a stunner. The thing was a metal box with a glossy, rhodium-plated surface. In general size and shape it bore a faint resemblance to an upended coffin, and had the same, brooding, ominous air of a casket waiting for its owner to give up the ghost.

There were a couple of small glass windows in its front through which could be seen a multitude of wheels as beautifully finished as those in a first-class watch. Elsewhere, several tiny lenses stared with sphinxlike indifference. There were three small trapdoors in one side, two in the other, and a large one in the front. From the top, two knobbed rods of metal stuck up like goat's horns, adding a satanic touch to the thing's vague air of yearning for midnight burial.

"It's an automatic layer-outer," I suggested, regarding the contraption with frank dislike. I pointed to one of the trapdoors. "You shove the shroud in there, and the corpse comes out the other side reverently composed and ready wrapped."

"So you don't like its air, either," Burman commented. He lugged open a drawer in a nearby tier, hauled out a mass of drawings. "These are its innards. It has an electric circuit, valves, condensers, and something that I can't quite understand, but which I suspect to be a tiny, extremely efficient electric furnace. It has parts I recognize as cog-cutters and pinion-shapers. It embodies several small-scale multiple stampers, apparently for dealing with sheet metal. There are vague suggestions of an assembly line ending in that large compartment shielded by the door in front. Have a look at the drawings yourself. You can see it's an extremely complicated device for manufacturing something only little less complicated."

The drawings showed him to be right. But they didn't show

everything. Any efficient machine designer could correctly have deduced the gadget's function if given complete details. Burman admitted this, saying that some parts he had made "on the spur of the moment," while others he had been "impelled to draw." Short of pulling the machine to pieces, there was enough data to whet the curiosity, but not enough to satisfy it.

"Start the damn thing and see what it does."

"I've tried," said Burman. "It won't start. There's no starting handle, nothing to suggest how it can be started. I tried everything I could think of, without result. The electric circuit ends in those antenna at the top, and I even sent current through those, but nothing happened."

"Maybe it's a self-starter," I ventured. Staring at it, a thought struck me. "Timed," I added.

"Eh?"

"Set for an especial time. When the dread hour strikes, it'll go of its own accord, like a bomb."

"Don't be so melodramatic," said Burman, uneasily.

Bending down, he peered into one of the tiny lenses.

"*Bz-z-z!*" murmured the contraption in a faint undertone that was almost inaudible.

Burman jumped a foot. Then he backed away, eyed the thing warily, turned his glance at me.

"Did you hear that?"

"Sure!" Getting the drawings, I mauled them around. That little lens took some finding, but it was there all right. It had a selenium cell behind it. "An eye," I said. "It saw you, and reacted. So it isn't dead even if it does just stand there seeing no evil, hearing no evil, speaking no evil." I put a white handkerchief against the lens.

"*Bz-z-z!*" repeated the coffin, emphatically.

Taking the handkerchief, Burman put it against the other lenses. Nothing happened. Not a sound was heard, not a funeral note. Just nothing.

"It beats me," he confessed.

I'd got pretty fed up by this time. If the crazy article had performed, I'd have written it up and maybe I'd have started another financial snowball rolling for Burman's benefit. But you can't do anything with a box that buzzes whenever it feels temperamental. Firm treatment was required, I decided.

"You've been all nice and mysterious about how you got hold of this brain wave," I said. "Why can't you go to the same source for information about what it's supposed to be?"

"I'll tell you—or, rather, I'll show you."

From his safe, Burman dragged out a box, and from the box he produced a gadget. This one was far simpler than the useless mass of works over by the wall. It looked just like one of those old-fashioned crystal sets, except that the crystal was very big, very shiny, and was set in a horizontal vacuum tube. There was the same single dial, the same cat's whisker. Attached to the lot by a length of flex was what might have been a pair of headphones, except in place of the phones were a pair of polished, smoothly rounded copper circles shaped to fit outside the ears and close against the skull.

"My one and only invention," said Burman, not without a justifiable touch of pride.

"What is it?"

"A time-traveling device."

"Ha, ha!" My laugh was very sour. I'd read about such things. In fact, I'd written about them. They were buncombe. Nobody could travel through time, either backward or forward. "Let me see you grow hazy and vanish into the future."

"I'll show you something very soon." Burman said it with assurance I didn't like. He said it with the positive air of a man who knows darned well that he can do something that everybody else knows darned well can't be done. He pointed to the crystal set. "It wasn't discovered at the first attempt. Thousands must have tried and failed. I was the lucky one. I must have picked a peculiarly individualistic crystal; I still don't know how it does what it does; I've never been able to repeat its performance even with a crystal apparently identical."

"And it enables you to travel in time?"

"Only forward. It won't take me backward, not even as much as one day. But it can carry me forward an immense distance, perhaps to the very crack of doom, perhaps everlastingly through infinity."

I had him now! I'd got him firmly entangled in his own absurdities. My loud chuckle was something I couldn't control.

"You can travel forward, but not backward, not even one day back. Then how the devil can you return to the present once you've gone into the future?"

"Because I never leave the present," he replied, evenly. "I don't partake of the future. I merely survey it from the vantage point of the present. All the same, it is time-traveling in the correct sense of the term." He seated himself. "Look here, Bill, what *are* you?"

"Who, me?"

"Yes, what are you." He went on to provide the answer. "Your name is Bill. You're a body and a mind. Which of them is Bill?"

"Both," I said, positively.

"True—but they're different parts of you. They're not the same even though they go around like Siamese twins." His voice grew serious. "Your body moves always in the present, the dividing line between the past and the future. But your mind is more free. It can think, and is in the present. It can remember, and at once is in the past. It can imagine, and at once is in the future, in its own choice of all the possible futures. *Your mind can travel through time!*"

He'd outwitted me. I could find points to pick upon and argue about, but I knew that fundamentally he was right. I'd not looked at it from his angle before, but he was correct in saying that anyone could travel through time within the limits of his own memory and imagination. At that very moment I could go back twelve years and see him in my mind's eye as a younger man, paler, thinner, more excitable, not so cool and self-possessed. The picture was as perfect as my memory was excellent. For that brief spell I was twelve years back in all but the flesh.

"I call this thing a psychophone," Burman went on. "When you imagine what the future will be like, you make a characteristic choice of all the logical possibilities, you pick your favorite from a multitude of likely futures. The psychophone, somehow —the Lord alone knows how—tunes you into future *reality*. It makes you depict within your mind the future as it will be shaped in actuality, eliminating all the alternatives that will not occur."

"An imagination-stimulator, a dream-machine," I scoffed, not feeling as sure of myself as I sounded. "How do you know it's giving you the McCoy?"

"Consistency," he answered, gravely. "It repeats the same features and the same trends far too often for the phenomena to be explained as mere coincidence. Besides," he waved a persuasive hand, "I got the battery from the future. It works, doesn't it?"

"It does," I agreed, reluctantly. I pointed to his psychophone. "I, too, may travel in time. How about letting me have a try? Maybe I'll solve your mystery for you."

"You can try if you wish," he replied, quite willingly. He pulled a chair into position. "Sit here, and I'll let you peer into the future."

Clipping the headband over my cranium, and fitting the copper rings against my skull where it sprouted ears, Burman connected his psychophone to the mains, switched it on; or rather he did some twiddling that I assumed was a mode of switching on.

"All you have to do," he said, "is to close your eyes, compose yourself, then try and permit your imagination to wander into the future."

He meddled with the cat's whisker. A couple of times he said, "Ah!" And each time he said it I got a peculiar dithery feeling around my unfortunate ears. After a few seconds of this, he drew it out to, "A-a-ah!" I played unfair, and peeped beneath lowered lids. The crystal was glowing like rats' eyes in a forgotten cellar. A furtive crimson.

Closing my own optics, I let my mind wander. Something was flowing between those copper electrodes, a queer, indescribable something that felt with stealthy fingers at some secret portion of my brain. I got the asinine notion that they were the dexterous digits of a yet-to-be-born magician who was going to shout, "Presto!" and pull my abused lump of think-meat out of a thirtieth-century hat—assuming they'd wear hats in the thirtieth century.

What was it like, or, rather, what would it be like in the thirtieth century? Would there be retrogression? Would humanity again be composed of scowling, fur-kilted creatures lurking in caves? Or had progress continued—perhaps even to the development of men like gods?

Then it happened! I swear it! I pictured, quite voluntarily, a savage, and then a huge-domed individual with glittering eyes —the latter being my version of the ugliness we hope to attain. Right in the middle of this erratic dreaming, those weird fingers warped my brain, dissolved my phantoms, and replaced them with a dictated picture which I witnessed with all the helplessness and clarity of a nightmare.

I saw a fat man spouting. He was quite an ordinary man as far as looks went. In fact, he was so normal that he looked henpecked. But he was attired in a Roman toga, and he wore a small, black box where his laurel wreath ought to have been. His audience was similarly dressed, and all were balancing their boxes like a convention of fish porters. What Fatty was orating sounded gabble to me, but he said his piece as if he meant it.

The crowd was in the open air, with great, curved rows of seats visible in the background. Presumably an outside auditorium of some sort. Judging by the distance of the back rows, it must have been a devil of a size. Far behind its sweeping ridge a great edifice jutted into the sky, a cubical erection with walls of glossy squares, like an immense glasshouse.

"F'wot?" bellowed Fatty, with obvious heat. "Wuk, wuk, wuk, mor, noon'n'ni'! Bok onned, ord this, ord that." He stuck an indignant finger against the mysterious object on his cranium. "Bok onned, wuk, wuk, wuk. F"wot?" he glared around. "F'nix!" The crowd murmured approval somewhat timidly. But it was enough for Fatty. Making up his mind, he flourished a plump fist and shouted, "Th'ell wit'm!" Then he tore his box from his pate.

Nobody said anything, nobody moved. Dumb and wide-eyed, the crowd just stood and stared as if paralyzed by the sight of a human being sans box. Something with a long, slender stream-lined body and broad wings soared gracefully upward in the distance, swooped over the auditorium, but still the crowd nei-ther moved nor uttered a sound.

A smile of triumph upon his broad face, Fatty bawled, "Lem see'm make wuk now! Lem see'm—"

He got no further. With a rush of mistiness from its tail, but in perfect silence, the soaring thing hovered and sent down a spear of faint, silvery light. The light touched Fatty. He rotted where he stood, like a victim of ultra-rapid leprosy. He rotted, collapsed, crumbled within his sagging clothes, became dust as once he had been dust. It was horrible.

The watchers did not flee in utter panic; not one expression of fear, hatred or disgust came from their tightly closed lips. In perfect silence they stood there, staring, just staring, like a horde of wooden soldiers. The thing in the sky circled to survey its handiwork, then dived low over the mob, a stubby antenna in its prow sparking furiously. As one man, the crowd turned left. As one man it commenced to march, left, right, left, right.

Tearing off the headband, I told Burman what I'd seen, or what his contraption had persuaded me to think that I'd seen. "What the deuce did it mean?"

"Automatons," he murmured. "Glasshouses and reaction ships." He thumbed through a big diary filled with notations in his own hands. "Ah, yes, looks like you were very early in the thirtieth century. Unrest was persistent for twenty years prior to the Antibox Rebellion."

"What rebellion?"

"The Antibox—the revolt of the automatons against the thirtieth-century Technocrats. Jackson-Dkj-99717, a successful and cunning schemer with a warped box, secretly warped hundreds of other boxes, and eventually led the rebels to victory in 3047. His great grandson, a greedy, thick-headed individual, caused the rebellion of the Boxless Freemen against his own clique of Jacksocrats."

I gaped at this recital, then said, "The way you tell it makes it sound like history."

"Of course it's history," he asserted. "History that is yet to be." He was pensive for a while. "Studying the future will seem a weird process to you, but it appears quite a normal procedure to me. I've done it for years, and maybe familiarity has bred contempt. Trouble was, though, that selectivity is poor. You can pick on some especial period twenty times in succession, but you'll never find yourself in the same month, or even the same year. In fact, you're fortunate if you strike twice in the same decade. Result is that my data is very erratic."

"I can imagine that," I told him. "A good guesser can guess the correct time to within a minute or two, but never to within ten or even fifty seconds."

"Quite!" he responded. "So the hell of it has been that mine was the privilege of watching the panorama of the future, but in a manner so sketchy that I could not grasp its prizes. Once I was lucky enough to watch a twenty-fifth-century power pack assembled from first to last. I got every detail before I lost the scene which I've never managed to hit upon again. But I made that power pack—and you know the result."

"So that's how you concocted your famous battery!"

"It is! But mine, good as it may be, isn't as good as the one I saw. Some slight factor is missing." His voice was suddenly tight when he added, "I missed something because I had to miss it!"

"Why?" I asked, completely puzzled.

"Because history, past or future, permits no glaring paradox. Because, having snatched this battery from the twenty-fifth century, I am recorded in that age as the twentieth-century inventor of the thing. They've made a mild improvement to it in those five centuries, but that improvement was automatically withheld from me. Future history is as fixed and unalterable by those of the present time as is the history of the past."

"Then," I demanded, "explain to me that complicated contraption which does nothing but say *bz-z-z.*"

"Damn it!" he said, with open ire, "that's just what's making me crazy! It can't be a paradox, it just can't." Then, more carefully, "So it must be a seeming paradox."

"O. K. You tell me how to market a seeming paradox, and the commercial uses thereof, and I'll give it a first-class write-up."

Ignoring my sarcasm, he went on. "I tried to probe the future as far as human minds can probe. I saw nothing, nothing but the vastness of a sterile floor upon which sat a queer machine, gleaming there in silent, solitary majesty. Somehow, it seemed aware of my scrutiny across the gulf of countless ages. It held my attention with a power almost hypnotic. For more than a day, for a full thirty hours, I kept that vision without losing it —the longest time I have ever kept a future scene."

"Well?"

"I drew it. I made complete drawings of it, performing the task with all the easy confidence of a trained machine draughtsman. Its insides could not be seen, but somehow they came to me, somehow I knew them. I lost the scene at four o'clock in the morning, finding myself with masses of very complicated drawings, a thumping head, heavy-lidded eyes, and a half-scared feeling in my heart." He was silent for a short time. "A year later I plucked up courage and started to build the thing I had drawn. It cost me a hell of a lot of time and a hell of a lot of money. But I did it—it's finished."

"And all it does is buzz," I remarked, with genuine sympathy.

"Yes," he sighed, doubtfully.

There was nothing more to be said. Burman gazed moodily at the wall, his mind far, far away. I fiddled aimlessly with the copper earpieces of the psychophone. My imagination, I reckoned, was as good as anyone's, but for the life of me I could neither imagine nor suggest a profitable market for a metal coffin filled with watchmaker's junk. No, not even if it did make odd noises.

A faint, smooth *whir* came from the coffin. It was a new sound that swung us round to face it pop-eyed. *Whir-r-r!* it went again. I saw finely machined wheels spin behind the window in its front.

"Good heavens!" said Burman.

Bz-z-z! Whir-r! Click! The whole affair suddenly slid sidewise on its hidden castors.

The devil you know isn't half so frightening as the devil you don't. I don't mean that this sudden demonstration of life and motion got us scared, but it certainly made us leery, and our hearts put in an extra dozen bumps a minute. This coffin-thing was, or might be, a devil we didn't know. So we stood there, side by side, gazing at it fascinatedly, feeling apprehensive of we knew not what.

Motion ceased after the thing had slid two feet. It stood there, silent, imperturbable, its front lenses eying us with glassy lack of expression. Then it slid another two feet. Another stop. More meaningless contemplation. After that, a swifter and farther slide that brought it right up to the laboratory table. At that point it ceased moving, began to emit varied but synchronized ticks like those of a couple of sympathetic grandfather clocks.

Burman said, quietly, "Something's going to happen!"

If the machine could have spoken it would have taken the words right out of his mouth. He'd hardly uttered the sentence when a trapdoor in the machine's side fell open, a jointed, metallic arm snaked cautiously through the opening and reached for a marine chronometer standing on the table.

With a surprised oath, Burman dashed forward to rescue the chronometer. He was too late. The arm grabbed it, whisked it into the machine, the trapdoor shut with a hard snap, like the vicious clash of a sprung bear trap. Simultaneously, another trapdoor in the front flipped open, another jointed arm shot out and in again, spearing with ultrarapid motion too fast to follow. That trapdoor also snapped shut, leaving Burman gaping down at his torn clothing from which his expensive watch and equally expensive gold chain had been ripped away.

"Good heavens!" said Burman, backing from the machine.

We stood looking at it a while. It didn't move again, just posed there ticking steadily as if ruminating upon its welcome meal. Its lenses looked at us with all the tranquil lack of interest of a well-fed cow. I got the idiotic notion that it was happily digesting a mess of cogs, pinions and wheels.

Because its subtle air of menace seemed to have faded away, or maybe because we sensed its entire preoccupation with the task in hand, we made an effort to rescue Burman's valuable timepiece. Burman tugged mightily at the trapdoor through which his watch had gone, but failed to move it. I tugged with him, without result. The thing was sealed as solidly as if welded in. A large screwdriver failed to pry it open. A crowbar, or a good jimmy would have done the job, but at that point Burman decided that he didn't want to damage the machine which had cost him more than the watch.

Tick-tick-tick! went the coffin, stolidly. We were back where we'd started, playing with our fingers, and no wiser than before. There was nothing to be done, and I felt that the accursed contraption knew it. So it stood there, gaping through its lenses, and jeered *tick-tick-tick.* From its belly, or where its belly would have been if it'd had one, a slow warmth radiated. According to Burman's drawings, that was the location of the tiny electric furnace.

The thing was functioning; there could be no doubt about that! If Burman felt the same way as I did, he must have been pretty mad. There we stood, like a couple of prize boobs, not knowing what the machine was supposed to do, and all the time it was doing under our very eyes whatever it was designed to do.

From where was it drawing its power? Were those antennae sticking like horns from its head busily sucking current from the atmosphere? Or was it, perhaps, absorbing radio power? Or did it have internal energy of its own? All the evidence suggested that it was making something, giving birth to something, but giving birth to what?

Tick-tick-tick! was the only reply.

Our questions were still unanswered, our curiosity was still unsatisfied, and the machine was still ticking industriously at the hour of midnight. We surrendered the problem until next morning. Burman locked and double-locked his laboratory before we left.

Police officer Burke's job was a very simple one. All he had to do was walk round and round the block, keeping a wary eye on the stores in general and the big jewel depot in particular, phoning headquarters once per hour from the post at the corner.

Night work suited Burke's taciturn disposition. He could wander along, communing with himself, with nothing to bother him or divert him from his inward ruminations. In that particular section nothing ever happened at night, nothing.

Stopping outside the gem-bedecked window, he gazed through the glass and the heavy grille behind it to where a low-power bulb shed light over the massive safe. There was a rajah's ransom in there. The guard, the grille, the automatic alarms and sundry ingenious traps preserved it from the adventurous fingers of anyone who wanted to ransom a rajah. Nobody had made the brash attempt in twenty years. Nobody had even made a try for the contents of the grille-protected window.

He glanced upward at a faintly luminescent path of cloud behind which lay the hidden moon. Turning, he strolled on. A cat sneaked past him, treading cautiously, silently, and hugging the angle of the wall. His sharp eyes detected its slinking shape even in the nighttime gloom, but he ignored it and progressed to the corner.

Back of him, the cat came below the window through which he just had stared. It stopped, one forefoot half-raised, its ears cocked forward. Then it flattened belly-low against the concrete, its burning orbs wide, alert, intent. Its tail waved slowly from side to side.

Something small and bright came skittering toward it, moving with mouselike speed and agility close in the angle of the wall. The cat tensed as the object came nearer. Suddenly, the thing was within range, and the cat pounced with lithe eagerness. Hungry paws dug at a surface that was not soft and furry, but hard, bright and slippery. The thing darted around like a clockwork toy as the cat vainly tried to hold it. Finally, with an angry snarl, the cat swiped it viciously, knocking it a couple of yards, where it rolled onto its back and emitted softly protesting clicks and tiny, urgent impulses that its feline attacker could not sense.

Gaining the gutter with a single leap, the cat crouched again. Something else was coming. The cat muscled, its eyes glowed. Another object slightly similar to the curious thing it had just captured, but a little bit bigger, a fraction noisier, and much different in shape. It resembled a small, gold-plated cylinder with a conical front from which projected a slender blade, and it slid along swiftly on invisible wheels.

Again the cat leaped. Down on the corner, Burke heard its brief shriek and following gargle. The sound didn't bother Burke—he'd heard cats and rats and other vermin make all sorts of queer noises in the night. Phlegmatically, he continued on his beat.

Three quarters of an hour later, Police Officer Burke had worked his way around to the fatal spot. Putting his flash on the body, he rolled the supine animal over with his foot. Its throat was cut. Its throat had been cut with an utter savagery that had half-severed its head from its body. Burke scowled down at it. He was no lover of cats himself, but he found difficulty in imagining anyone hating like that!

"Somebody," he muttered, "wants flaying alive."

His big foot shoved the dead cat back into the gutter where street cleaners could cart it away in the morning. He turned his attention to the window, saw the light still glowing upon the untouched safe. His mind was still on the cat while his eyes looked in and said that something was wrong. Then he dragged his attention back to business, realized what was wrong, and sweated at every pore. It wasn't the safe, it was the window.

In front of the window the serried trays of valuable rings still gleamed undisturbed. To the right, the silverware still shone untouched. But on the left had been a small display of delicate and extremely expensive watches. They were no longer there, not one of them. He remembered that right in front had rested a neat, beautiful calendar-chronometer priced at a year's salary. That, too, was gone.

The beam of his flash trembled as he tried the gate, found it fast, secure. The door behind it was firmly locked. The transom was closed, its heavy wire guard still securely fixed. He went over the window, eventually found a small, neat hole, about two inches in diameter, down in the corner on the side nearest the missing display.

Burke's curse was explosive as he turned and ran to the corner. His hand shook with indignation while it grabbed the telephone from its box. Getting headquarters, he recited his story. He thought he'd a good idea of what had happened, fancied he'd read once of a similar stunt being pulled elsewhere.

"Looks like they cut a disk with a rotary diamond, lifted it out with a suction cup, then fished through the hole with a telescopic rod." He listened a moment, then said, "Yes, yes. That's just what gets me—the rings are worth ten times as much."

His still-startled eyes looked down the street while he paid attention to the voice at the other end of the line. The eyes wandered slowly, descended, found the gutter, remained fixed on the dim shape lying therein. Another dead cat! Still clinging to his phone, Burke moved out as far as the cord would allow, extended a boot, rolled the cat away from the curb. The flash settled on it. Just like the other—ear to ear!

"And listen," he shouted into the phone, "some maniac's wandering around slaughtering cats."

Replacing the phone, he hurried back to the maltreated window, stood guard in front of it until the police car rolled up. Four piled out.

The first said, "Cats! I'll say somebody's got it in for cats! We passed two a couple of blocks away. They were bang in the middle of the street, flat in the headlights, and had been damn near guillotined. Their bodies were still warm."

The second grunted, approached the window, stared at the small, neat hole, and said, "The mob that did this would be too cute to leave a print."

"They weren't too cute to leave the rings," growled Burke.

"Maybe you've got something there," conceded the other. "If they've left the one, they might have left the other. We'll test for prints, anyway."

A taxi swung into the dark street, pulled up behind the police car. An elegantly dressed, fussy, and very agitated individual got out, rushed up to the waiting group. Keys jangled in his pale, moist hand.

"Maley, the manager—you phoned me," he explained, breathlessly. "Gentlemen, this is terrible, terrible! The window show is worth thousands, thousands! What a loss, what a loss!"

"How about letting us in?" asked one of the policemen, calmly.

"Of course, of course."

Jerkily, he opened the gate, unlocked the door, using about six keys for the job. They walked inside. Maley switched on the lights, stuck his head between the plate-glass shelves, surveyed the depleted window.

"My watches, my watches," he groaned.

"It's awful, it's awful!" said one of the policemen, speaking with beautiful solemnity. He favored his companions with a sly wink.

Maley leaned farther over, the better to inspect an empty corner. "All gone, all gone," he moaned, "all my show of the finest makes in—*Yeeouw!*" His yelp made them jump. Maley bucked as he tried to force himself through the obstructing shelves toward the grille and the window beyond it. "My watch! My own watch!"

The others tiptoed, stared over his shoulders, saw the gold buckle of a black velvet fob go through the hole in the window. Burke was the first outside, his ready flash searching the concrete. Then he spotted the watch. It was moving rapidly along, hugging the angle of the wall, but it stopped dead as his beam settled upon it. He fancied he saw something else, equally bright and metallic, scoot swiftly into the darkness beyond the circle of his beam.

Picking up the watch, Burke stood and listened. The noises of the others coming out prevented him from hearing clearly, but he could have sworn he'd heard a tiny whirring noise, and a swift, juicy ticking that was not coming from the instrument in his hand. Must have been only his worried fancy. Frowning deeply, he returned to his companions.

"There was nobody," he asserted. "It must have dropped out of your pocket and rolled."

Damn it, he thought, could a watch roll that far? What the devil was happening this night? Far up the street, something screeched, then it bubbled. Burke shuddered—he could make a shrewd guess at that! He looked at the others, but apparently they hadn't heard the noise.

The papers gave it space in the morning. The total was sixty watches and eight cats, also some oddments from the small stock of a local scientific instrument maker. I read about it on my way down to Burman's place. The details were fairly lavish, but not complete. I got them completely at a later time when we discovered the true significance of what had occurred.

Burman was waiting for me when I arrived. He appeared both annoyed and bothered. Over in the corner, the coffin was ticking away steadily, its noise much louder than it had been the previous day. The thing sounded a veritable hive of industry.

"Well?" I asked.

"It's moved around a lot during the night," said Burman. "It's smashed a couple of thermometers and taken the mercury out of them. I found some drawers and cupboards shut, some open, but I've an uneasy feeling that it's made a thorough search through the lot. A packet of nickel foil has vanished, a coil of copper wire has gone with it." He pointed an angry finger at the bottom of the door through which I'd just entered. "And I blame it for gnawing ratholes in that. They weren't there yesterday."

Sure enough, there were a couple of holes in the bottom of that door. But no rat made those—they were neat and smooth and round, almost as if a carpenter had cut them with a keyhole saw.

"Where's the sense in it making those?" I questioned. "It can't crawl through apertures that size."

"Where's the sense in the whole affair?" Burman countered. He glowered at the busy machine which stared back at him with its expressionless lenses and churned steadily on. *Tick-tick-tick!* persisted the confounded thing. Then, *whir-thump-click!*

I opened my mouth intending to voice a nice, sarcastic comment at the machine's expense when there came a very tiny, very subtle and extremely high-pitched whine. Something small, metallic, glittering shot through one of the ratholes, fled across the floor toward the churning monstrosity. A trapdoor opened and swallowed it with such swiftness that it had disappeared before I realized what I'd seen. The thing had been a cylindrical, polished object resembling the shuttle of a sewing machine, but about four times the size. And it had been dragging something also small and metallic.

Burman stared at me; I stared at Burman. Then he foraged around the laboratory, found a three-foot length of half-inch steel pipe. Dragging a chair to the door, he seated himself, gripped the pipe like a bludgeon, and watched the ratholes. Imperturbably, the machine watched him and continued to *tick-tick-tick*.

Ten minutes later, there came a sudden click and another tiny whine. Nothing darted inward through the holes, but the curious object we'd already seen—or another one exactly like it—dropped out of the trap, scooted to the door by which we were waiting. It caught Burman by surprise. He made a mad swipe with the steel as the thing skittered elusively past his feet and through a hole. It had gone even as the weapon walloped the floor.

"Damn!" said Burman, heartily. He held the pipe loosely in his grip while he glared at the industrious coffin. "I'd smash it to bits except that I'd like to catch one of these small gadgets first."

"Look out!" I yelled.

He was too late. He ripped his attention away from the coffin toward the holes, swinging up the heavy length of pipe, a startled look on his face. But his reaction was far too slow. Three of the little mysteries were through the holes and halfway across the floor before his weapon was ready to swing. The coffin swallowed them with the crash of a trapdoor.

The invading trio had rushed through in single file, and I'd got a better picture of them this time. The first two were golden shuttles, much like the one we'd already seen. The third was bigger, speedier, and gave me the notion that it could dodge around more dexterously. It had a long, sharp projection in front, a wicked, ominous thing like a surgeon's scalpel. Sheer speed deprived me of a good look at it, but I fancied that the tip of the scalpel had been tinged with red. My spine exuded perspiration.

Came an irritated scratching upon the outside of the door and a white-tipped paw poked tentatively through one of the holes. The cat backed to a safe distance when Burman opened the door, but looked lingeringly toward the laboratory. Its presence needed no explaining—the alert animal must have caught a glimpse of those infernal little whizzers. The same thought struck both of us; cats are quick on the pounce, very quick. Given a chance, maybe this one could make a catch for us.

We enticed it in with fair words and soothing noises. Its eagerness overcame its normal caution toward strangers, and it entered. We closed the door behind it; Burman got his length of pipe, sat by the door, tried to keep one eye on the holes and the other on the cat. He couldn't do both, but he tried. The cat sniffed and prowled around, mewed defeatedly. Its behavior suggested that it was seeking by sight rather than scent. There wasn't any scent.

With feline persistence, the animal searched the whole laboratory. It passed the buzzing coffin several times, but ignored it completely. In the end, the cat gave it up, sat on the corner of the laboratory table and started to wash its face.

Tick-tick-tick! went the big machine. Then *whir-thump!* A trap popped open, a shuttle fell out and raced for the door. A second one followed it. The first was too fast even for the cat, too fast for the surprised Burman as well. *Bang!* The length of steel tube came down viciously as the leading shuttle bulleted triumphantly through a hole.

But the cat got the second one. With a mighty leap, paws extended claws out, it caught its victim one foot from the door. It tried to handle the slippery thing, failed, lost it for an instant. The shuttle whisked around in a crazy loop. The cat got it again, lost it again, emitted an angry snarl, batted it against the skirting board. The shuttle lay there, upside down, four midget wheels in its underside spinning madly with a high, almost inaudible whine.

Eyes alight with excitement, Burman put down his weapon, went to pick up the shuttle. At the same time, the cat slunk toward it ready to play with it. The shuttle lay there, helplessly functioning upon its back, but before either could reach it the big machine across the room went *clunk!* opened a trap and ejected another gadget.

With astounding swiftness, the cat turned and pounced upon the newcomer. Then followed pandemonium. Its prey swerved agilely with a fitful gleam of gold; the cat swerved with it, cursed and spat. Black-and-white fur whirled around in a fighting haze in which gold occasionally glowed; the cat's hissings and spittings overlay a persistent whine that swelled and sank in the manner of accelerating or decelerating gears.

A peculiar gasp came from the cat, and blood spotted the floor. The animal clawed wildly, emitted another gasp followed by a gurgle. It shivered and flopped, a stream of crimson pouring from the great gash in its gullet.

We'd hardly time to appreciate the full significance of the ghastly scene when the victor made for Burman. He was standing by the skirting board, the still-buzzing shuttle in his hand. His eyes were sticking out with utter horror, but he retained enough presence of mind to make a frantic jump a second before the bulleting menace reached his feet.

He landed behind the thing, but it reversed in its own length and came for him again. I saw the mirrorlike sheen of its scalpel as it banked at terrific speed, and the sheen was drowned in sticky crimson two inches along the blade. Burman jumped over it again, reached the lab table, got up on that.

"Lord!" he breathed.

By this time I'd got the piece of pipe which he'd discarded. I hefted it, feeling its comforting weight, then did my best to bat the buzzing lump of wickedness through the window and over the roofs. It was too agile for me. It whirled, accelerated, dodged the very tip of the descending steel, and flashed twice around the table upon which Burman had taken refuge. It ignored me completely. Somehow, I felt that it was responding entirely to some mysterious call from the shuttle Burman had captured.

I swiped desperately, missed it again, though I swear I missed by no more than a millimeter. Something whipped through the holes in the door, fled past me into the big machine. Dimly, I heard traps opening and closing, and beyond all other sounds that steady, persistent *tick-tick-tick*. Another furious blow that accomplished no more than to dent the floor and jar my arm to the shoulder.

Unexpectedly, unbelievably, the golden curse ceased its insane gyrations on the floor and around the table. With a hard click, and a whir much louder than before, it raced easily up one leg of the table and reached the top.

Burman left his sanctuary in one jump. He was still clinging to the shuttle. I'd never seen his face so white.

"The machine!" he said, hoarsely. "Bash it to hell!"

Thunk! went the machine. A trap gaped, released another demon with a scalpel. *Tzz-z-z!* a third shot in through the holes in the door. Four shuttles skimmed through behind it, made for the machine, reached it safely. A fifth came through more slowly. It was dragging an automobile valve spring. I kicked the thing against the wall even as I struck a vain blow at one with a scalpel.

With another jump, Burman cleared an attacker. A second sheared off the toe of his right shoe as he landed. Again he reached the table from which his first foe had departed. All three things with scalpels made for the table with a reckless vim that was frightening.

"Drop that damned shuttle," I yelled.

He didn't drop it. As the fighting trio whirred up the legs, he flung the shuttle with all his might at the coffin that had given it birth. It struck, dented the casing, fell to the floor. Burman was off the table again. The thrown shuttle lay battered and noiseless, its small motive wheels stilled.

The armed contraptions scooting around the table seemed to change their purpose coincidently with the captured shuttle's smashing. Together, they dived off the table, sped through the holes in the door. A fourth came out of the machine, escorting two shuttles, and those too vanished beyond the door. A second or two later, a new thing, different from the rest, came in through one of the holes. It was long, round-bodied, snub-nosed, about half the length of a policeman's nightstick, had six wheels beneath, and a double row of peculiar serrations in front. It almost sauntered across the room while we watched it fascinatedly. I saw the serrations jerk and shift when it climbed the lowered trap into the machine. They were midget caterpillar tracks!

Burman had had enough. He made up his mind. Finding the steel pipe, he gripped it firmly, approached the coffin. Its lenses seemed to leer at him as he stood before it. Twelve years of intensive work to be destroyed at a blow. Endless days and nights of effort to be undone at one stroke. But Burman was past caring. With a ferocious swing he demolished the glass, with a fierce thrust he shattered the assembly of wheels and cogs behind.

The coffin shuddered and slid beneath his increasingly angry blows. Trapdoors dropped open, spilled out lifeless samples of the thing's metallic brood. Grindings and raspings came from the accursed object while Burman battered it to pieces. Then it was silent, stilled, a shapeless, useless mass of twisted and broken parts.

I picked up the dented shape of the object that had sauntered in. It was heavy, astonishingly heavy, and even after partial destruction its workmanship looked wonderful. It had a tiny, almost unnoticeable eye in front, but the miniature lens was cracked. Had it returned for repairs and overhaul?

"That," said Burman, breathing audibly, "is that!"

I opened the door to see if the noise had attracted attention. It hadn't. There was a lifeless shuttle outside the door, a second a yard behind it. The first had a short length of brass chain attached to a tiny hook projecting from its rear. The nose cap of the second had opened fanwise, like an iris diaphragm, and a pair of jointed metal arms were folded inside, hugging a medium-sized diamond. It looked as if they'd been about to enter when Burman destroyed the big machine.

Picking them up, I brought them in. Their complete inactivity, though they were undamaged, suggested that they had been controlled by the big machine and had drawn their motive power from it. If so, then we'd solved our problem simply, and by destroying the one had destroyed the lot.

Burman got his breath back and began to talk.

He said, "The Robot Mother! That's what I made—a duplicate of the Robot Mother. I didn't realize it, but I was patiently building the most dangerous thing in creation, a thing that is a terrible menace because it shares with mankind the ability to propagate. Thank Heaven we stopped it in time!"

"So," I remarked, remembering that he claimed to have got it from the extreme future, "that's the eventual master, or mistress, of Earth. A dismal prospect for humanity, eh?"

"Not necessarily. I don't know just how far I got, but I've an idea it was so tremendously distant in the future that Earth had become sterile from humanity's viewpoint. Maybe we'd emigrated to somewhere else in the cosmos, leaving our semi-intelligent slave machines to fight for existence or die. They fought —and survived."

"And then wangled things to try and alter the past in their favor," I suggested.

"No, I don't think so." Burman had become much calmer by now. "I don't think it was a dastardly attempt so much as an interesting experiment. The whole affair was damned in advance because success would have meant an impossible paradox. There are no robots in the next century, nor any knowledge of them. Therefore the intruders in this time must have been wiped out and forgotten."

"Which means," I pointed out, "that you must not only have destroyed the machine, but also all your drawings, all your notes, as well as the psychophone, leaving nothing but a few strange events and a story for me to tell."

"Exactly—I shall destroy everything. I've been thinking over the whole affair, and it's not until now I've understood that the psychophone can never be of the slightest use to me. It permits me to discover or invent only those things that history has decreed I shall invent, and which, therefore, I shall find with or without the contraption. I can't play tricks with history, past or future."

"Humph!" I couldn't find any flaw in his reasoning. "Did you notice," I went on, "the touch of bee-psychology in our antagonists? You built the hive, and from it emerged workers, warriors, and"—I indicated the dead saunterer—"one drone."

"Yes," he said, lugubriously. "And I'm thinking of the honey —eighty watches! Not to mention any other items the late papers may report, plus any claims for slaughtered cats. Good thing I'm wealthy."

"Nobody knows you've anything to do with those incidents. You can pay secretly if you wish."

"I shall," he declared.

"Well," I went on, cheerfully, "all's well that ends well. Thank goodness we've got rid of what we brought upon ourselves."

With a sigh of relief, I strolled toward the door. A high whine of midget motors drew my startled attention downward. While Burman and I stared aghast, a golden shuttle slid easily through one of the ratholes, sensed the death of the Robot Mother and scooted back through the other hole before I could stop it.

If Burman had been shaken before, he was doubly so now. He came over to the door, stared incredulously at the little exit just used by the shuttle, then at the couple of other undamaged but lifeless shuttles lying about the room.

"Bill," he mouthed, "your bee analogy was perfect. Don't you understand? There's another swarm! A queen got loose!"

There was another swarm all right. For the next forty-eight hours it played merry hell. Burman spent the whole time down at headquarters trying to convince them that his evidence wasn't just a fantastic story, but what helped him to persuade the police of his veracity was the equally fantastic reports that came rolling in.

To start with, old Gildersome heard a crash in his shop at midnight, thought of his valuable stock of cameras and miniature movie projectors, pulled on his pants and rushed downstairs. A razor-sharp instrument stabbed him through the right instep when halfway down, and he fell the rest of the way. He lay there, badly bruised and partly stunned, while things clicked, ticked and whirred in the darkness and the gloom. One by one, all the contents of his box of expensive lenses went through a hole in the door. A quantity of projector cogs and wheels went with them.

Ten people complained of being robbed in the night of watches and alarm clocks. Two were hysterical. One swore that the bandit was "a six-inch cockroach" which purred like a toy dynamo. Getting out of bed, he'd put his foot upon it and felt its cold hardness wriggle away from beneath him. Filled with revulsion, he'd whipped his foot back into bed "just as another cockroach scuttled toward him." Burman did not tell that agitated complainant how near he had come to losing his foot.

Thirty more reports rolled in next day. A score of houses had been entered and four shops robbed by things that had the agility and furtiveness of rats—except that they emitted tiny ticks and buzzing noises. One was seen racing along the road by a homing railway worker. He tried to pick it up, lost his forefinger and thumb, stood nursing the stumps until an ambulance rushed him away.

Rare metals and fine parts were the prey of these ticking marauders. I couldn't see how Burman or anyone else could wipe them out once and for all, but he did it. He did it by baiting them like rats. I went around with him, helping him on the job, while he consulted a map.

"Every report," said Burman, "leads to this street. An alarm clock that suddenly sounded was abandoned near here. Two automobiles were robbed of small parts near here. Shuttles have been seen going to or from this area. Five cats were dealt with practically on this spot. Every other incident has taken place within easy reach."

"Which means," I guessed, "that the queen is somewhere near this point?"

"Yes." He stared up and down the quiet, empty street over which the crescent moon shed a sickly light. It was two o'clock in the morning. "We'll settle this matter pretty soon!"

He attached the end of a reel of firm cotton to a small piece of silver chain, nailed the reel to the wall, dropped the chain on the concrete. I did the same with the movement of a broken watch. We distributed several small cogs, a few clock wheels, several camera fitments, some small, tangled bunches of copper wire, and other attractive oddments.

Three hours later, we returned accompanied by the police. They had mallets and hammers with them. All of us were wearing steel leg-and-foot shields knocked up at short notice by a handy sheet-metal worker.

The bait had been taken! Several cotton strands had broken after being unreeled a short distance, but others were intact. All of them either led to or pointed to a steel grating leading to a cellar below an abandoned warehouse. Looking down, we could see a few telltale strands running through the window frame beneath.

Burman said, "Now!" and we went in with a rush. Rusty locks snapped, rotten doors collapsed, we poured through the warehouse and into the cellar.

There was a small, coffin-shaped thing against one wall, a thing that ticked steadily away while its lenses stared at us with ghastly lack of emotion. It was very similar to the Robot Mother, but only a quarter of the size. In the light of a police torch, it was a brooding, ominous thing of dreadful significance. Around it, an active clan swarmed over the floor, buzzing and ticking in metallic fury.

Amid angry whirs and the crack of snapping scalpels on steel, we waded headlong through the lot. Burman reached the coffin first, crushing it with one mighty blow of his twelve-pound hammer, then bashing it to utter ruin with a rapid succession of blows. He finished exhausted. The daughter of the Robot Mother was no more, nor did her alien tribe move or stir.

Sitting down on a rickety wooden case, Burman mopped his brow and said, "Thank heavens that's done!"

Tick-tick-tick!

He shot up, snatched his hammer, a wild look in his eyes.

"Only my watch," apologized one of the policemen. "It's a cheap one, and it makes a hell of a noise." He pulled it out to show the worried Burman.

"Tick! tick!" said the watch, with mechanical aplomb.

"—AND HE BUILT A CROOKED HOUSE—"

Robert A. Heinlein

Robert A. Heinlein almost seems to have been invented to revolutionize science fiction. John Campbell is usually credited with "creating" modern science fiction, but it wasn't Campbell who wrote the stories that transformed the field—and among the writers who did create the stories in *Astounding* Heinlein stood pre-eminent.

Campbell had a clear idea of what he wanted in science fiction. In a 1942 *Writer's Digest* he wrote, "We want stories of the future told for scientifically trained, technically employed adults; central theme usually problems of an ordinary technician employed in an industry of fifty to fifty thousand years hence." And in a letter to Cleve Cartmill, one of the authors then beginning to write for *Astounding,* he put it more succinctly: "A science fiction story is a yarn lifted from the pages of a magazine of fifty, a hundred, or a thousand years from today."

Heinlein's "The Roads Must Roll," a perfect example of the first dictum, had been published two years before, and Campbell specifically cited Heinlein's work when he wrote to Cartmill. "Bob seemed to know how Campbell thought," says Cartmill. "And Campbell crowed and purred over Bob's stuff."

Heinlein may have been a born writer, but it took him nearly thirty-two years to discover this. Born in 1907 near Kansas City, Missouri, he attended the U.S. Naval Academy and graduated in 1929 standing twentieth in a class of six hundred. (He would have been fifth, says Heinlein, but "I got caught off-limits too many times

when I was out chasing girls.") For five years he served on active
duty as a line officer on destroyers and aircraft carriers, but was
retired from the Navy after he'd developed tuberculosis.

He enrolled at UCLA to study mathematics and physics, but his
health failed again and he moved to Colorado to recuperate. He
worked in silver mining, real estate and architecture, and ran unsuc-
cessfully for political office after he'd moved back to California. He
was accumulating the kind of experience on which writers can later
thrive; once, for instance, when he was about to close a sale on a
mine he owned, the deal fell through when the buyer was tommy-
gunned to death.

These were Depression years and money was scarce, so when he
saw an ad in *Thrilling Wonder Stories* offering a fifty-dollar first prize
for the best story by an amateur, he decided to try his hand. He wrote
"Life-Line" in four days. But, as he told Alfred Bester in a 1973
interview, "then I found out that *Astounding* was paying a cent a
word, and my story ran to 7000 words, so I submitted it to them and
they bought it." ("You son of a bitch," remarked Bester. "I won that
Thrilling Wonder contest and you beat me by twenty dollars.")

Heinlein reacted to the sale of his very first story just as Lester del
Rey had: How long has this been going on? He continued to write
science fiction, and by the end of 1941 had sold twenty-eight stories,
three of them full-length novels. They included many of the most
famous titles in sf history. " 'If This Goes On—,' " "Universe," "Beyond This Horizon" and the two stories included in the present book
are only a few. He never rewrote—Campbell never asked him to,
and on the few occasions when Campbell did reject a story he was
able to sell it quickly to the other magazines, usually *Astonishing* and
Super Science Stories. These appeared under the pen name "Lyle
Monroe."

(It was a common practice then for well-known writers to use
pseudonyms when they sold stories for less than top rates. Henry
Kuttner, Eando Binder, Edmond Hamilton and John Russell Fearn all
used pen names when they sold their work at half a cent a word;
when editors wanted to use their real names they had to double the
rate. Isaac Asimov once placed a story with Donald A. Wollheim for

Cosmic Stories, which began on a shoestring and relied on authors donating stories to help establish a new market; when a rival editor complained that such a practice allowed Wollheim to draw readers away from magazines that paid, Asimov gave Wollheim the option of running the story under a pen name or paying him a token five dollars. Wollheim paid the five dollars, pointing out that this was a record rate of $2.50 per word, since he was buying only Asimov's name.)

Heinlein's name was worth protecting in this way, for he had become the most popular writer in the science fiction field. In July 1941, just two years after the publication of his first story, Heinlein was Guest of Honor at the World Science Fiction Convention, a record for instant success that's never been approached by any other author.

Heinlein not only knew how to tell a story, he was a master at depicting the technology and sociology of future worlds. Usually he brought in the background as part of the basic story problem, so that it was integrated with the suspenseful build-up of the plot.

One of his most famous stories from this period is "Waldo," which described the kind of remote-control mechanical manipulators that later came to be used in atomic laboratories (and called "waldoes" by the technicians who used them). Willy Ley called this "one of the neatest predictions ever to come out of science fiction." Heinlein even envisioned the use of television to enable the operators to see what they were doing.

But Heinlein later explained how simple his method of prediction had been. He had read an article in *Popular Mechanics* in 1918 about a man "afflicted with myesthenia gravis, pathological muscular weakness so great that even handling a knife and fork is too much effort. . . . He devised complicated lever arrangements to enable him to use what little strength he had." Television, of course, had been invented years before Heinlein wrote his story. "As prophecies," said Heinlein, "these fictional predictions of mine were about as startling as for a man to look out a train window, see that another train is coming head-on toward his own on the same track—and predict a train wreck."

What sort of man was Robert A. Heinlein in the early 1940s? Jack Williamson met him in 1940, when they were both members of an informal Los Angeles group called the Mañana Literary Society. "I spent a good many evenings at his home in the Hollywood hills. He was a genial host, always neatly groomed, always courteous, but always a little reserved. An Annapolis graduate but retired from the Navy, he had the manner of a military aristocrat. . . . I remember thinking that he was the most highly civilized person I had ever met."

But he wasn't always so reserved. Isaac Asimov met Heinlein the same year when they were both visiting John Campbell at his home in New Jersey:

I refused a drink (I had never had anything to drink except a few drops of wine on occasional Passovers) and overcame my nervousness in my usual manner of talking and laughing loudly. Finally, Bob, who detected I was suffering, handed me a glass of something that looked like Coca-Cola. I sniffed at it cautiously and said, "What is it?"

"Coca-Cola," he said.

"It smells funny," I said.

"No, it doesn't," he said.

Afraid to argue, I drank it as I would drink Coca-Cola. Need I tell you it was a Cuba Libre? In five minutes, I was "high." . . . More scared than ever, I drifted to a corner, sat down and tried, in silence, to recover.

And after a few minutes, Bob whooped, "No wonder he doesn't drink. Alcohol sobers him up."

Sometimes the serious and the social sides of Heinlein worked together. Cleve Cartmill remembers a meeting of the Mañana Literary Society that "started when Jack Williamson and I mooched up Lookout Mountain Road to Heinlein's and announced that Jack had hit a snag on a story. The good guy kept wanting to act like a bastard.

"Bob got on the phone and presently a number of members with beer started arriving. We stationed ourselves around Bob's 40-foot living room and started kicking around the story idea that got stuck. Presently we worked it out in an acceptable fashion, and Jack later finished 'Backlash' and had it published in the August 1941 *Astounding*."

Heinlein was evidently a man who enjoyed a bull session enlivened by a civilized drink or two. He enjoyed a bit of fun in the stories he wrote too, so the slightly wacky tone of " '—And He Built a Crooked House—' " comes as no surprise. Quintus Teal, the story's overenthusiastic architect—who lived on Lookout Mountain Avenue, an address similar to ex-architect Heinlein's in this period—was by no means a stereotyped mad scientist of the sort that so often ranted through the pages of the science fiction pulps, but—

What, you don't believe there really were such things as mad scientists in the pulps? Then listen to Steck Davolio, the discredited paleontologist who, in a story by Robert Arthur, brought living specimens of Brontosaurus and Tyrannosaurus Rex to a modern fossil museum and refused to sell them:

". . . today I've opened the past to you, living, breathing, resurrected. For a quarter hour you have stared into the dead ages and seen creatures no living man could dare hope to see. . . . And now I'm taking it all away from you. You'll never rest again, never know satisfaction or contentment, knowing these creatures exist and you haven't got them. And I'll have a revenge I've been vindictive enough to long for for ten years."

Here's another warped genius bent on vengeance, from a 1940 story by Oscar J. Friend:

"They are robots I have built, robots that can function under my control. With them I shall conquer America, and then the entire world. I shall be supreme power. I'll teach them to laugh at my science, my theories—my inventions!"

To be sure, by the early 1940s mad scientists were on their way out, the readers having discredited them more effectively than their fictional colleagues could. But eccentric scientists were still popular: mavericks, loners and especially self-taught geniuses. Nelson S. Bond created one of the most popular of these in the person of Horse-Sense Hank, a gangling hayseed whose intuitive grasp of scientific principles carried him through a series of adventures in *Amazing Stories*. Challenged by the stuffy president of Midland University to explain Newton's laws of motion, he had to confess he'd never heard of Isaac Newton; but as for the natural laws that apply to things moving:

"Well, far's I can see, fust thing is that they can't get goin' by themselves, or if once they do, they can't stop less'n somethin' stops 'em. . . . Well, seems like everything in motion makes an equal motion like itself, an' it don't matter whether what it acts on is still or movin'. An' if there's anything else actin' along with it, both movements is goin' to have a say in the showdown. . . . Lastwise, pears like whenever there's a movement one way, there ought to be an equal kickback t'other way."

Quintus Teal, Heinlein's hero, was neither a rustic nor self-taught, but he'd probably have felt some affinity with Hank's individualistic approach. Certainly he was thrown back on his own wits when his imaginatively designed new house suddenly developed mystifying problems because of an earthquake. But does common sense apply in the fourth dimension?

REFERENCES:

John W. Campbell in *Writer's Digest,* quoted in *The Fantasite,* August-September 1942.
"A Rose Is a Rose Is a File Folder" by Cleve Cartmill. *Bixel,* December 1962.
"Interview with Robert A. Heinlein" by Alfred Bester. *Publishers' Weekly,* July 2, 1973.
Heinlein in Dimension by Alexei Panshin. Advent:Publishers, 1968.
"SF Bandwaggon" by Michael Ashley. *The History of the Science Fiction Magazine, Part 2, 1936–1945.* New English Library, 1975.
The Early Asimov by Isaac Asimov. Doubleday, 1972.
"Science Fiction: Its Nature, Faults and Virtues" by Robert A. Heinlein. *The Science Fiction Novel.* Advent:Publishers, 1959.
"The Campbell Era" by Jack Williamson. *Algol,* Summer 1975.
"Robert A. Heinlein" by Isaac Asimov. *MidAmeriCon Program Book,* 1976.
"The Tomb of Time" by Robert Arthur. *Thrilling Wonder Stories,* November 1940.
"The Worms Turn" by Oscar J. Friend. *Startling Stories,* July 1940.
"The Scientific Pioneer" by Nelson S. Bond. *Amazing Stories,* March 1940.

*　　*　　*

Americans are considered crazy anywhere in the world.

They will usually concede a basis for the accusation but point to California as the focus of the infection. Californians stoutly maintain that their bad reputation is derived solely from the acts of the inhabitants of Los Angeles County. Angelenos will, when pressed, admit the charge but explain hastily, "It's Hollywood. It's not our fault—we didn't ask for it; Hollywood just grew."

The people in Hollywood don't care; they glory in it. If you are interested, they will drive you up Laurel Canyon "—where we keep the violent cases." The Canyonites—the brown-legged women, the trunks-clad men constantly busy building and re-building their slap-happy unfinished houses—regard with faint contempt the dull creatures who live down in the flats, and treasure in their hearts the secret knowledge that they, and only they, know how to live.

Lookout Mountain Avenue is the name of a side canyon which twists up from Laurel Canyon. The other Canyonites don't like to have it mentioned; after all, one must draw the line somewhere!

High up on Lookout Mountain at number 8775, across the street from the Hermit—the original Hermit of Hollywood—lived Quintus Teal, graduate architect.

Even the architecture of southern California is different. Hot dogs are sold from a structure built like and designated "The Pup." Ice cream cones come from a giant stucco ice cream cone, and neon proclaims "Get the Chili Bowl Habit!" from the roofs of buildings which are indisputably chili bowls. Gasoline, oil, and free road maps are dispensed beneath the wings of tri-motored transport planes, while the certified rest rooms, inspected hourly for your comfort, are located in the cabin of the plane itself. These things may surprise, or amuse, the tourist, but the local residents, who walk bare-headed in the famous California noonday sun, take them as a matter of course.

Quintus Teal regarded the efforts of his colleagues in architecture as faint-hearted, fumbling, and timid.

"What is a house?" Teal demanded of his friend, Homer Bailey.

"Well—" Bailey admitted cautiously, "speaking in broad terms, I've always regarded a house as a gadget to keep off the rain."

"Nuts! You're as bad as the rest of them."

"I didn't say the definition was complete—"

"Complete! It isn't even in the right direction. From that point of view we might just as well be squatting in caves. But I don't blame you," Teal went on magnanimously, "you're no worse than the lugs you find practicing architecture. Even the Moderns—all they've done is to abandon the Wedding Cake School in favor of the Service Station School, chucked away the gingerbread and slapped on some chromium, but at heart they are as conservative and traditional as a county courthouse. Neutra! Schindler! What have those bums got? What's Frank Lloyd Wright got that I haven't got?"

"Commissions," his friend answered succinctly.

"Huh? Wha' d'ju say?" Teal stumbled slightly in his flow of words, did a slight double take, and recovered himself. "Commissions. Correct. And why? Because I don't think of a house as an upholstered cave; I think of it as a machine for living, a vital process, a live dynamic thing, changing with the mood of the dweller—not a dead, static, oversized coffin. Why should we be held down by the frozen concepts of our ancestors? Any fool with a little smattering of descriptive geometry can design a house in the ordinary way. Is the static geometry of Euclid the only mathematics? Are we to completely disregard the Picard-Vessiot theory? How about modular systems?—to say nothing of the rich suggestions of stereochemistry. Isn't there a place in architecture for transformation, for homomorphology, for actional structures?"

"Blessed if I know," answered Bailey. "You might just as well be talking about the fourth dimension for all it means to me."

"And why not? Why should we limit ourselves to the—Say!"

He interrupted himself and stared into distances. "Homer, I think you've really got something. After all, why not? Think of the infinite richness of articulation and relationship in four dimensions. What a house, what a house—" He stood quite still, his pale bulging eyes blinking thoughtfully.

Bailey reached up and shook his arm. "Snap out of it. What the hell are you talking about, four dimensions? Time is the fourth dimension; you can't drive nails into *that.*"

Teal shrugged him off. "Sure. Sure. Time is *a* fourth dimension, but I'm thinking about a fourth spatial dimension, like length, breadth and thickness. For economy of materials and convenience of arrangement you couldn't beat it. To say nothing of the saving of ground space—you could put an eight-room house on the land now occupied by a one-room house. Like a tesseract—"

"What's a tesseract?"

"Didn't you go to school? A tesseract is a hypercube, a square figure with four dimensions to it, like a cube has three, and a square has two. Here, I'll show you." Teal dashed out into the kitchen of his apartment and returned with a box of toothpicks which he spilled on the table between them, brushing glasses and a nearly empty Holland gin bottle carelessly aside. "I'll need some plasticine. I had some around here last week." He burrowed into a drawer of the littered desk which crowded one corner of his dining room and emerged with a lump of oily sculptor's clay. "Here's some."

"What are you going to do?"

"I'll show you." Teal rapidly pinched off small masses of the clay and rolled them into pea-sized balls. He stuck toothpicks into four of these and hooked them together into a square. "There! That's a square."

"Obviously."

"Another one like it, four more toothpicks, and we make a cube." The toothpicks were now arranged in the framework of a square box, a cube, with the pellets of clay holding the corners together. "Now we make another cube just like the first one, and the two of them will be two sides of the tesseract."

Bailey started to help him roll the little balls of clay for the second cube, but became diverted by the senuous feel of the docile clay and started working and shaping it with his fingers.

"Look," he said, holding up his effort, a tiny figurine, "Gypsy Rose Lee."

"Looks more like Gargantua; she ought to sue you. Now pay attention. You open up one corner of the first cube, interlock the second cube at one corner, and then close the corner. Then take eight more toothpicks and join the bottom of the first cube to the bottom of the second, on a slant, and the top of the first to the top of the second, the same way." This he did rapidly, while he talked.

"What's that supposed to be?" Bailey demanded suspiciously.

"That's a tesseract, eight cubes forming the sides of a hyper-cube in four dimensions."

"It looks more like a cat's cradle to me. You've only got two cubes there anyhow. Where are the other six?"

"Use your imagination, man. Consider the top of the first cube in relation to the top of the second; that's cube number three. Then the two bottom squares, then the front faces of each cube, the back faces, the right hand, the left hand—eight cubes." He pointed them out.

"Yeah, I see 'em. But they still aren't cubes; they're whatcha-mucallems—prisms. They are not square, they slant."

"That's just the way you look at it, in perspective. If you drew a picture of a cube on a piece of paper, the side squares would be slaunchwise, wouldn't they? That's perspective. When you look at a four-dimensional figure in three dimensions, naturally it looks crooked. But those are all cubes just the same."

"Maybe they are to you, brother, but they still look crooked to me."

Teal ignored the objections and went on. "Now consider this as the framework of an eight-room house; there's one room on the ground floor—that's for service, utilities, and garage. There are six rooms opening off it on the next floor, living room, dining room, bath, bedrooms, and so forth. And up at the top, completely inclosed and with windows on four sides, is your study. There! How do you like it?"

"Seems to me you have the bathtub hanging out of the living room ceiling. Those rooms are interlaced like an octopus."

"Only in perspective, only in perspective. Here, I'll do it another way so you can see it." This time Teal made a cube of toothpicks, then made a second of halves of toothpicks, and set it exactly in the center of the first by attaching the corners of the small cube to the large cube by short lengths of toothpick. "Now—the big cube is your ground floor, the little cube inside is your study on the top floor. The six cubes joining them are the living rooms. See?"

Bailey studied the figure, then shook his head. "I still don't see but two cubes, a big one and a little one. Those other six things, they look like pyramids this time instead of prisms, but they still aren't cubes."

"Certainly, certainly, you are seeing them in different perspective. Can't you see that?"

"Well, maybe. But that room on the inside, there. It's completely surrounded by the thingamujigs. I thought you said it had windows on four sides."

"It has—it just looks like it was surrounded. That's the grand feature about a tesseract house, complete outside exposure for every room, yet every wall serves two rooms and an eight-room house requires only a one-room foundation. It's revolutionary."

"That's putting it mildly. You're crazy, bud; you can't build a house like that. That inside room is on the inside, and there she stays."

Teal looked at his friend in controlled exasperation. "It's guys like you that keep architecture in its infancy. How many square sides has a cube?"

"Six."

"How many of them are inside?"

"Why, none of 'em. They're all on the outside."

"All right. Now listen—a tesseract has eight cubical sides, *all*

on the outside. Now watch me. I'm going to open up this tesseract like you can open up a cubical pasteboard box, until it's
flat. That way you'll be able to see all eight of the cubes."
Working very rapidly, he constructed four cubes, piling one on
top of the other in an unsteady tower. He then built out four
more cubes from the four exposed faces of the second cube in
the pile. The structure swayed a little under the loose coupling
of the clay pellets, but it stood, eight cubes in an inverted cross,
a double cross, as the four additional cubes stuck out in four
directions. "Do you see it now? It rests on the ground floor
room, the next six cubes are the living rooms, and there is your
study, up at the top."

Bailey regarded it with more approval than he had the other
figures. "At least I can understand it. You say that is a tesseract,
too?"

"That is a tesseract unfolded in three dimensions. To put it
back together you tuck the top cube onto the bottom cube, fold
those side cubes in till they meet the top cube and there you
are. You do all this folding through a fourth dimension of course;
you don't distort any of the cubes, or fold them into each other."

Bailey studied the wobbly framework further. "Look here,"
he said at last, "why don't you forget about folding this thing up
through a fourth dimension—you can't anyway—and build a
house like this?"

"What do you mean, I can't? It's a simple mathematical problem—"

"Take it easy, son. It may be simple in mathematics, but you
could never get your plans approved for construction. There
isn't any fourth dimension; forget it. But this kind of a house—
it might have some advantages."

Checked, Teal studied the model. "Hm-m-m—Maybe you
got something. We could have the same number of rooms, and
we'd save the same amount of ground space. Yes, and we would
set that middle cross-shaped floor northeast, southwest, and so
forth, so that every room would get sunlight all day long. That
central axis lends itself nicely to central heating. We'll put the

178 · ROBERT A. HEINLEIN

dining room on the northeast and the kitchen on the southeast, with big view windows in every room. O.K., Homer, I'll do it! Where do you want it built?"

"Wait a minute! Wait a minute! I didn't say you were going to build it for me—"

"Of course I am. Who else? Your wife wants a new house; this is it."

"But Mrs. Bailey wants a Georgian house—"

"Just an idea she has. Women don't know what they want—"

"Mrs. Bailey does."

"Just some idea an out-of-date architect has put in her head. She drives a 1941 car, doesn't she? She wears the very latest styles—why should she live in an eighteenth-century house? This house will be even later than a 1941 model; it's years in the future. She'll be the talk of the town."

"Well—I'll have to talk to her."

"Nothing of the sort. We'll surprise her with it. Have another drink."

"Anyhow, we can't do anything about it now. Mrs. Bailey and I are driving up to Bakersfield tomorrow. The company's bringing in a couple of wells tomorrow."

"Nonsense. That's just the opportunity we want. It will be a surprise for her when you get back. You can just write me a check right now, and your worries are over."

"I oughtn't to do anything like this without consulting her. She won't like it."

"Say, who wears the pants in your family anyhow?"

The check was signed about halfway down the second bottle.

Things are done fast in southern California. Ordinary houses there are usually built in a month's time. Under Teal's impassioned heckling the tesseract house climbed dizzily skyward in days rather than weeks, and its cross-shaped second story came jutting out at the four corners of the world. He had some trouble at first with the inspectors over these four projecting rooms but by using strong girders and folding money he had been able to convince them of the soundness of his engineering.

By arrangement, Teal drove up in front of the Bailey residence the morning after their return to town. He improvised on his two-tone horn. Bailey stuck his head out the front door. "Why don't you use the bell?"

"Too slow," answered Teal cheerfully. "I'm a man of action. Is Mrs. Bailey ready? Ah, there you are, Mrs. Bailey! Welcome home, welcome home. Jump in, we've got a surprise for you!"

"You know Teal, my dear," Bailey put in uncomfortably.

Mrs. Bailey sniffed. "I know him. We'll go in our own car, Homer."

"Certainly, my dear."

"Good idea," Teal agreed; " 'sgot more power than mine; we'll get there faster. I'll drive, I know the way." He took the keys from Bailey, slid into the driver's seat, and had the engine started before Mrs. Bailey could rally her forces.

"Never have to worry about my driving," he assured Mrs. Bailey, turning his head as he did so, while he shot the powerful car down the avenue and swung onto Sunset Boulevard, "it's a matter of power and control, a dynamic process, just my meat —I've never had a serious accident."

"You won't have but one," she said bitingly. "Will you *please* keep your eyes on the traffic?"

He attempted to explain to her that a traffic situation was a matter, not of eyesight, but intuitive integration of courses, speeds, and probabilities, but Bailey cut him short. "Where is the house, Quintus?"

"House?" asked Mrs. Bailey suspiciously. "What's this about a house, Homer? Have you been up to something without telling me?"

Teal cut in with his best diplomatic manner. "It certainly is a house, Mrs. Bailey. And what a house! It's a surprise for you from a devoted husband. Just wait till you see it—"

"I shall," she agreed grimly. "What style is it?"

"This house sets a new style. It's later than television, newer than next week. It must be seen to be appreciated. By the way," he went on rapidly, heading off any retort, "did you folks feel the earthquake last night?"

"Earthquake? What earthquake? Homer, was there an earthquake?"

"Just a little one," Teal continued, "about two A.M. If I hadn't been awake, I wouldn't have noticed it."

Mrs. Bailey shuddered. "Oh, this awful country! Do you hear that, Homer? We might have been killed in our beds and never have known it. Why did I ever let you persuade me to leave Iowa?"

"But my dear," he protested hopelessly, "you wanted to come out to California; you didn't like Des Moines."

"We needn't go into that," she said firmly. "You are a man; you should anticipate such things. Earthquakes!"

"That's one thing you needn't fear in your new home, Mrs. Bailey," Teal told her. "It's absolutely earthquake-proof; every part is in perfect dynamic balance with every other part."

"Well, I hope so. Where is this house?"

"Just around this bend. There's the sign now." A large arrow sign, of the sort favored by real estate promoters, proclaimed in letters that were large and bright even for southern California:

THE HOUSE OF THE FUTURE!!!

COLOSSAL—AMAZING—
REVOLUTIONARY

SEE HOW YOUR GRANDCHILDREN WILL LIVE!

Q. TEAL, ARCHITECT

"Of course that will be taken down," he added hastily, noting her expression, "as soon as you take possession." He slued around the corner and brought the car to a squealing halt in front of the House of the Future. *"Voilà!"* He watched their faces for response.

Bailey stared unbelievingly, Mrs. Bailey in open dislike. They saw a simple cubical mass, possessing doors and windows, but no other architectural features, save that it was decorated in intricate mathematical designs. "Teal," Bailey asked slowly, "what have you been up to?"

Teal turned from their faces to the house. Gone was the crazy tower with its jutting second-story rooms. No trace remained of the seven rooms above ground floor level. Nothing remained but the single room that rested on the foundations. "Great jumping cats!" he yelled, "I've been robbed!"

He broke into a run.

But it did him no good. Front or back, the story was the same: the other seven rooms had disappeared, vanished completely. Bailey caught up with him, and took his arm. "Explain yourself. What is this about being robbed? How come you built anything like this—it's not according to agreement."

"But I didn't. I built just what we had planned to build, an eight-room house in the form of a developed tesseract. I've been sabotaged; that's what it is! Jealousy! The other architects in town didn't dare let me finish this job; they knew they'd be washed up if I did."

"When were you last here?"

"Yesterday afternoon."

"Everything all right then?"

"Yes. The gardeners were just finishing up."

Bailey glanced around at the faultlessly manicured landscaping. "I don't see how seven rooms could have been dismantled and carted away from here in a single night without wrecking this garden."

Teal looked around, too. "It doesn't look it. I don't understand it."

Mrs. Bailey joined them. "Well? Well? Am I to be left to amuse myself? We might as well look it over as long as we are here, though I'm warning you, Homer, I'm not going to like it."

"We might as well," agreed Teal, and drew a key from his pocket with which he let them in the front door. "We may pick up some clues."

The entrance hall was in perfect order, the sliding screens that separated it from the garage space were back, permitting them to see the entire compartment. "This looks all right," observed Bailey. "Let's go up on the roof and try to figure out what happened. Where's the staircase? Have they stolen that, too?"

"Oh, no," Teal denied, "look—" He pressed a button below the light switch; a panel in the ceiling fell away and a light, graceful flight of stairs swung noiselessly down. Its strength members were the frosty silver of duralumin, its treads and risers transparent plastic. Teal wriggled like a boy who has successfully performed a card trick, while Mrs. Bailey thawed perceptibly.

It was beautiful.

"Pretty slick," Bailey admitted. "Howsomever it doesn't seem to go any place—"

"Oh, that—" Teal followed his gaze. "The cover lifts up as you approach the top. Open stairwells are anachronisms. Come on." As predicted, the lid of the staircase got out of their way as they climbed the flight and permitted them to debouch at the top, but not, as they had expected, on the roof of the single room. They found themselves standing in the middle one of the five rooms which constituted the second floor of the original structure.

For the first time on record Teal had nothing to say. Bailey echoed him, chewing on his cigar. Everything was in perfect order. Before them, through open doorway and translucent partition, lay the kitchen, a chef's dream of up-to-the-minute domestic engineering, monel metal, continuous counter space, concealed lighting, functional arrangement. On the left the formal, yet gracious and hospitable dining room awaited guests, its furniture in parade-ground alignment.

Teal knew before he turned his head that the drawing room and lounge would be found in equally substantial and impossible existence.

"Well, I must admit this *is* charming," Mrs. Bailey approved, "and the kitchen is just *too* quaint for words—though I would never have guessed from the exterior that this house had so much room upstairs. Of course *some* changes will have to be made. That secretary now—if we moved it over *here* and put the settle over *there*—"

"Stow it, Matilda," Bailey cut in brusquely. "Wha'd' yuh make of it, Teal?"

"Why, Homer Bailey! The very id—"

"Stow it, I said. Well, Teal?"

The architect shuffled his rambling body. "I'm afraid to say. Let's go on up."

"How?"

"Like this." He touched another button; a mate, in deeper colors, to the fairy bridge that had let them up from below offered them access to the next floor. They climbed it, Mrs. Bailey expostulating in the rear, and found themselves in the master bedroom. Its shades were drawn, as had been those on the level below, but the mellow lighting came on automatically. Teal at once activated the switch which controlled still another flight of stairs, and they hurried up into the top-floor study.

"Look, Teal," suggested Bailey when he had caught his breath, "can we get to the roof above this room? Then we could look around."

"Sure, it's an observatory platform." They climbed a fourth flight of stairs, but when the cover at the top lifted to let them reach the level above, they found themselves, not on the roof, but *standing in the ground floor room where they had entered the house.*

Mr. Bailey turned a sickly gray. "Angels in heaven," he cried, "this place is haunted. We're getting out of here." Grabbing his wife he threw open the front door and plunged out.

Teal was too much preoccupied to bother with their departure. There was an answer to all this, an answer that he did not believe. But he was forced to break off considering it because of hoarse shouts from somewhere above him. He lowered the staircase and rushed upstairs. Bailey was in the central room leaning over Mrs. Bailey, who had fainted. Teal took in the situation, went to the bar built into the lounge, and poured three fingers of brandy, which he returned with and handed to Bailey. "Here—this'll fix her up."

Bailey drank it.

"That was for Mrs. Bailey," said Teal.

"Don't quibble," snapped Bailey. "Get her another." Teal took the precaution of taking one himself before returning with a dose earmarked for his client's wife. He found her just opening her eyes.

"Here, Mrs. Bailey," he soothed, "this will make you feel better."

"I never touch spirits," she protested, and gulped it.

"Now tell me what happened," suggested Teal. "I thought you two had left."

"But we did—we walked out the front door and found ourselves up here, in the lounge."

"The hell you say! Hm-m-m—wait a minute." Teal went into the lounge. There he found that the big view window at the end of the room was open. He peered cautiously through it. He stared, not out at the California countryside, but into the ground floor room—or a reasonable facsimile thereof. He said nothing, but went back to the stairwell which he had left open and looked down it. The ground-floor room was still in place. Somehow, it managed to be in two different places at once, on different levels.

He came back into the central room and seated himself opposite Bailey in a deep, low chair, and sighted him past his upthrust bony knees. "Homer," he said impressively, "do you know what has happened?"

"No, I don't—but if I don't find out pretty soon, something is going to happen and pretty drastic, too!"

"Homer, this is a vindication of my theories. This house is a real tesseract."

"What's he talking about, Homer?"

"Wait, Matilda—now Teal, that's ridiculous. You've pulled some hanky-panky here and I won't have it—scaring Mrs. Bailey half to death, and making me nervous. All I want is to get out of here, with no more of your trapdoors and silly practical jokes."

"Speak for yourself, Homer," Mrs. Bailey interrupted, "I was *not* frightened; I was just took all over queer for a moment. It's my heart; all of my people are delicate and highstrung. Now about this tessy thing—explain yourself, Mr. Teal. Speak up."

He told her as well as he could in the face of numerous interruptions the theory back of the house. "Now as I see it, Mrs. Bailey," he concluded, "this house, while perfectly stable in three dimensions, was not stable in four dimensions. I had built a house in the shape of an unfolded tesseract; something happened to it, some jar or side thrust, and it collapsed into its normal shape—it folded up." He snapped his fingers suddenly. "I've got it! The earthquake!"

"Earthquake?"

"Yes, yes, the little shake we had last night. From a four-dimensional standpoint this house was like a plane balanced on edge. One little push and it fell over, collapsed along its natural joints into a stable four-dimensional figure."

"I thought you boasted about how safe this house was."

"It *is* safe—three-dimensionally."

"I don't call a house safe," commented Bailey edgily, "that collapses at the first little tremor."

"But look around you, man!" Teal protested. "Nothing has been disturbed, not a piece of glassware cracked. Rotation through a fourth dimension can't affect a three-dimensional figure any more than you can shake letters off a printed page. If you had been sleeping in here last night, you would never have awakened."

"That's just what I'm afraid of. Incidentally, has your great genius figured out any way for us to get out of this booby trap?"

"Huh? Oh, yes, you and Mrs. Bailey started to leave and landed back up here, didn't you? But I'm sure there is no real difficulty—we came in, we can go out. I'll try it." He was up and hurrying downstairs before he had finished talking. He flung open the front door, stepped through, and found himself staring at his companions, down the length of the second-floor lounge. "Well, there does seem to be some slight problem," he admitted blandly. "A mere technicality, though—we can always go out a window." He jerked aside the long drapes that covered the deep French windows set in one side wall of the lounge. He stopped suddenly.

"Hm-m-m," he said, "this is interesting—very."

"What is?" asked Bailey, joining him.

"This." The window stared directly into the dining room, instead of looking outdoors. Bailey stepped back to the corner where the lounge and the dining room joined the central room at ninety degrees.

"But that can't be," he protested, "that window is maybe fifteen, twenty feet from the dining room."

"Not in a tesseract," corrected Teal. "Watch." He opened the window and stepped through, talking back over his shoulder as he did so.

From the point of view of the Baileys he simply disappeared.

But not from his own viewpoint. It took him some seconds to catch his breath. Then he cautiously disentangled himself from the rosebush to which he had become almost irrevocably wedded, making a mental note the while never again to order landscaping which involved plants with thorns, and looked around him.

He was outside the house. The massive bulk of the ground floor room thrust up beside him. Apparently he had fallen off the roof.

He dashed around the corner of the house, flung open the front door and hurried up the stairs. "Homer!" he called out, "Mrs. Bailey! I've found a way out!"

Bailey looked annoyed rather than pleased to see him. "What happened to you?"

"I fell out. I've been outside the house. You can do it just as easily—just step through those French windows. Mind the rose-bush, though—we may have to build another stairway."

"How did you get back in?"

"Through the front door."

"Then we shall leave the same way. Come, my dear." Bailey set his hat firmly on his head and marched down the stairs, his wife on his arm.

Teal met them in the lounge. "I could have told you that wouldn't work," he announced. "Now here's what we have to do: As I see it, in a four-dimensional figure a three-dimensional man has two choices every time he crosses a line of juncture, like a wall or a threshold. Ordinarily he will make a ninety-degree turn through the fourth dimension, only he doesn't feel it with his three dimensions. Look." He stepped through the very window that he had fallen out of a moment before. Stepped through and arrived in the dining room, where he stood, still talking.

"I watched where I was going and arrived where I intended to." He stepped back into the lounge. "The time before I didn't watch and I moved on through normal space and fell out of the house. It must be a matter of subconscious orientation."

"I'd hate to depend on subconscious orientation when I step out for the morning paper."

"You won't have to; it'll become automatic. Now to get out of the house this time—Mrs. Bailey, if you will stand here with your back to the window, and jump backward, I'm pretty sure you will land in the garden."

Mrs. Bailey's face expressed her opinion of Teal and his ideas. "Homer Bailey," she said shrilly, "are you going to stand there and let him suggest such—"

"But Mrs. Bailey," Teal attempted to explain, "we can tie a rope on you and lower you down eas—"

"Forget it, Teal," Bailey cut him off brusquely. "We'll have to find a better way than that. Neither Mrs. Bailey nor I are fitted for jumping."

Teal was temporarily nonplused; there ensued a short silence. Bailey broke it with, "Did you hear that, Teal?"

"Hear what?"

"Someone talking off in the distance. D'you s'pose there

could be someone else in the house, playing tricks on us, maybe?"

"Oh, not a chance. I've got the only key."

"But I'm sure of it," Mrs. Bailey confirmed. "I've heard them ever since we came in. Voices. Homer, I can't stand much more of this. Do something."

"Now, now, Mrs. Bailey," Teal soothed, "don't get upset. There can't be anyone else in the house, but I'll explore and make sure. Homer, you stay here with Mrs. Bailey and keep an eye on the rooms on this floor." He passed from the lounge into the ground floor room and from there to the kitchen and on into the bedroom. This led him back to the lounge by a straight-line route, that is to say, by going straight ahead on the entire trip he returned to the place from which he started.

"Nobody around," he reported. "I opened all of the doors and windows as I went—all except this one." He stepped to the window opposite the one through which he had recently fallen and thrust back the drapes.

He saw a man with his back toward him, four rooms away. Teal snatched open the French window and dived through it, shouting, "There he goes now! Stop thief!"

The figure evidently heard him; it fled precipitately. Teal pursued, his gangling limbs stirred to unanimous activity, through drawing room, kitchen, dining room, lounge—room after room, yet in spite of Teal's best efforts he could not seem to cut down the four-room lead that the interloper had started with.

He saw the pursued jump awkwardly but actively over the low sill of a French window and in so doing knock off his hat. When he came up to the point where his quarry had lost his headgear, he stopped and picked it up, glad of an excuse to stop and catch his breath. He was back in the lounge.

"I guess he got away from me," he admitted. "Anyhow, here's his hat. Maybe we can identify him."

Bailey took the hat, looked at it, then snorted, and slapped it on Teal's head. It fitted perfectly. Teal looked puzzled, took the hat off, and examined it. On the sweat band were the initials "Q.T." It was his own.

Slowly comprehension filtered through Teal's features. He went back to the French window and gazed down the series of rooms through which he had pursued the mysterious stranger. They saw him wave his arms semaphore fashion. "What are you doing?" asked Bailey.

"Come see." The two joined him and followed his stare with their own. Four rooms away they saw the backs of three figures, two male and one female. The taller, thinner of the men was waving his arms in a silly fashion.

Mrs. Bailey screamed and fainted again.

Some minutes later, when Mrs. Bailey had been resuscitated and somewhat composed, Bailey and Teal took stock. "Teal," said Bailey, "I won't waste any time blaming you; recriminations are useless and I'm sure you didn't plan for this to happen, but I suppose you realize we are in a pretty serious predicament. How are we going to get out of here? It looks now as if we would stay until we starve; every room leads into another room."

"Oh, it's not that bad. I got out once, you know."

"Yes, but you can't repeat it—you tried."

"Anyhow we haven't tried all the rooms. There's still the study."

"Oh, yes, the study. We went through there when we first came in, and didn't stop. Is it your idea that we might get out through its windows?"

"Don't get your hopes up. Mathematically, it ought to look into the four side rooms on this floor. Still we never opened the blinds; maybe we ought to look."

" 'Twon't do any harm anyhow. Dear, I think you had best just stay here and rest—"

"Be left alone in this horrible place? I should say not!" Mrs. Bailey was up off the couch where she had been recuperating even as she spoke.

They went upstairs. "This is the inside room, isn't it, Teal?" Bailey inquired as they passed through the master bedroom and climbed on up toward the study. "I mean it was the little cube in your diagram that was in the middle of the big cube, and completely surrounded."

"That's right," agreed Teal. "Well, let's have a look. I figure this window ought to give into the kitchen." He grasped the cords of Venetian blinds and pulled them.

It did not. Waves of vertigo shook them. Involuntarily they fell to the floor and grasped helplessly at the pattern on the rug to keep from falling. "Close it! Close it!" moaned Bailey.

Mastering in part a primitive atavistic fear, Teal worked his way back to the window and managed to release the screen. The window had looked *down* instead of *out*, down from a terrifying height.

Mrs. Bailey had fainted again.

Teal went back after more brandy while Bailey chafed her wrists. When she had recovered, Teal went cautiously to the window and raised the screen a crack. Bracing his knees, he studied the scene. He turned to Bailey. "Come look at this, Homer. See if you recognize it."

"You stay away from there, Homer Bailey!"

"Now, Matilda, I'll be careful." Bailey joined him and peered out.

"See up there? That's the Chrysler Building, sure as shooting. And there's the East River, and Brooklyn." They gazed straight down the sheer face of an enormously tall building. More than a thousand feet away a toy city, very much alive, was spread out before them. "As near as I can figure it out, we are looking down the side of the Empire State Building from a point just above its tower."

"What is it? A mirage?"

"I don't think so—it's too perfect. I think space is folded over through the fourth dimension here and we are looking past the fold."

"You mean we aren't really seeing it?"

"No, we're seeing it all right. I don't know what would happen if we climbed out this window, but I for one don't want to try. But what a view! Oh, boy, what a view! Let's try the other windows."

They approached the next window more cautiously, and it was well that they did, for it was even more disconcerting, more reasonshaking, than the one looking down the gasping height of the skyscraper. It was a simple seascape, open ocean and blue sky—but the ocean was where the sky should have been, and contrariwise. This time they were somewhat braced for it, but they both felt seasickness about to overcome them at the sight of waves rolling overhead; they lowered the blind quickly without giving Mrs. Bailey a chance to be disturbed by it.

Teal looked at the third window. "Game to try it, Homer?"

"Hrrumph—well, we won't be satisfied if we don't. Take it easy." Teal lifted the blind a few inches. He saw nothing, and raised it a little more—still nothing. Slowly he raised it until the window was fully exposed. They gazed out at—nothing.

Nothing, nothing at all. What color is nothing? Don't be silly! What shape is it? Shape is an attribute of *something*. It had neither depth nor form. It had not even blackness. It was *nothing*.

Bailey chewed at his cigar. "Teal, what do you make of that?"

Teal's insouciance was shaken for the first time. "I don't know, Homer, I don't rightly know—but I think that window ought to be walled up." He stared at the lowered blind for a moment. "I think maybe we looked at a place where space *isn't*. We looked around a fourth-dimensional corner and there wasn't anything there." He rubbed his eyes. "I've got a headache."

They waited for a while before tackling the fourth window. Like an unopened letter, it might *not* contain bad news. The doubt left hope. Finally the suspense stretched too thin and Bailey pulled the cord himself, in the face of his wife's protests.

It was not so bad. A landscape stretched away from them, right side up, and on such a level that the study appeared to be a ground floor room. But it was distinctly unfriendly.

A hot, hot sun beat down from lemon-colored sky. The flat ground seemed burned a sterile, bleached brown and incapable of supporting life. Life there was, strange stunted trees that lifted knotted, twisted arms to the sky. Little clumps of spiky leaves grew on the outer extremities of these misshapen growths.

"Heavenly day," breathed Bailey, "where is that?"

Teal shook his head, his eyes troubled. "It beats me."

"It doesn't look like anything on Earth. It looks more like another planet—Mars, maybe."

"I wouldn't know. But, do you know, Homer, it might be worse than that, worse than another planet, I mean."

"Huh? What's that you say?"

"It might be clear out of our space entirely. I'm not sure that that is our Sun at all. It seems too bright."

Mrs. Bailey had somewhat timidly joined them and now gazed out at the outré scene. "Homer," she said in a subdued voice, "those hideous trees—they frighten me."

He patted her hand.

Teal fumbled with the window catch.

"What are you doing?" Bailey demanded.

"I thought if I stuck my head out the window I might be able to look around and tell a bit more."

"Well—all right," Bailey grudged, "but be careful."

"I will." He opened the window a crack and sniffed. "The air is all right, at least." He threw it open wide.

His attention was diverted before he could carry out his plan. An uneasy tremor, like the first intimation of nausea, shivered the entire building for a long second, and was gone.

"Earthquake!" They all said it at once. Mrs. Bailey flung her arms around her husband's neck.

Teal gulped and recovered himself, saying:

"It's all right, Mrs. Bailey. This house is perfectly safe. You know you can expect settling tremors after a shock like last night." He had just settled his features into an expression of reassurance when the second shock came. This one was no mild shimmy but the real seasick roll.

In every Californian, native born or grafted, there is a deep-rooted primitive reflex. An earthquake fills him with soul-shaking claustrophobia which impels him blindly to *get outdoors!* Model boy scouts will push aged grandmothers aside to obey it. It is a matter of record that Teal and Bailey landed on top of Mrs. Bailey. Therefore, she must have jumped through the window first. The order of precedence cannot be attributed to chivalry; it must be assumed that she was in readier position to spring.

They pulled themselves together, collected their wits a little, and rubbed sand from their eyes. Their first sensations were relief at feeling the solid sand of the desert land under them. Then Bailey noticed something that brought them to their feet and checked Mrs. Bailey from bursting into the speech that she had ready.

"Where's the house?"

It was gone. There was no sign of it at all. They stood in the center of flat desolation, the landscape they had seen from the window. But, aside from the tortured, twisted trees there was nothing to be seen but the yellow sky and the luminary overhead, whose furnacelike glare was already almost insufferable.

Bailey looked slowly around, then turned to the architect. "Well, Teal?" His voice was ominous.

Teal shrugged helplessly. "I wish I knew. I wish I could even be sure that we were on Earth."

"Well, we can't stand here. It's sure death if we do. Which direction?"

"Any, I guess. Let's keep a bearing on the Sun."

They had trudged on for an undetermined distance when Mrs. Bailey demanded a rest. They stopped. Teal said in an aside to Bailey, "Any ideas?"

"No . . . no, none. Say, do you hear anything?"

Teal listened. "Maybe—unless it's my imagination."

"Sounds like an automobile. Say, it *is* an automobile!"

They came to the highway in less than another hundred yards. The automobile, when it arrived, proved to be an elderly, puffing light truck, driven by a rancher. He crunched to a stop at their hail. "We're stranded. Can you help us out?"

"Sure. Pile in."

"Where are you headed?"

"Los Angeles."

"Los Angeles? Say, where is this place?"

"Well, you're right in the middle of the Joshua-Tree National Forest."

The return was as dispiriting as the Retreat from Moscow. Mr. and Mrs. Bailey sat up in front with the driver while Teal bumped along in the body of the truck, and tried to protect his head from the Sun. Bailey subsidized the friendly rancher to detour to the tesseract house, not because they wanted to see it again, but in order to pick up their car.

At last the rancher turned the corner that brought them back to where they had started. But the house was no longer there.

There was not even the ground floor room. It had vanished. The Baileys, interested in spite of themselves, poked around the foundations with Teal.

"Got any answers for this one, Teal?" asked Bailey.

"It must be that on that last shock it simply fell through into another section of space. I can see now that I should have anchored it at the foundations."

"That's not all you should have done."

"Well, I don't see that there is anything to get downhearted about. The house was insured, and we've learned an amazing lot. There are possibilities, man, possibilities! Why, right now I've got a great new revolutionary idea for a house—"

Teal ducked in time. He was always a man of action.

MICROCOSMIC GOD

Theodore Sturgeon

Theodore Sturgeon was one of the biggest "discoveries" made by John Campbell during the Golden Age, but, like A. E. van Vogt, he had already served an apprenticeship writing non–science fiction stories. Beginning in 1938, he had sold perhaps forty short-shorts to the McClure Newspaper Syndicate. Published under his own name in dozens of U.S. newspapers, they were human-interest vignettes, boy-meets-girl stories and the like.

He hadn't intended to be a writer. His boyhood dream was to become a gymnast with the Barnum & Bailey circus, but when he was fifteen he contracted acute rheumatic fever, which left him with a 16 per cent enlargement of the heart. "My heart used to push out between my ribs when it beat," he remembers. Gymnastics were now out of the question, and he went into a severe depression.

But he managed to finish high school, and won a scholarship in the Pennsylvania State Nautical School. After one term of being severely hazed as a cadet, he quit and got a job on a freighter plying East Coast waters from Miami to Boston. He stayed at sea for two and a half years, and began to write during his spare time.

One day he got an idea for a way to cheat the American Express Company out of several hundred thousand dollars. "I wrote to the company and found out precisely how they shipped this and that and the other things, got it all worked out and then wrote it as a short story because I didn't have quite the guts to do it myself." The idea paid off anyway, though the money was little: the McClure Syndicate accepted the story for five dollars payable on publication.

Sturgeon was so excited that he quit his job, went ashore in New York City and settled down to be a writer. The syndicate bought one or two stories a week; Sturgeon was paying $7.50 a week for his room, and eating on whatever was left. "I learned how to make a vegetable stew out of soup greens—six or seven cents would buy you a pack of soup greens: a turnip, a couple of tomatoes, a potato, some celery, and so on."

This went on for several months; then, early in 1939, a friend gave him a copy of the first issue of *Unknown,* saying, "This is what you ought to be writing for." Sturgeon read the issue, was delighted by it, and wrote a short story which he took to Campbell's office:

"I remember it was about a guy who got killed by a subway train, and he pointed out to me that it didn't have any story, that it described a situation. It was just promulgating the idea that at the moment of dying of violent death, time almost stops. And when you're getting hit by a subway train, you're hanging in mid-air, and the subway train comes and hits you and it crushes you to death, because you can't move out of the way, and it does it very slowly. But it had no story connected with it."

Sturgeon's experience writing vignettes for newspapers had evidently betrayed him: Campbell wanted fully developed stories. But he encouraged Sturgeon to try again, so Sturgeon wrote "A God in a Garden," and Campbell bought this one. It was published in the October 1939 *Unknown,* one month after Sturgeon's next story, "Ether Breather," had appeared in *Astounding.*

In the next two years Sturgeon sold twenty-six stories to Campbell. He was selling so regularly that eventually the front office raised its eyebrows at the number of checks made out to Theodore Sturgeon, wondering if Campbell might be playing favorites. So Sturgeon began using pen names, with the result that one month he had four stories in Campbell's magazines: the June 1941 *Astounding* carried stories by Theodore Sturgeon and "E. Waldo Hunter," as did the June 1941 *Unknown.*

(Sturgeon also used the name "E. Hunter Waldo." Waldo was his surname when he was born—he was then Edward Hamilton Waldo —but when his mother remarried, he legally changed his name to Theodore Sturgeon. Sturgeon was his stepfather's name, and since his real father's name had also been Edward, he'd always been called Teddy.)

His sales were coming so quickly that in 1940, at the age of twenty-two, Sturgeon decided he could support a family, so he married his high school sweetheart. He was at his most prolific now; he was even struck by a story idea during his honeymoon, and wrote the classic fantasy story "It" in one ten-hour session. Others followed, including "Microcosmic God," but in 1941 the wellsprings dried up and he found himself unable to write.

He took a job running a luxury resort hotel in Jamaica, hoping the change of scene would stimulate his imagination; but by the end of the year the United States was at war. Sturgeon's heart condition kept him out of the armed services, but he ran bulldozers for the Navy in Puerto Rico, working seventy hours a week. He managed to write only one story during the war, the famous novella "Killdozer," based on his experiences in Puerto Rico. It wasn't until 1946 that Sturgeon's byline again began to grace the pages of science fiction magazines.

He had made his mark during his first two years, though, and "Microcosmic God" was his most successful science fiction story of this period; its impact was so great that decades later the Science Fiction Writers of America voted it one of the five best sf stories of all time. Despite this, Sturgeon himself has never liked the story. When I told him I wanted to reprint it in this book he said, "Oh God, not that one! It's so badly written!"

This seemed odd, considering the story's popularity over nearly forty years, but the fact is that Theodore Sturgeon has always concerned himself with style—he was one of the very first science fiction writers whose prose was as important as his ideas—and it's the lack of "literary cadence" in the story that distresses him. Moreover, I found while putting together this book that several of the authors included were chagrined at the quality of writing in their stories: Eric Frank Russell felt "The Mechanical Mice" was poorly written, and Isaac Asimov feels that way even about "Nightfall."

As we've seen, Russell wrote his story under difficult circumstances, and Sturgeon and Asimov were both very young men when they wrote their stories. But their writing, despite any imperfections, was nevertheless superior to that in the vast majority of science fiction of the time.

The early 1940s were the end of the great era of pulp magazine publishing, a business which required professionals writing at a penny a word or less to turn out almost unbelievable quantities of fiction. Robert Bloch wrote 1500 to 2500 words an hour, all first draft; Henry Kuttner could write seven or eight thousand words an evening; and L. Ron Hubbard's pace was some 3000 to 4000 words an hour. (He wrote on an electric typewriter because no manually powered one could keep up with him.) Such haste seldom produced high-quality prose.

Moreover, pulp editors weren't interested in "good writing." One of the most prolific science fiction writers of the early 1940s was Frederic Arnold Kummer, Jr., who once commented, "Many letters in an author's mail accuse him of selling himself for gold, of not turning to the great work of which he is capable. I thought so once, myself. So I began turning out very well written pieces, character studies, ironic tales, laid on the various planets. No great inventions, no monsters . . . and no sales. I dreamed of the problems of people on other worlds, their loves, their hates, their twisted psychology. I still read over these yarns and admire their nice writing. But sell them? Never in a million years."

Raymond A. Palmer, then editor of *Amazing Stories* and *Fantastic Adventures,* was proud of the way he had directed the career of Robert Moore Williams: "He came into my office one afternoon, after having had a dozen straight rejects from me, to find out what was wrong. I told him very simply: 'Your stories are a lot of "pretty" writing. . . . If you'll take your next manuscript, blue-pencil *every* phrase that you consider to be *good* writing, I'll buy it.' " (Williams did, and became one of Palmer's most frequent contributors.)

The writing produced by authors working to pulp editors' demands was usually quite awful. Here's a sample of dialogue from the heroine of a story by Kummer:

"Oh, Eric, you were so right and I was so wrong! I know now why you fought against my father's invention! I've seen religion die out, seen women denied their most sacred mission.

"Famine, overcrowding, squalor! Men doomed to an eternity of endless routine, with no chance of advancement! No future, no children, no hope! Oh, if only there were some way to overthrow this dreadful curse!"

Nor was this sort of self-conscious melodrama confined to purely pulp-oriented authors and magazines. *Astounding* itself published prose like the following, written by two of its more accomplished authors.

Pathos:

Conn took her in his arms and kissed her. This, he thought, ought to be the last paragraph. Nothing else comes after this but "They lived happily ever after" and then "The End." He nestled his bruised cheek against her silky hair and tried to memorize its scent. At last he pushed Hilda gently away.

"I've got to go now," Conn said. "This is goodbye, Hilda, for a long time. Maybe forever—"

Nerve-shattering suspense:

. . . they were in this now, he as deep as she; and only the utmost boldness could hope to draw a fraction of victory from the defeat that loomed so starkly.

In truth, it's sometimes hard to conceive of the early forties as representing any sort of high point for science fiction, since the pulp mentality was evident in 99 per cent of the stories published then. You may not believe that such clichés as the following were ever actually published, yet they were there in the Golden Age.

"Follow that cab," I hissed at the hacker. "There's a ten spot in it for you if you don't lose it."

"Adam!" Eve whispered. "What does it all mean?"

"You are surprised that I speak your language?"

No such blemishes are to be found in "Microcosmic God." It may not be as smoothly written as Sturgeon's later work, but it's well crafted and explores a fascinating idea in the manner of the best science fiction. The story was written when Hitler's armies were overrunning Europe and Japan had invaded China. Sturgeon had been mulling over the idea of dictatorship, and he produced what even he admits is his most important early story. In contrast to the predominantly humorous stories he was writing then, "Microcosmic God" has, as Sturgeon once put it, "an element of heavy in it."

REFERENCES:

"Author! Author!" by Theodore Sturgeon. *The Fanscient,* Spring 1950.

Theodore Sturgeon: Storyteller by Paul Williams. Pendragon Press, 1978.

"Theodore Sturgeon: No More Than Human" by Sam Moskowitz. *Amazing Stories,* February 1962.

"Men Behind *Fantastic Adventures*" by Theodore Sturgeon. *Fantastic Adventures,* August 1951.

Unpublished interview with Theodore Sturgeon by Paul Williams, December 6, 1975.

Unpublished interview with Theodore Sturgeon by David Hartwell, September 4, 1972.

Introduction by Robert Silverberg. *The Science Fiction Hall of Fame.* Doubleday, 1970.

Letter from Eric Frank Russell, August 31, 1975.

"ALGOL Interview: Isaac Asimov" by Darrell Schweitzer. *Algol,* Winter 1977.

"Author! Author!" by Robert Bloch. *The Fanscient,* Summer 1949.

"C. L. Moore Talks to *Chacal.*" *Chacal,* Winter 1976.

"The Science of Science Fiction Writing" by John W. Campbell, Jr. *Of Worlds Beyond.* Fantasy Press, 1947.

"Readin' and Writhin' " by Damon Knight. *Science Fiction Quarterly,* February 1953.

"An Author Opens His Mail" by Frederic Arnold Kummer, Jr. *Fantascience Digest,* January-February 1940.

"Palmer tears his hair . . . out and down" by Raymond A. Palmer. *Stardust,* November 1940.

"Revolt Against Life" by Frederic Arnold Kummer, Jr. *Thrilling Wonder Stories,* January 1940.

"The Probable Man" by Alfred Bester. *Astounding Science-Fiction,* July 1941.

"Asylum" by A. E. van Vogt. *Astounding Science-Fiction,* May 1942.

"The Impossible Invention" by Robert Moore Williams. *Astonishing Stories,* June 1942.

"Adam Link in the Past" by Eando Binder. *Amazing Stories,* February 1941.

"Beyond Light" by Nelson S. Bond. *Planet Stories,* Winter 1940.
Introduction by Theodore Sturgeon to "Microcosmic God." *Without Sorcery.* Prime Press, 1948.

* * *

Here is a story about a man who had too much power, and a man who took too much, but don't worry; I'm not going political on you. The man who had the power was named James Kidder, and the other was his banker.

Kidder was quite a guy. He was a scientist and he lived on a small island off the New England coast all by himself. He wasn't the dwarfed little gnome of a mad scientist you read about. His hobby wasn't personal profit, and he wasn't a megalomaniac with a Russian name and no scruples. He wasn't insidious, and he wasn't even particularly subversive. He kept his hair cut and his nails clean and lived and thought like a reasonable human being. He was slightly on the baby-faced side; he was inclined to be a hermit; he was short and plump and—brilliant. His specialty was biochemistry, and he was always called *Mr.* Kidder. Not "Dr." Not "Professor." Just Mr. Kidder.

He was an odd sort of apple and always had been. He had never graduated from any college or university because he found them too slow for him, and too rigid in their approach to education. He couldn't get used to the idea that perhaps his professors knew what they were talking about. That went for his texts, too. He was always asking questions, and didn't mind very much when they were embarrassing. He considered Gregor Mendel a bungling liar, Darwin an amusing philosopher, and Luther Burbank a sensationalist. He never opened his mouth without grabbing a stickful of question marks. If he was talking to someone who had knowledge, he went in there and got it, leaving his victim feeling breathless. If he was talking to someone whose knowledge was already in his possession, he only asked repeatedly, "How do you know?" His most delectable pleasure was taken in cutting a fanatical eugenicist into conversational ribbons. So people left him alone and never, never asked him to tea. He was polite, but not politic.

He had a little money of his own, and with it he leased the island and built himself a laboratory. Now I've mentioned that he was a biochemist. But being what he was, he couldn't keep his nose in his own field. It wasn't too remarkable when he made an intellectual excursion wide enough to perfect a method of crystallizing Vitamin B_1 profitably by the ton—if anyone wanted it by the ton. He got a lot of money for it. He bought his island outright and put eight hundred men to work on an acre and a half of his ground, adding to his laboratory and building equipment. He got messing around with sisal fiber, found out how to fuse it, and boomed the banana industry by producing a practically unbreakable cord from the stuff.

You remember the popularizing demonstration he put on at Niagara, don't you? That business of running a line of the new cord from bank to bank over the rapids and suspending a ten-ton truck from the middle of it by razor edges resting on the cord? That's why ships now moor themselves with what looks like heaving line, no thicker than a lead pencil, that can be coiled on reels like garden hose. Kidder made cigarette money out of that, too. He went out and bought himself a cyclotron with part of it.

After that, money wasn't money any more. It was large numbers in little books. Kidder used to use little amounts of it to have food and equipment sent out to him, but after a while that stopped, too. His bank dispatched a messenger by seaplane to find out if Kidder was still alive. The man returned two days later in a bemused state, having been amazed something awesome at the things he'd seen out there. Kidder was alive, all right, and he was turning out a surplus of good food in an astonishingly simplified synthetic form. The bank wrote immediately and wanted to know if Mr. Kidder, in his own interest, was willing to release the secret of his dirtless farming. Kidder replied that he would be glad to, and inclosed the formulas. In a P. S. he said that he hadn't sent the information ashore because he hadn't realized anyone would be interested. That from a man who was responsible for the greatest sociological change in the second half of the twentieth century—factory farming. It made him richer; I mean it made his bank richer. He didn't give a rap.

But Kidder didn't really get started until about eight months after the bank messenger's visit. For a biochemist who couldn't even be called "Dr." he did pretty well. Here is a partial list of the things that he turned out:

A commercially feasible plan for making an aluminum alloy stronger than the best steel so that it could be used as a structural metal.

An exhibition gadget he called a light pump, which worked on the theory that light is a form of matter and therefore subject to physical and electromagnetic laws. Seal a room with a single light source, beam a cylindrical vibratory magnetic field to it from the pump, and the light will be led down it. Now pass the light through Kidder's "lens"—a ring which perpetuates an electric field along the lines of a high-speed iris-type camera shutter. Below this is the heart of the light pump—a ninety-eight-percent efficient light absorber, crystalline, which, in a sense, *loses* the light in its internal facets. The effect of darkening the room with this apparatus is slight but measurable. Pardon my layman's language, but that's the general idea.

Synthetic chlorophyll—by the barrel.

An airplane propeller efficient at eight times sonic speed.

A cheap goo you brush on over old paint, let harden, and then peel off like strips of cloth. The old paint comes with it. That one made friends fast.

A self-sustaining atomic disintegration of uranium's isotope 238, which is two hundred times as plentiful as the old stand-by, U-235.

That will do for the present. If I may repeat myself; for a biochemist who couldn't even be called Dr., he did pretty well.

204 · THEODORE STURGEON

Kidder was apparently unconscious of the fact that he held power enough on his little island to become master of the world. His mind simply didn't run to things like that. As long as he was left alone with his experiments, he was well content to leave the rest of the world to its own clumsy and primitive devices. He couldn't be reached except by a radiophone of his own design, and its only counterpart was locked in a vault of his Boston bank. Only one man could operate it—the bank president. The extraordinarily sensitive transmitter would respond only to President Conant's own body vibrations. Kidder had instructed Conant that he was not to be disturbed except by messages of the greatest moment. His ideas and patents, when Conant could pry one out of him, were released under pseudonyms known only to Conant—Kidder didn't care.

The result, of course, was an infiltration of the most astonishing advancements since the dawn of civilization. The nation profited—the world profited. But most of all, the bank profited. It began to get a little oversize. It began getting its fingers into other pies. It grew more fingers and had to bake more figurative pies. Before many years had passed, it was so big that, using Kidder's many weapons, it almost matched Kidder in power.

Almost.

Now stand by while I squelch those fellows in the lower left-hand corner who've been saying all this while that Kidder's slightly improbable; that no man could ever perfect himself in so many ways in so many sciences.

Well, you're right. Kidder was a genius—granted. But his genius was not creative. He was, to the core, a student. He applied what he knew, what he saw, and what he was taught. When first he began working in his new laboratory on his island he reasoned something like this:

"Everything I know is what I have been taught by the sayings and writings of people who have studied the sayings and writings of people who have—and so on. Once in a while someone stumbles on something new and he or someone cleverer uses the idea and disseminates it. But for each one that finds something really new, a couple of million gather and pass on information that is already current. I'd know more if I could get the jump on evolutionary trends. It takes too long to wait for the accidents that increase man's knowledge—my knowledge. If I had ambition enough now to figure out how to travel ahead in time, I could skim the surface of the future and just dip down when I saw something interesting. But time isn't that way. It can't be left behind or tossed ahead. What else is left?

"Well, there's the proposition of speeding intellectual evolution so that I can observe what it cooks up. That seems a bit inefficient. It would involve more labor to discipline human minds to that extent than it would to simply apply myself along those lines. But I can't apply myself that way. No one man can.

"I'm licked. I can't speed myself up, and I can't speed other men's minds up. Isn't there an alternative? There must be— somewhere, somehow, there's got to be an answer."

So it was on this, and not on eugenics, or light pumps, or botany, or atomic physics, that James Kidder applied himself. For a practical man, the problem was slightly on the metaphysical side, but he attacked it with typical thoroughness, using his own peculiar brand of logic. Day after day he wandered over the island, throwing shells impotently at sea gulls and swearing richly. Then came a time when he sat indoors and brooded. And only then did he get feverishly to work.

He worked in his own field, biochemistry, and concentrated mainly on two things—genetics and animal metabolism. He learned, and filed away in his insatiable mind, many things having nothing to do with the problem in hand, and very little of what he wanted. But he piled that little on what little he knew or guessed, and in time had quite a collection of known factors to work with. His approach was characteristically unorthodox. He did things on the order of multiplying apples by pears, and balancing equations by adding $\log \sqrt{-1}$ to one side and ∞ to the other. He made mistakes, but only one of a kind, and later, only one of a species. He spent so many hours at his microscope that he had to quit work for two days to get rid of a hallucination that his heart was pumping his own blood through the mike. He did nothing by trial and error because he disapproved of the method as sloppy.

And he got results. He was lucky to begin with, and even luckier when he formularized the law of probability and reduced it to such low terms that he knew almost to the item what experiments not to try. When the cloudy, viscous semifluid on the watch glass began to move of itself he knew he was on the right track. When it began to seek food on its own he began to be excited. When it divided and, in a few hours, redivided, and each part grew and divided again, he was triumphant, for he had created life.

He nursed his brain children and sweated and strained over them, and he designed baths of various vibrations for them, and inoculated and dosed and sprayed them. Each move he made taught him the next. And out of his tanks and tubes and incubators came amoebalike creatures, and then ciliated animalcules, and more and more rapidly he produced animals with eye spots, nerve cysts, and then—victory of victories—a real blastopod, possessed of many cells instead of one. More slowly he developed a gastropod, but once he had it, it was not too difficult for him to give it organs, each with a specified function, each inheritable.

Then came cultured mollusklike things, and creatures with more and more perfected gills. The day that a nondescript thing wriggled up an inclined board out of a tank, threw flaps over its gills and feebly breathed air, Kidder quit work and went to the other end of the island and got disgustingly drunk. Hangover and all, he was soon back in the lab, forgetting to eat, forgetting to sleep, tearing into his problem.

He turned into a scientific byway and ran down his other great triumph—accelerated metabolism. He extracted and refined the stimulating factors in alcohol, coca, heroin, and Mother Nature's prize dope runner, *cannabis indica*. Like the scientist who, in analyzing the various clotting agents for blood treatments, found that oxalic acid and oxalic acid alone was the active factor, Kidder isolated the accelerators and decelerators, the stimulants and soporifics, in every substance that ever undermined a man's morality and/or caused a "noble experiment." In the process he found one thing he needed badly—a colorless elixir that made sleep the unnecessary and avoidable waster of time it should be. Then and there he went on a twenty-four-hour shift.

He artificially synthesized the substances he had isolated, and in doing so sloughed away a great many useless components. He pursued the subject along the lines of radiations and vibrations. He discovered something in the longer reds which, when projected through a vessel full of air vibrating in the supersonics, and then polarized, speeded up the heartbeat of small animals twenty to one. They ate twenty times as much, grew twenty times as fast, and—died twenty times sooner than they should have.

Kidder built a huge hermetically sealed room. Above it was another room, the same length and breadth but not quite as high. This was his control chamber. The large room was divided into four sealed sections, each with its individual heat and atmosphere controls. Over each section were miniature cranes and derricks—handling machinery of all kinds. There were also trapdoors fitted with air locks leading from the upper to the lower room.

By this time the other laboratory had produced a warm-blooded, snake-skinned quadruped with an astonishingly rapid life cycle—a generation every eight days, a life span of about fifteen. Like the echidna, it was oviparous and mammalian. Its period of gestation was six hours; the eggs hatched in three; the young reached sexual maturity in another four days. Each female laid four eggs and lived just long enough to care for the young after they hatched. The males generally died two or three hours after mating. The creatures were highly adaptable. They were small—not more than three inches long, two inches to the shoulder from the ground. Their forepaws had three digits and a triple-jointed, opposed thumb. They were attuned to life in an atmosphere with a large ammonia content. Kidder bred four groups of the creatures and put one group in each section of the sealed room.

Then he was ready. With his controlled atmospheres he varied temperatures, oxygen content, humidity. He killed them off like flies with excesses of, for instance, carbon dioxide, and the survivors bred their physical resistance into the next generation. Periodically he would switch the eggs from one sealed section to another to keep the strains varied. And rapidly, under these controlled conditions, the creatures began to evolve.

This, then, was the answer to his problem. He couldn't speed up mankind's intellectual advancement enough to have it teach him the things his incredible mind yearned for. He couldn't speed himself up. So he created a new race—a race which would develop and evolve so fast that it would surpass the civilization of man; and from them he would learn.

They were completely in Kidder's power. Earth's normal atmosphere would poison them, as he took care to demonstrate to every fourth generation. They would make no attempt to escape from him. They would live their lives and progress and make their little trial-and-error experiments hundreds of times faster than man did. They had the edge on man, for they had Kidder to guide them. It took man six thousand years to really discover science, three hundred to really put it to work. It took Kidder's creatures two hundred days to equal man's mental attainments. And from then on—Kidder's spasmodic output made the late, great Tom Edison look like a home handicrafter.

He called them Neoterics, and he teased them into working for him. Kidder was inventive in an ideological way; that is, he could dream up impossible propositions providing he didn't have to work them out. For example, he wanted the Neoterics to figure out for themselves how to build shelters out of porous material. He created the need for such shelters by subjecting one of the sections to a high-pressure rainstorm which flattened the inhabitants. The Neoterics promptly devised waterproof shelters out of the thin waterproof material he piled in one corner. Kidder immediately blew down the flimsy structures with a blast of cold air. They built them up again so that they resisted both wind and rain. Kidder lowered the temperature so abruptly that they could not adjust their bodies to it. They heated their shelters with tiny braziers. Kidder promptly turned up the heat until they began to roast to death. After a few deaths, one of their bright boys figured out how to build a strong insulant house by using three-ply rubberoid, with the middle layer perforated thousands of times to create tiny air pockets.

Using such tactics, Kidder forced them to develop a highly advanced little culture. He caused a drought in one section and a liquid surplus in another, and then opened the partition between them. Quite a spectacular war was fought, and Kidder's notebooks filled with information about military tactics and weapons. Then there was the vaccine they developed against the common cold—the reason why that affliction has been absolutely stamped out in the world today, for it was one of the things that Conant, the bank president, got hold of. He spoke to Kidder over the radiophone one winter afternoon with a voice so hoarse from laryngitis that Kidder sent him a vial of the vaccine and told him briskly not to ever call him again in such a disgustingly inaudible state. Conant had it analyzed and again Kidder's accounts—and the bank's—swelled.

At first Kidder merely supplied them with the materials he thought the Neoterics might need, but when they developed an intelligence equal to the task of fabricating their own from the elements at hand, he gave each section a stock of raw materials. The process for really strong aluminum was developed when he built in a huge plunger in one of the sections, which reached from wall to wall and was designed to descend at the rate of four inches a day until it crushed whatever was at the bottom. The Neoterics, in self-defense, used what strong material they had in hand to stop the inexorable death that threatened them. But Kidder had seen to it that they had nothing but aluminum oxide and a scattering of other elements, plus plenty of electric power. At first they ran up dozens of aluminum pillars; when these were crushed and twisted they tried shaping them so that the soft metal would take more weight. When that failed they quickly built stronger ones; and when the plunger was halted, Kidder removed one of the pillars and analyzed it. It was hardened aluminum, stronger and tougher than molyb steel.

Experience taught Kidder that he had to make certain changes to increase his power over his Neoterics before they got too ingenious. There were things that could be done with atomic power that he was curious about; but he was not willing to trust his little superscientists with a thing like that unless they could be trusted to use it strictly according to Hoyle. So he instituted a rule of fear. The most trivial departure from what he chose to consider the right way of doing things resulted in instant death of half a tribe. If he was trying to develop a Diesel-type power plant, for instance, that would operate without a flywheel starter, and a bright young Neoteric used any of the materials for architectural purposes, half the tribe immediately died. Of course, they had developed a written language; it was Kidder's own. The teletype in a glass-inclosed area in a corner of each section was a shrine. Any directions that were given on it were obeyed, or else— After this innovation, Kidder's work was much simpler. There was no need for any more indirection. Anything he wanted done was done. No matter how impossible his commands, three or four generations of Neoterics could find a way to carry them out.

This quotation is from a paper that one of Kidder's high-speed telescopic cameras discovered being circulated among the younger Neoterics. It is translated from the highly simplified script of the Neoterics.

"These edicts shall be followed by each Neoteric upon pain of death, which punishment will be inflicted by the tribe upon the individual to protect the tribe against him.

"Priority of interest and tribal and individual effort is to be given the commands that appear on the word machine.

"Any misdirection of material or power, or use thereof for any other purpose than the carrying out of the machine's commands, unless no command appears, shall be punishable by death.

"Any information regarding the problem at hand, or ideas or experiments which might conceivably bear upon it, are to become the property of the tribe.

"Any individual failing to co-operate in the tribal effort, or who can be termed guilty of not expending his full efforts in the work; or the suspicion thereof, shall be subject to the death penalty."

Such are the results of complete domination. This paper impressed Kidder as much as it did because it was completely spontaneous. It was the Neoterics' own creed, developed by them for their own greatest good.

And so at last Kidder had his fulfillment. Crouched in the upper room, going from telescope to telescope, running off slowed-down films from his high-speed cameras, he found himself possessed of a tractable, dynamic source of information. Housed in the great square building with its four half-acre sections was a new world, to which he was god.

President Conant's mind was similar to Kidder's in that its approach to any problem was along the shortest distance between any two points, regardless of whether that approach was along the line of most or least resistance. His rise to the bank presidency was a history of ruthless moves whose only justification was that they got him what he wanted. Like an overefficient general, he would never vanquish an enemy through sheer force of numbers alone. He would also skillfully flank his enemy, not on one side, but on both. Innocent bystanders were creatures deserving no consideration.

The time he took over a certain thousand-acre property, for instance, from a man named Grady, he was not satisfied with only the title to the land. Grady was an airport owner—had been all his life, and his father before him. Conant exerted every kind of pressure on the man and found him unshakable. Finally judicious persuasion led the city officials to dig a sewer right across the middle of the field, quite efficiently wrecking Grady's business. Knowing that this would supply Grady, who was a wealthy man, with motive for revenge, Conant took over Grady's bank at half again its value and caused it to fold up. Grady lost every cent he had and ended his life in an asylum. Conant was very proud of his tactics.

Like many another who has had Mammon by the tail, Conant did not know when to let go. His vast organization yielded him more money and power than any other concern in history, and yet he was not satisfied. Conant and money were like Kidder and knowledge. Conant's pyramided enterprises were to him what the Neoterics were to Kidder. Each had made his private world; each used it for his instruction and profit. Kidder, though, disturbed nobody but his Neoterics. Even so, Conant was not wholly villainous. He was a shrewd man, and had discovered early the value of pleasing people. No man can rob successfully over a period of years without pleasing the people he robs. The technique for doing this is highly involved, but master it and you can start your own mint.

Conant's one great fear was that Kidder would some day take an interest in world events and begin to become opinionated. Good heavens—the potential power he had! A little matter like swinging an election could be managed by a man like Kidder as easily as turning over in bed. The only thing he could do was to call him periodically and see if there was anything that Kidder needed to keep himself busy. Kidder appreciated this. Conant, once in a while, would suggest something to Kidder that intrigued him, something that would keep him deep in his hermitage for a few weeks. The light pump was one of the results of Conant's imagination. Conant bet him it couldn't be done. Kidder did it.

One afternoon Kidder answered the squeal of the radiophone's signal. Swearing mildly, he shut off the film he was watching and crossed the compound to the old laboratory. He went to the radiophone, threw a switch. The squealing stopped.

"Well?"

"Hello, Kidder," said Conant. "Busy?"

"Not very," said Kidder. He was delighted with the pictures his camera had caught, showing the skillful work of a gang of Neoterics synthesizing rubber out of pure sulphur. He would rather have liked to tell Conant about it, but somehow he had never got around to telling Conant about the Neoterics, and he didn't see why he should start now.

Conant said, "Er . . . Kidder, I was down at the club the other day and a bunch of us were filling up an evening with loose talk. Something came up which might interest you."

"What?"

"Couple of the utilities boys there. You know the power set-up in this country, don't you? Thirty percent atomic, the rest hydro-electric, Diesel and steam?"

"I hadn't known," said Kidder, who was as innocent as a babe of current events.

"Well, we were arguing about what chance a new power source would have. One of the men there said it would be smarter to produce a new power and then talk about it. Another one waived that; said he couldn't name that new power, but he could describe it. Said it would have to have everything that present power sources have, plus one or two more things. It could be cheaper, for instance. It could be more efficient. It might supersede the others by being easier to carry from the power plant to the consumer. See what I mean? Any one of these factors might prove a new source of power competitive to the others. What I'd like to see is a new power with *all* of these factors. What do you think of it?"

"Not impossible."

"Think not?"

"I'll try it."

"Keep me posted." Conant's transmitter clicked off. The

switch was a little piece of false front that Kidder had built into the set, which was something that Conant didn't know. The set switched itself off when Conant moved from it. After the switch's sharp crack, Kidder heard the banker mutter, "If he does it, I'm all set. If he doesn't, at least the crazy fool will keep himself busy on the isl—"

Kidder eyed the radiophone for an instant with raised eyebrows, and then shrugged them down again with his shoulders. It was quite evident that Conant had something up his sleeve, but Kidder wasn't worried. Who on earth would want to disturb him? He wasn't bothering anybody. He went back to the Neoterics' building, full of the new power idea.

Eleven days later Kidder called Conant and gave specific instructions on how to equip his receiver with a facsimile set which would enable Kidder to send written matter over the air. As soon as this was done and Kidder informed, the biochemist for once in his life spoke at some length.

"Conant—you inferred that a new power source that would be cheaper, more efficient and more easily transmitted than any now in use did not exist. You might be interested in the little generator I have just set up.

"It has power, Conant—unbelievable power. Broadcast. A beautiful little tight beam. Here—catch this on the facsimile recorder." Kidder slipped a sheet of paper under the clips on his transmitter and it appeared on Conant's set. "Here's the wiring diagram for a power receiver. Now listen. The beam is so tight, so highly directional, that not three thousandths of one percent of the power would be lost in a two-thousand-mile transmission. The power system is closed. That is, any drain on the beam returns a signal along it to the transmitter, which automatically steps up to increase the power output. It has a limit, but it's way up. And something else. This little gadget of mine can send out eight different beams with a total horse-power output of around eight thousand per minute per beam. From each beam you can draw enough power to turn the page of a book or fly a superstratosphere plane. Hold on—I haven't finished yet. Each beam, as I told you before, returns a signal from receiver to transmitter. This not only controls the power output of the beam, but directs it. Once contact is made, the beam will never let go. It will follow the receiver anywhere. You can power land, air or water vehicles with it, as well as any stationary plant. Like it?"

Conant, who was a banker and not a scientist, wiped his shining pate with the back of his hand and said, "I've never known you to steer me wrong yet, Kidder. How about the cost of this thing?"

"High," said Kidder promptly. "As high as an atomic plant. But there are no high-tension lines, no wires, no pipelines, no nothing. The receivers are little more complicated than a radio set. The transmitter is—well, that's quite a job."

"Didn't take you long," said Conant.

"No," said Kidder, "it didn't, did it?" It was the lifework of nearly twelve hundred highly cultured people, but Kidder wasn't going into that. "Of course, the one I have here's just a model."

Conant's voice was strained. "A—model? And it delivers—"

"Over sixty thousand horsepower," said Kidder gleefully.

"Good heavens! In a full-sized machine—why, one transmitter would be enough to—" The possibilities of the thing choked Conant for a moment. "How is it fueled?"

"It isn't," said Kidder. "I won't begin to explain it. I've tapped a source of power of unimaginable force. It's—well, big. So big that it can't be misused."

"What?" snapped Conant. "What do you mean by that?"

Kidder cocked an eyebrow. Conant *had* something up his sleeve, then. At this second indication of it, Kidder, the least suspicious of men, began to put himself on guard. "I mean just what I say," he said evenly. "Don't try too hard to understand me—I barely savvy it myself. But the source of this power is a monstrous resultant caused by the unbalance of two previously equalized forces. Those equalized forces are cosmic in quantity.

Actually, the forces are those which make suns, crush atoms the way they crushed those that compose the companion of Sirius. It's not anything you can fool with."

"I don't—" said Conant, and his voice ended puzzledly.

"I'll give you a parallel of it," said Kidder. "Suppose you take two rods, one in each hand. Place their tips together and push. As long as your pressure is directly along their long axes, the pressure is equalized; right and left hands cancel each other out. Now I come along; I put out one finger and touch the rods ever so lightly where they come together. They snap out of line violently; you break a couple of knuckles. The resultant force is at right angles to the original force you exerted. My power transmitter is on the same principle. It takes an infinitesimal amount of energy to throw those forces out of line. Easy enough when you know how to do it. The important question is whether or not you can control the resultant when you get it. I can."

"I—see." Conant indulged in a four-second gloat. "Heaven help the utility companies. I don't intend to. Kidder—I want a full-size power transmitter."

Kidder clucked into the radiophone. "Ambitious, aren't you? I haven't a staff out here, Conant—you know that. And I can't be expected to build four or five thousand tons of apparatus myself."

"I'll have five hundred engineers and laborers out there in forty-eight hours."

"You will not. Why bother me with it? I'm quite happy here, Conant, and one of the reasons is that I've no one to get in my hair."

"Oh, now, Kidder—don't be like that. I'll pay you—"

"You haven't got that much money," said Kidder briskly. He flipped the switch on his set. *His* switch worked.

Conant was furious. He shouted into the phone several times, then began to lean on the signal button. On his island, Kidder let the thing squeal and went back to his projection room. He was sorry he had sent the diagram of the receiver to Conant. It would have been interesting to power a plane or a car with the model transmitter he had taken from the Neoterics. But if Conant was going to be that way about it—well, anyway, the receiver would be no good without the transmitter. Any radio engineer would understand the diagram, but not the beam which activated it. And Conant wouldn't get his beam.

Pity he didn't know Conant well enough.

Kidder's days were endless sorties into learning. He never slept, nor did his Neoterics. He ate regularly every five hours, exercised for half an hour in every twelve. He did not keep track of time, for it meant nothing to him. Had he wanted to know the date, or the year, even, he knew he could get it from Conant. He didn't care, that's all. The time that was not spent in observation was used in developing new problems for the Neoterics. His thoughts just now ran to defense. The idea was born in his conversation with Conant; now the idea was primary, its motivation something of no importance. The Neoterics were working on a vibration field of quasi-electrical nature. Kidder could see little practical value in such a thing—an invisible wall which would kill any living thing which touched it. But still—the idea was intriguing.

He stretched and moved away from the telescope in the upper room through which he had been watching his creations at work. He was profoundly happy here in the large control room. Leaving it to go to the old laboratory for a bite to eat was a thing he hated to do. He felt like bidding it good-by each time he walked across the compound, and saying a glad hello when he returned. A little amused at himself, he went out.

There was a black blob—a distant power boat—a few miles off the island, toward the mainland. Kidder stopped and stared distastefully at it. A white petal of spray was affixed to each side of the black body—it was coming toward him. He snorted, thinking of the time a yacht load of silly fools had landed out of curiosity one afternoon, spewed themselves over his beloved island, peppered him with lame-brained questions, and thrown his nervous equilibrium out for days. Lord, how he hated *people!*

The thought of unpleasantness bred two more thoughts that played half-consciously with his mind as he crossed the compound and entered the old laboratory. One was that perhaps it might be wise to surround his buildings with a field of force of some kind and post warnings for trespassers. The other thought was of Conant and the vague uneasiness the man had been sending to him through the radiophone these last weeks. His suggestion, two days ago, that a power plant be built on the island—horrible idea!

Conant rose from his seat on a laboratory bench as Kidder walked in.

They looked at each other wordlessly for a long moment. Kidder hadn't seen the bank president in years. The man's presence, he found, made his scalp crawl.

"Hello," said Conant genially. "You're looking fit."

Kidder grunted. Conant eased his unwieldy body back onto the bench and said, "Just to save you the energy of asking questions, Mr. Kidder, I arrived two hours ago on a small boat. Rotten way to travel. I wanted to be a surprise to you; my two men rowed me the last couple of miles. You're not very well equipped here for defense, are you? Why, anyone could slip up on you the way I did."

"Who'd want to?" growled Kidder. The man's voice edged annoyingly into his brain. He spoke too loudly for such a small room; at least, Kidder's hermit's ears felt that way. Kidder shrugged and went about preparing a light meal for himself.

"Well," drawled the banker, "I might want to." He drew out a Dow-metal cigar case. "Mind if I smoke?"

"I do," said Kidder sharply.

Conant laughed easily and put the cigars away. "I might," he said, "want to urge you to let me build that power station on this island."

"Radiophone work?"

"Oh, yes. But now that I'm here you can't switch me off. Now —how about it?"

"I haven't changed my mind."

"Oh, but you should, Kidder, you should. Think of it—think of the good it would do for the masses of people that are now paying exorbitant power bills!"

"I hate the masses! Why do you have to build here?"

"Oh, that. It's an ideal location. You own the island; work could begin here without causing any comment whatsoever. The plant would spring full-fledged on the power markets of the country, having been built in secret. The island can be made impregnable."

"I don't want to be bothered."

"We wouldn't bother you. We'd build on the north end of the island—a mile and a quarter from you and your work. Ah—by the way—where's the model of the power transmitter?"

Kidder, with his mouth full of synthesized food, waved a hand at a small table on which stood the model, a four-foot, amazingly intricate device of plastic and steel and tiny coils.

Conant rose and went over to look at it. "Actually works, eh?" He sighed deeply and said, "Kidder, I really hate to do this, but I want to build that plant rather badly. Corson! Robbins!"

Two bull-necked individuals stepped out from their hiding places in the corners of the room. One idly dangled a revolver by its trigger guard. Kidder looked blankly from one to the other of them.

"These gentlemen will follow my orders implicitly, Kidder. In half an hour a party will land here—engineers, contractors. They will start surveying the north end of the island for the construction of the power plant. These boys here feel about the same way I do as far as you are concerned. Do we proceed with your co-operation or without it? It's immaterial to me whether or not you are left alive to continue your work. My engineers can duplicate your model."

Kidder said nothing. He had stopped chewing when he saw the gunmen, and only now remembered to swallow. He sat crouched over his plate without moving or speaking.

Conant broke the silence by walking to the door. "Robbins—can you carry that model there?" The big man put his gun away, lifted the model gently, and nodded. "Take it down to the beach and meet the other boat. Tell Mr. Johansen, the engineer, that that is the model he is to work from." Robbins went out. Conant turned to Kidder. "There's no need for us to anger ourselves," he said oilily. "I think you are stubborn, but I don't hold it against you. I know how you feel. You'll be left alone; you have my promise. But I mean to go ahead on this job, and a small thing like your life can't stand in my way."

Kidder said, "Get out of here." There were two swollen veins throbbing at his temples. His voice was low, and it shook.

"Very well. Good day, Mr. Kidder. Oh—by the way—you're a clever devil." No one had ever referred to the scholastic Mr. Kidder that way before. "I realize the possibility of your blasting us off the island. I wouldn't do it if I were you. I'm willing to give you what you want—privacy. I want the same thing in return. If anything happens to me while I'm here, the island will be bombed by someone who is working for me. I'll admit they might fail. If they do, the United States government will take a hand. You wouldn't want that, would you? That's rather a big thing for one man to fight. The same thing goes if the plant is sabotaged in any way after I go back to the mainland. You might be killed. You will most certainly be bothered interminably. Thanks for your . . . er . . . co-operation." The banker smirked and walked out, followed by his taciturn gorilla.

Kidder sat there for a long time without moving. Then he shook his head, rested it in his palms. He was badly frightened; not so much because his life was in danger, but because his privacy and his work—his world—were threatened. He was hurt and bewildered. He wasn't a businessman. He couldn't handle men. All his life he had run away from humans and what they represented to him. He was like a frightened child when men closed in on him.

Cooling a little, he wondered vaguely what would happen

when the power plant opened. Certainly the government would be interested. Unless—unless by then Conant was the government. That plant was an unimaginable source of power, and not only the kind of power that turned wheels. He rose and went back to the world that was home to him, a world where his motives were understood, and where there were those who could help him. Back at the Neoterics' building, he escaped yet again from the world of men into his work.

Kidder called Conant the following week, much to the banker's surprise. His two days on the island had gotten the work well under way, and he had left with the arrival of a shipload of laborers and material. He kept in close touch by radio with Johansen, the engineer in charge. It had been a blind job for Johansen and all the rest of the crew on the island. Only the bank's infinite resources could have hired such a man, or the picked gang with him.

Johansen's first reaction when he saw the model had been ecstatic. He wanted to tell his friends about this marvel; but the only radio set available was beamed to Conant's private office in the bank, and Conant's armed guards, one to every two workers, had strict orders to destroy any other radio transmitter on sight. About that time he realized that he was a prisoner on the island. His instant anger subsided when he reflected that being a prisoner at fifty thousand dollars a week wasn't too bad. Two of the laborers and an engineer thought differently, and got disgruntled a couple of days after they arrived. They disappeared one night—the same night that five shots were fired down on the beach. No questions were asked, and there was no more trouble.

Conant covered his surprise at Kidder's call and was as offensively jovial as ever. "Well, now! Anything I can do for you?"

"Yes," said Kidder. His voice was low, completely without expression. "I want you to issue a warning to your men not to pass the white line I have drawn five hundred yards north of my buildings, right across the island."

"Warning? Why, my dear fellow, they have orders that you are not to be disturbed on any account."

"You've ordered them. All right. Now warn them. I have an electric field surrounding my laboratories that will kill anything living which penetrates it. I don't want to have murder on my conscience. There will be no deaths unless there are trespassers. You'll inform your workers?"

"Oh, now, Kidder," the banker expostulated. "That was totally unnecessary. You won't be bothered. Why—" But he found he was talking into a dead mike. He knew better than to call back. He called Johansen instead and told him about it. Johansen didn't like the sound of it, but he repeated the message and signed off. Conant liked that man. He was, for a moment, a little sorry that Johansen would never reach the mainland alive.

But that Kidder—he was beginning to be a problem. As long as his weapons were strictly defensive he was no real menace. But he would have to be taken care of when the plant was operating. Conant couldn't afford to have genius around him unless it was unquestionably on his side. The power transmitter and Conant's highly ambitious plans would be safe as long as Kidder was left to himself. Kidder knew that he could, for the time being, expect more sympathetic treatment from Conant than he could from a horde of government investigators.

Kidder only left his own inclosure once after the work began on the north end of the island, and it took all of his unskilled diplomacy to do it. Knowing the source of the plant's power, knowing what could happen if it were misused, he asked Conant's permission to inspect the great transmitter when it was nearly finished. Insuring his own life by refusing to report back to Conant until he was safe within his own laboratory again, he turned off his shield and walked up to the north end.

He saw an awe-inspiring sight. The four-foot model was duplicated nearly a hundred times as large. Inside a massive three-hundred-foot tower a space was packed nearly solid with the same bewildering maze of coils and bars that the Neoterics had built so delicately into their machine. At the top was a globe of polished golden alloy, the transmitting antenna. From it would stream thousands of tight beams of force, which could be tapped to any degree by corresponding thousands of receivers placed anywhere at any distance. Kidder learned that the receivers had already been built, but his informant, Johansen, knew little about that end of it and was saying less. Kidder checked over every detail of the structure, and when he was through he shook Johansen's hand admiringly.

"I didn't want this thing here," he said shyly, "and I don't. But I will say that it's a pleasure to see this kind of work."

"It's a pleasure to meet the man that invented it."

Kidder beamed. "I didn't invent it," he said. "Maybe some day I'll show you who did. I—well, good-by." He turned before he had a chance to say too much and marched off down the path.

"Shall I?" said a voice at Johansen's side. One of Conant's guards had his gun out.

Johansen knocked the man's arm down. "No." He scratched his head. "So that's the mysterious menace from the other end of the island. Eh! Why, he's a hell of a nice little feller!"

Built on the ruins of Denver, which was destroyed in the great Battle of the Rockies during the Western War, stands the most beautiful city in the world—our nation's capital, New Washington. In a circular room deep in the heart of the white house, the president, three army men and a civilian sat. Under the president's desk a dictaphone unostentatiously recorded every word that was said. Two thousand and more miles away, Conant hung over a radio receiver, turned to receive the signals of the tiny transmitter in the civilian's side pocket.

One of the officers spoke.

"Mr. President, the 'impossible claims' made for this gentleman's product are absolutely true. He has proved beyond doubt each item on his prospectus."

224 · THEODORE STURGEON

The president glanced at the civilian, back at the officer. "I won't wait for your report," he said. "Tell me—what happened?"

Another of the army men mopped his face with a khaki bandanna. "I can't ask you to believe us, Mr. President, but it's true all the same. Mr. Wright here has in his suitcase three or four dozen small . . . er . . . bombs—"

"They're not bombs," said Wright casually.

"All right. They're not bombs. Mr. Wright smashed two of them on an anvil with a sledge hammer. There was no result. He put two more in an electric furnace. They burned away like so much tin and cardboard. We dropped one down the barrel of a field piece and fired it. Still nothing." He paused and looked at the third officer, who picked up the account.

"We really got started then. We flew to the proving grounds, dropped one of the objects and flew to thirty thousand feet. From there, with a small hand detonator no bigger than your fist, Mr. Wright set the thing off. I've never seen anything like it. Forty acres of land came straight up at us, breaking up as it came. The concussion was terrific—you must have felt it here, four hundred miles away."

The president nodded. "I did. Seismographs on the other side of the Earth picked it up."

"The crater it left was a quarter of a mile deep at the center. Why, one plane load of those things could demolish any city! There isn't even any necessity for accuracy!"

"You haven't heard anything yet," another officer broke in. "Mr. Wright's automobile is powered by a small plant similar to the others. He demonstrated it to us. We could find no fuel tank of any kind, or any other driving mechanism. But with a power plant no bigger than six cubic inches, that car, carrying enough weight to give it traction, outpulled an army tank!"

"And the other test!" said the third excitedly. "He put one of the objects into a replica of a treasury vault. The walls were twelve feet thick, super-reinforced concrete. He controlled it from over a hundred yards away. He . . . he burst that vault! It wasn't an explosion—it was as if some incredibly powerful expansive force inside filled it and flattened the walls from inside. They cracked and split and powdered, and the steel girders and rods came twisting and shearing out like . . . like—*whew!* After that he insisted on seeing you. We knew it wasn't usual, but he said he has more to say and would say it only in your presence."

The president said gravely. "What is it, Mr. Wright?"

Wright rose, picked up his suitcase, opened it and took out a small cube, about eight inches on a side, made of some light-absorbent red material. Four men edged nervously away from it.

"These gentlemen," he began, "have seen only part of the things this device can do. I'm going to demonstrate to you the delicacy of control that is possible with it." He made an adjustment with a tiny knob on the side of the cube, set it on the edge of the president's desk.

"You have asked me more than once if this is my invention or if I am representing someone. The latter is true. It might also interest you to know that the man who controls this cube is right now several thousand miles from here. He, and he alone, can prevent it from detonating now that I"—he pulled his detonator out of the suitcase and pressed a button—"have done this. It will explode the way the one we dropped from the plane did, completely destroying this city and everything in it, in just four hours. It will also explode"—he stepped back and threw a tiny switch on his detonator—"if any moving object comes within three feet of it or if anyone leaves this room but me—it can be compensated for that. If, after I leave, I am molested, it will detonate as soon as a hand is laid on me. No bullets can kill me fast enough to prevent me from setting it off."

The three army men were silent. One of them swiped nervously at the beads of cold sweat on his forehead. The others did not move. The president said evenly,

"What's your proposition?"

"A very reasonable one. My employer does not work in the open, for obvious reasons. All he wants is your agreement to carry out his orders; to appoint the cabinet members he chooses, to throw your influence in any way he dictates. The public—Congress—anyone else—need never know anything about it. I might add that if you agree to this proposal, this 'bomb,' as you call it, will not go off. But you can be sure that thousands of them are planted all over the country. You will never know when you are near one. If you disobey, it means instant annihilation for you and everyone else within three or four square miles.

"In three hours and fifty minutes—that will be at precisely seven o'clock—there is a commercial radio program on Station RPRS. You will cause the announcer, after his station identification, to say 'Agreed.' It was pass unnoticed by all but my employer. There is no use in having me followed; my work is done. I shall never see nor contact my employer again. That is all. Good afternoon, gentlemen!"

Wright closed his suitcase with a businesslike snap, bowed, and left the room. Four men sat frozen, staring at the little red cube.

"Do you think he can do all he says?" asked the president.

The three nodded mutely. The president reached for his phone.

There was an eavesdropper to all of the foregoing. Conant, squatting behind his great desk in the vault, where he had his sanctum sanctorum, knew nothing of it. But beside him was the compact bulk of Kidder's radiophone. His presence switched it on, and Kidder, on his island, blessed the day he had thought of that device. He had been meaning to call Conant all morning, but was very hesitant. His meeting with the young engineer Johansen had impressed him strongly. The man was such a thorough scientist, possessed of such complete delight in the work he did, that for the first time in his life Kidder found himself actually wanting to see someone again. But he feared for Johansen's life if he brought him to the laboratory, for Johansen's work was done on the island, and Conant would most certainly have the engineer killed if he heard of his visit, fearing that Kidder would influence him to sabotage the great transmitter. And if Kidder went to the power plant he would probably be shot on sight.

All one day Kidder wrangled with himself, and finally determined to call Conant. Fortunately he gave no signal, but turned up the volume on the receiver when the little red light told him that Conant's transmitter was functioning. Curious, he heard everything that occurred in the president's chamber three thousand miles away. Horrified, he realized what Conant's engineers had done. Built into tiny containers were tens of thousands of power receivers. They had no power of their own, but, by remote control, could draw on any or all of the billions of horsepower the huge plant on the island was broadcasting.

Kidder stood in front of his receiver, speechless. There was nothing he could do. If he devised some means of destroying the power plant, the government would certainly step in and take over the island, and then—what would happen to him and his precious Neoterics?

Another sound grated out of the receiver—a commercial radio program. A few bars of music, a man's voice advertising stratoline fares on the installment plan, a short silence, then:

"Station RPRS, voice of the nation's Capital, District of South Colorado."

The three-second pause was interminable.

"The time is exactly . . . er . . . *agreed*. The time is exactly seven p.m., Mountain Standard Time."

Then came a half-insane chuckle. Kidder had difficulty believing it was Conant. A phone clicked. The banker's voice:

"Bill? All set. Get out there with your squadron and bomb up the island. Keep away from the plant, but cut the rest of it to ribbons. Do it quick and get out of there."

Almost hysterical with fear, Kidder rushed about the room and then shot out the door and across the compound. There were five hundred innocent workmen in barracks a quarter mile from the plant. Conant didn't need them now, and he didn't need Kidder. The only safety for anyone was in the plant itself, and Kidder wouldn't leave his Neoterics to be bombed. He flung himself up the stairs and to the nearest teletype. He banged out, "Get me a defense. I want an impenetrable shield. Urgent!"

The words rippled out from under his fingers in the functional script of the Neoterics. Kidder didn't think of what he wrote, didn't really visualize the thing he ordered. But he had done what he could. He'd have to leave them now, get to the barracks, warn those men. He ran up the path toward the plant, flung himself over the white line that marked death to those who crossed it.

A squadron of nine clip-winged, mosquito-nosed planes rose out of a cove on the mainland. There was no sound from the engines, for there were no engines. Each plane was powered with a tiny receiver and drew its unmarked, light-absorbent wings through the air with power from the island. In a matter of minutes they raised the island. The squadron leader spoke briskly into a microphone.

"Take the barracks first. Clean 'em up. Then work south."

Johansen was alone on a small hill near the center of the island. He carried a camera, and though he knew pretty well that his chances of ever getting ashore again were practically nonexistent, he liked angle shots of his tower, and took innumerable pictures. The first he knew of the planes was when he heard their whining dive over the barracks. He stood transfixed, saw a shower of bombs hurtle down and turn the barracks into a smashed ruin of broken wood, metal and bodies. The picture of Kidder's earnest face flashed into his mind. Poor little guy— if they ever bombed his end of the island he would—But his tower! Were they going to bomb the plant?

He watched, utterly appalled, as the planes flew out to sea, cut back and dove again. They seemed to be working south. At the third dive he was sure of it. Not knowing what he could do, he nevertheless turned and ran toward Kidder's place. He rounded a turn in the trail and collided violently with the little biochemist. Kidder's face was scarlet with exertion, and he was the most terrified-looking object Johansen had ever seen.

Kidder waved a hand northward. "Conant!" he screamed over the uproar. "It's Conant! He's going to kill us all!"

"The plant?" said Johansen, turning pale.

"It's safe. He won't touch *that!* But . . . my place . . . what about all those men?"

"Too late!" shouted Johansen.

"Maybe I can—Come on!" called Kidder, and was off down the trail, heading south.

Johansen pounded after him. Kidder's little short legs became a blur as the squadron swooped overhead, laying its eggs in the spot where they had met.

As they burst out of the woods, Johansen put on a spurt, caught up with the scientist and knocked him sprawling not six feet from the white line.

"Wh . . . wh—"

"Don't go any farther, you fool! Your own damned force field —it'll kill you!"

"Force field? But—I came through it on the way up— Here. Wait. If I can—" Kidder began hunting furiously about in the grass. In a few seconds he ran up to the line, clutching a large grasshopper in his hand. He tossed it over. It lay still.

"See?" said Johansen. "It—"

"Look! It jumped! Come on! I don't know what went wrong, unless the Neoterics shut it off. They generated that field—I didn't."

"Neo—huh?"

"Never mind," snapped the biochemist, and ran.

They pounded gasping up the steps and into the Neoterics' control room. Kidder clapped his eyes to a telescope and shrieked in glee. "They've done it! They've done it!"

"Who's—"

"My little people! The Neoterics! They've made the impenetrable shield! Don't you see—it cut through the lines of force that start up that field out there! Their generator is still throwing it up, but the vibrations can't get out! They're safe! They're safe!" And the overwrought hermit began to cry. Johansen looked at him pityingly and shook his head.

"Sure—you're little men are all right. But we aren't," he added as the floor shook at the detonation of a bomb.

Johansen closed his eyes, got a grip on himself and let his curiosity overcome his fear. He stepped to the binocular telescope, gazed down it. There was nothing there but a curved sheet of gray material. He had never seen a gray quite like that. It was absolutely neutral. It didn't seem soft and it didn't seem hard, and to look at it made his brain reel. He looked up.

Kidder was pounding the keys of a teletype, watching the blank yellow tape anxiously.

"I'm not getting through to them," he whimpered. "I don't know what's the mat— Oh, of *course!*"

"What?"

"The shield is absolutely impenetrable! The teletype impulses can't get through or I could get them to extend the screen over the building—over the whole island! There's nothing those people can't do!"

"He's crazy," Johansen said under his breath. "Poor little—"

The teletype began clicking sharply. Kidder dove at it, practically embraced it. He read off the tape as it came out. Johansen saw the characters, but they meant nothing to him.

"Almighty," Kidder read falteringly, "pray have mercy on us and be forbearing until we have said our say. Without orders we have lowered the screen you ordered us to raise. We are lost, O great one. Our screen is truly impenetrable, and so cut off your words on the word machine. We have never, in the memory of any Neoteric, been without your word before. Forgive us our action. We will eagerly await your answer."

Kidder's fingers danced over the keys. "You can look now," he gasped. "Go on—the telescope!"

Johansen, trying to ignore the whine of sure death from above, looked.

He saw what looked like land—fantastic fields under cultivation, a settlement of some sort, factories, and—beings. Everything moved with incredible rapidity. He couldn't see one of the inhabitants except as darting pinky-white streaks. Fascinated, he stared for a long minute. A sound behind him made him whirl. It was Kidder, rubbing his hands together briskly. There was a broad smile on his face.

"They did it," he said happily. "You see?"

Johansen didn't see until he began to realize that there was a dead silence outside. He ran to a window. It was night outside —the blackest night—when it should have been dusk. "What happened?"

"The Neoterics," said Kidder, and laughed like a child. "My friends downstairs there. They threw up the impenetrable shield over the whole island. We can't be touched now!"

And at Johansen's amazed questions, he launched into a description of the race of beings below them.

Outside the shell, things happened. Nine airplanes suddenly went dead-stick. Nine pilots glided downward, powerless, and some fell into the sea, and some struck the miraculous gray shell that loomed in place of an island; slid off and sank.

And ashore, a man named Wright sat in a car, half dead with fear, while government men surrounded him, approached cautiously, daring instant death from a now-dead source.

In a room deep in the White House, a high-ranking army officer shrieked, "I can't stand it any more! I can't!" and leaped up, snatched a red cube off the president's desk, ground it to ineffectual litter under his shining boots.

And in a few days they took a broken old man away from the bank and put him in an asylum, where he died within a week.

The shield, you see, was truly impenetrable. The power plant was untouched and sent out its beams; but the beams could not get out, and anything powered from the plant went dead. The story never became public, although for some years there was heightened naval activity off the New England coast. The navy, so the story went, had a new target range out there—a great hemi-ovoid of gray material. They bombed it and shelled it and rayed it and blasted all around it, but never even dented its smooth surface.

Kidder and Johansen let it stay there. They were happy enough with their researches and their Neoterics. They did not hear or feel the shelling, for the shield was truly impenetrable. They synthesized their food and their light and air from the materials at hand, and they simply didn't care. They were the only survivors of the bombing, with the exception of three poor maimed devils that died soon afterward.

All this happened many years ago, and Kidder and Johansen may be alive today, and they may be dead. But that doesn't matter too much. The important thing is that that great gray shell will bear watching. Men die, but races live. Some day the Neoterics, after innumerable generations of inconceivable advancement, will take down their shield and come forth. When I think of that I feel frightened.

NIGHTFALL

Isaac Asimov

By mid-1941, the heart of the Golden Age, John Campbell's editorial direction had paid off handsomely. We've seen the explosion of new talents like del Rey, van Vogt, Heinlein and Sturgeon; now we come to a writer whose career began more slowly but was now reaching fruition.

Isaac Asimov was born in Petrovichi, Russia, around the beginning of 1920; the exact date is unknown because Russia was then on the Julian calendar, with thirteen days' discrepancy from our Gregorian one. And neither the then-new Communist regime nor his parents (who dated things according to the holy days of the Jewish calendar) could supply a definite record. Asimov celebrates his birthday on January 2.

Late in 1922 his family emigrated from Russia (where anti-Semitism was in force then too) and arrived in New York City in February 1923. Before long Asimov's father opened a candy store in Brooklyn, and Isaac worked there after school. There was a newsstand in the store and Isaac was allowed to read the science fiction magazines as long as he kept them in pristine condition so that they could still be sold. He began writing to the letter columns, eventually joining a fan club that included Frederik Pohl and Donald A. Wollheim, and finally decided to try writing science fiction himself.

He submitted his first manuscript to *Astounding,* delivering it to Campbell in person on June 21, 1938. Campbell spent over an hour talking with him, and promised to read the story that night. He did, and rejected it with a thoughtful two-page letter that encouraged Asimov to continue trying.

"Many years later," Asimov says, "I asked Campbell . . . why he had bothered with me at all, since that first story was surely utterly impossible.

" 'It was,' he said frankly, for he never flattered. 'On the other hand, I saw something in *you*. You were eager and you listened and I knew you wouldn't quit no matter how many rejections I handed you. As long as you were willing to work hard at improving, I was willing to work with you.' "

Campbell rejected Asimov's first eight stories; however, Raymond A. Palmer accepted one of them, "Marooned Off Vesta," for *Amazing Stories*. Palmer's rate of a penny a word was the same as Campbell's, but Asimov had little respect for *Amazing,* so the joy of his professional debut in the March 1939 *Amazing* was less than it might have been.

Fortunately, by the time the story was published Asimov had managed to sell to *Astounding*. He'd submitted a story titled "Ad Astra" and Campbell had liked it enough to discuss a rewrite; Asimov followed his suggestions, and on January 31, 1939, he received his first acceptance from Campbell, who changed the title to "Trends" and published it in the July 1939 *Astounding.*

The publication of "Trends," Asimov's first important story, coincided with his graduation from Columbia with a bachelor of science degree in chemistry. L. Sprague de Camp remembers meeting him in June: "a slim, good-looking stripling of medium height, with blue eyes, dark-brown hair, and a downy mustache." Campbell introduced Asimov as "one of his newest writers," which must have buoyed Asimov's spirits.

Asimov was asked to say a few words from the platform of the First World Science Fiction Convention in July, and Campbell, who was sitting in an aisle seat, waved him forward delightedly. Asimov good-naturedly called himself "the worst science fiction writer unlynched."

Obviously he wasn't that bad, but Campbell did reject the next seven stories Asimov showed him. Asimov succeeded in selling many of Campbell's rejects, mostly to newly founded magazines like *Future Fiction* and *Astonishing Stories,* but by March 1941, more than two years after Campbell accepted "Trends," he'd still sold only four stories to *Astounding.*

Then, on March 17, 1941, Asimov went to Campbell's office with a new story idea; Campbell countered by quoting to Asimov the passage from Ralph Waldo Emerson that was to become the beginning of "Nightfall." Campbell asked him what he thought would happen if the stars appeared only at very long intervals. When Asimov was unable to come up with a good answer, Campbell said thoughtfully, "I think men would go mad."

They discussed the notion for quite a while, even deciding on the title of the story, and Asimov began writing it that night. He worked on it for three weeks, off and on, submitted it to Campbell and did some slight revision, and on April 24 Campbell bought it. He was so delighted with the story that he paid a bonus of a quarter of a cent a word, the first bonus Asimov had received. When it was published in the September 1941 *Astounding,* Asimov found the story illustrated by a beatuiful cover painting by Hubert Rogers, and Asimov's name on the cover. The readers loved the story, and in one month a "hopeful third-rater," as Asimov considered himself, became a major science fiction writer. Years later, "Nightfall" was voted the best sf short story or novelette of all time by the Science Fiction Writers of America, by a wide margin.

(There's an ironic sidelight to this: Ralph Waldo Emerson was an ancestor of Theodore Sturgeon, born Edward Hamilton Waldo; though Sturgeon was one of Campbell's "regulars" at the time, it was Asimov to whom he gave this story idea.)

Isaac Asimov is such a towering figure in science fiction today that it's difficult to imagine how surprised most readers were when "Nightfall" first appeared. He was only twenty-one, and his role in science fiction till then had been characterized by humorously brash letters to the sf magazines and a dozen or so stories, most of them minor efforts in the lesser pulps. A fan magazine of the time commented, " 'Nightfall' by that conceited and precocious brat, Asimov, is an excellent story"—a typical reaction.

But Campbell had accurately seen Asimov's potential, which was evident in more than his willingness to work hard. Asimov was basically a scientist who had a facility for storytelling, so he wrote science fiction to help finance his college education (he was now a graduate student at Columbia). Scientific content was important to him, and he had little patience with authors or editors who didn't agree. When Palmer deleted the science from his second story in *Amazing,* preserving only the most unavoidable information in footnotes, Asimov put *Amazing* at the bottom of his submissions list thereafter.

He faced a problem in writing "Nightfall," though, because the story needed a good deal of background information: how to explain the astronomy of a multiple-star system without forcing the story to a grinding halt? He took refuge in a device that was common in science fiction then, the use of a newspaper reporter as hero.

Reporters were familiar as characters not only in science fiction, of course, but also in movies, detective stories and many other forms of popular entertainment. The young reporter out to prove himself by getting a "scoop" for his paper was a phenomenon of the time when any major city might have half a dozen newspapers vying day to day for circulation. The reporter was also a useful character because his job required him to investigate strange happenings, ask for explanations, even chase after criminals and secretive scientists in quest of the all-important news story that might earn him a bonus or a raise.

Thus the science fiction magazines were rife with reporter-narrators saying, "I had to bet the boss a bottle of Scotch I'd get a headline exclusive story," and ending with dialogue like "Why, it's the greatest story the System's ever known. They'll give it headlines two feet high."

(Another reason for the prevalence of reporters as heroes was the fact that so many pulp writers earned their daily livings as reporters themselves: Clifford D. Simak and Cleve Cartmill, for instance. One of Robert A. Heinlein's early stories featured a reporter named Cleve Carter.)

These fictional reporters went to foolhardy lengths to provide their newspapers, and their authors, with stories. In A. E. van Vogt's "The Seesaw," a building from the future suddenly materialized in a city of 1941. While hundreds of people, both private citizens and police, stared in consternation, a doughty reporter went to the door and found it open: "Pure reporter's instinct made him step forward toward the blackness that pressed from beyond the rectangle of door."

That reporter didn't live to write his scoop; he was catapulted onto a time journey that ended in the remote past when, charged with "stupendous temporal energy," his body exploded and caused the formation of the Solar System. But the hero of Harry Bates's famous story "Farewell to the Master" (later adapted into the movie *The Day the Earth Stood Still*) fared better when he trespassed overnight in a museum to investigate a robot from some far planet. After watching the supposedly dormant robot kill a gorilla and bring a dead scientist back to life, he was found by the police, who asked what had been going on.

" 'Gentlemen, I'd tell you gladly—only business first,' Cliff answered. 'There's been some fantastic goings on in this room, and I saw them and have the story, but'—he smiled—'I must decline to answer without advice of counsel until I've sold my story to one of the news syndicates. You know how it is.' "

Allowed by the police to make a call, "Cliff made a deal which would bring him more money than he had ever before earned in a year." (He got thrown in jail for a night "on general principles," but he'd achieved his scoop in the best tradition of heroic journalism.)

The veteran reporter in L. Ron Hubbard's "The Professor Was a Thief" also went in for trespassing, with the aid of wire cutters on the gate of an eccentric scientist. Though he'd been fired by the boss's jealous son-in-law, he got his story and saved New York City from a plague of disappearing buildings too: Grant's Tomb, the Empire State Building, Grand Central Station. The boss himself stepped in at the end to rehire him, this time as managing editor: "Maybe you can make this son-in-law of mine amount to something if you train him right."

Asimov's newspaperman in "Nightfall" wasn't this sort of dauntless news hound, but he served a somewhat more sophisticated purpose: he enabled readers to understand the story situation not only from the explanations he gathered, but also by the very questions he asked. And the situation was one of the most fascinating in all of science fiction. What do *you* think would happen if you lived on a world where no one in memory had ever seen the stars—and suddenly they crowded into the sky?

238 · ISAAC ASIMOV

REFERENCES:

The Early Asimov by Isaac Asimov. Doubleday, 1972.

Introduction by Isaac Asimov to *Before the Golden Age*. Doubleday, 1974.

"Isaac Asimov: Genius in the Candy Store" by Sam Moskowitz. *Amazing Stories,* April 1962.

"You Can't Beat Brains" by L. Sprague de Camp. *Fantasy and Science Fiction,* October 1966.

Theodore Sturgeon: Storyteller by Paul Williams. Pendragon Press, 1978.

"Among the Hams and Pros" by Joseph Gilbert. *The Fantasite,* September 1941.

"Improbability" by "Paul Edmonds" (Henry Kuttner). *Astonishing Stories,* June 1940.

"Spaceship in a Flask" by Clifford D. Simak. *Astounding Science-Fiction,* July 1941.

"My Object All Sublime" by "Lyle Monroe" (Robert A. Heinlein). *Future combined with Science Fiction,* February 1942.

"The Seesaw" by A. E. van Vogt. *Astounding Science-Fiction,* July 1941.

"Farewell to the Master" by Harry Bates. *Astounding Science-Fiction,* October 1940.

"The Professor Was a Thief" by L. Ron Hubbard. *Astounding Science-Fiction,* February 1940.

*   *   *

If the stars should appear one night in a thousand years, how would men believe and adore, and preserve for many generations the remembrance of the city of God!

—Emerson

Aton 77, director of Saro University, thrust out a belligerent lower lip and glared at the young newspaperman in a hot fury.

Theremon 762 took that fury in his stride. In his earlier days, when his now widely syndicated column was only a mad idea in a cub reporter's mind, he had specialized in "impossible" interviews. It had cost him bruises, black eyes, and broken bones; but it had given him an ample supply of coolness and self-confidence.

So he lowered the outthrust hand that had been so pointedly ignored and calmly waited for the aged director to get over the worst. Astronomers were queer ducks, anyway, and if Aton's actions of the last two months meant anything, this same Aton was the queer-duckiest of the lot.

Aton 77 found his voice, and though it trembled with restrained emotion, the careful, somewhat pedantic, phraseology, for which the famous astronomer was noted, did not abandon him.

"Sir," he said, "you display an infernal gall in coming to me with that impudent proposition of yours."

The husky telephotographer of the Observatory, Beenay 25, thrust a tongue's tip across dry lips and interposed nervously, "Now, sir, after all—"

The director turned to him and lifted a white eyebrow. "Do not interfere, Beenay. I will credit you with good intentions in bringing this man here; but I will tolerate no insubordination now."

Theremon decided it was time to take a part. "Director Aton, if you'll let me finish what I started saying I think—"

"I don't believe, young man," retorted Aton, "that anything you could say now would count much as compared with your daily columns of these last two months. You have led a vast newspaper campaign against the efforts of myself and my colleagues to organize the world against the menace which it is now too late to avert. You have done your best with your highly personal attacks to make the staff of this Observatory objects of ridicule."

The director lifted the copy of the Saro City *Chronicle* on the table and shook it at Theremon furiously. "Even a person of your well-known impudence should have hesitated before coming to me with a request that he be allowed to cover today's events for his paper. Of all newsmen, you!"

Aton dashed the newspaper to the floor, strode to the window and clasped his arms behind his back.

"You may leave," he snapped over his shoulder. He stared moodily out at the skyline where Gamma, the brightest of the planet's six suns, was setting. It had already faded and yellowed into the horizon mists, and Aton knew he would never see it again as a sane man.

He whirled. "No, wait, come here!" He gestured peremptorily. "I'll give you your story."

The newsman had made no motion to leave, and now he approached the old man slowly. Aton gestured outward, "Of the six suns, only Beta is left in the sky. Do you see it?"

The question was rather unnecessary. Beta was almost at zenith; its ruddy light flooding the landscape to an unusual orange as the brilliant rays of setting Gamma died. Beta was at aphelion. It was small; smaller than Theremon had ever seen it before, and for the moment it was undisputed ruler of Lagash's sky.

Lagash's own sun, Alpha, the one about which it revolved, was at the antipodes; as were the two distant companion pairs. The red dwarf Beta—Alpha's immediate companion—was alone, grimly alone.

Aton's upturned face flushed redly in the sunlight. "In just under four hours," he said, "civilization, as we know it, comes to an end. It will do so because, as you see, Beta is the only sun in the sky." He smiled grimly. "Print that! There'll be no one to read it."

"But if it turns out that four hours pass—and another four— and nothing happens?" asked Theremon softly.

"Don't let that worry you. Enough will happen."

"Granted! And *still*—if nothing happens?"

For a second time, Beenay 25 spoke. "Sir, I think you ought to listen to him."

Theremon said, "Put it to a vote, Director Aton."

There was a stir among the remaining five members of the Observatory staff, who till now had maintained an attitude of wary neutrality.

"That," stated Aton flatly, "is not necessary." He drew out his pocket watch. "Since your good friend, Beenay, insists so urgently, I will give you five minutes. Talk away."

"Good! Now, just what difference would it make if you allowed me to take down an eyewitness account of what's to come? If your prediction comes true, my presence won't hurt; for in that case my column would never be written. On the other hand, if nothing comes of it, you will just have to expect ridicule or worse. It would be wise to leave that ridicule to friendly hands."

Aton snorted. "Do you mean yours when you speak of friendly hands?"

"Certainly!" Theremon sat down and crossed his legs. "My columns may have been a little rough at times, but I gave you people the benefit of the doubt every time. After all, this is not the century to preach 'the end of the world is at hand' to Lagash. You have to understand that people don't believe the 'Book of Revelations' any more, and it annoys them to have scientists turn about face and tell us the Cultists are right after all—"

"No such thing, young man," interrupted Aton. "While a great deal of our data has been supplied us by the Cult, our results contain none of the Cult's mysticism. Facts are facts, and the Cult's so-called 'mythology' *has* certain facts behind it. We've exposed them and ripped away their mystery. I assure you that the Cult hates us now worse than you do."

"I don't hate you. I'm just trying to tell you that the public is in an ugly humor. They're angry."

Aton twisted his mouth in derision. "Let them be angry."

"Yes, but what about tomorrow?"

"There'll be no tomorrow!"

"But if there is. Say that there is—just to see what happens. That anger might take shape into something serious. After all, you know, business has taken a nose dive these last two months. Investors don't really believe the world is coming to an end, but just the same they're being cagy with their money until it's all over. Johnny Public doesn't believe you, either, but the new spring furniture might as well wait a few months—just to make sure.

"You see the point. Just as soon as this is all over, the business interests will be after your hide. They'll say that if crackpots— begging your pardon—can upset the country's prosperity any time they want simply by making some cockeyed prediction— it's up to the planet to prevent them. The sparks will fly, sir."

The director regarded the columnist sternly. "And just what were you proposing to do to help the situation?"

"Well," grinned Theremon, "I was proposing to take charge of the publicity. I can handle things so that only the ridiculous side will show. It would be hard to stand, I admit, because I'd have to make you all out to be a bunch of gibbering idiots, but if I can get people laughing at you, they might forget to be angry. In return for that, all my publisher asks is an exclusive story."

Beenay nodded and burst out, "Sir, the rest of us think he's right. These last two months we've considered everything but the million-to-one chance that there is an error somewhere in our theory or in our calculations. We ought to take care of that, too."

There was a murmur of agreement from the men grouped about the table, and Aton's expression became that of one who found his mouth full of something bitter and couldn't get rid of it.

"You may stay if you wish, then. You will kindly refrain, however, from hampering us in our duties in any way. You will also remember that I am in charge of all activities here, and in spite of your opinions as expressed in your columns, I will ex- pect full co-operation and full respect—"

His hands were behind his back, and his wrinkled face thrust forward determinedly as he spoke. He might have continued indefinitely but for the intrusion of a new voice.

"Hello, hello, hello!" It came in a high tenor, and the plump cheeks of the newcomer expanded in a pleased smile. "What's this morguelike atmosphere about here? No one's losing his nerve, I hope."

Aton started in consternation and said peevishly, "Now what the devil are you doing here, Sheerin? I thought you were going to stay behind in the Hideout."

Sheerin laughed and dropped his tubby figure into a chair. "Hideout be blowed! The place bored me. I wanted to be here, where things are getting hot. Don't you suppose I have my share of curiosity? I want to see these Stars the Cultists are forever speaking about." He rubbed his hands and added in a soberer tone, "It's freezing outside. The wind's enough to hang icicles on your nose. Beta doesn't seem to give any heat at all, at the distance it is."

The white-haired director ground his teeth in sudden exasperation, "Why do you go out of your way to do crazy things, Sheerin? What kind of good are you around here?"

"What kind of good am I around there?" Sheerin spread his palms in comical resignation. "A psychologist isn't worth his salt in the Hideout. They need men of action and strong, healthy women that can breed children. Me? I'm a hundred pounds too heavy for a man of action, and I wouldn't be a success at breeding children. So why bother then with an extra mouth to feed? I feel better over here."

Theremon spoke briskly, "Just what is the Hideout, sir?"

Sheerin seemed to see the columnist for the first time. He frowned and blew his ample cheeks out, "And just who in Lagash are you, redhead?"

Aton compressed his lips and then muttered sullenly, "That's Theremon 762, the newspaper fellow. I suppose you've heard of him."

The columnist offered his hand. "And, of course, you're Sheerin 501 of Saro University. I've heard of *you*." Then he repeated, "What is this Hideout, sir?"

"Well," said Sheerin, "we have managed to convince a few people of the validity of our prophecy of—er—doom, to be spectacular about it, and those few have taken proper measures. They consist mainly of the immediate members of the families of the Observatory staff, certain of the faculty of Saro University and a few outsiders. Altogether, they number about three hundred, but three quarters are women and children."

"I see! They're supposed to hide where the Darkness and the —er—Stars can't get at them, and then hold out when the rest of the world goes poof."

"If they can. It won't be easy. With all of mankind insane; with the great cities going up in flames—environment will not be conducive to survival. But they have food, water, shelter, and weapons—"

"They've got more," said Aton. "They've got all our records, except for what we will collect today. Those records will mean everything to the next cycle, and *that's* what must survive. The rest can go hang."

Theremon whistled a long, low whistle and sat brooding for several minutes. The men about the table had brought out a multichess board and started a six-member game. Moves were made rapidly and in silence. All eyes bent in furious concentration on the board. Theremon watched them intently and then rose and approached Aton, who sat apart in whispered conversation with Sheerin.

"Listen," he said, "Let's go somewhere where we won't bother the rest of the fellows. I want to ask some questions."

The aged astronomer frowned sourly at him, but Sheerin chirped up, "Certainly. It will do me good to talk. It always does. Aton was telling me about your ideas concerning world reaction to a failure of the prediction—and I agree with you. I read your column pretty regularly, by the way, and as a general thing I like your views."

"Please, Sheerin," growled Aton.

"Eh? Oh, all right. We'll go into the next room. It has softer chairs, anyway."

There *were* softer chairs in the next room. There were also thick red curtains on the windows and a maroon carpet on the floor. With the bricky light of Beta pouring in, the general effect was one of dried blood.

Theremon shuddered, "Say, I'd give ten credits for a decent

dose of white light for just a second. I wish Gamma or Delta were in the sky."

"What are your questions?" asked Aton. "Please remember that our time is limited. In a little over an hour and a quarter we're going upstairs, and after that there will be no time for talk."

"Well, here it is." Theremon leaned back and folded his hands on his chest. "You people seem so all-fired serious about this that I'm beginning to believe you. Would you mind explaining what it's all about?"

Aton exploded, "Do you mean to sit there and tell me that you've been bombarding us with ridicule without even finding out what we've been trying to say?"

The columnist grinned sheepishly. "It's not that bad, sir. I've got the general idea. You say that there is going to be a world-wide Darkness in a few hours and that all mankind will go violently insane. What I want now is the science behind it."

"No, you don't. No, you don't," broke in Sheerin. "If you ask Aton for that—supposing him to be in the mood to answer at all—he'll trot out pages of figures and volumes of graphs. You won't make head or tail of it. Now if you were to ask *me*, I could give you the layman's standpoint."

"All right; I ask you."

"Then first I'd like a drink." He rubbed his hands and looked at Aton.

"Water?" grunted Aton.

"Don't be silly!"

"Don't you be silly. No alcohol today. It would be too easy to get my men drunk. I can't afford to tempt them."

The psychologist grumbled wordlessly. He turned to Theremon, impaled him with his sharp eyes, and began.

"You realize, of course, that the history of civilization on Lagash displays a cyclic character—but I mean, *cyclic!*"

"I know," replied Theremon cautiously, "that that is the current archaeological theory. Has it been accepted as a fact?"

"Just about. In this last century it's been generally agreed upon. This cyclic character is—or, rather, was—one of *the* great mysteries. We've located series of civilizations, nine of them definitely, and indications of others as well, all of which have reached heights comparable to our own, and all of which, without exception, were destroyed by fire at the very height of their culture.

"And no one could tell why. All centers of culture were thoroughly gutted by fire, with nothing left behind to give a hint as to the cause."

Theremon was following closely. "Wasn't there a Stone Age, too?"

"Probably, but as yet, practically nothing is known of it, except that men of that age were little more than rather intelligent apes. We can forget about that."

"I see. Go on!"

"There have been explanations of these recurrent catastrophes, all of a more or less fantastic nature. Some say that there are periodic rains of fire; some that Lagash passes through a sun every so often; some even wilder things. But there is one theory, quite different from all of these, that has been handed down over a period of centuries."

"I know. You mean this myth of the 'Stars' that the Cultists have in their 'Book of Revelations.' "

"Exactly," rejoined Sheerin with satisfaction. "The Cultists said that every two thousand and fifty years Lagash entered a huge cave, so that all the suns disappeared, and there came *total darkness all over the world!* And then, they say, things called Stars appeared, which robbed men of their souls and left them unreasoning brutes, so that they destroyed the civilization they themselves had built up. Of course, they mix all this up with a lot of religio-mystic notions, but that's the central idea."

There was a short pause in which Sheerin drew a long breath. "And now we come to the Theory of Universal Gravitation." He pronounced the phrase so that the capital letters sounded—and at that point Aton turned from the window, snorted loudly, and stalked out of the room.

The two stared after him, and Theremon said, "What's wrong?"

"Nothing in particular," replied Sheerin. "Two of the men were due several hours ago and haven't shown up yet. He's terrifically short-handed, of course, because all but the really essential men have gone to the Hideout."

"You don't think the two deserted, do you?"

"Who? Faro and Yimot? Of course not. Still, if they're not back within the hour, things would be a little sticky." He got to his feet suddenly, and his eyes twinkled. "Anyway, as long as Aton is gone—"

Tiptoeing to the nearest window, he squatted, and from the low window box beneath withdrew a bottle of red liquid that gurgled suggestively when he shook it.

"I *thought* Aton didn't know about this," he remarked as he trotted back to the table. "Here! We've only got one glass so, as the guest, you can have it. I'll keep the bottle." And he filled the tiny cup with judicious care.

Theremon rose to protest, but Sheerin eyed him sternly. "Respect your elders, young man."

The newsman seated himself with a look of pain and anguish on his face. "Go ahead, then, you old villain."

The psychologist's Adam's apple wobbled as the bottle upended, and then, with a satisfied grunt and a smack of the lips, he began again.

"But what do you know about gravitation?"

"Nothing, except that it is a very recent development, not too well established, and that the math is so hard that only twelve men in Lagash are supposed to understand it."

"*Tcha!* Nonsense! Boloney! I can give you all the essential math in a sentence. The Law of Universal Gravitation states that there exists a cohesive force among all bodies of the universe, such that the amount of this force between any two given bodies is proportional to the product of their masses divided by the square of the distance between them."

"Is that all?"

"That's enough! It took four hundred years to develop it."

"Why that long? It sounded simple enough, the way you said it."

"Because great laws are not divined by flashes of inspiration, whatever you may think. It usually takes the combined work of a world full of scientists over a period of centuries. After Genovi 41 discovered that Lagash rotated about the sun Alpha, rather than vice versa—and that was four hundred years ago—astronomers have been working. The complex motions of the six suns were recorded and analyzed and unwoven. Theory after theory was advanced and checked and counterchecked and modified and abandoned and revived and converted to something else. It was a devil of a job."

Theremon nodded thoughtfully and held out his glass for more liquor. Sheerin grudgingly allowed a few ruby drops to leave the bottle.

"It was twenty years ago," he continued after remoistening his own throat, "that it was finally demonstrated that the Law of Universal Gravitation accounted exactly for the orbital motions of the six suns. It was a great triumph."

Sheerin stood up and walked to the window, still clutching his bottle. "And now we're getting to the point. In the last decade, the motions of Lagash about Alpha were computed according to gravity, and *it did not account for the orbit observed;* not even when all perturbations due to the other suns were included. Either the law was invalid, or there was another, as yet unknown, factor involved."

Theremon joined Sheerin at the window and gazed out past the wooded slopes to where the spires of Saro City gleamed bloodily on the horizon. The newsman felt the tension of uncertainty grow within him as he cast a short glance at Beta. It glowered redly at zenith, dwarfed and evil.

"Go ahead, sir," he said softly.

Sheerin replied, "Astronomers stumbled about for years, each proposed theory more untenable than the one before—until Aton had the inspiration of calling in the Cult. The head of the Cult, Sor 5, had access to certain data that simplified the problem considerably. Aton set to work on a new track.

"What if there were another non-luminous planetary body such as Lagash? If there were, you know, it would shine only by reflected light, and if it were composed of bluish rock, as Lagash itself largely is, then, in the redness of the sky, the eternal blaze of the suns would make it invisible—drown it out completely."

Theremon whistled, "What a screwy idea!"

"You think *that's* screwy? Listen to this: Suppose this body rotated about Lagash at such a distance and in such an orbit and had such a mass that its attraction would exactly account for the deviations of Lagash's orbit from theory—do you know what would happen?"

The columnist shook his head.

"Well, sometimes this body would get in the way of a sun." And Sheerin emptied what remained in the bottle at a draft.

"And it does, I suppose," said Theremon flatly.

"Yes! But only one sun lies in its plane of revolutions." He jerked a thumb at the shrunken sun above. "Beta! And it has been shown that the eclipse will occur only when the arrangement of the suns is such that Beta is alone in its hemisphere and at maximum distance, at which time the moon is invariably at minimum distance. The eclipse that results, with the moon seven times the apparent diameter of Beta, covers all of Lagash and lasts well over half a day, so that no spot on the planet escapes the effects. *That eclipse comes once every two thousand and forty-nine years.*"

Theremon's face was drawn into an expressionless mask. "And that's my story?"

The psychologist nodded. "That's all of it. First the eclipse—which will start in three quarters of an hour—then universal Darkness, and, maybe, these mysterious Stars—then madness, and end of the cycle."

He brooded. "We had two months' leeway—we at the Observatory—and that wasn't enough time to persuade Lagash of the danger. Two centuries might not have been enough. But our records are at the Hideout, and today we photograph the eclipse. The next cycle will *start off* with the truth, and when the *next* eclipse comes, mankind will at last be ready for it. Come to think of it, that's part of your story, too."

A thin wind ruffled the curtains at the window as Theremon opened it and leaned out. It played coldly with his hair as he stared at the crimson sunlight on his hand. Then he turned in sudden rebellion.

"What is there in Darkness to drive *me* mad?"

Sheerin smiled to himself as he spun the empty liquor bottle with abstracted motions of his hand. "Have you ever experienced Darkness, young man?"

The newsman leaned against the wall and considered. "No. Can't say I have. But I know what it is. Just—uh—" He made vague motions with his fingers, and then brightened. "Just no light. Like in caves."

"Have you ever been in a cave?"

"In a *cave!* Of course not!"

"I thought not. *I* tried last week—just to see—but I got out in a hurry. I went in until the mouth of the cave was just visible as a blur of light, with black everywhere else. I never thought a person my weight could run that fast."

Theremon's lip curled. "Well, if it comes to that, I guess I wouldn't have run, if I had been there."

The psychologist studied the young man with an annoyed frown.

"My, don't you talk big! I dare you to draw the curtain."

Theremon looked his surprise and said, "What for? If we had four or five suns out there we might want to cut the light down a bit for comfort, but now we haven't enough light as it is."

"That's the point. Just draw the curtain; then come here and sit down."

"All right." Theremon reached for the tasseled string and jerked. The red curtain slid across the wide window, the brass rings hissing their way along the crossbar, and a dusk-red shadow clamped down on the room.

Theremon's footsteps sounded hollowly in the silence as he made his way to the table, and then they stopped halfway. "I can't see you, sir," he whispered.

"Feel your way," ordered Sheerin in a strained voice.

"But I can't see you, sir." The newsman was breathing harshly. "I can't see anything."

"What did you expect?" came the grim reply. "Come here and sit down!"

The footsteps sounded again, waveringly, approaching slowly. There was the sound of someone fumbling with a chair. Theremon's voice came thinly, "Here I am. I feel . . . *ulp* . . . all right."

"You like it, do you?"

"N-no. It's pretty awful. The walls seem to be—" He paused. "They seem to be closing in on me. I keep wanting to push them away. But I'm not going *mad!* In fact, the feeling isn't as bad as it was."

"All right. Draw the curtain back again."

There were cautious footsteps through the dark, the rustle of Theremon's body against the curtain as he felt for the tassel, and then the triumphant *ro-o-o-osh* of the curtain slithering back. Red light flooded the room, and with a cry of joy Theremon looked up at the sun.

Sheerin wiped the moistness off his forehead with the back of a hand and said shakily, "And that was just a dark room."

"It can be stood," said Theremon lightly.

"Yes, a dark room can. But were you at the Jonglor Centennial Exposition two years ago?"

"No, it so happens I never got around to it. Six thousand miles was just a bit too much to travel, even for the exposition."

"Well, I was there. You remember hearing about the 'Tunnel of Mystery' that broke all records in the amusement area—for the first month or so, anyway?"

"Yes. Wasn't there some fuss about it?"

"Very little. It was hushed up. You see, that Tunnel of Mystery was just a mile-long tunnel—with no lights. You got into a little open car and jolted along through Darkness for fifteen minutes. It was very popular—while it lasted."

"Popular?"

"Certainly. There's a fascination in being frightened *when it's part of a game.* A baby is born with three instinctive fears: of loud noises, of falling, and of the absence of light. That's why it's considered so funny to jump at someone and shout 'Boo!' That's why it's such fun to ride a roller coaster. And that's why that Tunnel of Mystery started cleaning up. People came out of that Darkness shaking, breathless, half dead with fear, but they kept on paying to get in."

"Wait awhile, I remember now. Some people came out dead, didn't they? There were rumors of that after it shut down."

The psychologist snorted. "Bah! Two or three died. That was nothing! They paid off the families of the dead ones and argued the Jonglor City Council into forgetting it. After all, they said, if people with weak hearts want to go through the tunnel, it was at their own risk—and besides, it wouldn't happen again. So they put a doctor in the front office and had every customer go through a physical examination before getting into the car. That actually *boosted* ticket sales."

"Well, then?"

"But, you see, there was something else. People sometimes came out in perfect order, except that they refused to go into buildings—any buildings; including palaces, mansions, apartment houses, tenements, cottages, huts, shacks, lean-tos, and tents."

Theremon looked shocked. "You mean they refused to come in out of the open. Where'd they sleep?"

"In the open."

"They should have *forced* them inside."

"Oh, they did, they did. Whereupon these people went into violent hysterics and did their best to bat their brains out against the nearest wall. Once you got them inside, you couldn't keep them there without a strait jacket and a shot of morphine."

"They must have been crazy."

"Which is exactly what they were. One person out of every ten who went into that tunnel came out that way. They called in the psychologists, and we did the only thing possible. We closed down the exhibit." He spread his hands.

"What was the matter with these people?" asked Theremon finally.

"Essentially the same thing that was the matter with you when you thought the walls of the room were crushing in on you in the dark. There is a psychological term for mankind's instinctive fear of the absence of light. We call it 'claustrophobia,' because the lack of light is always tied up with inclosed places, so that fear of one is fear of the other. You see?"

"And those people of the tunnel?"

"Those people of the tunnel consisted of those unfortunates whose mentality did not quite possess the resiliency to overcome the claustrophobia that overtook them in the Darkness. Fifteen minutes without light is a long time; you only had two or three minutes, and I believe you were fairly upset.

"The people of the tunnel had what is called a 'claustrophobic fixation.' Their latent fear of Darkness and inclosed places had crystallized and become active, and, as far as we can tell, permanent. *That's* what fifteen minutes in the dark will do."

There was a long silence, and Theremon's forehead wrinkled slowly into a frown. "I don't believe it's that bad."

"You mean you don't want to believe," snapped Sheerin. "You're afraid to believe. Look out the window!"

Theremon did so, and the psychologist continued without pausing, "Imagine Darkness—everywhere. No light, as far as you can see. The houses, the trees, the fields, the earth, the sky —*black!* And Stars thrown in, for all I know—whatever *they* are. Can you conceive it?"

"Yes, I can," declared Theremon truculently.

And Sheerin slammed his fist down upon the table in sudden passion. "You lie! You can't conceive that. Your brain wasn't built for the conception any more than it was built for the conception of infinity or of eternity. You can only talk about it. A fraction of the reality upsets you, and when the real thing comes, your brain is going to be presented with a phenomenon outside its limits of comprehension. You will go mad, completely and permanently! There is no question of it!"

He added sadly, "And another couple of millenniums of painful struggle comes to nothing. Tomorrow there won't be a city standing unharmed in all Lagash."

Theremon recovered part of his mental equilibrium. "That doesn't follow. I still don't see that I can go loony just because there isn't a Sun in the sky—but even if I did, and everyone else did, how does that harm the cities? Are we going to blow them down?"

But Sheerin was angry, too. "If you were in Darkness, what would you want more than anything else; what would it be that every instinct would call for? Light, damn you, *light!*"

"Well?"

"And how would you get light?"

"I don't know," said Theremon flatly.

"What's the *only* way to get light, short of the sun?"

"How should I know?"

They were standing face to face and nose to nose.

Sheerin said, "You burn something, mister. Ever see a forest fire? Ever go camping and cook a stew over a wood fire? Heat isn't the only thing burning wood gives off, you know. It gives off light, and people know that. And when it's dark they want light, and they're going to *get it.*"

"So they burn wood?"

"So they burn whatever they can get. They've got to have light. They've got to burn something, and wood isn't handy—so they'll burn whatever is nearest. They'll have their light—and every center of habitation goes up in flames!"

Eyes held each other as though the whole matter were a personal affair of respective will powers, and then Theremon broke away wordlessly. His breathing was harsh and ragged, and he scarcely noted the sudden hubbub that came from the adjoining room behind the closed door.

Sheerin spoke, and it was with an effort that he made it sound matter-of-fact. "I think I heard Yimot's voice. He and Faro are probably back. Let's go in and see what kept them."

"Might as well!" muttered Theremon. He drew a long breath and seemed to shake himself. The tension was broken.

The room was in an uproar, with members of the staff clustering about two young men who were removing outer garments even as they parried the miscellany of questions being thrown at them.

Aton bustled through the crowd and faced the newcomers angrily. "Do you realize that it's less than half an hour before deadline. Where have you two been?"

Faro 24 seated himself and rubbed his hands. His cheeks were red with the outdoor chill. "Yimot and I have just finished carrying through a little crazy experiment of our own. We've been trying to see if we couldn't construct an arrangement by which we could simulate the appearance of Darkness and Stars so as to get an advance notion as to how it looked."

There was a confused murmur from the listeners, and a sudden look of interest entered Aton's eyes. "There wasn't anything said of this before. How did you go about it?"

"Well," said Faro, "the idea came to Yimot and myself long ago, and we've been working it out in our spare time. Yimot knew of a low one-story house down in the city with a domed roof—it had once been used as a museum, I think. Anyway, we bought it—"

"Where did you get the money?" interrupted Aton peremptorily.

"Our bank accounts," grunted Yimot 70. "It cost two thousand credits." Then, defensively, "Well, what of it? Tomorrow, two thousand credits will be two thousand pieces of paper. That's all."

"Sure," agreed Faro. "We bought the place and rigged it up with black velvet from top to bottom so as to get as perfect a Darkness as possible. Then we punched tiny holes in the ceiling and through the roof and covered them with little metal caps, all of which could be shoved aside simultaneously at the close of a switch. At least, we didn't do that part ourselves; we got a carpenter and an electrician and some others—money didn't count. The point was that we could get the light to shine through those holes in the roof, so that we could get a starlike effect."

Not a breath was drawn during the pause that followed. Aton said stiffly:

"You had no right to make a private—"

Faro seemed abashed. "I know, sir—but, frankly, Yimot and I thought the experiment was a little dangerous. If the effect really worked, we half expected to go mad—from what Sheerin says about all this, we thought that would be rather likely. We wanted to take the risk ourselves. Of course, if we found we could retain sanity, it occurred to us that we might develop immunity to the real thing, and then expose the rest of you to the same thing. But things didn't work out at all—"

"Why, what happened?"

It was Yimot who answered. "We shut ourselves in and allowed our eyes to get accustomed to the dark. It's an extremely creepy feeling because the total Darkness makes you feel as if the walls and ceiling are crushing in on you. But we got over that and pulled the switch. The caps fell away and the roof glittered all over with little dots of light—"

"Well?"

"Well—nothing. That was the whacky part of it. Nothing happened. It was just a roof with holes in it, and that's just what it looked like. We tried it over and over again—that's what kept us so late—but there just isn't any effect at all."

There followed a shocked silence, and all eyes turned to Sheerin, who sat motionless, mouth open.

Theremon was the first to speak. "You know what this does to this whole theory you've built up, Sheerin, don't you?" He was grinning with relief.

But Sheerin raised his hand. "Now wait a while. Just let me think this through." And then he snapped his fingers, and when he lifted his head there was neither surprise nor uncertainty in his eyes. "Of course—"

He never finished. From somewhere up above there sounded a sharp clang, and Beenay, starting to his feet, dashed up the stairs with a "What the devil!"

The rest followed after.

Things happened quickly. Once up in the dome, Beenay cast one horrified glance at the shattered photographic plates and at the man bending over them; and then hurled himself fiercely at the intruder, getting a death grip on his throat. There was a wild threshing, and as others of the staff joined in, the stranger was swallowed up and smothered under the weight of half a dozen angry men.

Aton came up last, breathing heavily. "Let him up!"

There was a reluctant unscrambling and the stranger, panting harshly, with his clothes torn and his forehead bruised, was hauled to his feet. He had a short yellow beard curled elaborately in the style affected by the Cultists.

Beenay shifted his hold to a collar grip and shook the man savagely. "All right, rat, what's the idea? These plates—"

"I wasn't after *them*," retorted the Cultist coldly. "That was an accident."

Beenay followed his glowering stare and snarled, "I see. You were after the cameras themselves. The accident with the plates was a stroke of luck for you, then. If you had touched Snapping Bertha or any of the others, you would have died by slow torture. As it is—" He drew his fist back.

Aton grabbed his sleeve. "Stop that! Let him go!"

The young technician wavered, and his arm dropped reluctantly. Aton pushed him aside and confronted the Cultist. "You're Latimer, aren't you?"

The Cultist bowed stiffly and indicated the symbol upon his hip. "I am Latimer 25, adjutant of the third class to his serenity, Sor 5."

"And"—Aton's white eyebrows lifted—"you were with his

serenity when he visited me last week, weren't you?"

Latimer bowed a second time.

"Now, then, what do you want?"

"Nothing that you would give me of your own free will."

"Sor 5 sent you, I suppose—or is this your own idea?"

"I won't answer that question."

"Will there be any further visitors?"

"I won't answer that, either."

Aton glanced at his timepiece and scowled. "Now, man, what is it your master wants of me. I have fulfilled my end of the bargain."

Latimer smiled faintly, but said nothing.

"I asked him," continued Aton angrily, "for data only the Cult could supply, and it was given to me. For that, thank you. In return, I promised to prove the essential truth of the creed of the Cult."

"There was no need to prove that," came the proud retort. "It stands proven by the 'Book of Revelations.'"

"For the handful that constitute the Cult, yes. Don't pretend to mistake my meaning. I offered to present scientific backing for your beliefs. And I did!"

The Cultist's eyes narrowed bitterly. "Yes, you did—with a fox's subtlety, for your pretended explanation backed our beliefs, and at the same time removed all necessity for them. You made of the Darkness and of the Stars a natural phenomenon, and removed all its real significance. That was blasphemy."

"If so, the fault isn't mine. The facts exist. What can I do but state them?"

"Your 'facts' are a fraud and a delusion."

Aton stamped angrily. "How do *you* know?"

And the answer came with the certainty of absolute faith. "I *know!*"

The director purpled and Beenay whispered urgently. Aton waved him silent. "And what does Sor 5 want us to do. He still thinks, I suppose, that in trying to warn the world to take measures against the menace of madness, we are placing innumerable souls in jeopardy. We aren't succeeding, if that means anything to him."

"The attempt itself has done harm enough, and your vicious effort to gain information by means of your devilish instruments must be stopped. We obey the will of the Stars, and I only regret that my clumsiness prevented me from wrecking your infernal devices."

"It wouldn't have done you too much good," returned Aton. "All our data, except for the direct evidence we intend collecting right now, is already safely cached and well beyond possibility of harm." He smiled grimly. "But that does not affect your present status as an attempted burglar and criminal."

He turned to the men behind him. "Someone call the police at Saro City."

There was a cry of distaste from Sheerin. "Damn it, Aton, what's wrong with you? There's no time for that. Here"—he bustled his way forward—"let me handle this."

Aton stared down his nose at the psychologist. "This is not the time for your monkeyshines, Sheerin. Will you please let me handle this my own way? Right now you are a complete outsider here, and don't forget it."

Sheerin's mouth twisted eloquently. "Now why should we go to the impossible trouble of calling the police—with Beta's eclipse a matter of minutes from now—when this young man here is perfectly willing to pledge his word of honor to remain and cause no trouble whatsoever."

The Cultist answered promptly, "I will do no such thing. You're free to do what you want, but it's only fair to warn you that just as soon as I get my chance I'm going to finish what I came out here to do. If it's my word of honor you're relying on, you'd better call the police."

Sheerin smiled in a friendly fashion. "You're a determined cuss, aren't you? Well, I'll explain something. Do you see that young man at the window? He's a strong, husky fellow, quite handy with his fists, and he's an outsider besides. Once the eclipse starts there will be nothing for him to do except keep an eye on you. Besides him, there will be myself—a little too stout for active fisticuffs, but still able to help."

"Well, what of it?" demanded Latimer frozenly.

"Listen and I'll tell you," was the reply. "Just as soon as the eclipse starts, we're going to take you, Theremon and I, and deposit you in a little closet with one door, to which is attached one giant lock and no windows. You will remain there for the duration."

"And afterward," breathed Latimer fiercely, "there'll be no one to let me out. I know as well as you do what the coming of the Stars means—I know it far better than you. With all your minds gone, you are not likely to free me. Suffocation or slow starvation, is it? About what I might have expected from a group of scientists. But I don't give my word. It's a matter of principle, and I won't discuss it further."

Aton seemed perturbed. His faded eyes were troubled. "Really, Sheerin, locking him—"

"Please!" Sheerin motioned him impatiently to silence. "I don't think for a moment things will go that far. Latimer has just tried a clever little bluff, but I'm not a psychologist just because I like the sound of the word." He grinned at the Cultist. "Come now, you don't really think I'm trying anything as crude as slow starvation. My dear Latimer, if I lock you in the closet, you are not going to see the Darkness, and you are not going to see the Stars. It does not take much of a knowledge of the fundamental creed of the Cult to realize that for you to be hidden from the Stars when they appear means the loss of your immortal soul. Now, I believe you to be an honorable man. I'll accept your word of honor to make no further effort to disrupt proceedings if you'll offer it."

A vein throbbed in Latimer's temple, and he seemed to shrink within himself as he said thickly, "You have it!" And then he added with swift fury, "But it is my consolation that you will all be damned for your deeds of today." He turned on his heel and stalked to the high three-legged stool by the door.

Sheerin nodded to the columnist. "Take a seat next to him, Theremon—just as a formality. Hey, Theremon!"

But the newspaperman didn't move. He had gone pale to the lips. "Look at that!" The finger he pointed toward the sky shook, and his voice was dry and cracked.

There was one simultaneous gasp as every eye followed the pointing finger and, for one breathless moment, stared frozenly.

Beta was chipped on one side!

The tiny bit of encroaching blackness was perhaps the width of a fingernail, but to the staring watchers it magnified itself into the crack of doom.

Only for a moment they watched, and after that there was a shrieking confusion that was even shorter of duration and which gave way to an orderly scurry of activity—each man at his prescribed job. At the crucial moment there was no time for emotion. The men were merely scientists with work to do. Even Aton had melted away.

Sheerin said prosaically, "First contact must have been made fifteen minutes ago. A little early, but pretty good considering the uncertainties involved in the calculation." He looked about him and then tiptoed to Theremon, who still remained staring out the window, and dragged him away gently.

"Aton is furious," he whispered, "so stay away. He missed first contact on account of this fuss with Latimer, and if you get in his way he'll have you thrown out the window."

Theremon nodded shortly and sat down. Sheerin stared in surprise at him.

"The devil, man," he exclaimed, "you're shaking."

"Eh?" Theremon licked dry lips and then tried to smile. "I don't feel very well, and that's a fact."

The psychologist's eyes hardened. "You're not losing your nerve?"

"No!" cried Theremon in a flash of indignation. "Give me a chance, will you? I haven't really believed this rigmarole—not way down beneath, anyway—till just this minute. Give me a chance to get used to the idea. *You've* been preparing yourself for two months or more."

"You're right, at that," replied Sheerin thoughtfully. "Listen!

Have you got a family—parents, wife, children?"

Theremon shook his head. "You mean the Hideout, I suppose. No, you don't have to worry about that. I have a sister, but she's two thousand miles away. I don't even know her exact address."

"Well, then, what about yourself? You've got time to get there, and they're one short anyway, since I left. After all, you're not needed here, and you'd make a darned fine addition—"

Theremon looked at the other wearily. "You think I'm scared stiff, don't you? Well, get this, mister, I'm a newspaperman and I've been assigned to cover a story. I intend covering it."

There was a faint smile on the psychologist's face. "I see. Professional honor, is that it?"

"You might call it that. But, man, I'd give my right arm for another bottle of that sockeroo juice even half the size of the one *you* hogged. If ever a fellow needed a drink, I do."

He broke off. Sheerin was nudging him violently. "Do you hear that? Listen!"

Theremon followed the motion of the other's chin and stared at the Cultist, who, oblivious to all about him, faced the window, a look of wild elation on his face, droning to himself the while in singsong fashion.

"What's he saying?" whispered the columnist.

"He's quoting 'Book of Revelations,' fifth chapter," replied Sheerin. Then, urgently, "Keep quiet and listen, I tell you."

The Cultist's voice had risen in a sudden increase of fervor:

" 'And it came to pass that in those days the Sun, Beta, held lone vigil in the sky for ever longer periods as the revolutions passed; until such time as for full half a revolution, it alone, shrunken and cold, shone down upon Lagash.

" 'And men did assemble in the public squares and in the highways, there to debate and to marvel at the sight, for a strange depression had seized them. Their minds were troubled and their speech confused, for the souls of men awaited the coming of the Stars.

" 'And in the city of Trigon, at high noon, Vendret 2 came

forth and said unto the men of Trigon, "Lo, ye sinners! Though ye scorn the ways of righteousness, yet will the time of reckoning come. Even now the Cave approaches to swallow Lagash; yea, and all it contains."

" 'And even as he spoke the lip of the Cave of Darkness passed the edge of Beta so that to all Lagash it was hidden from sight. Loud were the cries of men as it vanished, and great the fear of soul that fell upon them.

" 'It came to pass that the Darkness of the Cave fell upon Lagash, and there was no light on all the surface of Lagash. Men were even as blinded, nor could one man see his neighbor, though he felt his breath upon his face.

" 'And in this blackness there appeared the Stars, in countless numbers, and to the strains of ineffable music of a beauty so wondrous that the very leaves of the trees turned to tongues that cried out in wonder.

" 'And in that moment the souls of men departed from them, and their abandoned bodies became even as beasts; yea, even as brutes of the wild; so that through the blackened streets of the cities of Lagash they prowled with wild cries.

" 'From the Stars there then reached down the Heavenly Flame, and where it touched, the cities of Lagash flamed to utter destruction, so that of man and of the works of man nought remained.

" 'Even then—' "

There was a subtle change in Latimer's tone. His eyes had not shifted, but somehow he had become aware of the absorbed attention of the other two. Easily, without pausing for breath, the timber of his voice shifted and the syllables became more liquid.

Theremon, caught by surprise, stared. The words seemed on the border of familiarity. There was an elusive shift in the accent, a tiny change in the vowel stress; nothing more—yet Latimer had become thoroughly unintelligible.

Sheerin smiled slyly. "He shifted to some old-cycle tongue, probably their traditional second cycle. That was the language in which the 'Book of Revelations' had originally been written, you know."

"It doesn't matter; I've heard enough." Theremon shoved his chair back and brushed his hair back with hands that no longer shook. "I feel much better now."

"You do?" Sheerin seemed mildly surprised.

"I'll say I do. I had a bad case of jitters just a while back. Listening to you and your gravitation and seeing that eclipse start almost finished me. But this"—he jerked a contemptuous thumb at the yellow-bearded Cultist—"*this* is the sort of thing my nurse used to tell me. I've been laughing at that sort of thing all my life. I'm not going to let it scare me *now.*"

He drew a deep breath and said with a hectic gaiety, "But if I expect to keep on the good side of myself, I'm going to turn my chair away from the window."

Sheerin said, "Yes, but you'd better talk lower. Aton just lifted his head out of that box he's got it stuck into and gave you a look that should have killed you."

Theremon made a mouth. "I forgot about the old fellow." With elaborate care he turned the chair from the window, cast one distasteful look over his shoulder and said, "It has occurred to me that there must be considerable immunity against this Star madness."

The psychologist did not answer immediately. Beta was past its zenith now, and the square of bloody sunlight that outlined the window upon the floor had lifted into Sheerin's lap. He stared at its dusky color thoughtfully and then bent and squinted into the sun itself.

The chip in its side had grown to a black encroachment that covered a third of Beta. He shuddered, and when he straightened once more his florid cheeks did not contain quite as much color as they had had previously.

With a smile that was almost apologetic, he reversed his chair also. "There are probably two million people in Saro City that are all trying to join the Cult at once in one gigantic revival." Then, ironically, "The Cult is in for an hour of unexampled prosperity. I trust they'll make the most of it. Now, what was it you said?"

"Just this. How do the Cultits manage to keep the 'Book of Revelations' going from cycle to cycle, and how on Lagash did it get written in the first place? There must have been some sort of immunity, for if everyone had gone mad, who would be left to write the book?"

Sheerin stared at his questioner ruefully. "Well, now, young man, there isn't any eyewitness answer to that, but we've got a few damned good notions as to what happened. You see, there are three kinds of people who might remain relatively unaffected. First, the very few who don't see the Stars at all; the blind, those who drink themselves into a stupor at the beginning of the eclipse and remain so to the end. We leave them out —because they aren't really witnesses.

"Then there are children below six, to whom the world as a whole is too new and strange for them to be *too* frightened at Stars and Darkness. They would be just another item in an already surprising world. You see that, don't you?"

The other nodded doubtfully. "I suppose so."

"Lastly, there are those whose minds are too coarsely grained to be entirely toppled. The very insensitive would be scarcely affected—oh, such people as some of our older, work-broken peasants. Well, the children would have fugitive memories, and that, combined with the confused, incoherent babblings of the half-mad morons, formed the basis for the 'Book of Revelations.'

"Naturally, the book was based, in the first place, on the testimony of those least qualified to serve as historians; that is, children and morons; and was probably extensively edited and re-edited through the cycles."

"Do you suppose," broke in Theremon, "that they carried the book through the cycles the way we're planning on handing on the secret of gravitation?"

Sheerin shrugged. "Perhaps, but their exact method is unimportant. They do it, somehow. The point I was getting at was that the book can't help but be a mass of distortion, even if it is based on fact. For instance, do you remember the experiment with the holes in the roof that Faro and Yimot tried—the one that didn't work?"

"Yes."

"You know why it didn't w—" He stopped and rose in alarm, for Aton was approaching, his face a twisted mask of consternation. *What's happened?"*

Aton drew him aside and Sheerin could feel the fingers on his elbow twitching.

"Not so loud!" Aton's voice was low and tortured. "I've just gotten word from the Hideout on the private line."

Sheerin broke in anxiously, "They are in trouble?"

"Not *they.*" Aton stressed the pronoun significantly. "They sealed themselves off just a while ago, and they're going to stay buried till day after tomorrow. They're safe. But the *city*, Sheerin—it's a shambles. You have no idea—" He was having difficulty in speaking.

"Well?" snapped Sheerin impatiently. "What of it? It will get worse. What are you shaking about?" Then, suspiciously, "How do you feel?"

Aton's eyes sparked angrily at the insinuation, and then faded to anxiety once more. "You don't understand. The Cultists are active. They're rousing the people to storm the Observatory—promising them immediate entrance into grace, promising them salvation, promising them anything. What are we to do, Sheerin?"

Sheerin's head bent, and he stared in long abstraction at his toes. He tapped his chin with one knuckle, then looked up and said crisply, "Do? What is there to do? Nothing at all! Do the men know of this?"

"No, of course not!"

"Good! Keep it that way. How long till totality?"

"Not quite an hour."

"There's nothing to do but gamble. It will take time to organize any really formidable mob, and it will take more time to get them out here. We're a good five miles from the city—"

He glared out the window, down the slopes to where the farmed patches gave way to clumps of white houses in the suburbs; down to where the metropolis itself was a blur on the horizon—a mist in the waning blaze of Beta.

He repeated without turning, "It will take time. Keep on working and pray that totality comes first."

Beta was cut in half, the line of division pushing a slight concavity into the still-bright portion of the Sun. It was like a gigantic eyelid shutting slantwise over the light of a world.

The faint clatter of the room in which he stood faded into oblivion, and he sensed only the thick silence of the fields outside. The very insects seemed frightened mute. And things were dim.

He jumped at the voice in his ear. Theremon said, "Is something wrong?"

"Eh? Er—no. Get back to the chair. We're in the way." They slipped back to their corner, but the psychologist did not speak for a time. He lifted a finger and loosened his collar. He twisted his neck back and forth but found no relief. He looked up suddenly.

"Are you having any difficulty in breathing?"

The newspaperman opened his eyes wide and drew two or three long breaths. "No. Why?"

"I looked out the window too long, I suppose. The dimness got me. Difficulty in breathing is one of the first symptoms of a claustrophobic attack."

Theremon drew another long breath. "Well, it hasn't got me yet. Say, here's another of the fellows."

Beenay had interposed his bulk between the light and the pair in the corner, and Sheerin squinted up at him anxiously. "Hello, Beenay."

The astronomer shifted his weight to the other foot and smiled feebly. "You won't mind if I sit down awhile and join in on the talk. My cameras are set, and there's nothing to do till totality." He paused and eyed the Cultist, who fifteen minutes earlier had drawn a small, skinbound book from his sleeve and had been poring intently over it ever since. "That rat hasn't been making trouble, has he?"

Sheerin shook his head. His shoulders were thrown back and he frowned his concentration as he forced himself to breathe regularly. He said, "Have you had any trouble breathing, Beenay?"

Beenay sniffed the air in his turn. "It doesn't seem stuffy to me."

"A touch of claustrophobia," explained Sheerin apologetically.

"Oh-h-h! It worked itself differently with me. I get the impression that my eyes are going back on me. Things seem to blur and—well, nothing is clear. And it's cold, too."

"Oh, it's cold, all right. That's no illusion." Theremon grimaced. "My toes feel as if I've been shipping them cross country in a refrigerating car."

"What we need," put in Sheerin, "is to keep our minds busy with extraneous affairs. I was telling you a while ago, Theremon, why Faro's experiments with the holes in the roof came to nothing."

"You were just beginning," replied Theremon. He encircled a knee with both arms and nuzzled his chin against it.

"Well, as I started to say, they were misled by taking the 'Book of Revelations' literally. There probably wasn't any sense in attaching any physical significance to the Stars. It might be, you know, that in the presence of total Darkness, the mind finds it absolutely necessary to create light. This illusion of light might be all the Stars there really are."

"In other words," interposed Theremon, "you mean the Stars are the results of the madness and not one of the causes. Then, what good will Beenay's photographs be?"

"To prove that it is an illusion, maybe; or to prove the opposite, for all I know. Then again—"

But Beenay had drawn his chair closer, and there was an expression of sudden enthusiasm on his face. "Say, I'm glad you two got on to this subject." His eyes narrowed and he lifted one finger. "I've been thinking about these Stars and I've got a really cute notion. Of course, it's strictly ocean foam, and I'm not trying to advance it seriously, but I think it's interesting. Do you want to hear it?"

He seemed half reluctant, but Sheerin leaned back and said, "Go ahead! I'm listening."

"Well, then, supposing there were other suns in the universe." He broke off a little bashfully. "I mean suns that are so far away that they're too dim to see. It sounds as if I've been reading some of that fantastic fiction, I suppose."

"Not necessarily. Still, isn't that possibility eliminated by the fact that, according to the Law of Gravitation, they would make themselves evident by their attractive forces?"

"Not if they were far enough off," rejoined Beenay, "really far off—maybe as much as four light years, or even more. We'd never be able to detect perturbations then, because they'd be too small. Say that there were a lot of suns that far off; a dozen or two, maybe."

Theremon whistled melodiously. "What an idea for a good Sunday supplement article. Two dozen suns in a universe eight light years across. Wow! That would shrink *our* universe into insignificance. The readers would eat it up."

"Only an idea," said Beenay with a grin, "but you see the point. During eclipse, these dozen suns would become visible, because there'd be no *real* sunlight to drown them out. Since they're so far off, they'd appear small, like so many little marbles. Of course, the Cultists talk of millions of Stars, but that's probably exaggeration. There just isn't any place in the universe you could put a million suns—unless they touch each other."

Sheerin had listened with gradually increasing interest. "You've hit something there, Beenay. And exaggeration is just exactly what would happen. Our minds, as you probably know, can't grasp directly any number higher than five; above that there is only the concept of 'many.' A dozen would become a million just like that. A damn good idea!"

"And I've got another cute little notion," Beenay said. "Have you ever thought what a simple problem gravitation would be if only you had a sufficiently simple system? Supposing you had a universe in which there was a planet with only one sun. The planet would travel in a perfect ellipse and the exact nature of the gravitational force would be so evident it could be accepted as an axiom. Astronomers on such a world would start off with gravity probably before they even invent the telescope. Naked-eye observation would be enough."

"But would such a system be dynamically stable?" questioned Sheerin doubtfully.

"Sure! They call it the 'one-and-one' case. It's been worked out mathematically, but it's the philosophical implications that interest me."

"It's nice to think about," admitted Sheerin, "as a pretty abstraction—like a perfect gas or absolute zero."

"Of course," continued Beenay, "there's the catch that life would be impossible on such a planet. It wouldn't get enough heat and light, and if it rotated there would be total Darkness half of each day. You couldn't expect life—which is fundamentally dependent upon light—to develop under those conditions. Besides—"

Sheerin's chair went over backward as he sprang to his feet in a rude interruption. "Aton's brought out the lights."

Beenay said, "Huh," turned to stare, and then grinned half-way around his head in open relief.

There were half a dozen foot-long, inch-thick rods cradled in Aton's arms. He glared over them at the assembled staff members.

"Get back to work, all of you. Sheerin, come here and help me!"

Sheerin trotted to the older man's side and, one by one, in utter silence, the two adjusted the rods in makeshift metal holders suspended from the walls.

With the air of one carrying through the most sacred item of a religious ritual, Sheerin scraped a large, clumsy match into spluttering life and passed it to Aton, who carried the flame to the upper end of one of the rods.

It hesitated there awhile, playing futilely about the tip, until a sudden, crackling flare cast Aton's lined face into yellow highlights. He withdrew the match and a spontaneous cheer rattled the window.

The rod was topped by six inches of wavering flame! Methodically, the other rods were lighted, until six independent fires turned the rear of the room yellow.

The light was dim, dimmer even than the tenuous sunlight. The flames reeled crazily, giving birth to drunken, swaying shadows. The torches smoked devilishly and smelled like a bad day in the kitchen. But they emitted yellow light.

There is something *to* yellow light—after four hours of somber, dimming Beta. Even Latimer had lifted his eyes from his book and stared in wonder.

Sheerin warmed his hands at the nearest, regardless of the soot that gathered upon them in a fine, gray powder, and muttered ecstatically to himself, "Beautiful! Beautiful! I never realized before what a wonderful color yellow is."

But Theremon regarded the torches suspiciously. He wrinkled his nose at the rancid odor, and said, "What are those things?"

"Wood," said Sheerin shortly.

"Oh, no, they're not. They aren't burning. The top inch is charred and the flame just keeps shooting up out of nothing."

"That's the beauty of it. This is a really efficient artificial-light mechanism. We made a few hundred of them, but most went to the Hideout, of course. You see"—he turned and wiped his blackened hands upon his handkerchief—"you take the pithy core of coarse water reeds, dry them thoroughly and soak them in animal grease. Then you set fire to it and the grease burns, little by little. These torches will burn for almost half an hour without stopping. Ingenious, isn't it? It was developed by one of our own young men at Saro University."

After the momentary sensation, the dome had quieted. Latimer had carried his chair directly beneath a torch and continued reading, lips moving in the monotonous recital of invocations to the Stars. Beenay had drifted away to his cameras once more, and Theremon seized the opportunity to add to his notes on the article he was going to write for the Saro City *Chronicle* the next day—a procedure he had been following for the last two hours in a perfectly methodical, perfectly conscientious and, as he was well aware, perfectly meaningless fashion.

But, as the gleam of amusement in Sheerin's eyes indicated, careful note taking occupied his mind with something other than the fact that the sky was gradually turning a horrible deep purple-red, as if it were one gigantic, freshly peeled beet; and so it fulfilled its purpose.

The air grew, somehow, denser. Dusk, like a palpable entity, entered the room, and the dancing circle of yellow light about the torches etched itself into ever-sharper distinction against the gathering grayness beyond. There was the odor of smoke and the presence of little chuckling sounds that the torches made as they burned; the soft pad of one of the men circling the table at which he worked, on hesitant tiptoes; the occasional indrawn breath of someone trying to retain composure in a world that was retreating into the shadow.

It was Theremon who first heard the extraneous noise. It was a vague, unorganized *impression* of sound that would have gone unnoticed but for the dead silence that prevailed within the dome.

The newsman sat upright and replaced his notebook. He held his breath and listened; then, with considerable reluctance, threaded his way between the solaroscope and one of Beenay's cameras and stood before the window.

The silence ripped to fragments at his startled shout:
"Sheerin!"

Work stopped! The psychologist was at his side in a moment. Aton joined him. Even Yimot 70, high in his little lean-back seat at the eyepiece of the gigantic solaroscope, paused and looked downward.

Outside, Beta was a mere smoldering splinter, taking one last desperate look at Lagash. The eastern horizon, in the direction of the city, was lost in Darkness, and the road from Saro to the Observatory was a dull-red line bordered on both sides by wooded tracts, the trees of which had somehow lost individuality and merged into a continuous shadowy mass.

But it was the highway itself that held attention, for along it there surged another, and infinitely menacing, shadowy mass.

Aton cried in a cracked voice, "The madmen from the city! They've come!"

"How long to totality?" demanded Sheerin.

"Fifteen minutes, but . . . but they'll be here in five."

"Never mind, keep the men working. We'll hold them off. This place is built like a fortress. Aton, keep an eye on our young Cultist just for luck. Theremon, come with me."

Sheerin was out the door, and Theremon was at his heels. The stairs stretched below them in tight, circular sweeps about the central shaft, fading into a dank and dreary grayness.

The first momentum of their rush had carried them fifty feet down, so that the dim, flickering yellow from the open door of the dome had disappeared and both up above and down below the same dusky shadow crushed in upon them.

Sheerin paused, and his pudgy hand clutched at his chest. His eyes bulged and his voice was a dry cough. "I can't . . . breathe . . . go down . . . yourself. Close all doors—"

Theremon took a few downward steps, then turned. "Wait! Can you hold out a minute?" He was panting himself. The air passed in and out his lungs like so much molasses, and there was a little germ of screeching panic in his mind at the thought of making his way into the mysterious Darkness below by himself.

Theremon, after all, was afraid of the dark!

"Stay here," he said. "I'll be back in a second." He dashed upward two steps at a time, heart pounding—not altogether from the exertion—tumbled into the dome and snatched a torch from its holder. It was foul smelling, and the smoke smarted his eyes almost blind, but he clutched that torch as if he wanted to kiss it for joy, and its flame streamed backward as he hurtled down the stairs again.

Sheerin opened his eyes and moaned as Theremon bent over him. Theremon shook him roughly. "All right, get a hold on yourself. We've got light."

He held the torch at tiptoe height and, propping the tottering psychologist by an elbow, made his way downward in the middle of the protecting circle of illumination.

The offices on the ground floor still possessed what light there was, and Theremon felt the horror about him relax.

"Here," he said brusquely, and passed the torch to Sheerin. "You can hear *them* outside."

And they could. Little scraps of hoarse, wordless shouts.

But Sheerin was right; the Observatory *was* built like a fortress. Erected in the last century, when the neo-Gavottian style of architecture was at its ugly height, it had been designed for stability and durability, rather than for beauty.

The windows were protected by the grillework of inch-thick iron bars sunk deep into the concrete sills. The walls were solid masonry that an earthquake couldn't have touched, and the main door was a huge oaken slab reinforced with iron at the strategic points. Theremon shot the bolts and they slid shut with a dull clang.

At the other end of the corridor, Sheerin cursed weakly. He pointed to the lock of the back door which had been neatly jimmied into uselessness.

"That must be how Latimer got in," he said.

"Well, don't stand there," cried Theremon impatiently. "Help drag up the furniture—and keep that torch out of my eyes. The smoke's killing me."

He slammed the heavy table up against the door as he spoke, and in two minutes had built a barricade which made up for what it lacked in beauty and symmetry by the sheer inertia of its massiveness.

Somewhere, dimly, far off, they could hear the battering of naked fists upon the door; and the screams and yells from outside had a sort of half reality.

That mob had set off from Saro City with only two things in mind: the attainment of Cultist salvation by the destruction of the Observatory, and a maddening fear that all but paralyzed them. There was no time to think of ground cars, or of weapons, or of leadership, or even of organization. They made for the Observatory on foot and assaulted it with bare hands.

And now that they were there, the last flash of Beta, the last ruby-red drop of flame, flickered feebly over a humanity that had left only stark, universal fear!

Theremon groaned, "Let's get back to the dome!"

In the dome, only Yimot, at the solaroscope, had kept his place. The rest were clustered about the cameras, and Beenay was giving his instructions in a hoarse, strained voice.

"Get it straight, all of you. I'm snapping Beta just before totality and changing the plate. That will leave one of you to each camera. You all know about . . . about times of exposure—"

There was a breathless murmur of agreement.

Beenay passed a hand over his eyes. "Are the torches still burning? Never mind, I see them!" He was leaning hard against the back of a chair. "Now remember, don't . . . don't try to look for good shots. Don't waste time trying to get t-two stars at a time in the scope field. One is enough. And . . . and if you feel yourself going, *get away from the camera.*"

At the door, Sheerin whispered to Theremon, "Take me to Aton. I don't see him."

The newsman did not answer immediately. The vague forms of the astronomers wavered and blurred, and the torches overhead had become only yellow spotches.

"It's dark," he whimpered.

Sheerin held out his hand. "Aton." He stumbled forward. "Aton!"

Theremon stepped after and seized his arm. "Wait, I'll take you." Somehow he made his way across the room. He closed his eyes against the Darkness and his mind against the chaos within it.

No one heard them or paid attention to them. Sheerin stumbled against the wall. "Aton!"

The psychologist felt shaking hands touching him, then withdrawing, and a voice muttering, "Is that you, Sheerin?"

"Aton!" He strove to breathe normally. "Don't worry about the mob. The place will hold them off."

Latimer, the Cultist, rose to his feet, and his face twisted in desperation. His word was pledged, and to break it would mean placing his soul in mortal peril. Yet that word had been forced from him and had not been given freely. The Stars would come soon; he could not stand by and allow— And yet his word was pledged.

Beenay's face was dimly flushed as it looked upward at Beta's last ray, and Latimer, seeing him bend over his camera, made his decision. His nails cut the flesh of his palms as he tensed himself.

He staggered crazily as he started his rush. There was nothing before him but shadows; the very floor beneath his feet lacked substance. And then someone was upon him and he went down with clutching fingers at his throat.

He doubled his knee and drove it hard into his assailant. "Let me up or I'll kill you."

Theremon cried out sharply and muttered through a blinding haze of pain, "You double-crossing rat!"

The newsman seemed conscious of everything at once. He heard Beenay croak, "I've got it. At your cameras, men!" and then there was the strange awareness that the last thread of sunlight had thinned out and snapped.

Simultaneously he heard one last choking gasp from Beenay, and a queer little cry from Sheerin, a hysterical giggle that cut off in a rasp—and a sudden silence, a strange, deadly silence from outside.

And Latimer had gone limp in his loosening grasp. Theremon peered into the Cultist's eyes and saw the blankness of them, staring upward, mirroring the feeble yellow of the torches. He saw the bubble of froth upon Latimer's lips and heard the low animal whimper in Latimer's throat.

With the slow fascination of fear, he lifted himself on one arm and turned his eyes toward the blood-curdling blackness of the window.

Through it shone the Stars!

Not Earth's feeble thirty-six hundred Stars visible to the eye—Lagash was in the center of a giant cluster. Thirty thousand mighty suns shone down in a soul-searing splendor that was more frighteningly cold in its awful indifference than the bitter wind that shivered across the cold, horribly bleak world.

Theremon staggered to his feet, his throat constricting him to breathlessness, all the muscles of his body writhing in a tensity of terror and sheer fear beyond bearing. He was going mad, and knew it, and somewhere deep inside a bit of sanity was screaming, struggling to fight off the hopeless flood of black terror. It was very horrible to go mad and know that you were going mad —to know that in a little minute you would be here physically and yet all the real essence would be dead and drowned in the black madness. For this was the Dark—the Dark and the Cold and the Doom. The bright walls of the universe were shattered and their awful black fragments were falling down to crush and squeeze and obliterate him.

He jostled someone crawling on hands and knees, but stumbled somehow over him. Hands groping at his tortured throat, he limped toward the flame of the torches that filled all his mad vision.

"Light!" he screamed.

Aton, somewhere, was crying, whimpering horribly like a terribly frightened child. "Stars—all the Stars—we didn't know at all. We didn't know anything. We thought six stars in a universe is something the Stars didn't notice is Darkness forever and ever and ever and the walls are breaking in and we didn't know we couldn't know and anything—"

Someone clawed at the torch, and it fell and snuffed out. In the instant, the awful splendor of the indifferent Stars leaped nearer to them.

On the horizon outside the window, in the direction of Saro City, a crimson glow began growing, strengthening in brightness, that was not the glow of a sun.

The long night had come again.

BY HIS BOOTSTRAPS

Robert A. Heinlein

It would be impossible to limit Robert A. Heinlein's representation in this book to one story. He dominated science fiction in the early forties, writing so well and so prolifically that at the beginning of 1941 he adopted the pen name "Anson MacDonald" for many of his stories in *Astounding*. Between the February and October issues, he had two stories in the same issue five times; he even took a third name, "Caleb Saunders," for one of them.

By the time "By His Bootstraps" appeared, even John Campbell had become confused. He'd announced it as by Heinlein, but when he published it in the October issue the byline was MacDonald. (The name was derived from Heinlein's middle name and the maiden name of his wife at the time, Leslyn McDonald.)

In all, Heinlein's contributions to *Astounding* during 1941 totaled 20 per cent or more of the wordage in the magazine. But it was a situation that was not to continue, for when the United States entered World War II at the end of the year, Heinlein joined the war effort.

"A former shipmate of mine, [later Rear Admiral] A. B. Scoles, was then engaged in aviation research and development . . . he sent for me, put me in charge of a high-altitude laboratory of which one of the projects was the development of a space suit (then called a high-altitude pressure suit)." Heinlein arranged to hire L. Sprague de Camp and Isaac Asimov, and for three and a half years the three worked together, "fighting the Axis with slide rule and requisition forms in quintuplicate," as de Camp has described it.

Heinlein did no science fiction writing during this time, but after the war he wrote *Rocket Ship Galileo,* the first of his enormously popular juvenile sf novels, in which he described space suits similar to those on which he and de Camp had worked at the Philadelphia Navy Yard. The story was adapted into the movie *Destination Moon,* with Heinlein as technical adviser, and he sent for a photo of one of the space suits developed during that project; it was copied as closely as possible for the movie. (The actual space suits used by modern astronauts aren't greatly different.)

But in "By His Bootstraps" Heinlein concerned himself with time travel rather than trips into space, producing one of the classic stories of time paradoxes. In fact, it so thoroughly explored the idea of a man coming back in time to meet himself that it delayed the career of William Tenn for nearly five years. Tenn had just written a story called "Me, Myself and I" when "By His Bootstraps" appeared; Tenn read it with a sinking feeling, realizing that Heinlein had beaten him to the punch, and he didn't submit his story. It wasn't until Tenn had sold his first story to *Astounding* in 1946 that he was encouraged enough to dig out "Me, Myself and I" and sell it to *Planet Stories* under the pen name "Kenneth Putnam." ("William Tenn" is also a pen name—his real name is Philip Klass—but never mind.)

Heinlein also made a small breakthrough when he included in "By His Bootstraps" a scene in which Bob Wilson visited his girlfriend for over an hour and came away "wearing the expression of the canary that ate the cat." This was about as close to an explicit sex scene as any writer was allowed to come in the science fiction magazines of 1941, especially since it was preceded by a one-line space, the equivalent of those old movie scenes in which the camera panned from two people kissing to a blazing fireplace.

Pulp magazines had always avoided explicit sex scenes, because of the stringent censorship laws of the time. Even under-the-counter magazines such as *Spicy Adventure,* which had begun during the 1930s, resorted to such fadeouts. ("An hour later a door opened into a narrow alley in the rear of Woon Yuen's antique shop, and Arline was thrust roughly out, her breasts almost bare, her dress ripped to shreds." Robert E. Howard wrote that under a pen name.)

But the science fiction magazines were the most puritanical of all, for their readership consisted mostly of teenagers. Moreover, these young readers dreamed of higher things than lust—they sought heroic adventures among the stars and in the far reaches of the future. As Charles Hornig, then editor of *Science Fiction* and *Future Fiction* (and just twenty-three years old), put it in 1940:

> In order for a story to be true-to-life, it must take into account that people are human and fall in love, even though they may be great scientists. . . . Many times it is necessary to have clinches in order to make the characters appear real, but there is no need to go further than the surface of their love-lives. The love (or "sex") interest in science-fiction stories should be wholesome and ideal—nothing lewd. . . . Good science-fiction stories tend to place the fan on a higher mental plane, a psychic condition that broadens his horizons . . . *Now:* the sex-mood does just the opposite. It . . . spoils the illusion of glorious psychic expansion, and, in fact, reduces the reader to a lustful, very down-to-earth personality.

Henry Kuttner, in an article titled "Eunuchs in the Pulps" later the same year, disagreed, though his argument was couched in similarly high moral terms:

> The typical criminal pervert is outwardly extremely moral. Any form of sex is anathema to him; normal emotional life is warped and suppressed rigidly. Eventually the dam bursts and the newspapers have another sensational headline. Sanity, common sense and health make their own rules, which may not be broken. The characters in science fiction are, as a rule, potential rapists. . . .
> Pornography is unnecessary. Human beings are vital. But we shall have no human beings in science fiction till readers outgrow their opinionated adolescence and become more adult and sophisticated in outlook. [Kuttner was twenty-six.]

One science fiction magazine had tried in 1938 to inject sex into its stories, but not for the purpose of sophisticated characterization. The first two issues of *Marvel Science Stories* featured several stories in which the author, on editorial demand, had inserted lurid sexual passages. The stories brought a storm of protest and *Marvel* quickly switched to straight science fiction. (Ironically, the author involved was Henry Kuttner, though he hid the worst of these stories under pen names.)

But a year later the publishers decided to try the experiment again, no doubt because they had been successful in combining sex with weird fiction in *Mystery Tales* and *Uncanny Tales*. They changed the title of their science fiction magazine to *Marvel Tales* and published two issues whose sexual content was heavy, not to mention appalling.

One example will suffice: "Mistress of Machine-Age Madness" by Nils O. Sonderlund. The story began, "Shrieking with terror, and quite aware of her complete nudity, Ann Tancred appeared in a second-story window. The weird greenish glare of the laboratory conflagration spotlighted the full roundness of her young breasts."

Thereafter, Ann Tancred was repeatedly subjected to torture with a whip wielded by the villainous laboratory assistant who had murdered her scientist-father: "Then, naked, she stood up to wait for the whip. Craig heard the cruel hissing of it, and the vicious cracks. He saw red marks spring across the firm upturned breasts of the girl, her smooth white back, and the gleaming columns of her thighs."

Hero and heroine were forced to accompany the villain on an exploration of the depths of the Earth; they found an underworld cavern and hideous monsters, eventually escaping when the monsters destroyed the villain. But even their escape, which should have led to a completely happy ending when Ann revealed that she had hidden several priceless "red pearls" in her hair, was perverted by this final touch:

" 'I'll forgive you, this time,' whispered Craig. 'But, any more deceit—'

"She shuddered deliciously."

The only cheering thing about *Marvel* is the fact that it was a complete failure. Its sadistic-sex policy was again abandoned, but even after its return to ordinary science fiction the magazine lasted only two issues before dying. Whether Hornig was right in saying that sex undermined the appeal of science fiction, or Kuttner in his contention that sf readers were too adolescent, it's clear that there was no market for sexual sadism in science fiction's Golden Age.

"By His Bootstraps" indulged in none of *Marvel*'s sexual bullying, of course (though one has to wonder about the scantily clad maidservants who were "slaves by nature"); sex was no more than implied in it, and the emphasis throughout was on the fascinating

intellectual puzzle of a man meeting himself . . . and meeting himself
. . . and meeting himself . . .

What sexual pleasures could compare? (On paper, at least.)

REFERENCES:

Heinlein in Dimension by Alexei Panshin. Advent:Publishers, 1968.
"In Times to Come" by John W. Campbell, Jr. *Astounding Science-Fiction,*
August 1941.
"Robert A. Heinlein" by Isaac Asimov. *MidAmeriCon Program Book,* 1976.
"Science Fiction: Its Nature, Faults and Virtues" by Robert A. Heinlein. *The
Science Fiction Novel.* Advent:Publishers, 1959.
"You Can't Beat Brains" by L. Sprague de Camp. *Fantasy and Science
Fiction,* October 1966.
"Shooting 'Destination Moon' " by Robert A. Heinlein. *Astounding Science
Fiction,* July 1950.
Conversation with Philip Klass, January 1, 1975.
The Pulps by Tony Goodstone. Bonanza Books, 1970.
"The Purple Heart of Erlik" by "Sam Walser" (Robert E. Howard). *Spicy
Adventure,* 1936.
The Encyclopedia of Science Fiction and Fantasy, Vol. 1 by Donald H. Tuck.
Advent:Publishers, 1974.
"Sex in Science Fiction" by Charles Hornig. *Stardust,* March 1940.
"Eunuchs in the Pulps" by Henry Kuttner. *Sweetness and Light,* Winter
1940.
"The Secret Lives of Henry Kuttner" by Sam Moskowitz. *Amazing Stories,*
October 1962.
The Shudder Pulps by Robert Kenneth Jones. FAX Collector's Editions, 1975.
"Mistress of Machine-Age Madness" by Nils O. Sonderlund. *Marvel Tales,*
May 1940.

* * *

Bob Wilson did not see the circle grow.

Nor, for that matter, did he see the stranger who stepped out
of the circle and stood staring at the back of Wilson's neck—

stared, and breathed heavily, as if laboring under strong and unusual emotion.

Wilson had no reason to suspect that anyone else was in his room; he had every reason to expect the contrary. He had locked himself in his room for the purpose of completing his thesis in one sustained drive. He *had* to—tomorrow was the last day for submission, yesterday the thesis had been no more than a title: "An Investigation into Certain Mathematical Aspects of a Rigor of Metaphysics."

Fifty-two cigarettes, four pots of coffee, and thirteen hours of continuous work had added seven thousand words to the title. As to the validity of his thesis he was far too groggy to give a damn. Get it done, was his only thought, get it done, turn it in, take three stiff drinks and sleep for a week.

He glanced up and let his eyes rest on his wardrobe door, behind which he had cached a gin bottle, nearly full. No, he admonished himself, one more drink and you'll never finish it, Bob, old son.

The stranger behind him said nothing.

Wilson resumed typing. "—nor is it valid to assume that a conceivable proposition is necessarily a possible proposition, even when it is possible to formulate mathematics which describes the proposition with exactness. A case in point is the concept "Time Travel.' Time travel may be imagined and its necessities may be formulated under any and all theories of time, formulae which resolve the paradoxes of each theory. Nevertheless, we know certain things about the empirical nature of time which preclude the possibility of the conceivable proposition. Duration is an attribute of consciousness and not of the plenum. It has no *ding an sicht*. Therefore—"

A key of the typewriter stuck, three more jammed up on top of it. Wilson swore dully and reached forward to straighten out the cantankerous machinery. "Don't bother with it," he heard a voice say. "It's a lot of utter hogwash anyhow."

Wilson sat up with a jerk, then turned his head slowly around.

He fervently hoped that there was someone behind him. Otherwise—

He perceived the stranger with relief. "Thank God," he said to himself. "For a moment I thought I had come unstuck." His relief turned to extreme annoyance. "What the devil are you doing in my room?" he demanded. He shoved back his chair, got up and strode over to the one door. It was still locked, and bolted on the inside.

The windows were no help; they were adjacent to his desk and three stories above a busy street. "How *did* you get in?" he added.

"Through that," answered the stranger, hooking a thumb toward the circle. Wilson noticed it for the first time, blinked his eyes and looked again. There it hung between them and the wall, a great disk of nothing, of the color one sees when the eyes are shut tight.

Wilson shook his head vigorously. The circle remained. "Gosh," he thought, "I was right the first time. I wonder when I slipped my trolley?" He advanced toward the disk, put out a hand to touch it.

"Don't!" snapped the stranger.

"Why not?" said Wilson edgily. Nevertheless he paused.

"I'll explain. But let's have a drink first." He walked directly to the wardrobe, opened it, reached in and took out the bottle of gin without looking.

"Hey!" yelled Wilson. "What are you doing there? That's *my* liquor."

"*Your* liquor—" The stranger paused for a moment. "Sorry. You don't mind if I have a drink, do you?"

"I suppose not," Bob Wilson conceded in a surly tone. "Pour me one while you're about it."

"O. K.," agreed the stranger, "then I'll explain."

"It had better be good," Wilson said ominously. Nevertheless he drank his drink and looked the stranger over.

He saw a chap about the same size as himself and much the same age—perhaps a little older, though a three-day growth of beard may have accounted for that impression. The stranger had a black eye and a freshly cut and badly swollen upper lip. Wilson decided he did not like the chap's face. Still, there was something familiar about the face; he felt that he should have recognized it, that he had seen it many times before under different circumstances.

"Who are you?" he asked suddenly.

"Me?" said his guest. "Don't you recognize me?"

"I'm not sure," admitted Wilson. "Have I ever seen you before?"

"Well—not exactly," the other temporized. "Skip it—you wouldn't know about it."

"What's your name?"

"My name? Uh . . . just call me Joe."

Wilson set down his glass. "O. K., Joe Whatever-your-name-is, trot out that explanation and make it snappy."

"I'll do that," agreed Joe. "That dingus I came through"—he pointed to the circle—"that's a Time Gate."

"A what?"

"A Time Gate. Time flows along side by side on each side of the Gate, but some thousands of years apart—just how many thousands I don't know. But for the next couple of hours that Gate is open. You can walk into the future just by stepping through that circle." The stranger paused.

Bob drummed on the desk. "Go ahead. I'm listening. It's a nice story."

"You don't believe me, do you? I'll show you." Joe got up, went again to the wardrobe and obtained Bob's hat, his prized and only hat, which he had mistreated into its present battered grandeur through six years of undergraduate and graduate life. Joe chucked it toward the impalpable disk.

It struck the surface, went on through with no apparent resistance, disappeared from sight.

Wilson got up, walked carefully around the circle and examined the bare floor. "A neat trick," he conceded. "Now I'll thank you to return to me my hat."

The stranger shook his head. "You can get it for yourself when you pass through."

"Huh?"

"That's right. Listen—" Briefly the stranger repeated his explanation about the Time Gate. Wilson, he insisted, had an opportunity that comes once in a millennium—if he would only hurry up and climb through that circle. Furthermore, though Joe could not explain in detail at the moment, it was very important that Wilson go through.

Bob Wilson helped himself to a second drink, and then a third. He was beginning to feel both good and argumentative. "Why?" he said flatly.

Joe looked exasperated. "Dammit, if you'd just step through once, explanations wouldn't be necessary. However—" According to Joe, there was an old guy on the other side who needed Wilson's help. With Wilson's help the three of them would run the country. The exact nature of the help Joe could not or would not specify. Instead he bore down on the unique possibilities for high adventure. "You don't want to slave your life away teaching numskulls in some fresh-water college," he insisted. "This is your chance. Grab it!"

Bob Wilson admitted to himself that a Ph.D. and an appointment as an instructor was not his ideal of existence. Still, it beat working for a living. His eye fell on the gin bottle, its level now deplorably lowered. That explained it. He got up unsteadily.

"No, my dear fellow," he stated, "I'm not going to climb on your merry-go-round. You know why?"

"Why?"

"Because I'm drunk, that's why. You're not there at all. *That* ain't there." He gestured widely at the circle. "There ain't anybody here but me, and I'm drunk. Been working too hard," he added apologetically. "I'm goin' to bed."

"You're not drunk."

"I *am* drunk. Peter Piper pepped a pick of pippered peckles." He moved toward his bed.

Joe grabbed his arm. "You can't do that," he said.

"Let him alone!"

They both swung around. Facing them, standing directly in front of the circle was a third man. Bob looked at the newcomer, looked back at Joe, blinked his eyes and tried to focus them. The two looked a good bit alike, he thought, enough alike to be brothers. Or maybe he was seeing double. Bad stuff, gin. Should 'ave switched to rum a long time ago. Good stuff, rum. You could drink it, or take a bath in it No, that was gin—he meant Joe.

How silly! Joe was the one with the black eye. He wondered why he had ever been confused.

Then who was this other lug? Couldn't a couple of friends have a quiet drink together without people butting in?

"Who are you?" he said with quiet dignity.

The newcomer turned his head, then looked at Joe. *"He* knows me," he said meaningly.

Joe looked him over slowly. "Yes," he said, "yes, I suppose I do. But what the deuce are you here for? And why are you trying to bust up the plan?"

"No time for long-winded explanations. I know more about it than you do—you'll concede that—and my judgment is bound to be better than yours. He doesn't go through the Gate."

"I don't concede anything of the sort—"

The telephone rang.

"Answer it!" snapped the newcomer.

Bob was about to protest the peremptory tone, but decided he wouldn't. He lacked the phlegmatic temperament necessary to ignore a ringing telephone. "Hello?"

"Hello," he was answered. "Is that Bob Wilson?"

"Yes. Who is this?"

"Never mind. I just wanted to be sure you were there. I *thought* you would be. You're right in the groove, kid, right in the groove."

Wilson heard a chuckle, then the click of disconnection. "Hello," he said. "Hello!" He jiggled the bar a couple of times, then hung up.

"What was it?" asked Joe.

"Nothing. Some nut with a misplaced sense of humor." The telephone bell rang again. Wilson added, "There he is again," and picked up the receiver. "Listen, you butterfly-brained ape! I'm a busy man, and this is *not* a public telephone."

"Why, Bob!" came a hurt feminine voice.

"Huh? Oh, it's you, Genevieve. Look—I'm sorry. I apologize—"

"Well, I should think you would!"

"You don't understand, honey. A guy has been pestering me over the phone and I thought it was him. You know I wouldn't talk that way to you, Babe."

"Well, I should think not. Particularly after all you said to me this afternoon, and all we *meant* to each other."

"Huh? This afternoon? Did you say this afternoon?"

"Of course. But what I called up about was this: You left your hat in my apartment. I noticed it a few minutes after you had gone and just thought I'd call and tell you where it is. Anyhow," she added coyly, "it gave me an excuse to hear your voice again."

"Sure. Fine," he said mechanically. "Look, Babe, I'm a little mixed up about this. Trouble I've had all day long, and more trouble now. I'll look you up tonight and straighten it out. But I *know* I didn't leave your hat in my apartment—"

"*Your* hat, silly!"

"Huh? Oh, sure! Anyhow, I'll see you tonight. 'By." He rang off hurriedly. Gosh, he thought, that woman is getting to be a problem. Hallucinations. He turned to his two companions.

"Very well, Joe. I'm ready to go if you are." He was not sure just when or why he had decided to go through the time gadget, but he had. Who did this other mug think he was, anyhow, trying to interfere with a man's freedom of choice?

"Fine!" said Joe, in a relieved voice. "Just step through. That's all there is to it."

"No, you don't!" It was the ubiquitous stranger. He stepped between Wilson and the Gate.

Bob Wilson faced him. "Listen, you! You come butting in here like you think I was a bum. If you don't like it, go jump in the lake—and I'm just the kind of guy who can do it! You and who else?"

The stranger reached out and tried to collar him. Wilson let go a swing, but not a good one. It went by nothing faster than parcel post. The stranger walked under it and let him have a mouthful of knuckles—large, hard ones. Joe closed in rapidly, coming to Bob's aid. They traded punches in a free-for-all, with Bob joining in enthusiastically but inefficiently. The only punch he landed was on Joe, theoretically his ally. However, he had intended it for the third man.

It was this *faux pas* which gave the stranger an opportunity to land a clean left jab on Wilson's face. It was inches higher than the button, but in Bob's bemused condition it was sufficient to cause him to cease taking part in the activities.

Bob Wilson came slowly to awareness of his surroundings. He was seated on a floor which seemed a little unsteady. Someone was bending over him. "Are you all right?" the figure inquired.

"I guess so," he answered thickly. His mouth pained him; he put his hand to it, got it sticky with blood. "My head hurts."

"I should think it would. You came through head over heels. I think you hit your head when you landed."

Wilson's thoughts were coming back into confused focus. Came through? He looked more closely at his succorer. He saw a middle-aged man with gray-shot busy hair and a short, neatly trimmed beard. He was dressed in what Wilson took to be purple lounging pajamas.

But the room in which he found himself bothered him even more. It was circular and the ceiling was arched so subtly that it was difficult to say how high it was. A steady glareless light filled the room from no apparent source. There was no furniture save for a high dais or pulpit-shaped object near the wall facing him. "Came through? Came through what?"

"The Gate, of course." There was something odd about the

man's accent. Wilson could not place it, save for a feeling that English was not a tongue he was accustomed to speaking.

Wilson looked over his shoulder in the direction of the other's gaze, and saw the circle.

That made his head ache even more. "Oh Lord," he thought, "now I really am nuts. Why don't I wake up?" He shook his head to clear it.

That was a mistake. The top of his head did not quite come off—not quite. And the circle stayed where it was, a simple locus hanging in the air, its flat depth filled with the amorphous colors and shapes of no-vision. "Did I come through that?"

"Yes."

"Where am I?"

"In the Hall of the Gate in the High Palace of Norkaal. But what is more important is *when* you are. You have gone forward a little more than thirty thousand years."

"Now I know I'm crazy," thought Wilson. He got up unsteadily and moved toward the Gate.

The older man put a hand on his shoulder. "Where are you going?"

"Back!"

"Not so fast. You will go back all right—I give you my word on that. But let me dress your wounds first. And you should rest. I have some explanations to make to you, and there is an errand you can do for me when you get back—to our mutual advantage. There is a great future in store for you and me, my boy —a great future!"

Wilson paused uncertainly. The elder man's insistence was vaguely disquieting. "I don't like this."

The other eyed him narrowly. "Wouldn't you like a drink before you go?"

Wilson most assuredly would. Right at the moment a stiff drink seemed the most desirable thing on earth—or in time. "O. K."

"Come with me." The older man led him back of the structure near the wall and through a door which led into a passageway. He walked briskly; Wilson hurried to keep up.

"By the way," he asked, as they continued down the long passage, "what is your name?"

"My name? You may call me Diktor—everyone else does."

"O. K., Diktor. Do you want my name?"

"Your name?" Diktor chuckled. "I know your name. It's Bob Wilson."

"Huh? Oh—I suppose Joe told you."

"Joe? I know no one by that name."

"You don't? He seemed to know you. Say—maybe you aren't the guy I was supposed to see."

"But I am. I have been expecting you—in a way, Joe . . . Joe —Oh!" Diktor chuckled. "It had slipped my mind for a moment. He told you to call him Joe, didn't he?"

"Isn't it his name?"

"It's as good a name as any other. Here we are." He ushered Wilson into a small, but cheerful, room. It contained no furniture of any sort, but the floor was soft and warm as live flesh. "Sit down. I'll be back in a moment."

Bob looked around for something to sit on, then turned to ask Diktor for a chair. But Diktor was gone, furthermore the door through which they had entered was gone. Bob sat down on the comfortable floor and tried not to worry.

Diktor returned promptly. Wilson saw the door dilate to let him in, but did not catch on to how it was done. Diktor was carrying a carafe, which gurgled pleasantly, and a cup. "Mud in your eye," he said heartily and poured a good four fingers. "Drink up."

Bob accepted the cup. "Aren't you drinking?"

"Presently. I want to attend to your wounds first."

"O. K." Wilson tossed off the first drink in almost indecent haste—it was good stuff, a little like Scotch, he decided, but smoother and not as dry—while Diktor worked deftly with salves that smarted at first, then soothed. "Mind if I have another?"

"Help yourself."

Bob drank more slowly the second cup. He did not finish it; it slipped from relaxed fingers, spilling a ruddy, brown stain across the floor. He snored.

Bob Wilson woke up feeling fine and completely rested. He was cheerful without knowing why. He lay relaxed, eyes still closed, for a few moments and let his soul snuggle back into his body. This was going to be a good day, he felt. Oh, yes—he had finished that double-damned thesis. No, he hadn't either! He sat up with a start.

The sight of the strange walls around him brought him back into continuity. But before he had time to worry—at once, in fact—the door relaxed and Diktor stepped in. "Feeling better?"

"Why, yes, I do. Say, what is this?"

"We'll get to that. How about some breakfast?"

In Wilson's scale of evaluations breakfast rated just after life itself and ahead of the chance of immortality. Diktor conducted him to another room—the first that he had seen possessing windows. As a matter of fact half the room was open, a balcony hanging high over a green countryside. A soft, warm, summer breeze wafted through the place. They broke their fast in luxury, Roman style, while Diktor explained.

Bob Wilson did not follow the explanations as closely as he might have done, because his attention was diverted by the maidservants who served the meal. The first came in bearing a great tray of fruit on her head. The fruit was gorgeous. So was the girl. Search as he would he could discern no fault in her.

Her costume lent itself to the search.

She came first to Diktor, and with a single, graceful movement dropped to one knee, removed the tray from her head, and offered it to him. He helped himself to a small, red fruit and waved her away. She then offered it to Bob in the same delightful manner.

"As I was saying," continued Diktor, "it is not certain where the High Ones came from or where they went when they left Earth. I am inclined to think they went away into Time. In any case they ruled more than twenty thousand years and completely obliterated human culture as you knew it. What is more important to you and to me is the effect they had on the human psyche. One twentieth-century-style go-getter can accomplish just about anything he wants to accomplish around here—Aren't you listening?"

"Huh? Oh, yes, sure. Say, that's one mighty pretty girl." His eyes still rested on the exit through which she had disappeared.

"Who? Oh, yes, I suppose so. She's not exceptionally beautiful as women go around here."

"That's hard to believe. I could learn to get along with a girl like that."

"You like her? Very well, she is yours."

"Huh?"

"She's a slave. Don't get indignant. They are slaves by nature. If you like her, I'll make you a present of her. It will make her happy." The girl had just returned. Diktor called to her in a language strange to Bob. "Her name is Arma," he said in an aside, then spoke to her briefly.

Arma giggled. She composed her face quickly, and, moving over to where Wilson reclined, dropped on both knees to the floor and lowered her head, with both hands cupped before her. "Touch her forehead," Diktor instructed.

Bob did so. The girl arose and stood waiting placidly by his side. Diktor spoke to her. She looked puzzled, but moved out of the room. "I told her that, notwithstanding her new status, you wished her to continue serving breakfast."

Diktor resumed his explanations while the service of the meal continued. The next course was brought in by Arma and another girl. When Bob saw the second girl he let out a low whistle. He realized he had been a little hasty in letting Diktor give him Arma. Either the standard of pulchritude had gone up incredibly, he decided, or Diktor went to a lot of trouble in selecting his servants.

"—for that reason," Diktor was saying, "it is necessary that you go back through the Time Gate at once. Your first job is to bring this other chap back. Then there is one other task for you to do, and we'll be sitting pretty. After that it is share and share alike for you and me. And there is plenty to share, I—You aren't listening!"

"Sure I was, chief. I heard every word you said." He fingered his chin. "Say, have you got a razor I could borrow? I'd like to shave."

Diktor swore softly in two languages. "Keep your eyes off those wenches and listen to me! There's work to be done."

"Sure, sure. I understand that—and I'm your man. When do we start?" Wilson had made up his mind some time ago—just shortly after Arma had entered with the tray of fruit, in fact. He felt as if he had walked into some extremely pleasant dream. If co-operation with Diktor would cause that dream to continue, so be it. To hell with an academic career!

Anyhow, all Diktor wanted was for him to go back where he started and persuade another guy to go through the Gate. The worst that could happen was for him to find himself back in the twentieth century. What could he lose?

Diktor stood up. "Let's get on with it," he said shortly, "before you get your attention diverted again. Follow me." He set off at a brisk pace with Wilson behind him.

Diktor took him to the Hall of the Gate and stopped. "All you have to do," he said, "is to step through the Gate. You will find yourself back in your own room, in your own time. Persuade the man you find there to go through the Gate. We have need of him. Then come back yourself."

Bob held up a hand and pinched thumb and forefinger together. "It's in the bag, boss. Consider it done." He started to step through the Gate.

"Wait!" commanded Diktor. "You are not used to time travel. I warn you that you are going to get one hell of a shock when you step through. This other chap—you'll recognize him."

"Who is he?"

"I won't tell you because you wouldn't understand. But you will when you see him. Just remember this—There are some very strange paradoxes connected with time travel. Don't let anything you see throw you. You do what I tell you to and you'll be all right."

"Paradoxes don't worry me," Bob said confidently. "Is that all? I'm ready."

"One minute." Diktor stepped behind the raised dais. His head appeared above the side a moment later. "I've set the controls. O. K. Go!"

Bob Wilson stepped through the locus known as the Time Gate.

There was no particular sensation connected with the transition. It was like stepping through a curtained doorway into a darker room. He paused for a moment on the other side and let his eyes adjust to the dimmer light. He was, he saw, indeed in his own room.

There was a man in it, seated at his own desk. Diktor had been right about that. This, then, was the chap he was to send back through the Gate. Diktor had said he would recognize him. Well, let's see who it is.

He felt a passing resentment at finding someone at *his* desk in *his* room, then thought better of it. After all, it was just a rented room; when he disappeared, no doubt it had been rented again. He had no way of telling how long he had been gone—shucks, it might be the middle of next week!

The chap did look vaguely familiar, although all he could see was his back. Who was it? Should he speak to him, cause him to turn around? He felt vaguely reluctant to do so until he knew who it was. He rationalized the feeling by telling himself that it was desirable to know with whom he was dealing before he attempted anything as outlandish as persuading this man to go through the Gate.

The man at the desk continued typing, paused to snuff out a cigarette by laying it in an ash tray, then stamping it with a paper weight.

Bob Wilson knew that gesture.

Chills trickled down his back. "If he lights his next one," he whispered to himself, "the way I think he is going to—"

The man at the desk took out another cigarette, tamped it on one end, turned it and tamped the other, straightened and crimped the paper on one end carefully against his left thumb-nail and placed that end in his mouth.

Wilson felt the blood beating in his neck. *Sitting there with his back to him was himself, Bob Wilson!*

He felt that he was going to faint. He closed his eyes and steadied himself on a chair back. "I knew it," he thought, "the whole thing is absurd. I'm crazy. I know I'm crazy. Some sort of split personality. I shouldn't have worked so hard."

The sound of typing continued.

He pulled himself together, and reconsidered the matter. Diktor had warned him that he was due for a shock, a shock that could not be explained ahead of time, because it could not be believed. "All right—suppose I'm not crazy. If time travel can happen at all, there is no reason why I can't come back and see myself doing something I did in the past. If I'm sane, that is what I'm doing.

"And if I am crazy, it doesn't make a damn bit of difference what I do!

"And furthermore," he added to himself, "if I'm crazy, maybe I can stay crazy and go back through the Gate! No, that does not make sense. Neither does anything else—the hell with it!"

He crept forward softly and peered over the shoulder of his double. "Duration is an attribute of the consciousness," he read, "and not of the plenum."

"That tears it," he thought, "right back where I started, and watching myself write my thesis."

The typing continued. "It has no *ding an sicht.* Therefore—" A key stuck, and others piled up on top of it. His double at the desk swore and reached out a hand to straighten the keys.

"Don't bother with it," Wilson said on sudden impulse. "It's a lot of utter hogwash anyhow."

The other Bob Wilson sat up with a jerk, then looked slowly around. An expression of surprise gave way to annoyance. "What the devil are you doing in my room?" he demanded. Without waiting for an answer he got up, went quickly to the door and examined the lock. "How did you get in?".

"This," thought Wilson, "is going to be difficult."

"Through that," Wilson answered, pointing to the Time Gate. His double looked where he had pointed, did a double take, then advanced cautiously and started to touch it.

"Don't!" yelled Wilson.

The other checked himself. "Why not?" he demanded.

Just why he must not permit his other self to touch the Gate was not clear to Wilson, but he had had an unmistakable feeling of impending disaster when he saw it about to happen. He temporized by saying, "I'll explain. But let's have a drink." A drink was a good idea in any case. There had never been a time when he needed one more than he did right now. Quite automatically he went to his usual cache of liquor in the wardrobe and took out the bottle he expected to find there.

"Hey!" protested the other. "What are you doing there? That's *my* liquor."

"*Your* liquor—" Hell's bells! It was *his* liquor. No, it wasn't; it was—*their* liquor. Oh, the devil! It was much too mixed up to try to explain. "Sorry. You don't mind if I have a drink, do you?"

"I suppose not," his double said grudgingly. "Pour me one while you're about it."

"O. K.," Wilson assented, "then I'll explain." It was going to be much, much too difficult to explain until he had had a drink, he felt. As it was, he couldn't explain it fully to himself.

"It had better be good," the other warned him, and looked Wilson over carefully while he drank his drink.

Wilson watched his younger self scrutinizing him with confused and almost insupportable emotions. Couldn't the stupid fool recognize his own face when he saw it in front of him? If he could not *see* what the situation was, how in the world was he ever going to make it clear to him?

It had slipped his mind that his face was barely recognizable in any case, being decidedly battered and unshaven. Even more important, he failed to take into account the fact that a person does not look at his own face, even in mirrors, in the same frame of mind with which he regards another's face. No sane person ever expects to see his own face hanging on another.

Wilson could see that his companion was puzzled by his appearance, but it was equally clear that no recognition took place. "Who are you?" the other man asked suddenly.

"Me?" replied Wilson. "Don't you recognize me?"

"I'm not sure. Have I ever seen you before?"

"Well—not exactly," Wilson stalled. How did you go about telling another guy that the two of you were a trifle closer than twins? "Skip it—you wouldn't know about it."

"What's your name?"

"My name? Uh—" Oh, oh! This was going to be sticky! The whole situation was utterly ridiculous. He opened his mouth, tried to form the words "Bob Wilson," then gave up with a feeling of utter futility. Like many a man before him, he found himself forced into a lie because the truth simply would not be believed. "Just call me Joe," he finished lamely.

He felt suddenly startled at his own words. It was at this point that he realized that he was *in fact* "Joe," the Joe whom he had encountered once before. That he had landed back in his own room at the very time at which he had ceased working on his thesis he already realized, but he had not had time to think the matter through. Hearing himself refer to himself as Joe slapped him in the face with the realization that this was not simply a similar scene, but the *same* scene he had lived through once before—save that he was living through it from a different viewpoint.

At least he thought it was the same scene. Did it differ in any respect? He could not be sure, as he could not recall, word for word, what the conversation had been.

For a complete transcript of the scene that lay dormant in his memory he felt willing to pay twenty-five dollars cash, plus sales tax.

Wait a minute now—he was under no compulsion. He was sure of that. Everything he did and said was the result of his own free will. Even if he couldn't remember the script, there were some things he *knew* "Joe" hadn't said. "Mary had a little lamb," for example. He would recite a nursery rhyme and get off this damned repetitious treadmill. He opened his mouth—

"O. K., Joe Whatever-your-name-is," his alter ego remarked, setting down a glass which had contained, until recently, a quarter pint of gin, "trot out that explanation and make it snappy."

He opened his mouth again to answer the question, then closed it. "Steady, son, steady," he told himself. "You're a free agent. You want to recite a nursery rhyme—go ahead and do it. Don't answer him; go ahead and recite it—and break this vicious circle."

But under the unfriendly, suspicious eye of the man opposite him he found himself totally unable to recall any nursery rhyme. His mental processes stuck on dead center.

He capitulated. "I'll do that. That dingus I came through— that's a Time Gate."

"A what?"

"A Time Gate. Time flows along side by side on each side—" As he talked he felt sweat breaking out on him; he felt reasonably sure that he was explaining in exactly the same words in which the explanation had first been offered to *him*. "—into the future just by stepping through that circle." He stopped and wiped his forehead.

"Go ahead," said the other implacably. "I'm listening. It's a nice story."

Bob suddenly wondered if the other man *could* be himself. The stupid arrogant dogmatism of the man's manner infuriated him. All right, all right! He'd show him. He strode suddenly over to the wardrobe, took out his hat and threw it through the Gate.

His opposite number watched the hat snuff out of existence with expressionless eyes, then stood up and went around in back of the Gate, walking with the careful steps of a man who is a little bit drunk, but determined not to show it. "A neat trick," he applauded, after satisfying himself that the hat was gone, "now I'll thank you to return to me my hat."

Wilson shook his head. "You can get it for yourself when you pass through," he answered absent-mindedly. He was pondering the problem of how many hats there were on the other side of the Gate.

"Huh?"

"That's right. Listen—" Wilson did his best to explain persuasively what it was he wanted his earlier *persona* to do. Or rather to cajole. Explanations were out of the question, in any honest sense of the word. He would have preferred attempting to explain tensor calculus to an Australian aborigine, even though he did not understand that esoteric mathematics himself.

The other man was not helpful. He seemed more interested in nursing the gin than he did in following Wilson's implausible protestations.

"Why?" he interrupted pugnaciously.

"Dammit," Wilson answered, "if you'd just step through once, explanations wouldn't be necessary. However—" He continued with a synopsis of Diktor's proposition. He realized with irritation that Diktor had been exceedingly sketchy with *his* explanations. He was forced to hit only the high spots in the logical parts of his argument, and bear down on the emotional appeal. He was on safe ground there—no one knew better than he did himself how fed up the earlier Bob Wilson had been with the pretty drudgery and stuffy atmosphere of an academic career. "You don't want to slave your life away teaching numskulls in some fresh-water college," he concluded. "This is your chance. Grab it!"

Wilson watched his companion narrowly and thought he detected a favorable response. He definitely seemed interested. But the other set his glass down carefully, stared at the gin bottle, and at last replied:

"My dear fellow, I am not going to climb on your merry-go-round. You know why?"

"Why?"

"Because I'm drunk, that's why. You're not there at all. *That* ain't there." He gestured widely at the Gate, nearly fell, and recovered himself with effort. "There ain't anybody here but me, and I'm drunk. Been working too hard," he mumbled, "I'm goin' to bed."

"You're not drunk," Wilson protested unhopefully. "Damnation," he thought, "a man who can't hold his liquor shouldn't drink."

"I am drunk. Peter Piper pepped a pick of pippered peckles." He lumbered over toward the bed.

Wilson grabbed his arm. "You can't do that."

"Let him alone!"

Wilson swung around, saw a third man standing in front of the Gate—recognized him with a sudden shock. His own recollection of the sequence of events was none too clear in his memory, since he had been somewhat intoxicated—damned near boiled, he admitted—the first time he had experienced this particular busy afternoon. He realized that he should have anticipated the arrival of a third party. But his memory had not prepared him for who the third party would turn out to be.

He recognized himself—another carbon copy.

He stood silent for a minute, trying to assimilate this new fact and force it into some reasonable integration. He closed his eyes helplessly. This was just a little too much. He felt that he wanted to have a few plain words with Diktor.

"Who the hell are you?" He opened his eyes to find that his other self, the drunk one, was addressing the latest edition. The newcomer turned away from his interrogator and looked sharply at Wilson.

"*He* knows me."

Wilson took his time about replying. This thing was getting out of hand. "Yes," he admitted, "yes, I suppose I do. But what the deuce are you here for? And why are you trying to bust up the plan?"

His facsimile cut him short. "No time for long-winded explanations. I know more about it than you do—you'll concede that

—and my judgment is bound to be better than yours. He doesn't go through the Gate."

The offhand arrogance of the other antagonized Wilson. "I don't concede anything of the sort—" he began.

He was interrupted by the telephone bell. "Answer it!" snapped Number Three.

The tipsy Number One looked belligerent but picked up the handset. "Hello. . . . Yes. Who is this? . . . Hello. . . . Hello!" He tapped the bar of the instrument, then slammed the receiver back into its cradle.

"Who was that?" Wilson asked, somewhat annoyed that he had not had a chance to answer it himself.

"Nothing. Some nut with a misplaced sense of humor." At that instant the telephone rang again. "There he is again!" Wilson tried to answer it, but his alcoholic counterpart beat him to it, brushed him aside. "Listen, you butterfly-brained ape! I'm a busy man and this is *not* a public telephone. . . . Huh? Oh, it's you, Genevieve. Look—I'm sorry. I apologize— . . . You don't understand, honey. A guy has been pestering me over the phone and I thought it was him. You know I wouldn't talk to you that way, Babe. . . . Huh? This afternoon? Did you say *this* afternoon? . . . Sure. Fine. Look, Babe, I'm a little mixed up about this. Trouble I've had all day long and more trouble now. I'll look you up tonight and straighten it out. But I *know* I didn't leave your hat in my apartment— . . . Huh? Oh, sure! Anyhow, I'll see you tonight. 'By."

It almost nauseated Wilson to hear his earlier self catering to the demands of that clinging female. Why didn't he just hang up on her? The contrast with Arma—there was a dish!—was acute; it made him more determined than ever to go ahead with the plan, despite the warning of the latest arrival.

After hanging up the phone his earlier self faced him, pointedly ignoring the presence of the third copy. "Very well, Joe," he announced. "I'm ready to go if you are."

"Fine!" Wilson agreed with relief. "Just step through. That's all there is to it."

"No, you don't!" Number Three barred the way.

Wilson started to argue, but his erratic comrade was ahead of him. "Listen, you! You come butting in here like you think I was a bum. If you don't like it, go jump in the lake—and I'm just the kind of a guy who can do it! You and who else?"

They started trading punches almost at once. Wilson stepped in warily, looking for an opening that would enable him to put the slug on Number Three with one decisive blow.

He should have watched his drunken ally as well. A wild swing from that quarter glanced off his already damaged features and caused him excruciating pain. His upper lip, cut, puffy, and tender from his other encounter, took the blow and became an area of pure agony. He flinched and jumped back.

A sound cut through his fog of pain, a dull *Smack!* He forced his eyes to track and saw the feet of a man disappear through the Gate. Number Three was still standing by the Gate. "Now you've done it!" he said bitterly to Wilson, and nursed the knuckles of his left hand.

The obviously unfair allegation reached Wilson at just the wrong moment. His face still felt like an experiment in sadism. "Me?" he said angrily. "*You* knocked him through. I never laid a finger on him."

"Yes, but it's your fault. If you hadn't interfered, I wouldn't have had to do it."

"*Me* interfere? Why, you bald-faced hypocrite—*you* butted in and tried to queer the pitch. Which reminds me—you owe me some explanations and I damn well mean to have 'em. What's the idea of—"

But his opposite number cut in on him. "Stow it," he said gloomily. "It's too late now. He's gone through."

"Too late for what?" Wilson wanted to know.

"Too late to put a stop to this chain of events."

"Why should we?"

"Because," Number Three said bitterly, "Diktor has played me—I mean has played *you* . . . *us*—for a dope, for a couple of dopes. Look, he told you that he was going to set you up as a big shot over *there*"—he indicated the Gate—"didn't he?"

"Yes," Wilson admitted.

"Well, that's a lot of malarkey. All he means to do is to get us so incredibly tangled up in this Time Gate thing that we'll never get straightened out again."

Wilson felt a sudden doubt nibbling at his mind. It *could* be true. Certainly there had not been much sense to what had happened so far. After all, why should Diktor want his help, want it bad enough to offer to split with him, even-Stephen, what was obviously a cushy spot? "How do you know?" he demanded.

"Why go into it?" the other answered wearily. "Why don't you just take my word for it?"

"Why should I?"

His companion turned a look of complete exasperation on him. "If you can't take my word, whose word can you take?"

The inescapable logic of the question simply annoyed Wilson. He resented this interloping duplicate of himself anyhow; to be asked to follow his lead blindly irked him. "I'm from Missouri," he said. "I'll see for myself." He moved toward the Gate.

"Where are you going?"

"Through! I'm going to look up Diktor and have it out with him."

"Don't!" the other said. "Maybe we can break the chain even now." Wilson felt and looked stubborn. The other sighed. "Go ahead," he surrendered. "It's your funeral. I wash my hands of you."

Wilson paused as he was about to step through the Gate. "It is, eh? Hm-m-m—how can it be *my* funeral unless it's *your* funeral, too?"

The other man looked blank, then an expression of apprehension raced over his face. That was the last Wilson saw of him as he stepped through.

The Hall of the Gate was empty of other occupants when Bob Wilson came through on the other side. He looked for his hat, but did not find it, then stepped around back of the raised platform, seeking the exit he remembered. He nearly bumped into Diktor.

"Ah, there you are!" the older man greeted him. "Fine! Fine! Now there is just one more little thing to take care of, then we will be all squared away. I must say I am pleased with you, Bob, very pleased indeed."

"Oh, you are, are you?" Bob faced him truculently. "Well, it's too bad I can't say the same about you! I'm not a damn bit pleased. What was the idea of shoving me into that . . . that daisy chain without warning me? What's the meaning of all this nonsense? Why didn't you warn me?"

"Easy, easy," said the older man, "don't get excited. Tell the truth now—if I had told you that you were going back to meet yourself face to face, would you have believed me? Come now, 'fess up."

Wilson admitted that he would not have believed it.

"Well, then," Diktor continued with a shrug, "there was no point in me telling you, was there? If I had told you, you would not have believed me, which is another way of saying that you would have believed false data. Is it not better to be in ignorance than to believe falsely?"

"I suppose so, but—"

"Wait! I did not intentionally deceive you. I did not deceive you at all. But had I told you the full truth, you would have been deceived because you would have rejected the truth. It was better for you to learn the truth with your own eyes. Otherwise—"

"Wait a minute! Wait a minute!" Wilson cut in. "You're getting me all tangled up. I'm willing to let bygones be bygones, if you'll come clean with me. Why did you send me back at all?"

" 'Let bygones be bygones,' " Diktor repeated. "Ah, if we only could! But we can't. That's why I sent you back—in order that you might come through the Gate in the first place."

"Huh? Wait a minute—I already *had* come through the Gate."

Diktor shook his head. "Had you, now? Think a moment.

When you got back into your own time and your own place you found your earlier self there, didn't you?"

"Mmmm—yes."

"*He*—your earlier self—had not yet been through the Gate, had he?"

"No. I—"

"How could you have *been* through the Gate, unless you persuaded him to *go* through the Gate?"

Bob Wilson's head was beginning to whirl. He was beginning to wonder who did what to whom and who got paid. "But that's impossible! You are telling me that I did something because I was going to do something."

"Well, didn't you? You were there."

"No, I didn't—no . . . well, maybe I did, but it didn't *feel* like it."

"Why should you expect it to? It was something totally new to your experience."

"But . . . but—" Wilson took a deep breath and got control of himself. Then he reached back into his academic philosophical concepts and produced the notion he had been struggling to express. "It denies all reasonable theories of causation. You would have me believe that causation can be completely circular. I went through because I came back from going through to persuade myself to go through. That's silly."

"Well, didn't you?"

Wilson did not have an answer ready for that one. Diktor continued with, "Don't worry about it. The causation you have been accustomed to is valid enough in its own field but is simply a special case under the general case. *Causation in a plenum need not be and is not limited by a man's perception of duration.*"

Wilson thought about that for a moment. It sounded nice, but there was something slippery about it. "Just a second," he said. "How about entropy? You can't get around entropy."

"Oh, for Heaven's sake," protested Diktor, "shut up, will you? You remind me of the mathematicians that proved that airplanes couldn't fly." He turned and started out the door. "Come on. There's work to be done."

Wilson hurried after him. "Dammit, you can't do this to me. What happened to the other two?"

"The other two what?"

"The other two of me? Where are they? How am I ever going to get unsnarled?"

"You aren't snarled up. You don't feel like more than one person, do you?"

"No, but—"

"Then don't worry about it."

"But I've got to worry about it. What happened to the guy that came through just ahead of me?"

"You remember, don't you? However—" Diktor hurried on ahead, led him down a passageway, and dilated a door. "Take a look inside," he directed.

Wilson did so. He found himself looking into a small window-less unfurnished room, a room that he recognized. Sprawled on the floor, snoring steadily, was another edition of himself.

"When you first came through the Gate," explained Diktor at his elbow, "I brought you in here, attended to your hurts, and gave you a drink. The drink contained a soporific which will cause you to sleep about thirty-six hours, sleep that you badly needed. When you wake up, I will give you breakfast and ex-plain to you what needs to be done."

Wilson's head started to ache again. "Don't do that," he pleaded. "Don't refer to that guy as if he were me. *This* is *me*, standing here."

"Have it your own way," said Diktor. "That is the man you *were*. You remember the things that are about to happen to him, don't you?"

"Yes, but it makes me dizzy. Close the door, please."

"O. K.," said Diktor, and complied. "We've got to hurry, anyhow. Once a sequence like this is established there is no time to waste. Come on." He led the way back to the Hall of the Gate.

"I want you to return to the twentieth century and obtain certain things for us, things that can't be obtained on this side but which will be very useful to us in, ah, developing—yes, that is the word—developing this country."

"What sort of things?"

"Quite a number of items. I've prepared a list for you—certain reference books, certain items of commerce. Excuse me, please. I must adjust the controls of the Gate." He mounted the raised platform from the rear. Wilson followed him and found that the structure was boxlike, open at the top, and had a raised floor. The Gate could be seen by looking over the high sides.

The controls were unique.

Four colored spheres the size of marbles hung on crystal rods arranged with respect to each other as the four major axes of a tetrahedron. The three spheres which bounded the base of the tetrahedron were red, yellow, and blue; the fourth at the apex was white. "Three spatial controls, one time control," explained Diktor. "It's very simple. Using here-and-now as zero reference, displacing any control away from the center moves the other end of the Gate farther from here-and-now. Forward or back, right or left, up or down, past or future—they are all controlled by moving the proper sphere in or out on its rod."

Wilson studied the system. "Yes," he said, "but how do you tell where the other end of the Gate is? Or when? I don't see any graduations."

"You don't need them. You can see where you are. Look." He touched a point under the control framework on the side toward the Gate. A panel rolled back and Wilson saw there was a small image of the Gate itself. Diktor made another adjustment and Wilson found that he could see through the image.

He was gazing into his own room, as if through the wrong end of a telescope. He could make out two figures, but the scale was too small for him to see clearly what they were doing, nor could he tell which editions of himself were there present—if they were in truth himself! He found it quite upsetting. "Shut it off," he said.

Diktor did so and said, "I must not forget to give you your list." He fumbled in his sleeve and produced a slip of paper which he handed to Wilson. "Here—take it."

Wilson accepted it mechanically and stuffed it into his pocket. "See here," he began, "everywhere I go I keep running into myself. I don't like it at all. It's disconcerting. I feel like a whole batch of guinea pigs. I don't half understand what this is all about and now you want to rush me through the Gate again with a bunch of half-baked excuses. Come clean. Tell me what it's all about."

Diktor showed temper in his face for the first time. "You are a stupid and ignorant young fool. I've told you all that you are able to understand. This is a period in history entirely beyond your comprehension. It would take weeks before you would even begin to understand it. I am offering you half a world in return for a few hours' co-operation and you stand there arguing about it. Stow it, I tell you. Now—where shall we set you down?" He reached for the controls.

"Get away from those controls!" Wilson rapped out. He was getting the glimmering of an idea. "Who are you, anyhow?"

"Me? I'm Diktor."

"That's not what I mean and you know it. How did you learn English?"

Diktor did not answer. His face became expressionless.

"Go on," Wilson persisted. "You didn't learn it here; that's a cinch. You're from the twentieth century, *aren't you?*"

Diktor smiled sourly. "I wondered how long it would take you to figure that out."

Wilson nodded. "Maybe I'm not bright, but I'm not as stupid as you think I am. Come on. Give me the rest of the story."

Diktor shook his head. "It's immaterial. Besides, we're wasting time."

Wilson laughed. "You've tried to hurry me with that excuse once too often. How can we waste time when we have *that?*" He pointed to the controls and to the Gate beyond it. "Unless you lied to me, we can use any slice of time we want to, any time. No, I think I know why you tried to rush me. Either you want to get me out of the picture here, or there is something devilishly dangerous about the job you want me to do. And I know how to settle it—you're going with me!"

"You don't know what you're saying," Diktor answered slowly. "That's impossible. I've got to stay here and manage the controls."

"That's just what you aren't going to do. You could send me through and lose me. I prefer to keep you in sight."

"Out of the question," answered Diktor. "You'll have to trust me." He bent over the controls again.

"Get away from there!" shouted Wilson. "Back out of there before I bop you one." Under Wilson's menacing fist Diktor withdrew from the control pulpit entirely. "There. That's better," he added when both of them were once more on the floor of the hall.

The idea which had been forming in his mind took full shape. The controls, he knew, were still set on his room in the boardinghouse where he lived—or had lived—back in the twentieth century. From what he had seen through the speculum of the controls, the time control was set to take him right back to the day in 1942 from which he had started. "Stand there," he commanded Diktor. "I want to see something."

He walked over to the Gate as if to inspect it. Instead of stopping when he reached it, he stepped on through.

He was better prepared for what he found on the other side than he had been on the two earlier occasions of time translation—"earlier" in the sense of sequence in his memory track. Nevertheless it is never too easy on the nerves to catch up with one's self.

For he had done it again. He was back in his own room, but there were two of himself there before him. They were very much preoccupied with each other; he had a few seconds in which to get them straightened out in his mind. One of them had a beautiful black eye and a badly battered mouth. Beside that he was very much in need of a shave. That tagged him. He had been through the Gate at least once. The other, though somewhat in need of shaving himself, showed no marks of a fist fight.

He had them sorted out now, and knew where and *when* he was. It was all still most damnably confusing, but after former —no, not *former*, he amended—*other* experiences with time translation he knew better what to expect. He was back at the beginning again; this time he would put a stop to the crazy nonsense once and for all.

The other two were arguing. One of them swayed drunkenly toward the bed. The other grabbed him by the arm. "You can't do that," he said.

"Let him alone!" snapped Wilson.

The other two swung around and looked him over. Wilson watched the more sober of the pair size him up, saw his expression of amazement change to startled recognition. The other, the earliest Wilson, seemed to have trouble in focusing on him at all. "This is going to be a job," thought Wilson. "The man is positively stinking." He wondered why anyone would be foolish enough to drink on an empty stomach. It was not only stupid, it was a waste of good liquor.

He wondered if they had left a drink for him.

"Who are you?" demanded his drunken double.

Wilson turned to "Joe." "He knows me," he said significantly.

"Joe," studied him. "Yes," he conceded, "Yes, I suppose I do. But what the deuce are you here for? And why are you trying to bust up the plan?"

Wilson interrupted him. "No time for long-winded explanations. I know more about it than you do—you'll concede that— and my judgment is bound to be better than yours. He doesn't go through the Gate."

"I don't concede anything of the sort—"

The ringing of the telephone checked the argument. Wilson greeted the interruption with relief, for he realized that he had started out on the wrong tack. Was it possible that he was really as dense himself as this lug appeared to be? Did *he* look that way to other people? But the time was too short for self-doubts and soul-searching. "Answer it!" he commanded Bob (Boiled) Wilson.

The drunk looked belligerent, but acceded when he saw that Bob (Joe) Wilson was about to beat him to it.

"Hello. . . .Yes. Who is this? . . . Hello. . . . Hello!"

"Who was that?" asked Joe."

"Nothing. Some nut with a misplaced sense of humor." The telephone rang again. "There he is again." The drunk grabbed the phone before the others could reach it. "Listen, you butterfly-brained ape! I'm a busy man and this is *not* a public telephone. . . . Huh? Oh, it's you, Genevieve—" Wilson paid little attention to the telephone conversation—he had heard it too many times before, and he had too much on his mind. His earliest *persona* was much too drunk to be reasonable, he realized; he must concentrate on some argument that would appeal to "Joe"—otherwise he was outnumbered. "—Huh? Oh, sure!" the call concluded. "Anyhow, I'll see you tonight. 'By."

Now was the time, thought Wilson, before this dumb yap can open his mouth. What would he say? What would sound convincing?

But the boiled edition spoke first. "Very well, Joe," he stated, "I'm ready to go if you are."

"Fine!" said "Joe." "Just step through. That's all there is to it."

This was getting out of hand, not the way he had planned it at all. "No, you don't!" he barked and jumped in front of the Gate. He would have to make them realize, and quickly.

But he got no chance to do so. The drunk cussed him out, then swung on him; his temper snapped. He knew with sudden fierce exultation that he had been wanting to take a punch at someone for some time. Who did they think they were to be taking chances with his future?

The drunk was clumsy; Wilson stepped under his guard and hit him hard in the face. It was a solid enough punch to have convinced a sober man, but his opponent shook his head and came back for more. "Joe" closed in. Wilson decided that he would have to put his original opponent away in a hurry, and give his attention to "Joe"—by far the more dangerous of the two.

A slight mix-up between the two allies gave him his chance. He stepped back, aimed carefully, and landed a long jab with his left, one of the hardest blows he had ever struck in his life. It lifted his target right off his feet.

As the blow landed Wilson realized his orientation with respect to the Gate, knew with bitter certainty that he had again played through the scene to its inescapable climax.

He was alone with "Joe"; their companion had disappeared through the Gate.

His first impulse was the illogical but quite human and very common feeling of look-what-you-made-me-do. "Now you've done it!" he said angrily.

"Me?" "Joe" protested. "You knocked him through. I never laid a finger on him."

"Yes," Wilson was forced to admit. "But it's your fault," he added, "if you hadn't interfered, I wouldn't have had to do it."

"*Me* interfere? Why, you bald-faced hypocrite, you butted in and tried to queer the pitch. Which reminds me—you owe me some explanations and I damn well mean to have them. What's the idea of—"

"Stow it," Wilson headed him off. He hated to be wrong and he hated still more to have to admit that he was wrong. It had been hopeless from the start, he now realized. He felt bowed down by the utter futility of it. "It's too late now. He's gone through."

"Too late for what?"

"Too late to put a stop to this chain of events." He was aware now that it always had been too late, regardless of what time it was, what year it was, or how many times he came back and tried to stop it. He *remembered* having gone through the first time, he had *seen* himself asleep on the other side. Events would have to work out their weary way.

"Why should we?"

It was not worth while to explain, but he felt the need for self-justification. "Because," he said, "Diktor has played me—I mean has played *you* . . . us—for a dope, for a couple of dopes. Look, he told you that he was going to set you up as a big shot over there, didn't he?"

"Yes—"

"Well, that's a lot of malarkey. All he means to do is to get us so incredibly tangled up in this Gate thing that we'll never get straightened out again."

"Joe" looked at him sharply. "How do you know?"

Since it was largely hunch, he felt pressed for reasonable explanation. "Why go into it?" he evaded. "Why don't you just take my word for it?"

"Why should I?"

Why should you? Why, you lunk, can't you see? I'm yourself, older and more experienced—you *have* to believe me. Aloud he answered, "If you can't take my word, whose word can you take?"

"Joe" grunted. "I'm from Missouri," he said. "I'll see for myself."

Wilson was suddenly aware that "Joe" was about to step through the Gate. "Where are you going?"

"Through! I'm going to look up Diktor and have it out with him."

"Don't!" Wilson pleaded. "Maybe we can break the chain even now." But the stubborn sulky look on the other's face made him realize how futile it was. He was still enmeshed in inevitability; it *had* to happen. "Go ahead," he shrugged. "It's your funeral. I wash my hands of you."

"Joe" paused at the Gate. "It is, eh? Hm-m-m—how can it be *my* funeral unless it's *your* funeral, too?"

Wilson stared speechlessly while "Joe" stepped through the Gate. Whose funeral? He had not thought of it in quite that way. He felt a sudden impulse to rush through the Gate, catch up with his alter ego, and watch over him. The stupid fool might do anything. Suppose he got himself killed? Where would that leave Bob Wilson? Dead, of course.

Or would it? Could the death of a man thousands of years in the future kill *him* in the year 1942? He saw the absurdity of the situation suddenly, and felt very much relieved. "Joe's" actions could not endanger him; he remembered everything that "Joe" had done—was going to do. "Joe" would get into an argument with Diktor and, in due course of events, would come back through the Time Gate. No, *had* come back through the Time Gate. He was "Joe." It was hard to remember that.

Yes, he was "Joe." As well as the first guy. They would thread their courses, in and out and roundabout, and end up here, with *him*. Had to.

Wait a minute—in that case the whole crazy business was straightened out. He had gotten away from Diktor, had all of his various personalities sorted out, and was back where he started from, no worse for the wear except for a crop of whiskers and, possibly, a scar on his lip. Well, he knew when to let well enough alone. Shave, and get back to work, kid.

As he shaved he stared at his face and wondered why he had failed to recognize it the first time. He had to admit that he had never looked at it objectively before. He had always taken it for granted.

He acquired a crick in his neck from trying to look at his own profile through the corner of one eye.

On leaving the bathroom the Gate caught his eye forcibly. For some reason he had assumed that it would be gone. It was not. He inspected it, walked around it, carefully refrained from touching it. Wasn't the damned thing ever going to go away? It had served its purpose; why didn't Diktor shut it off?

He stood in front of it, felt a sudden surge of the compulsion that leads men to jump from high places. What would happen if he went through? What would he find? He thought of Arma. And the other one—what was her name? Perhaps Diktor had not told him. The other maidservant, anyhow, the second one.

But he restrained himself and forced himself to sit back down at the desk. If he was going to stay here—and of course he was, he was resolved on that point—he must finish the thesis. He had to eat; he needed the degree to get a decent job. Now where was he?

Twenty minutes later he had come to the conclusion that the thesis would have to be rewritten from one end to the other. His prime theme, the application of the empirical method to the problems of speculative metaphysics and its expression in rigorous formulae, was still valid, he decided, but he had acquired a mass of new and not yet digested data to incorporate in it. In re-reading his manuscript he was amazed to find how dogmatic he had been. Time after time he had fallen into the pathetic fallacy of Descartes, mistaking clear reasoning for correct reasoning.

He tried to brief a new version of the thesis, but discovered that there were two problems he was forced to deal with which were decidedly not clear in his mind: the problem of the ego and the problem of free will. When there had been three of him in the room, which one was the ego—was *himself*? And how was it that he had been unable to change the course of events?

An absurdly obvious answer to the first question occurred to him at once. The ego was himself. Self is self, an unproved and unprovable first statement, directly experienced. What, then, of the other two? Surely they had been equally sure of ego-being —he remembered it. He thought of a way to state it: Ego is the point of consciousness, the latest term in a continuously expanding series along the line of memory duration. That sounded like a general statement, but he was not sure; he would have to try to formulate it mathematically before he could trust it. Verbal language had such queer booby traps in it.

The telephone rang.

He answered it absent-mindedly. "Yes?"

"Is that you, Bob?"

"Yes. Who is this?"

"Why, it's Genevieve, of course, darling. What's come over

you today? That's the second time you've failed to recognize my voice."

Annoyance and frustration rose up in him. Here was another problem he had failed to settle—well, he'd settle it now. He ignored her complaint. "Look here, Genevieve, I've told you not to telephone me while I'm working. Good-by!"

"Well, of all the—You can't talk that way to me, Bob Wilson! In the first place, you weren't working today. In the second place, what makes you think you can use honey and sweet words on me and two hours later snarl at me? I'm not any too sure I want to marry you."

"Marry you? What put that silly idea in your head?"

The phone sputtered for several seconds. When it had abated somewhat he resumed with, "Now just calm down. This isn't the Gay Nineties, you know. You can't assume that a fellow who takes you out a few times intends to marry you."

There was a short silence. "So that's the game, is it?" came an answer at last in a voice so cold and hard and completely shrewish that he almost failed to recognize it. "Well, there's a way to handle men like you. A woman isn't unprotected in this State!"

"You ought to know," he answered savagely. "You've hung around the campus enough years."

The receiver clicked in his ear.

He wiped the sweat from his forehead. That dame, he knew, was quite capable of causing him lots of trouble. He had been warned before he ever started running around with her, but he had been so sure of his own ability to take care of himself. He should have known better—but then he had not expected anything quite as raw as this.

He tried to get back to work on his thesis, but found himself unable to concentrate. The deadline of 10 A.M. the next morning seemed to be racing toward him. He looked at his watch. It had stopped. He set it by the desk clock—four fifteen in the afternoon. Even if he sat up all night he could not possibly finish it properly.

Besides there was Genevieve—

The telephone rang again. He let it ring. It continued; he took the receiver off the cradle. He would *not* talk to her again.

He thought of Arma. There was a proper girl with the right attitude. He walked over to the window and stared down into the dusty, noisy street. Half subconsciously he compared it with the green and placid countryside he had seen from the balcony where he and Diktor had breakfasted. This was a crummy world full of crummy people. He wished poignantly that Diktor had been on the up-and-up with him.

An idea broke surface in his brain and plunged around frantically. The Gate was still open. *The Gate was still open!* Why worry about Diktor? He was his own master. Go back and play it out—everything to gain, nothing to lose.

He stepped up to the Gate, then hesitated. Was he wise to do it? After all, how much did he know about the future?

He heard footsteps climbing the stairs, coming down the hall, no—yes, stopping at his door. He was suddenly convinced that it was Genevieve; that decided him. He stepped through.

The Hall of the Gate was empty on his arrival. He hurried around the control box to the door and was just in time to hear, "Come on. There's work to be done." Two figures were retreating down the corridor. He recognized both of them and stopped suddenly.

That was a near thing, he told himself; I'll just have to wait until they get clear. He looked around for a place to conceal himself, but found nothing but the control box. That was useless; they were coming back. Still—

He entered the control box with a plan vaguely forming in his mind. If he found that he could dope out the controls, the Gate might give him all the advantage he needed. First he needed to turn on the speculum gadget. He felt around where he recalled having seen Diktor reach to turn it on, then reached in his pocket for a match.

Instead he pulled out a piece of paper. It was the list that Diktor had given him, the things he was to obtain in the twentieth century. Up to the present moment there had been too much going on for him to look it over.

His eyebrows crawled up his forehead as he read. It was a funny list, he decided. He had subconsciously expected it to call for technical reference books, samples of modern gadgets, weapons. There was nothing of the sort. Still, there was a sort of mad logic to the assortment. After all, Diktor knew these people better than he did. It might be just what was needed.

He revised his plans, subject to being able to work the Gate. He decided to make one more trip back and do the shopping Diktor's list called for—but for his own benefit, not Diktor's. He fumbled in the semidarkness of the control booth, seeking the switch or control for the speculum. His hand encountered a soft mass. He grasped it, and pulled it out.

It was his hat.

He placed it on his head, guessing idly that Diktor had stowed it there, and reached again. This time he brought forth a small notebook. It looked like a find—very possibly Diktor's own notes on the operation of the controls. He opened it eagerly.

It was not what he had hoped. But it did contain page after page of handwritten notes. There were three columns to the page; the first was in English, the second in international phonetic symbols, the third in a completely strange sort of writing. It took no brilliance for him to identify it as a vocabulary. He slipped it into a pocket with a broad smile; it might have taken Diktor months or even years to work out the relationship between the two languages; he would be able to ride on Diktor's shoulders in the matter.

The third try located the control and the speculum lighted up. He felt again the curious uneasiness he had felt before, for he was gazing again into his own room and again it was inhabited by two figures. He did not want to break into that scene again, he was sure. Cautiously he touched one of the colored beads.

The scene shifted, panned out through the walls of the boardinghouse and came to rest in the air, three stories above the campus. He was pleased to have gotten the Gate out of the house, but three stories was too much of a jump. He fiddled with the other two colored beads and established that one of them caused the scene in the speculum to move toward him or away from him while the other moved it up or down.

He wanted a reasonably inconspicuous place to locate the Gate, some place where it would not attract the attention of the curious. This bothered him a bit; there was no ideal place, but he compromised on a blind alley, a little court formed by the campus powerhouse and the rear wall of the library. Cautiously and clumsily he maneuvered his flying eye to the neighborhood he wanted and set it down carefully between the two buildings. He then readjusted his position so that he stared right into a blank wall. Good enough!

Leaving the controls as they were, he hurried out of the booth and stepped unceremoniously back into his own period.

He bumped his nose against the brick wall. "I cut that a little too fine," he mused as he slid cautiously out from between the confining limits of the wall and the Gate. The Gate hung in the air, about fifteen inches from the wall and roughly parallel to it. But there was room enough, he decided—no need to go back and readjust the controls. He ducked out of the areaway and cut across the campus toward the Students' Co-op, wasting no time. He entered and went to the cashier's window.

"Hi, Bob."

"H'lo, Soupy. Cash a check for me?"

"How much?"

"Twenty dollars."

"Well—I suppose so. Is it a good check?"

"Not very. It's my own."

"Well, I might invest in it as a curiosity." He counted out a ten, a five, and five ones.

"Do that," advised Wilson. "My autographs are going to be rare collectors' items." He passed over the check, took the money, and proceeded to the bookstore in the same building.

Most of the books on the list were for sale there. Ten minutes later he had acquired title to:

"The Prince," by Niccolo Machiavelli.

"Behind the Ballots," by James Farley.

"Mein Kampf" (unexpurgated), by Adolf Schicklgruber.

"How to Make Friends and Influence People," by Dale Carnegie.

The other titles he wanted were not available in the bookstore; he went from there to the university library where he drew out "Real Estate Broker's Manual," "History of Musical Instruments," and a quarto title "Evolution of Dress Styles." The latter was a handsome volume with beautiful colored plates and was classified as reference. He had to argue a little to get a twenty-four-hour permission for it.

He was fairly well loaded down by then; he left the campus, went to a pawnshop and purchased two used, but sturdy, suitcases into one of which he packed the books. From there he went to the largest music store in the town and spent forty-five minutes in selecting and rejecting phonograph records, with emphasis on swing and boogie-woogie—highly emotional stuff, all of it. He did not neglect classical and semi-classical, but he applied the same rule to those categories—a piece of music had to be sensuous and compelling, rather than cerebral. In consequence his collection included such strangely assorted items as the "Marseillaise," Ravel's "Bolero," four Cole Porters, and "L'Après-midi d'un Faun."

He insisted on buying the best mechanical reproducer on the market in the face of the clerk's insistence that what he needed was an electrical one. But he finally got his own way, wrote a check for the order, packed it all in his suitcases, and had the clerk get a taxi for him.

He had a bad moment over the check. It was pure rubber, as the one he had cashed at the Students' Co-op had cleaned out his balance. He had urged them to phone the bank, since that was what he wished them not to do. It had worked. He had established, he reflected, the alltime record for kiting checks—thirty thousand years.

When the taxi drew up opposite the court where he had located the Gate, he jumped out and hurried in.

The Gate was gone.

He stood there for several minutes, whistling softly, and assessing—unfavorably—his own abilities, mental processes, et cetera. The consequences of writing bad checks no longer seemed quite so hypothetical.

He felt a touch at his sleeve. "See here, Bud, do you want my hack, or don't you? The meter's still clicking."

"Huh? Oh, sure." He followed the driver, climbed back in. "Where to?"

That was a problem. He glanced at his watch, then realized that the usually reliable instrument had been through a process which rendered its reading irrelevant. "What time is it?"

"Two fifteen." He reset his watch.

Two fifteen. There would be a jamboree going on in his room at that time of a particularly confusing sort. He did not want to go *there*—not yet. Not until his blood brothers got through playing happy fun games with the Gate.

The Gate!

It would be in his room until sometime after four fifteen. If he timed it right—"Drive to the corner of Fourth and McKinley," he directed, naming the intersection closest to his boardinghouse.

He paid off the taxi driver there, and lugged his bags into the filling station at that corner, where he obtained permission from the attendant to leave them and assurance that they would be safe. He had nearly two hours to kill. He was reluctant to go very far from the house for fear some hitch would upset his timing.

It occurred to him that there was one piece of unfinished business in the immediate neighborhood—and time enough to take care of it. He walked briskly to a point two streets away, whistling cheerfully, and turned in at an apartment house.

In response to his knock the door of Apartment 211 was opened a crack, then wider. "Bob darling! I thought you were working today."

"Hi, Genevieve. Not at all—I've got time to burn."

She glanced back over her shoulder. "I don't know whether I should let you come in—I wasn't expecting you. I haven't washed the dishes, or made the bed. I was just putting on my make-up."

"Don't be coy." He pushed the door open wide, and went on in.

When he came out he glanced at his watch. Three thirty— plenty of time. He went down the street wearing the expression of the canary that ate the cat.

He thanked the service station salesman and gave him a quarter for his trouble, which left him with a lone nickel. He looked at this coin, grinned to himself, and inserted it in the pay phone in the office of the station. He dialed his own number.

"Hello," he heard.

"Hello," he replied. "Is that Bob Wilson?"

"Yes. Who is this?"

"Never mind," he chuckled. "I just wanted to be sure you were there. I *thought* you would be. You're right in the groove, kid, right in the groove." He replaced the receiver with a grin.

At four ten he was too nervous to wait any longer. Struggling under the load of the heavy suitcases he made his way to the boardinghouse. He let himself in and heard a telephone ringing upstairs. He glanced at his watch—four fifteen. He waited in the hall for three interminable minutes, then labored up the stairs and down the upper hallway to his own door. He unlocked the door and let himself in.

The room was empty, the Gate still there.

Without stopping for anything, filled with apprehension lest the Gate should flicker and disappear while he crossed the floor, he hurried to it, took a firm grip on his bags, and strode through it.

The Hall of the Gate was empty, to his great relief. What a break, he told himself thankfully. Just five minutes, that's all I ask. Five uninterrupted minutes. He set the suitcases down near the Gate to be ready for a quick departure. As he did so he noticed that a large chunk was missing from a corner of one case. Half a book showed through the opening, sheared as neatly as with a printer's trimmer. He identified it as "Mein Kampf."

He did not mind the loss of the book but the implications made him slightly sick at his stomach. Suppose he had not described a clear arc when he had first been knocked through the Gate, had hit the edge, half in and half out? Man Sawed in Half —and no illusion!

He wiped his face and went to the control booth. Following Diktor's simple instructions he brought all four spheres together at the center of the tetrahedron. He glanced over the side of the booth and saw that the Gate had disappeared entirely. "Check!" he thought. "Everything on zero—no Gate." He moved the white sphere slightly. The Gate reappeared. Turning on the speculum he was able to see that the miniature scene showed the inside of the Hall of the Gate itself. So far so good—but he would not be able to tell what time the Gate was set for by looking into the Hall. He displaced a space control slightly; the scene flickered past the walls of the palace and hung in the open air. Returning the white time control to zero he then displaced it very, very slightly. In the miniature scene the sun became a streak of brightness across the sky; the days flickered past like light from a low frequency source of illumination. He increased the displacement a little, saw the ground become sere and brown, then snow-covered, and finally green again.

Working cautiously, steadying his right hand with his left, he made the seasons march past. He had counted ten winters when he became aware of voices somewhere in the distance. He stopped and listened, then very hastily returned the space controls to zero, leaving the time control as it was—set for ten years in the past—and rushed out of the booth.

He hardly had time to grasp his bags, lift them, and swing them through the Gate, himself with them. This time he was exceedingly careful not to touch the edge of the circle.

He found himself, as he had planned to, still in the Hall of the Gate, but, if he had interpreted the controls correctly, ten years away from the events he had recently participated in. He had intended to give Diktor a wider berth than that, but there had been no time for it. However, he reflected, since Diktor was, by his own statement and the evidence of the little notebook Wilson had lifted from him, a native of the twentieth century, it was quite possible that ten years was enough. Diktor might not be in this era. If he was, there was always the Time Gate for a getaway. But it was reasonable to scout out the situation first before making any more jumps.

It suddenly occurred to him that Diktor might be looking at him through the speculum of the Time Gate. Without stopping to consider that speed was no protection—since the speculum could be used to view *any* time sector—he hurriedly dragged his two suitcases into the cover of the control booth. Once inside the protecting walls of the booth he calmed down a bit. Spying could work both ways. He found the controls set at zero; making use of the same process he had used once before, he ran the scene in the speculum forward through ten years, then cautiously hunted with the space controls on zero. It was a very difficult task; the time scale necessary to hunt through several months in a few minutes caused any figure which might appear in the speculum to flash past at an apparent speed too fast for his eye to follow. Several times he thought he detected flitting shadows which might be human beings but he was never able to find them when he stopped moving the time control.

He wondered in great exasperation why whoever had built the double-damned gadget had failed to provide it with graduations and some sort of delicate control mechanism—a vernier, or the like. It was not until much later that it occurred to him that the creator of the Time Gate might have no need of such gross aids to his senses. He would have given up, was about to give up, when, purely by accident, one more fruitless scanning happened to terminate with a figure in the field.

It was himself, carrying two suitcases. He saw himself walking directly into the field of view, grow larger, disappear. He looked over the rail, half expecting to see himself step out of the Gate.

But nothing came out of the Gate. It puzzled him, until he recalled that it was the setting at *that* end, ten years in the future, which controlled the time of egress. But he had what he wanted; he sat back and watched. Almost immediately Diktor and another edition of himself appeared in the scene. He recalled the situation when he saw it portrayed in the speculum. It was Bob Wilson number three, about to quarrel with Diktor and make his escape back to the twentieth century.

That was that—Diktor had not seen him, did not know that he had made unauthorized use of the Gate, did not know that he was hiding ten years in the "past," would not look for him there. He returned the controls to zero, and dismissed the matter.

But other matters needed his attention—food, especially. It seemed obvious, in retrospect, that he should have brought along food to last him for a day or two at least. And maybe a .45. He had to admit that he had not been very foresighted. But he easily forgave himself—it was hard to be foresighted when the future kept slipping up behind one. "All right, Bob, old boy," he told himself aloud, "let's see if the natives are friendly—as advertised."

A cautious reconnoiter of the small part of the Palace with which he was acquainted turned up no human beings, nor life of any sort, not even insect life. The place was dead, sterile, as static and unlived-in as a window display. He shouted once, just to hear a voice. The echoes caused him to shiver; he did not do it again.

The architecture of the place confused him. Not only was it

strange to his experience—he had expected that—but the place, with minor exceptions, seemed totally unadapted to the uses of human beings. Great halls large enough to hold ten thousand people at once—had there been floors for them to stand on. For there frequently were no floors in the accepted meaning of a level or reasonably level platform. In following a passageway he came suddenly to one of the great mysterious openings in the structure and almost fell in before he realized that his path had terminated. He crawled gingerly forward and looked over the edge. The mouth of the passage debouched high up on a wall of the place; below him the wall was cut back so that there was not even a vertical surface for the eye to follow. Far below him, the wall curved back and met its mate of the opposite side—not decently, in a horizontal plane, but at an acute angle.

There were other openings scattered around the walls, openings as unserviceable to human beings as the one in which he crouched. "The High Ones," he whispered to himself. All his cockiness was gone out of him. He retraced his steps through the fine dust and reached the almost friendly familiarity of the Hall of the Gate.

On his second try he attempted only those passages and compartments which seemed obviously adapted to men. He had already decided what such parts of the Palace must be—servants' quarters, or, more probably, slaves' quarters. He regained his courage by sticking to such areas. Though deserted completely, by contrast with the rest of the great structure a room or a passage which seemed to have been built for men was friendly and cheerful. The sourceless ever-present illumination and the unbroken silence still bothered him, but not to the degree to which he had been upset by the Gargantuan and mysteriously convoluted chambers of the "High Ones."

He had almost despaired of finding his way out of the Palace and was thinking of retracing his steps when the corridor he was following turned and he found himself in bright sunlight.

He was standing at the top of a broad steep ramp which

spread fanlike down to the base of the building. Ahead of him and below him, distant at least five hundred yards, the pavement of the ramp met the green of sod and bush and tree. It was the same placid, lush, and familiar scene he had looked out over when he breakfasted with Diktor—a few hours ago and ten years in the future.

He stood quietly for a short time, drinking in the sunshine, soaking up the heart-lifting beauty of the warm, spring day. "This is going to be all right," he exulted. "It's a grand place."

He moved slowly down the ramp, his eyes searching for human beings. He was halfway down when he saw a small figure emerge from the trees into a clearing near the foot of the ramp. He called out to it in joyous excitement. The child—it was a child he saw—looked up, stared at him for a moment, then fled back into the shelter of the trees.

"Impetuous, Robert—that's what you are," he chided himself. "Don't scare 'em. Take it easy." But he was not made downhearted by the incident. Where there were children there would be parents, society, opportunities for a bright, young fellow who took a broad view of things. He moved on down at a leisurely pace.

A man showed up at the point where the child had disappeared. Wilson stood still. The man looked him over and advanced hesitantly a step or two. "Come here!" Wilson invited in a friendly voice. "I won't hurt you."

The man could hardly have understood his words, but he advanced slowly. At the edge of the pavement he stopped, eyed it and would not proceed farther.

Something about the behavior pattern clicked in Wilson's brain, fitted in with what he had seen in the Palace, and with the little that Diktor had told him. "Unless," he told himself, "the time I spent in 'Anthropology I' was totally wasted, this Palace is tabu, the ramp I'm standing on is tabu, and, by contagion, I'm tabu. Play your cards, son, play your cards!"

He advanced to the edge of the pavement, being careful not to step off it. The man dropped to his knees and cupped his hands in front of him, head bowed. Without hesitation Wilson touched him on the forehead. The man got back to his feet, his face radiant.

"This isn't even sporting," Wilson said. "I ought to shoot him on the rise."

His Man Friday cocked his head, looked puzzled, and answered in a deep, melodious voice. The words were liquid and strange and sounded like a phrase from a song. "You ought to commercialize that voice," Wilson said admiringly. "Some stars get by on less. However— Get along now, and fetch something to eat. Food." He pointed to his mouth.

The man looked hesitant, spoke again. Bob Wilson reached into his pocket and took out the stolen notebook. He looked up "eat," then looked up "food." It was the same word. "Blellan," he said carefully.

"Blellaaaan?"

"Blellaaaaaaaan," agreed Wilson. "You'll have to excuse my accent. Hurry up." He tried to find "hurry" in the vocabulary, but it was not there. Either the language did not contain the idea or Diktor had not thought it worth while to record it. But we'll soon fix that, Wilson thought—if there isn't such a word, I'll give 'em one.

The man departed.

Wilson sat himself down Turk-fashion and passed the time by studying the notebook. The speed of his rise in these parts, he decided, was limited only by the time it took him to get into full communication. But he had only time enough to look up a few common substantives when his first acquaintance returned, in company.

The procession was headed by an extremely elderly man, white-haired but beardless. All of the men were beardless. He walked under a canopy carried by four male striplings. Only he of all the crowd wore enough clothes to get by anywhere but on a beach. He was looking uncomfortable in a sort of toga effect which appeared to have started life as a Roman-striped awning. That he was the head man was evident.

Wilson hurriedly looked up the word for "chief."

The word for chief was "Diktor."

It should not have surprised him, but it did. It was, of course, a logical probability that the word "Diktor" was a title rather than a proper name. It simply had not occurred to him.

Diktor—*the* Diktor—had added a note under the word. "One of the few words," Wilson read, "which shows some probability of having been derived from the dead languages. This word, a few dozen others, and the grammatical structure of the language itself, appear to be the only link between the language of the 'Forsaken Ones' and the English language."

The chief stopped in front of Wilson, just short of the pavement. "O. K., Diktor," Wilson ordered, "kneel down. You're not exempt." He pointed to the ground. The chief knelt down. Wilson touched his forehead.

The food that had been fetched along was plentiful and very palatable. Wilson ate slowly and with dignity, keeping in mind the importance of face. While he ate he was serenaded by the entire assemblage. The singing was excellent he was bound to admit. Their ideas of harmony he found a little strange and the performance, as a whole, seemed primitive, but their voices were all clear and mellow and they sang as if they enjoyed it.

The concert gave Wilson an idea. After he had satisfied his hunger he made the chief understand, with the aid of the indispensable little notebook, that he and his flock were to wait where they were. He then returned to the Hall of the Gate and brought back from there the phonograph and a dozen assorted records. He treated them to a recorded concert of "modern" music.

The reaction exceeded his hopes. "Begin the Beguine" caused tears to stream down the face of the old chief. The first movement of Tschaikowsky's "Concerto Number One in B Flat Minor" practically stampeded them. They jerked. They held their heads and moaned. They shouted their applause. Wilson refrained from giving them the second movement, tapered them off instead with the compelling monotony of the "Bolero."

"Diktor," he said—he was not thinking of the old chief—
"Diktor, old chum, you certainly had these people doped out
when you sent me shopping. By the time you show up—if you
ever do—I'll own the place.

This is not an account of how Boosterism came to Arcadia.
Wilson's rise to power was more in the nature of a triumphal
progress than a struggle for supremacy; it contained little that
was dramatic. Whatever it was that the High Ones had done to
the human race it had left them with only physical resemblance
and with temperament largely changed. The docile friendly
children with whom Wilson dealt had little in common with the
brawling, vulgar, lusty, dynamic swarms who had once called
themselves the People of the United States.

The relationship was like that of Jersey cattle to longhorns, or
cocker spaniels to wolves. The fight was gone out of them. It was
not that they lacked intelligence, nor civilized arts; it was the
competitive spirit that was gone, the will-to-power.

Wilson had a monopoly on that.

But even he lost interest in playing a game that he always
won. Having established himself as boss man by taking up residence in the Palace and representing himself as the viceroy of
the departed High Ones, he, for a time, busied himself in organ-
izing certain projects intended to bring the culture "up-to-
date"—the reinvention of musical instruments, establishment
of a systematic system of mail service, redevelopment of the
idea of styles in dress and a tabu against wearing the same
fashion more than one season. There was cunning in the latter
project. He figured that arousing a hearty interest in display in
the minds of the womenfolk would force the men to hustle to
satisfy their wishes. What the culture lacked was drive—it was
slipping downhill. He tried to give them the drive they lacked.

His subjects co-operated with his wishes, but in a bemused
fashion, like a dog performing a trick, not because he under-
stands it, but because his master and godhead desires it.

He soon tired of it.

But the mystery of the High Ones, and especially the mystery of their Time Gate, still remained to occupy his mind. His was a mixed nature, half hustler, half philosopher. The philosopher had his inning.

It was intellectually necessary to him that he be able to construct in his mind a physio-mathematical model for the phenomena exhibited by the Time Gate. He achieved one, not a good one perhaps, but one which satisfied all of the requirements. Think of a plane surface, a sheet of paper, or, better yet, a silk handkerchief—silk, because it has no rigidity, folds easily, while maintaining all of the relational attributes of a two-dimensional continuum on the surface of the silk itself. Let the threads of the woof be the dimension—or direction—of time; let the threads of the warp represent all three of the space dimensions.

An ink spot on the handkerchief becomes the Time Gate. By folding the handkerchief that spot may be superposed on any other spot on the silk. Press the two spots together between thumb and forefinger; the controls are set, the Time Gate is open, a microscopic inhabitant of this piece of silk may crawl from one fold to the other without traversing any other part of the cloth.

The model is imperfect; the picture is static—but a physical picture is necessarily limited by the sensory experience of the person visualizing it.

He could not make up his mind whether or not the concept of folding the four-dimensional continuum—three of space, one of time—back on itself so that the Gate was "open" required the concept of higher dimensions through which to fold it. It seemed so, yet it might simply be an intellectual shortcoming of the human mind. Nothing but empty space was required for the "folding," but "empty space" was itself a term totally lacking in meaning—he was enough of a mathematician to know that.

If higher dimensions were required to "hold" a four-dimensional continuum, then the number of dimensions of space and of time were necessarily infinite; each order requires the next higher order to maintain it.

But "infinite" was another meaningless term. "Open series" was a little better, but not much.

Another consideration forced him to conclude that there was probably at least one more dimension than the four his senses could perceive—the Time Gate itself. He became quite skilled in handling its controls, but he never acquired the foggiest notion of how it worked, or how it had been built. It seemed to him that the creatures who built it must necessarily have been able to stand outside the limits that confined him in order to anchor the Gate to the structure of space time. The concept escaped him.

He suspected that the controls he saw were simply the part that stuck through into the space he knew. The very Palace itself might be no more than a three-dimensional section of a more involved structure. Such a condition would help to explain the otherwise inexplicable nature of its architecture.

He became possessed of an overpowering desire to know more about these strange creatures, the "High Ones," who had come and ruled the human race and built this Palace and this Gate, and gone away again—and in whose backwash he had been flung out of his setting some thirty millennia. To the human race they were no more than a sacred myth, a contradictory mass of tradition. No picture of them remained, no trace of their writing, nothing of their works save the High Palace of Norkaal and the Gate. And a sense of irreparable loss in the hearts of the race they had ruled, a loss expressed by their own term for themselves—the Forsaken Ones.

With controls and speculum he hunted back through time, seeking the Builders. It was slow work, as he had found before. A passing shadow, a tedious retracing—and failure.

Once he was sure that he had seen such a shadow in the miniature Hall reflected in the speculum. He set the controls back far enough to be sure that he had repassed it, armed himself with food and drink and waited.

He waited three weeks.

The shadow might have passed during the hours he was forced to take out for sleep. But he felt sure that he was in the right period; he kept up the vigil.

He saw it.

It was moving toward the Gate.

When he pulled himself together he was halfway down the passageway leading away from the Hall. He realized that he had been screaming. He still had an attack of the shakes.

Somewhat later he forced himself to return to the Hall, and, with eyes averted, enter the control booth and return the spheres to zero. He backed out hastily and left the Hall for his apartment. He did not touch the controls nor enter the Hall for more than two years.

It had not been fear of physical menace that had shaken his reason, nor the appearance of the creature—he could recall nothing of *how* it looked. It had been a feeling of sadness infinitely compounded which had flooded through him at the instant, a sense of tragedy, of grief insupportable and unescapable, of infinite weariness. He had been flicked with emotions many times too strong for his spiritual fiber and which he was no more fitted to experience than an oyster is to play a violin.

He felt that he had learned all about the High Ones a man could learn and still endure. He was no longer curious. The shadow of that vicarious emotion ruined his sleep, brought him sweating out of dreams.

One other problem bothered him—the problem of himself and his meanders through time. It still worried him that he had met himself coming back, so to speak, had talked with himself, fought with himself.

Which one was *himself?*

He was all of them, he knew, for he remembered being each one. How about the times when there had been more than one present?

By sheer necessity he was forced to expand the principle of

nonidentity—"Nothing is identical with anything else, not even with itself"—to include the ego. In a four-dimensional continuum each event is an absolute individual, it has its space co-ordinates and its date. The Bob Wilson he was right now was *not* the Bob Wilson he had been ten minutes ago. Each was a discrete section of a four-dimensional process. One resembled the other in many particulars, as one slice of bread resembles the slice next to it. But they were *not* the same Bob Wilson— they differed by a length of time.

When he had doubled back on himself, the difference had become apparent, for the separation was now in space rather than in time, and he happened to be so equipped as to be able to *see* a space length, whereas he could only remember a time difference. Thinking back he could remember a great many different Bob Wilsons, baby, small child, adolescent, young man. They were all different—he knew that. The only thing that bound them together into a feeling of identity was continuity of memory.

And that was the same thing that bound together the three —no, four, Bob Wilsons on a certain crowded afternoon, a memory track that ran through all of them. The only thing about it that remained remarkable was time travel itself.

And a few other little items—the nature of "free will," the problem of entropy, the law of the conservation of energy and mass. The last two, he now realized, needed to be extended or generalized to include the cases in which the Gate, or something like it, permitted a leak of mass, energy, or entropy from one neighborhood in the continuum to another. They were otherwise unchanged and valid. Free will was another matter. It could not be laughed off, because it could be directly experienced—yet his own free will had worked to create the same scene over and over again. Apparently human will must be considered as one of the factors which make up the processes in the continuum—"free" to the ego, mechanistic from the outside.

And yet his last act of evading Diktor had apparently changed the course of events. He was here and running the country, had been for many years, but Diktor had not showed up. Could it be that each act of "true" free will created a new and different future? Many philosophers had thought so.

This future appeared to have no such person as Diktor—*the* Diktor—in it, anywhere or anywhen.

As the end of his first ten years in the future approached, he became more and more nervous, less and less certain of his opinion. Damnation, he thought, if Diktor is going to show up it was high time that he did so. He was anxious to come to grips with him, establish which was to be boss.

He had agents posted throughout the country of the Forsaken Ones with instructions to arrest any man with hair on his face and fetch him forthwith to the Palace. The Hall of the Gate he watched himself.

He tried fishing the future for Diktor, but had no significant luck. He thrice located a shadow and tracked it down; each time it was himself. From tedium and partly from curiosity he attempted to see the other end of the process; he tried to relocate his original home, thirty thousand years in the past.

It was a long chore. The further the time button was displaced from the center, the poorer the control became. It took patient practice to be able to stop the image within a century or so of the period he wanted. It was in the course of his experimentation that he discovered what he had once looked for, a fractional control—a vernier, in effect. It was as simple as the primary control, but twist the bead instead of moving it directly.

He steadied down on the twentieth century, approximated the year by the models of automobiles, types of architecture, and other gross evidence, and stopped in what he believed to be 1942. Careful displacement of the space controls took him to the university town where he had started—after several false tries; the image did not enable him to read road signs.

He located his boardinghouse, brought the Gate into his own room. It was vacant, no furniture in it.

He panned away from the room, and tried again, a year

earlier. Success—his own room, his own furniture, but empty. He ran rapidly back, looking for shadows.

There! He checked the swing of the image. There were three figures in the room, the image was too small, the light too poor for him to be sure whether or not one of them was himself. He leaned over and studied the scene.

He heard a dull thump outside the booth. He straightened up and looked over the side.

Sprawled on the floor was a limp human figure. Near it lay a crushed and battered hat.

He stood perfectly still for an uncounted time, staring at the two redundant figures, hat and man, while the winds of unreason swept through his mind and shook it. He did not need to examine the unconscious form to identify it. He knew . . . *he knew*—it was his younger self, knocked willy-nilly through the Time Gate.

It was not that fact in itself which shook him. He had not particularly expected it to happen, having come tentatively to the conclusion that he was living in a different, an alternative, future from the one in which he had originally transitted the Time Gate. He had been aware that it might happen nevertheless, that it did happen did not surprise him.

When it did happen, *he himself had been the only spectator!*

He was Diktor. He was *the* Diktor. He was *the only* Diktor!

He would never find Diktor, nor have it out with him. He need never fear his coming. There never had been, never would be, any other person called Diktor, because Diktor never had been nor ever would be anyone but himself.

In review, it seemed obvious that he must be Diktor; there were so many bits of evidence pointing to it. And yet it had not been obvious. Each point of similarity between himself and the Diktor, he recalled, had arisen from rational causes—usually from his desire to ape the gross characteristics of the "other" and thereby consolidate his own position of power and authority before the "other" Diktor showed up. For that reason he had established himself in the very apartments that "Diktor" had used—so that they would be "his" first.

To be sure, his people called him Diktor, but he had thought nothing of that—they called anyone who ruled by that title, even the little subchieftains who were his local administrators.

He had grown a beard, such as Diktor had worn, partly in imitation of the "other" man's precedent, but more to set him apart from the hairless males of the Forsaken Ones. It gave him prestige, increased his tabu. He fingered his bearded chin. Still, it seemed strange that he had not recalled that his own present appearance checked with the appearance of "Diktor." "Diktor" had been an older man. He himself was only thirty-two, ten here, twenty-two *there*.

Diktor he had judged to be about forty-five. Perhaps an unprejudiced witness would believe himself to be that age. His hair and beard were shot with gray—had been, ever since the year he had succeeded too well in spying on the High Ones. His face was lined. Uneasy lies the head and so forth. Running a country, even a peaceful Arcadia, will worry a man, keep him awake nights.

Not that he was complaining—it had been a good life, a grand life, and it beat anything the ancient past had to offer.

In any case, he had been looking for a man in his middle forties, whose face he remembered dimly after ten years and whose picture he did not have. It had never occurred to him to connect that blurred face with his present one. Naturally not.

But there were other little things. Arma, for example. He had selected a likely-looking lass some three years back and made her one of his household staff, renaming her Arma in sentimental memory of the girl he had once fancied. It was logically necessary that they were the same girl, not two Armas, but one.

But, as he recalled her, the "first" Arma had been much prettier.

Hm-m-m—it must be his own point of view that had changed. He admitted that he had had much more opportunity to become bored with exquisite female beauty than his young friend over there on the floor. He recalled with a chuckle how he had found it necessary to surround himself with an elaborate system of tabus to keep the nubile daughters of his subjects out of his hair—most of the time. He had caused a particular pool in the river adjacent to the Palace to be dedicated to his use in order that he might swim without getting tangled up in mermaids.

The man on the floor groaned, but did not open his eyes.

Wilson, the Diktor, bent over him but made no effort to revive him. That the man was not seriously injured he had reason to be certain. He did not wish him to wake up until he had had time to get his own thoughts entirely in order.

For he had work to do, work which must be done meticulously, without mistake. Everyone, he thought with a wry smile, makes plans to provide for their future.

He was about to provide for his past.

There was the matter of the setting of the Time Gate when he got around to sending his early self back. When he had tuned in on the scene in his room a few minutes ago, he had picked up the action just before his early self had been knocked through. In sending him back he must make a slight readjustment in the time setting to an instant around two o'clock of that particular afternoon. That would be simple enough; he need only search a short sector until he found his early self alone and working at his desk.

But the Time Gate had appeared in that room at a later hour; he had just caused it to do so. He felt confused.

Wait a minute, now—if he changed the setting of the time control, the Gate would appear in his room at the earlier time, remain there, and simply blend into its "reappearance" an hour or so later. Yes, that was right. To a person in the room it would simply be as if the Time Gate had been there all along, from about two o'clock.

Which it had been. He would see to that.

Experienced as he was with the phenomena exhibited by the Time Gate, it nevertheless required a strong and subtle intellectual effort to think other than in durational terms, to take an *eternal* viewpoint.

And there was the hat. He picked it up and tried it on. It did not fit very well, no doubt because he was wearing his hair longer now. The hat must be placed where it would be found — Oh, yes, in the control booth. And the notebook, too.

The notebook, the notebook—Mm-m-m— Something funny, there. When the notebook he had stolen had become dog-eared and tattered almost to illegibility some four years back, he had carefully recopied its contents in a new notebook—to refresh his memory of English rather than from any need for it as a guide. The worn-out notebook he had destroyed; it was the new one he intended to obtain, and leave to be found.

In that case, *there never had been two notebooks.* The one he had now would become, after being taken through the Gate to a point ten years in the past, the notebook from which he had copied it. They were simply different segments of the same physical process, manipulated by means of the Gate to run concurrently, side by side, for a certain length of time.

As he had himself—one afternoon.

He wished that he had not thrown away the worn-out notebook. If he had it at hand, he could compare them and convince himself that they were identical save for the wear and tear of increasing entropy.

But when had he learned the language, in order that he might prepare such a vocabulary? To be sure, when he copied it he then *knew* the language—copying had not actually been necessary.

But he *had* copied it.

The physical process he had all straightened out in his mind, but the intellectual process it represented was completely circular. His older self had taught his younger self a language which the older self knew because the younger self, after being taught, grew up to be the older self and was, therefore, capable of teaching.

But where had it started?

Which comes first, the hen or the egg?

You feed the rats to the cats, skin the cats, and feed the carcasses of the cats to the rats who are in turn fed to the cats. The perpetual motion fur farm.

If God created the world, who created God?

342 · ROBERT A. HEINLEIN

Who wrote the notebook? Who started the chain?

He felt the intellectual desperation of any honest philosopher. He knew that he had about as much chance of understanding such problems as a collie has of understanding how dog food gets into cans. Applied psychology was more his size —which reminded him that there were certain books which his early self would find very useful in learning how to deal with the political affairs of the country he was to run. He made a mental note to make a list.

The man on the floor stirred again, sat up. Wilson knew that the time had come when he must insure his past. He was not worried; he felt the sure confidence of the gambler who is "hot," who *knows* what the next roll of the dice will show.

He bent over his alter ego. "Are you all right?" he asked.

"I guess so," the younger man mumbled. He put his hand to his bloody face. "My head hurts."

"I should think it would," Wilson agreed. "You came through head over heels. I think you hit your head when you landed."

His younger self did not appear fully to comprehend the words at first. He looked around dazedly, as if to get his bearings. Presently he said, "Came through? Came through what?"

"The Gate, of course," Wilson told him. He nodded his head toward the Gate, feeling that the sight of it would orient the still groggy younger Bob.

Young Wilson looked over his shoulder in the direction indicated, sat up with a jerk, shuddered and closed his eyes. He opened them again after what seemed to be a short period of prayer, looked again, and said, "Did I come through that?"

"Yes," Wilson assured him.

"Where am I?"

"In the Hall of the Gate in the High Palace of Norkaal. But what is more important," Wilson added, "is *when* you are. You have gone forward a little more than thirty thousand years."

The knowledge did not seem to reassure him. He got up and stumbled toward the Gate. Wilson put a restraining hand on his shoulder. "Where are you going?"

"Back!"

"Not so fast." He did not dare let him go back yet, not until the Gate had been reset. Besides he was still drunk—his breath was staggering. "You will go back all right—I give you my word on that. But let me dress your wounds first. And you should rest. I have some explanations to make to you, and there is an errand you can do for me when you get back—to our mutual advantage. There is a great future in store for you and me, my boy —a great future!"

A great future!

CHILD OF THE GREEN LIGHT

Leigh Brackett

Women did not figure prominently in the Golden Age. Science fiction then was primarily a male literature, based on the appeal of science and adventure, neither of which was considered a proper subject for feminine interest. Though John Campbell de-emphasized the importance of swashbuckling action in *Astounding* in favor of sociological extrapolation of the effects of new technology, he still relied on logical, "masculine" thinking, and he was obviously aware that most of his readers were male. (When he previewed A. E. van Vogt's "Slan!" he wrote, "Gentlemen, it's a lulu!")

To be sure, there had been women writers of science fiction such as Clare Winger Harris and Amelia Reynolds Long, and one major sf writer who was a woman: C. L. Moore. But they were exceptions; the future was considered a male province. Sewell Peaslee Wright had stated it succinctly in a story published eight years before: "Women have their great and proper place, even in a man's universe."

Leigh Brackett began to claim her place in science fiction in the early 1940s with stories that combined suspenseful action and poetic descriptions of alien locales; she quickly established herself as "the acknowledged mistress of the flamboyant interplanetary adventure," as Anthony Boucher has said. Space opera wasn't John Campbell's style; nevertheless it was he who discovered her, buying her first two stories in one week late in 1939 during the same period he was buying the first sf stories by Heinlein, Sturgeon, van Vogt and the rest of the writers who helped make him famous.

Born December 7, 1915—a birthday that she didn't feel like celebrating when Japan bombed Pearl Harbor on that date in 1941—

Brackett began to write when she was nine, and by the age of thirteen was submitting "heavy problem novels," short stories and poems to editors. None of them was bought, which isn't surprising considering the fact that the manuscripts were in longhand on ruled paper.

She spent most of her childhood living with her grandfather on a beach in Southern California, and he had so much faith in her writing talent that he continued to support her "when I was quite old enough to make my own living." She met Henry Kuttner, who gave her invaluable advice about writing, "part of which was a gentle insistence on buying more purple pencils to cope with my purple prose."

She learned well, and after her initial breakthrough in the pages of *Astounding* (her first story, "Martian Quest," was in the February 1940 issue) she sold frequently to magazines like *Planet Stories, Super Science Stories, Startling Stories* and *Amazing*—wherein Raymond A. Palmer, who had bought her story through her agent, introduced her as a man. She continued to submit stories to Campbell first, though, "because *Astounding* was *the* prestige market." But she didn't know enough about science and her storytelling abilities were more suited to the swashbuckling mode of *Planet Stories.* She sold only one more story to *Astounding.*

Brackett's agent, Julius Schwartz, visited Los Angeles in 1940 and introduced her to Edmond Hamilton and Jack Williamson. She was completely overawed: "They were both looking thoroughly auctorial . . . I nearly fell through the floor." She and Hamilton began dating (he took her to a meeting of the Los Angeles Science Fantasy Society on their first date), and after the war they were married.

Brackett sold dozens of science fiction stories during the Golden Age, but her success was viewed dimly by fans of Serious Science Fiction. She told me of an occasion when she was among a group of *Astounding* writers "and a worshipful fan sitting at the feet gathered from the conversation that I also was a writer, though he had not caught my name. He asked it. I told him. 'Brackett?' he said. 'The Brackett who writes those things for *Planet Stories?'* I was forced to admit it. 'My God,' he said, and moved hurriedly away as if he might catch something."

She gained steadily in accomplishment and prestige, however. In

1944, she suddenly found herself collaborating simultaneously with Ray Bradbury and William Faulkner. She had finished half of a novella for *Planet Stories* when she was given the call to work on a screenplay with Faulkner, so she gave the novella to Bradbury to finish. "Lorelei of the Red Mist," the Brackett-Bradbury story, became a space opera classic; and the screenplay on which she worked with Faulkner eventually emerged as *The Big Sleep,* one of Humphrey Bogart's most famous films.

She went on to write many more screenplays—shortly before her death in 1978 she wrote the first draft to the sequel of *Star Wars*— plus critically acclaimed suspense and Western novels, and a large body of science fiction that led to her being named co–Guest of Honor with Edmond Hamilton at the World Science Fiction Convention in 1964.

So Leigh Brackett proved that a woman, even one whose talents didn't fit the requirements of *Astounding,* could become a major science fiction writer. She traveled a long way from the science fiction world of the early forties, when women were routinely portrayed in stories saying things like "I'm sure of that. Even if it isn't logic. Even if it does sound feminine and everything!"

Even heroes in love had a surprisingly low opinion of women then. In a 1942 story by S. D. Gottesman, the narrator said, "Art and I were desperately in love with Miss Earle. Despite her obvious physical charms, we discovered . . . that she was a woman of much brain-capacity."

It's enough to make you wonder if the standards of feminine beauty in those days included a sloping forehead and a small brainpan. ("Gottesman" was a pseudonym used in this case by C. M. Kornbluth, Frederik Pohl and Robert W. Lowndes, so it's difficult to guess which one it was who had a yen for Neanderthal women.)

Nelson S. Bond told of an inventor who'd built a time machine; when his fiancée saw it, "Helen, being a woman, got right down to fundamentals. 'It's not streamlined,' she said. 'I don't like the color, and the dashboard isn't pretty. Where's the cigarette lighter?' "

But it was in the pages of *Astounding* that this smug male chauvinism reached its nadir. Frank Belknap Long reported a conversation between a scientific explorer and his fiancée:

He: "The urge to reach out, to cross new frontiers, is a biological constant."

She: "It isn't in me. A woman seeks new frontiers in a man's arms."

Some writers did try to portray sensible, self-reliant women in those old pulp stories, if only for the sake of novelty. In fact there were two woman characters who were so "different" that each was featured in a series of stories: Gerry Carlyle, interplanetary huntress, and Violet Ray, "the Golden Amazon."

The Carlyle series was written by Arthur K. Barnes, who made no bones about the strength of her character: "Gerry Carlyle had fought her way to the top of the most exacting of all professions. Success was not won by resort to feminine stratagem, nor by use of her amazing beauty. Gerry scorned such wiles. In a man's world, she competed with men on their own terms. Her success was due to hard work, brains, courage, and the overwhelming effect of her forceful personality."

Nevertheless, when the climactic fight scene came in this story, it was Carlyle's fiancé, Tommy Strike, who stepped forward. As Barnes described it: "Gerry stood staring at Strike with her lips parted, her eyes shining. She was experiencing that strange emotion—a compound of awe, fright and admiration—that every woman knows when she sees the man she loves in two-fisted action."

The Golden Amazon had no need for male help in her fights with villains; lost on Venus as a baby, she had become superstrong and supersmart as a result of solar radiations. In one story she burst a chain with her bare hands; in another, after catching the kidnappers of her children, she broke the villain's neck with one punch. "No quarter this time! It's not plain crime anymore but massacre and baby snatching—*my* babies!" Superwomen were acceptable only if they showed, when the chips were down, that they were still "feminine." (The author, John Russell Fearn, did his best to help the Golden Amazon by referring to her throughout as a "girl.")

There were a few woman characters who transcended the stereotypes of the time without apologies from their authors. Lester del

Rey, in "Nerves," included a woman who was a doctor (not a nurse); and Robert A. Heinlein's " '—We Also Walk Dogs' " concerned an agency that could handle any job, big or small. One of its best troubleshooters was a woman, and Heinlein treated this as perfectly natural.

But it was Leigh Brackett who dismissed the image of helpless, dependent women in one brief dialogue. In "Out of the Sea," tentacled monsters came from the Pacific Ocean to attack humans, including the heroine, who fought her way free. This conversation ensued:

Hero: "Why haven't you fainted?"

Heroine: "I haven't had time."

Brackett's "Child of the Green Light" was less an action story than one of mood; her heroine was ethereal, but she had brains and inner strength. The story offers a contrast to the determinedly common-sense style of *Astounding,* showing that Campbell's approach wasn't the only one that could produce good fiction.

Alden H. Norton, who had replaced Frederik Pohl as editor of *Super Science Stories,* bought "Child of the Green Light" for his February 1942 issue. Brackett had written it because "I got to wondering what it would be like to live in space free of all hampering life-support sytems; to *belong,* as it were, to the universe. . . . This is the part of science fiction I have always enjoyed the most . . . the opportunity to be, in imagination, all sorts of, or any sort of, creature, human, non-human, you name it, in an unlimited choice of life-styles."

Brackett's protagonist was faced with a choice of lives; the story hinged on his decision.

REFERENCES:

"In Times to Come" by John W. Campbell, Jr. *Astounding Science-Fiction,* August 1940.

"Priestess of the Flame" by Sewell Peaslee Wright. *Astounding Stories,* June 1932.

Introduction by Anthony Boucher to "The Tweener" by Leigh Brackett. *Fantasy and Science Fiction,* February 1955.

Letter from Leigh Brackett, March 26, 1976.

"Meet the Author" by Leigh Brackett. *Startling Stories,* Fall 1944.

"Who's Who in Science Fiction" by Leigh Brackett. *Destiny,* Summer 1954.

"The Observatory" by Raymond A. Palmer. *Amazing Stories,* April 1941.

"Beyond Our Narrow Skies" by Leigh Brackett. *The Best of Planet Stories #1.* Ballantine Books, 1975.

"Leigh Brackett" by Donald A. Wollheim. *Pacificon II Program Book,* 1964.

"An Interview with Leigh Brackett and Edmond Hamilton" by David Truesdale with Paul McGuire. *Tangent,* Summer 1976.

"The Tomb of Time" by Robert Arthur. *Thrilling Wonder Stories,* November 1940.

"The Extrapolated Dimwit" by S. D. Gottesman. *Future Fantasy and Science Fiction,* October 1942.

Index to the Science-Fiction Magazines by Donald B. Day. Perri Press, 1952.

"Horsesense Hank in the Parallel Worlds" by Nelson S. Bond. *Amazing Stories,* August 1942.

"Brown" by Frank Belknap Long. *Astounding Science-Fiction,* July 1941.

"Trouble on Titan" by Arthur K. Barnes. *Thrilling Wonder Stories,* February 1941.

"The Golden Amazon" by "Thornton Ayre" (John Russell Fearn). *Fantastic Adventures,* July 1939.

"The Golden Amazon Returns" by "Thornton Ayre" (John Russell Fearn). *Fantastic Adventures,* January 1941.

"Nerves" by Lester del Rey. *Astounding Science-Fiction,* September 1942.

" '—We Also Walk Dogs' " by "Anson MacDonald" (Robert A. Heinlein). *Astounding Science-Fiction,* July 1941.

"Out of the Sea" by Leigh Brackett. *Astonishing Stories,* June 1942.

* * *

Son felt the distant, ringing shiver of the metal under him. The whole close-packed mass of broken hulks shifted slightly with the impact, turning wheel-like around the shining Light.

Son half rose. He'd been sprawled full length on the crest of the wheel, trying to make the Veil get thin enough to see through. They had both seen that it was thinner than ever, and Aona, on the other side of it, had danced for him, a misty shifting light beyond the queer darkness.

Several times he thought he had almost seen her outlines.

He could hear her mind now, tickling his brain with impish thought-fingers.

She must have heard his own thought change, because she asked, "What is it, Son? What's happened?"

"Another ship, I think." Son rose lazily, the green Light from below rippling around him like clear water.

He looked out over his domain, feeling the savage sun-fire and the spatial cold of the shadows touch his naked body with little whips of ecstasy. His face was a boy's face, handsome and bright-eyed. His fair head burned like a torch in the blinding glare.

The sun made a blazing canopy across half the sky. The rest was open space, velvet dark and boundless, flecked with the little fires of the stars.

Between sun and space lay the wheel, built of space ships that lay side by side, over and under and sometimes through, broken and bent and dead, bound close by the power of the Light.

The Light, lying below Son's naked feet at the very heart of the wheel, burning green through the packed hulks—the Light that was his bridge to Aona.

Son's blue eyes, unshaded, looked for the wreck. He knew it would be a wreck. Only one ship in the wheel, the one in which his memories began, was whole.

Then he stood quite still, staring, feeling every muscle tense and tighten.

He saw the ship, lying high on the outer rim of the wheel. It was not broken. Tubes burned red at the front end. There was a door opening in the side. Things began to come out of it.

Things shaped like Son, only thick and clumsy, with queer gleaming bulbs on their heads.

A strange contracting shiver ran through Son. Since sound

and breath had gone, and the effigies that lay in his ship had ceased to move, nothing had stirred on the wheel but Son himself.

In the broken ships there was never anything but scraps of odd substance, scattered as though by some bursting inner force. Son and Aona had talked idly of living beings, but Son hadn't bothered his head about them much.

He was Himself. He had the sun, and space, and Aona. It was sufficient.

Aona said impatiently, "Well, Son?"

"It's a ship," he answered, with his mind. "Only it isn't wrecked. Aona, there are living things coming out of it."

He stood staring at the Veil, and the misty light beyond.

"Aona," his mind whispered. "In my head I'm cold and hot all at once. I want to go and do, but I don't know where or what. What's the matter with me, Aona?"

"It's fear," she told him softly. "I have it, too."

Son could feel it, pulsing from her mind. In all the years of life he had never felt it before. Now it had him by the throat.

Aona cried, "What if these creatures should harm you, or the Light?"

"You have said that nothing in this universe could harm me now. And"—Son shivered—"no one would do what has to be done to destroy the Light."

"But these creatures—we don't know what knowledge they may have. Son, if anything should happen . . ."

Son raised his arms to the darkness.

"I don't want you to be afraid, Aona. Tear away the Veil!"

"I can't, darling. You know neither of us can, until the Veil of itself passes behind you."

"How long, Aona?"

She laughed, with an attempt at her old sweet teasing. "How long is 'long' in your world, Son? How long have you lived? How long have we talked? No one knows. Only, the Veil grows thinner every time we meet, every time we talk like this.

"Stay by the Light, Son. Don't let anyone harm it!"

Son's blue eyes narrowed. "I love you," he said quietly. "No one shall harm the Light."

"I'll stay with you," she said. "They won't be able to see—yet."

Son turned and went, across the tumbled plain of dead ships, with Aona's misty light following beyond the blurred and pulsing dark.

There were seven of the invaders. They stood in a close knot beside their ship, staring at the green fire of the Light. Three of them began to dance clumsily. The others placed shapeless hands on each other's shapeless shoulders and shook and pounded.

Son's eyes were as sharp as the spear-points of the stars. He lay behind a steering-jet housing, watching, and he saw with shock that there were faces under the glittering helmets.

Faces very like his own.

There were three round, smooth faces. They belonged to the ones who danced. There was one deeply lined face with bushy eyebrows and a framing straggle of white hair. Then there were two others, which Son sensed to be of different races.

One was round and green and small, with shining eyes the color of space, and a mouth like a thin wound. The other differed from the first three only in subtle points of line and shape, but its face was like a mask beaten out of dark iron, with deepset, sullen eyes.

The seventh face drove all the others out of Son's mind. It was bronzed and grim and strong, with some driving inner force about it that was like the pulse Son felt beating in space, when he lay on the crest of the wheel watching the sun and the burning stars.

This last man seemed to be the leader. He turned to the others, his mouth moving. Then the mouths of the others moved also. Presently five of the invaders turned. Son thought they were going away again.

But two of them—the white-haired one and the one with the

dark, vital face—started together, out across the broken plain of ships. And Son tensed where he lay.

They were heading toward the heart of the wheel, where the glow of the Light danced like the fire-veils of the sun.

Who knew what knowledge, what powers they might have? Son called to Aona, and followed, keeping out of sight, his blue eyes narrowed and hard.

They were almost over the Light when Son heard the first human thought-voice, as though the power of the Light brought it out. It was faint and indistinct. He could catch only fragments.

". . . here, inside Mercury's orbit . . . heat! . . . found it, after five years . . ."

That was the bronzed man speaking. Then—

"Yes, thank God! Now if we can . . ."

Son wished the voices were clearer. There was a terrible, disturbing urgency about them.

The invaders paused where the green light was strongest, at the heart of the wheel.

The mind of the grim, dark man said, "Down there."

He started to lower himself into a crevice between two hulls. And Son, driven by a sudden stab of anger, leaped up.

He came striding across the searing metal, naked and erect and beautiful, his fair head burning in the sunlight.

He flung up one corded arm, and his mind cried out, "No! You can't go down."

The invaders straightened, staring. The face of the bronzed, strong man went white, the lines of it blurring into slackness. The white-haired man swayed on his feet.

"The radiation's getting me, Ransome," he whispered. "I'm having hallucinations."

"No. No, I see it, too." The eyes of the bronzed man burned into Son's. "A man, naked in open space."

He stumbled forward, his gaze fixed on the powerful body outlined against the stars.

Son watched him come, conscious of a curious pulsing excitement. Anger, resentment, fear for the Light, and something else. Something like the first time he had spoken to Aona through the Veil.

The bronzed man stopped before him. His lips moved in that queer way they had. Son heard his mind speaking, faintly.

"What are you?"

"I am Son," he answered simply. "What do you want with the Light?"

Again he heard the faint mind-voice. "You can't understand me, of course. I don't know what you are, god or demon, but don't try to stop us! For God's sake, don't make it any harder!"

"But I do understand. You can't go down there."

Ransome turned. "Dick," he said, "Lord only knows what this —this creature is, or what it will do. But we've got to get down there and study this thing. If it tries to stop us, I'll kill it."

Dick nodded his white head. His face was lined and very tired. "Surely nothing will stop us now," he said. "Not now."

"I'll cover you," said Ransome. Dick slid down into the crevice. The bronzed man drew something from his belt and waited.

Son stepped forward, anger and fear cording his muscles.

The dark man said, "I don't want to kill you. I have no right to kill you, because of what you are. But that thing down there is going to be destroyed."

Son stopped, quite still. A great flaming pulse shot through him. And then he gathered himself.

The spring of his corded thighs carried him full over the crack down which the white-haired man had gone. One long arm reached down. The hand closed angrily on smooth glass.

The helmet shattered. Son had a momentary glimpse of a lined, weary face upturned, faded eyes staring in unbelieving horror. Then the flesh of the face split into crimson ribbons, and the body under the space suit altered strangely.

Son got up slowly, feeling strange and unsteady in his thoughts. He hadn't wanted to destroy the man, only to make him come back.

He became aware, then, of Ransome, standing with a metal thing in his hand, staring at him with eyes like the savage, dying red stars.

"It didn't touch him," Ransome's mind was saying. "A heat ray strong enough to fuse steel, and it didn't touch him. And Dick's dead."

Ransome hurled the gun suddenly into Son's face.

"Do you know what you've done?" his mind shouted. "Dick was a physicist—about the only one with any knowledge that hasn't died of old age. He might have found the way to destroy that thing. Now, if our weapons don't work on it . . .

"The effect is accelerating. Every child born since the Cloud is horribly susceptible. There isn't any time any more for anything. There won't be anyone to follow us, because now there's no time to learn."

Ransome stepped close to Son. His head was thrown back, his face a grim, hard mask streaked suddenly by little shining things that ran from those savage eyes.

"You don't know what that means, do you? You don't know how old Dick was, with his white hair and his wrinkles. Thirty-six! Or me. I'm nineteen—nineteen. And my life is already half gone.

"All over the Solar System it's like that, because of this hellish thing that came in the Cloud. We've hunted the System over for five years, all of us that could, for a thing that wouldn't react to any test or show on any instrument. And when we found it . . ."

He stopped, the veins knotted across his forehead, a little muscle twitching in one lean cheek.

Then, very calmly, he said, "Get him, boys."

Son jerked around, but it was too late. The five who had stayed in the ship were all around him. For a long time Son had been conscious only of these two men, and the strange confusion in his mind—a confusion made worse, somehow, by those mysterious crystal drops running from Ransome's eyes. They caught him, somewhere, deep.

Ropes of light metal fell around him. He fought like a Titan in the naked blaze of the sun. But they were experts with their ropes. They caught his wrists and ankles, dividing his power, baffling him with tenuous cords of elastic strength.

Son knew that his mass was still sufficiently in phase to be subject to such laws as gravity and tension. He fought. But presently he was spread-eagled on the burning metal, helpless.

The man with the face like beaten metal and the sullen eyes said, "We were watching from the ship. We thought we must be crazy when we saw this—man standing out here. Then we thought you might need help."

He stopped, staring at Son. "The heat ray didn't touch him."

"No," said Ransome quietly. "That's how he got Dickson."

The one with the queer green face snapped, "Dickson's dead?"

Ransome nodded. "Down in the crack there. We were trying to get down to study the light. He—it didn't want us to go."

The green-faced one said, "My God!"

"Quite. Arun, you and one of the boys guard the ship. Teck, you mount guard here with the other. Greenough, come with me."

One of the round-faced ones stepped forward. His eyes were light blue, oddly empty in spite of their brightness. He looked down at the crevice where Dickson's body was, and his mind said, "I'm afraid. I don't want to go down there. I'm afraid."

"Come on, Greenough," Ransome snapped. His lips started to move again, and stopped abruptly.

Son caught the thought, "Got to hurry. God knows what this radiation will do to us, right on top of it."

"Sir," said Greenough jerkily, "what if there are more like him down there?"

Ransome turned his grim, hard face on the boy. Son felt again that force, the strength that pulsed between the stars.

"Well," said Ransome, "what if there are?"

He turned and slid down into the crevice.

Greenough closed his pale, scared eyes, licked his lips, and followed.

Teck, the man with the sullen eyes, laughed—a biting mind-sound as hard as his jaw-line. "Hell of a gunnery officer."

Arun said absently, "He's only eleven." His eyes, purple-black and opaque as a dark nebula, swung jerkily from Son to the crevice where Dickson lay, and back again.

Teck was a big man, as big as Son, but Arun topped him by a foot. He was very slender, moving with a queer rubbery grace.

"What if we can't do it?" he said suddenly. "What if our weapons won't work on it any more than they did on *him*?"

"Then," answered Teck evenly, "the last generation of mankind will die of old age within fifty years." His sullen gaze roved over Son, over and over, and his mind was whispering to itself.

"Mutation," he said abruptly. "That's it. Complete change of cellular structure, metabolism, brain tissue, everything. Mutation in the living individual. I wonder how long . . ."

"Look at that green light," whispered Arun. "Remember how it filled the whole sky when we came into the Cloud? Cosmic dust, the scientist said. Temporary effect. But it stayed, when the Cloud went."

His long thin arms came up in a blind sort of gesture. "We were millions of miles away, then. What will it do to us now?"

Teck studied his hands. "We're not aging, anyway. Concentrated effect is probably different. Feel anything?"

"Deep. Deep inside me. I—"

"Your cellular structure is different from ours, anyway."

Arun swayed slightly, watching the green light pulse up from below. Beads of sweat ran down his face.

"Yes," he whispered. "Different. You know how the Cloud affected us on Tethys. If our life-span were not almost three times as long as yours—"

He bent suddenly over Son, and more of the queer shining things were trickling out of his eyes.

"For five years we've watched our people die, hunting for this thing. Dickson was our only chance. And you, you damned freak—"

He lifted his long arms again, as though to cover his head. "I'll get back to the ship now," he said abruptly, and turned.

Teck hesitated for a heartbeat, scowling at Arun. Then he stepped in front of him, the thing they called a heat gun in his hand.

"Sit down, Arun."

"You heard Ransome's orders." The Tethysman was trembling.

"In the Martian Drylands, where I come from," murmured Teck, "men sometimes get what we call *esht*—desert-fear. They take other men's water and *vaards,* and run away. You're the engineer, Arun, and even without me to do the navigating. . . . Sit down, Arun."

The Tethysman sat, a fluid folding of thin length. The two round-faced boys stood by, not moving or speaking, the fear so strong in their minds that Son could hear it shouting.

He saw and heard all this with a small part of his brain. Most of it was thinking of the Light and the men working their way down to the queer hole where it lay among the tangled ships.

This talk of age and years and dying and humanity meant nothing to him. In all his universe there was only himself, the wheel, the sun, the distant stars, and Aona. There was no day or night, no time.

He was angry and afraid, full of hatred and resentment and a queer tearing at his throat, as though he had lost some vital part of him—the Light. Were they going to take the horrible way of destruction that Aona had told him of? Or did they know another way?

He tensed his corded body against the metal ropes, and his mind cried out, "Aona!" as though he were seeing her vanish forever beyond the Veil.

The Martian said, softly, "He used to be human. I wonder . . ." He leaned forward suddenly. "Can you hear me?"

Son answered, "Yes." He was beginning to realize something. The mouth-movements of these men had something to do with speaking, and their clearest, loudest thoughts came with them.

Teck must have caught the motion of his eyes, for he cried out.

"Yes! But you can't speak, because you don't breathe air. Probably lost both lungs and vocal cords. You must be a telepath. I'll bet that's what you are!"

The Martian's dark-iron mask of a face was eager; his sullen eyes full of little sparks.

"You hear me think, is that it? Nod your head once, if you do."

Son hesitated, studying the men with narrow eyes. If he talked with them, he might find out how much they knew. He nodded.

Teck was quite still for a moment. Arun sat rigid, staring with eerie purple eyes at the Light.

"How long have you been here?" asked Teck.

Son shook his head.

"Where did you come from?" Again Son shook his head, and Teck asked, "You know no other place than this?"

Again the negative.

Teck drew a long breath.

"You must have been born here, then. In one of the first ships swept up by the magnetic force of this thing as it passed through the Solar System. Then your ship cannot have been wrecked. Probably the counter-pull of some planet saved it, as our new Elker drive saved us."

His deep eyes blazed. "Your body was the same as mine, once. How long would it take to change me to a being like you?"

Arun got up suddenly. "I've got to get back to the ship."

Teck's gun hand was steady. "Sit down!"

Arun's thought rose tightly. "But I've got to! Something's wrong—" Teck's gun thrust forward menacingly. Arun sat down again, slowly. The green light wavered around him, making his face curiously indistinct.

Teck's thought hammered at Son.

"You know what the light is?"

Son hesitated, sending Aona a rapid question.

Her mind said, "No! Don't tell, Son. It might help them destroy it."

He shook his head. "No."

Teck's lips drew back. "You're lying," he said, and then whirled around, his dark hard face taut.

Arun had risen, and the single wild shriek in his mind stabbed Son's brain so that he writhed in his shackles.

The two boys backed off, their faces white and staring. Even Teck drew back a bit, and his gun hand trembled.

Arun was changing. Son watched tensely, forgetting for a moment even his agony of fear for the Light.

The lines of the green, smooth face of the Tethysman blurred and shifted in the green light, like something seen under water. Strange writhing tremors shook his body.

His mind cried out with his moving lips: "Something's happening to me. Oh, God! And all for nothing . . ."

He staggered forward. His eyes were night-black and luminous, horribly steady in that blurred face, fixed on Son.

Son knew, lying there chained, that he was in deadly peril. Because Arun was on his own plane, though a little past him.

"All for nothing—mankind lost," wailed the thought-voice. "I'm going blind. No. *No!* I'm seeing—*through* . . ."

His scream shivered cold as space along Son's nerve-channels. The tall rubbery form loomed over him, bending closer . . .

One of the boys fainted quietly, rolling like an ungainly bundle into a deep shaft between two wrecks. Teck caught his breath.

"I'm not through with him yet," he muttered, and raised his gun.

The glassite helmet melted and ran. The head and the glowing purple eyes beneath it were untouched.

And then no one moved, nor spoke. Arun's head and face quivered, merging imperceptibly into the blurred darkness of the Veil.

Aona cried out suddenly, "He's coming through!" And then, "No!" The change was too swift. Too many atoms in transition. He's caught . . ."

Shivering against Son's mind, like the single wild shaft of a distant comet, came Arun's thought.

"No, not here! Not here—*between!*"

And then he was gone. His space suit crumpled down, quite empty.

Teck swayed, the dark hardness of his face bleached and rigid. "What did he mean—'between'?"

Son lay quite still, hearing Aona sob beyond the Veil. He knew. Aona had told him. Between universes—the darkness, the nothingness, the nowhere. He felt the cold dark crawling in his mind.

Teck laughed suddenly, biting and defiant. His deep eyes were fixed on Son, sprawled like a young god in the raw blaze of the sun.

"By the gods," he whispered, "it's worth the risk!"

Greenough came stumbling up out of the crevice.

He looked more like a child than ever. His round face was dazed and bewildered, screwed up strangely. Even to Son, there was something terrible and unholy in that child's shallow-eyed face on a man's strong body.

Teck drew a slow breath. Son felt a dark, iron strength in him, different from the strength of the bronzed Ransome, that was like the beat of space itself, but great, too. Great, and dangerous.

"What did you find out?" asked Teck. "Where's Ransome?"

Son's brain burned within him with fear, though he saw that the green Light was still unchanged.

"Down there," said Greenough, and whimpered. He blinked his eyes, moving his head and pawing at his helmet as though to clear it.

"I only looked at it a minute. It was too little and too big all at once, and I was frightened."

Teck caught him by the shoulders and shook him roughly. "Looked at what?" he demanded. "What's happened?"

"At the light," said Greenough, in a far-away voice. "We found it inside a ship. We could look right through the metal. I only looked a minute because I was frightened. I was frightened, I was . . ."

Teck's strong hands snapped his teeth together. "What was it?"

Greenough's shallow eyes wandered to his. "Ransome says it's part of another universe. He's still there, looking. Only . . ."

Greenough's voice broke in a little hiccough. "Only he can't see any more."

Son felt a great surge of relief. The Light was safe, so far.

Greenough slipped suddenly from Teck's hands, sitting wide-legged on the battered hull.

"I'm scared," he said. "I want Mama." Big slow drops ran down his cheeks, and again Son was stirred by something deep and strange.

Teck turned slowly to Son. "He was six years old when the Cloud came. You can build a man's body in eleven years, but not his brain." He was silent, looking down with deep, intense eyes.

He spoke, after a bit, slowly and deliberately.

"So it's part of another universe. Diluted by distance, its radiation speeds human metabolism, causing swift age. Concentrated, it changes the human organism into an alien metabolism, alien flesh.

"Slim almost made it through, but his peculiar chemical balance destroyed him. You must be in the same transition stage, but much slower, being passed by the changing of your basic vibratory rate into another space-time continuum."

Son couldn't hide the sudden flicker in his eyes. He hated this dark Martian suddenly, this man who guessed so much.

"So it's true," said Teck. "Confirmation of the old conception of coexisting universes on different vibratory planes. But how would you know, unless—unless you can talk to that other universe?"

He laughed at the bitter look in Son's blue eyes.

"Afraid, aren't you? That means you have something to hide, or protect." He dropped suddenly to one knee, catching his fingers in Son's fair hair.

"Look at me. I want to watch your eyes. You do know what

that light is, and how it can be destroyed. If I could get a body like yours, and still not cross over . . .

"Do you feed on the green light, or the sun?"

The question came so quickly that Son's eyes flicked to the canopy of fire overhead, before he could stop them. Teck sat back on his heels with a long, slow sigh.

"That's all I needed," he murmured. "Your friends on the other side evidently can't help you, or you'd be free now." He rose abruptly. "Greenough! You, there, sailor! Help me get this loose hull-section over here."

The two pale, empty-eyed boys rose obediently and helped. The heavy metal plates, uptilted by the force of the original crash, were not far from Son. They had only to heat the bottom with cutting torches and bend it.

Son lay, then, in black, utter dark.

"Now then," said Teck. "Back to the ship, both of you."

The boys stumbled off across the broken ships. Son could see them, out in the glare beyond his prison shadow. Teck waited until their backs were well turned.

The beam of his heat gun flickered briefly, twice. Two crumpled shapes fell and were still. Teck turned, smiling tightly.

"No need to have a whole race of supermen." He inspected the spiderweb of metal ropes that bound Son, and nodded, satisfied.

"When you get hungry enough for energy, you'll tell me how to destroy the light. And then—" His hard dark face was cut deep with triumph, his eyes fierce with dreams.

"After I destroy the light, the aging process will stop. People will start to live again. And I'll be virtually a god, untouchable, impervious."

He laughed, softly and deep within him, rolling Son's head with his foot.

"You wouldn't know what that means, would you? Think it over while I'm down taking care of Ransome!"

He turned and slid down into the crevice.

Son cried out in anguish, "Aona!"

The Veil, the darkness that was everywhere and nowhere, that was all through the wheel and yet not of it, shimmered and swirled.

"Son! Son, what has happened?"

His mind had been too busy to tell her before. Now he hesitated, thinking of Teck clambering down to kill the man with the strength of the stars in him; thinking of Arun's agony and Greenough's fear and the tired face of the man he had killed; thinking most of all of the strange shining drops that ran from their eyes.

"Aona, what is age?"

"We had it, long ago. The legends hardly remember, except that it was ugly, and sad."

"What are years?" He tried to give her the thought as he had taken it from their minds. But the idea was so alien to him, the time-concept so vague in itself, that he couldn't make himself clear.

She said, "I don't know, Son."

"And Aona—what is death?"

"No one knows that, Son. It's like sleep, only one never wakens. But we live so long before it comes, there's time for everything. And even in the little part of our universe that's left, there are so many worlds to see."

Already, there in the shadow, he was hungry for the sun. He would starve for energy if he couldn't get free. He gathered himself to try . . .

And then, quite suddenly, it happened. The thing he'd waited all his life for. He looked into the shimmering blur of the Veil and cried, "Aona! Aona! I can see you!"

He surged against his ropes, aflame inside him with a joy like the fire of the sun itself.

The Veil was still there, hiding most of Beyond. But it was closer and thinner. He could see the slim silver shaft of her standing against soft blurred colors, could almost see the luminous brightness of her eyes.

"Oh darling," she cried. "Almost!"

Everything, all memory of the invaders and their alien troubles, left Son's mind. He stared hungrily into the Veil, watching the pale blur of her face steady, become clear.

"You're beautiful," he whispered. "Beautiful as a blue star."

"And you . . . Oh Son, go down to the Light. The force is strongest there. The Veil will pass more quickly."

"But I can't. I'm tied." He told her briefly what had happened.

She laughed. "You've changed since then. The ratio has changed. More of your atoms are vibrating in phase with my universe than with yours. From now on the change will be very swift. Try again!"

He tried, pitting his strength against the ropes. Slowly their resistance slackened. His wrists and ankles slid through them, as though they were heavy smoke.

He rose and shook himself, and looked once more at the wheel and the stars and the blazing sun. Then he turned to Aona, and a pulse of joy rose in him until he thought surely his head would burst.

He plunged downward, toward the Light.

He found that he had no need to clamber through the broken ships.

The matter of their metal walls resisted him as water resists a swimmer, no more. He went downward through the green light that grew stronger as he went, until it was like the water at the bottom of a green lake.

Aona followed, running on little white feet across pale blue grass, with a great sweep of sky growing clearer behind her. Her silver draperies whipped in something she had called a wind. Her eyes were silvery, too, tilted with impish piquancy, and there was a crest of some feathery stuff on her head, burning red-gold like his own sun.

His mind shouted to hers and hers laughed back, and the barrier between their universes was growing thin.

It was almost a shock to Son to see Teck crawling through a doorway in the wrecked saloon of a liner, just above the Light itself.

Ransome crouched on the deck before him, his back turned, quite still.

The Martian's hard lips smiled. He drew his heat gun.

Son stopped, the sheer happiness of the moment shattered. His dark hatred for this man came back, his instinctive loathing of what the fingers of his mind had brushed against in Teck's brain. Also, dimly, it had to do with Ransome.

Hardly realizing what he was doing, he sprang at Teck.

His arm sheared harmlessly through the matter of Teck's helmet and head. Son realized then that he had no more power over the stuff of his universe.

But Teck started and cried out, and his aim was spoiled. The heat beam flicked across Ransome's shoulder, melting a little hole in the fabric of his space suit.

The Martian's sullen, fiery eyes were wide.

"You've changed," he whispered. "Like Arun. I can see through you."

Then, furiously he shouted, "Damn you! *Look out!*"

He lurched sideways, but he was just too late. A searching tongue of heat ranged across him, across Son and the metal wall behind him, leaving a little molten trail. It rose and fell methodically, weaving a net of death across that whole space.

Teck's space suit collapsed. Son witnessed again, this time with a curious satisfaction, the disruption of an alien organism.

Alien. Yes. And yet . . .

He turned to see Ransome crouched on one knee, holding the shoulder of his suit with one hand and the heat gun—not firing now—in the other.

His eyes were open, but they didn't see. Son knew what had happened. Ransome had looked too long at the Light, and the distances, the planes and angles and curves of it had pulled his sight too far.

Son said, "He's dead."

Ransome nodded. "I heard his mind die. This thing down here—I can hear you, too. I couldn't, up there."

A strange, subtle thrill crept along Son's consciousness. Something in him reached out to that mind, strong even now, strong as the pulse-beat of space.

"You're not bad," said Ransome. "You just don't understand. I don't suppose you could, although you were human once."

He dropped the gun, as though it didn't matter any more. "I'm going to die, you know. There's a hole in my suit. In a few minutes the air will leak out. But there's no time here, is there? And you've forgotten what air is, or why I need it."

The bronzed, grim face smiled, but it was not humorous. "So humanity dies, because one of its sons has no conception of time."

"Son!" It was Aona calling, peering through the thinning Veil. Ransome lifted his head. "Who's that?"

Son said, "It's Aona. She's waiting for me." His surroundings were getting indistinct.

The Veil was passing.

"Aona. Someone you love. Son—that's what she called you, isn't it? Son, what is this light? Where did it come from?"

The strength of Ransome's mind was bright and terrible. It was like the fire of a dying star.

"It's— Aona, you tell him." Son's thoughts were strangely chaotic.

"It's a part of my universe," she said slowly. There was a quality of stillness in her thought, a subtle forerunner of fear. "Something happened, in one small corner of space, to the electrical tension that holds the fabric of the universe together. There was a release of energy so unthinkably vast . . ."

Her burning crest drooped as she shivered. "Scraps of our universe were hurled right through the walls of vibration that separate us from other space-time continua. Only a very little bit of ours survived.

"The bit of our universe in yours, vibrating at a different basic rate, makes a sort of bridge between us, by altering atomic speeds. Son has changed almost completely. Only a few of his atoms now vibrate in phase with your universe."

Ransome nodded. "And that alien vibration is destroying us. Can't you take it back?"

Aona shook her glowing head. "We could not possibly generate enough energy to draw it back." Her silvery, tilted eyes went to Son, and the terror in them stabbed him.

"I hear you," said Ransome softly. "Then there is a way."

Aona whispered, "Yes."

All Son's being went out to her. And yet, some tiny scrap of his mind clung to Ransome's, as though to something he must not lose.

"I don't understand," he said slowly. "Years, age, time—they mean nothing."

"No." Ransome's grim dark head strained back in his helmet. His face was veined and glistening with sweat.

"Think of it this way. You love Aona. She's beautiful—I can hear that in your mind. Suppose that now, while you looked at her, she were to wither and crumple and die . . ."

He broke off, as though fighting for strength. Not the pulsing strength of his mind, but the power of his body. When his thought came again, it was weaker.

"Look at your own body, Son. Think of it, now, growing weak and ugly and bent . . ."

He staggered up suddenly, his eyes like the last embers of a dying sun, fixed on nothingness.

"You're mankind's only hope, Son. Son. Remember the people who called you that. They were human. Remember. Son— of humanity."

Ransome's suit collapsed with a rush. Son shut his eyes.

"Son," he whispered. "His thought said—" He couldn't phrase it clearly, only that it meant coming from something, being a part of it, as he, already, was part of Aona.

And Aona whispered, "I feel it growing in your mind. Oh, Son . . ."

He could see the flowers around her feet now, the distant fires of some great sun. A strange tremor shook his body, a shifting and changing. The Veil was thinner.

"Son, they're not your people any longer. You couldn't even understand."

"No. No, but I could *feel.*" He turned abruptly. "There's something I have to do. Quickly."

He plunged off, rushing through the dissolving matter of his universe. Up, and into the ship he thought of as his, though he had left it long ago. He hated it, down here away from the sun.

Aona followed him, her feet like little white stars in the grass.

Things grew dimmer, more vague. Son had only to wait, to put off thinking until it was too late. But something drove him on.

Presently he stood in the cabin of his ship, looking down at the still effigies. The people who had called him Son.

He shivered with something more than the shock of change. These still faces—Dickson's face, and Arun's, and Ransome's.

These still shapes, that had touched him and called him Son and shed queer shining drops from their eyes.

Something caught at him, wrung him so that he cried out.

"I don't want to. Aona, I don't want to. But I must!"

Her thought was a mere tremor across his mind. "I think I knew, when he spoke to you. I try to think, if they were my people, suffering and dying—"

"I don't want to, Aona. But he said—Son of humanity."

Only to postpone, to wait until it was too late. The Veil was so thin. Son beat his hands together, very softly. Then, blindly, he rushed back toward the Light.

Something had got hold of him, was driving him. He knew it was right. But he wanted to fight it, to hold it off until it couldn't hurt him.

And he was afraid.

He stopped in the ship above the Light, where Ransome lay dead. He raised his corded arms and cried, "No! I can't. I don't understand!"

He saw Aona watching him on her shining hilltop, not moving or speaking. And slow silver drops rolled from her tilted eyes and down her cheeks.

Then he knew. Then he was calm and steady, and not very much afraid. Because he understood why the bright drops had rolled from the eyes of the strange men.

He smiled at Aona. He took a long, sweeping look at the sun and the sky and the blowing grass, and the silver shaft of her standing in the midst of it.

Then he went slowly down toward the Light.

He knew what would happen. Aona had told him. Most of his substance was in her universe now. Part of it was still in his own. But there were atoms in him just changing. Atoms that were—Between.

Because of the atoms that matched its own, he could penetrate the Light. The atoms in transition would set up a vibration in the Light that had not been in Son, because of the balancing pull of two universes.

The vibratory balance of the Light would be destroyed, because Son's universe had no hold on it. It would be pushed back through the wall of that universe, but not back to its own.

A little green roundness that could be held in his hand, that yet was not round at all and that stretched into soaring distance. Color and line and form that melted and flowed and were not.

Son went, without stopping, straight into the heart of the Light.

For an instant, or an eternity, he was lost in chaos. He knew nothing—whether he moved or was still, whether he saw the black-green rushing darkness or whether it was only the picture of his own fear.

He didn't fight. He caught only two things to him in his mind—Ransome's strength and Aona, standing on her shining hilltop.

An instant, or an eternity. And then there was stillness, a cessation. Son opened his eyes and looked about—at the space Between.

VICTORY UNINTENTIONAL

Isaac Asimov

It might be possible to limit Isaac Asimov to one story in this book, but it would be less fun. Asimov didn't become recognized as a top writer till late in 1941, but he produced a good number of stories and, unlike some of the famous writers of the time, he was always entertaining even when his stories fell short of classic stature.

His early robot stories fall into this category. Though he became famous for them later, when his ingenuity in exploring the ramifications of robot intelligence had produced a definitive series, individually they were usually simple problems in logic, entertaining but not particularly striking. A fan-magazine review of one of these early stories shows how they were received at the time: "Asimov okay, though he'd better be warned if he has ideas of running a series. . . . The days of the wacky robot stuff are gone."

In a sense they were, for 1942 saw the end of the famous Adam Link series by Eando Binder, which had been appearing in *Amazing Stories* since 1939. The reason wasn't lack of popularity, however: Binder had been hired by Fawcett Publications to write comic book stories for *Captain Marvel* and other characters of the burgeoning comics industry. His Adam Link stories, concerning a powerful robot with human emotions, were charming but rather simple-minded adventures. As Nelson S. Bond noted when he wrote a satire on robot stories late in 1942, Adam Link was "a robot who far outdoes anything for which Mankind would ever wish to create mechanical servants; he becomes, in effect, a plate-armored superman whose pistoned heart churns with emotion, whose sponge-iridium brain palpitates with love of his flesh-and-blood brothers."

(Bond couldn't resist adding that " 'sponge-iridium' is one of the least stable of all forms of matter; it fuses easily and has a tendency to break down under even such slight changes as a rise in temperature or a volt of electricity. Perhaps this will explain to you the completely irrational actions of a certain fictional robot known to all fans.")

But if emotional robots like Adam Link and Lester del Rey's Helen O'Loy had had their day, the field was still wide open for exploration of the situations that could be created by robots that behaved purely logically. Since he'd written his earliest stories, Asimov had been hoping to create a character or characters around whom he could establish a series. "For one thing," he explained later, "you had a definite background that was carried on from story to story, so that half your work was done for you. Secondly, if the series became popular, it would be difficult to reject new stories that fit into it." But when he did manage to start a successful series, the robot stories, it was almost by accident—the first story, "Robbie," wasn't conceived as the beginning of a series—and the stories weren't based on particular characters but rather on ideas, the exploration of robot mentality.

This was typical of Asimov's approach to fiction (the "Foundation" series was also based on an idea), but most of the successful series in science fiction then featured characters who were remarkable in some intriguing way. Thus we had Gerry Carlyle and the Golden Amazon, "superwomen"; Bond's Horsesense Hank, the bucolic scientific genius; and Binder's emotional robot, Adam Link. There were also A. R. McKenzie's Juggernaut Jones, a spaceship salesman; L. Sprague de Camp's Johnny Black, an ape with human intelligence; James Norman's Martian detective, Oscar (with a tulip-nose that could smell thoughts); and Henry Kuttner's Hollywood on the Moon series featuring Anthony Quade, cameraman for Nine Planets Films.

Some series characters were just that: "characters." There was the free-wheeling con man Pete Manx, who traveled into the past and stumbled into creating the legends of Hercules, King Arthur, etc. (Henry Kuttner and Arthur K. Barnes took turns writing these stories.)

Nelson S. Bond's most successful character was Lancelot Biggs, a spaceship navigator who spoke like this: "Any time a ship gets within umpteen miles of Jupiter, pal, it's hold your hat and give the prayerbook a quick riffle. That hunk of red goo has gravitational power—spelled with a capital 'Phew!' More spaceships than you have corpuscles have fallen within old Jupe's drag, crashed on the planet."

Robert Bloch wrote a Damon Runyonesque series about Lefty Feep, a lowlife gambler who said, on learning that he'd slept two decades into the future, "So I do a twenty-year stretch on the grass. Well, there are worse places. But I see where I am plenty behind on current events. What do you hear from the mob?"

But the most flamboyant series character of all was Edmond Hamilton's Captain Future, who was featured in a series of novels in a magazine of the same name. *Captain Future* was a companion magazine of *Thrilling Wonder Stories* and *Startling Stories,* both of which had relied heavily on series (Gerry Carlyle, Hollywood on the Moon, Pete Manx among them) to hold the readers without resorting to serialized novels. The editorial director, Leo Margulies, attended the First World Science Fiction Convention in July 1939 and remarked, "I didn't think you fans could be so damn sincere." He laid plans for *Captain Future* on the spot: "There must be a super-scientist hero. There must also be aides: a robot and an android and, of course, a beautiful female assistant. Each story must be a crusade to bring to justice an arch villain; and, in each novel, the hero must be captured and escape three times."

The formula was aimed at the lowest teenage bracket of readers, prompting sf historian Michael Ashley to wonder "just what Margulies's opinion of the fans really was!" Whatever Margulies expected, *Captain Future* never sold as well as its companion sf magazines, and was canceled in 1944.

Raymond A. Palmer was the other editor who was most receptive to series stories; an issue of *Amazing Stories* or *Fantastic Adventures* without Adam Link, Lancelot Biggs, the Golden Amazon, Lefty Feep or others seemed completely atypical. Palmer even managed to acquire a dozen Edgar Rice Burroughs stories about John Carter of Mars, Carson Napier of Venus and David Innes of Pellucidar; these were thinly disguised installments of then-forthcoming novels.

Palmer says this emphasis on series wasn't a deliberate policy, and Robert Bloch confirms him, saying that when he began writing about Lefty Feep, "I had no thought of doing a series; it's just that the first Feep story seemed to inspire a sequel, so I wrote it immediately and Palmer accepted it at once. . . . I never discussed a series concept and Palmer never suggested any further ideas; I merely wrote further stories as they occurred to me." But the various series were enormously popular and contributed heavily to the fact that *Amazing* was *Astounding's* only competitor in science fiction circulation.

Notwithstanding the success of series stories, John Campbell didn't always buy a story even if it was part of a series he'd been running. Early in February 1942, Isaac Asimov wrote "Victory Unintentional," a robot story that was a sequel to an earlier *non*-robot story published in *Astounding,* but neither of these considerations moved Campbell to buy it: he returned the manuscript with the succinct notation "$CH_3C_2CH_2CH_2SH$." As Campbell expected, Asimov recognized this as the formula for butyl mercaptan, which gives the skunk its smell. (Asimov was entitled to take comfort from the reflection that only a friendly editor who admired his talent would send such a pungent rejection.)

Asimov sold the story instead to Alden Norton for *Super Science Stories,* where it proved to be one of the most popular stories in the August 1942 issue. Readers called it "Number One in any language" and "Asimov's best story of the year, no doubt about it." (Even though "Foundation" had appeared several months before.) Campbell's judgment was not necessarily always correct.

As it happened, "Victory Unintentional" was the last story Asimov wrote during the Golden Age. Early in 1942 he joined Heinlein and de Camp doing research for the Navy, and in July he got married. He was working a six-day, fifty-four-hour week, and the excitement of a new marriage occupied what time was left, so it was fourteen months before he wrote another story.

At that time Asimov had no idea that he would ever become a professional writer. "I never thought of my writing as anything but a way to help out with my college tuition. . . . My career was to be chemistry." And so it was for some years. Though he wrote a few stories during the war and began selling novels in the late 1940s, it wasn't until 1958 that Asimov became a full-time writer. His talent, knowledge and productivity have since become legendary, and he's currently approaching the publication of his two hundredth book. He's won awards for both fiction and nonfiction, is the editorial director of *Isaac Asimov's Science Fiction Magazine,* and is so well known even to the non–science fiction public that he's hired to do television commercials. Isaac Asimov has become one of the most successful writers ever to come out of science fiction.

"Victory Unintentional" is an example of his early writing, produced less than four years after his first story. But it deftly combines wonders and humor, showing that Asimov had already mastered this technique in 1942. It can stand beside the work of anyone, including the Asimov of today.

REFERENCES:

"Among the Hams and Pros" by John Chapman. *The Fantasite,* March-April 1942.
Fantasy Times, Second November 1941 issue.
"The Story Behind the Story" by Nelson S. Bond. *Thrilling Wonder Stories,* October 1942.
The Early Asimov by Isaac Asimov. Doubleday, 1972.
"The Ghost of Lancelot Biggs" by Nelson S. Bond. *Weird Tales,* January 1942.
"Time Wounds All Heels" by Robert Bloch. *Fantastic Adventures,* April 1942.
"Mort Weisinger: The Superman Behind Superman" by Sam Moskowitz. *Amazing Stories,* August 1964.
"Edmond Hamilton" by Sam Moskowitz. *Amazing Stories,* October 1963.
"SF Bandwaggon" by Michael Ashley. *The History of the Science Fiction Magazine, Part 2, 1936–1945.* New English Library, 1975.
Conversation with Leo Margulies, October 19, 1974.
Letter from Raymond A. Palmer, August 1975.
Letter from Robert Bloch, February 20, 1975.
Introduction by Isaac Asimov to "Victory Unintentional." *The Rest of the Robots.* Doubleday, 1964.

A. R. Brown and Joe Fortier in "Missives and Missiles." *Super Science Stories,* November 1942.

*   *   *

The spaceship leaked, as the saying goes, like a sieve.

It was supposed to! In fact, that was the whole idea!

The result, of course, was that during the journey from Ganymede to Jupiter, the ship was crammed just as full as it could be with the very hardest space vacuum. And since the ship also lacked heating devices, this space vacuum was at normal temperature, which is a fraction of a degree above absolute zero.

This, also, was according to plan. Little things like the absence of heat and air didn't annoy anyone at all on that particular spaceship.

The first near vacuum wisps of Jovian atmosphere began percolating into the ship several thousand miles above the Jovian surface. It was practically all hydrogen, though perhaps a careful gas analysis might have located a trace of helium as well. The pressure gauges began creeping skywards.

That creep continued at an accelerating pace as the ship dropped downwards in a Jupiter-circling spiral. The pointers of successive gauges, each designed for progressively higher pressures, began to move until they reached the neighborhood of a million or so atmospheres, where figures lost most of their meaning. The temperature, as recorded by thermocouples, rose slowly and erratically, and finally steadied at about seventy below zero, Centigrade.

The ship moved slowly towards the end, plowing its way heavily through a maze of gas molecules that crowded together so closely that hydrogen itself was squeezed to the density of a liquid. Ammonia vapor, drawn from the incredibly vast oceans of that liquid, saturated the horrible atmosphere. The wind, which had begun a thousand miles higher, had risen to a pitch inadequately described as a hurricane.

It was quite plain long before the ship landed on a fairly large Jovian island, perhaps seven times the size of Asia, that Jupiter was not a very pleasant world.

And yet the three members of the crew thought it was. They were quite convinced it was. But then, the three members of the crew were not exactly human. And neither were they exactly Jovian.

They were simply robots designed on Earth, for Jupiter!

ZZ Three said, "It appears to be a rather desolate place."

ZZ Two joined him and regarded the wind-blasted landscape somberly. "There are structures of some sort in the distance," he said, "which are obviously artificial. I suggest we wait for the inhabitants to come to us."

Across the room, ZZ One listened, but made no reply. He was the first constructed of the three, and half experimental. Consequently, he spoke a little less frequently than his two companions.

The wait was not too long. An air vessel of queer design swooped overhead. More followed. And then a line of ground vehicles approached, took position, and disgorged organisms. Along with these organisms came various inanimate accessories, that might have been weapons. Some of these were borne by a single Jovian, some by several, and some advanced under their own power, with Jovians perhaps inside.

The robots couldn't tell.

ZZ Three said, "They're all around us now. The logical peaceful gesture would be to come out in the open. Agreed?"

It was, and ZZ One shoved open the heavy door, which was not double, nor, for that matter, particularly airtight.

Their appearance through the door was the signal for an excited stir among the surrounding Jovians. Things were done to several of the very largest of the inanimate accessories, and ZZ Three became aware of a temperature rise on the outer rind of his beryllium-iridium-bronze body.

He glanced at ZZ Two, "Do you feel it? They're aiming heat energy at us, I believe."

ZZ Two indicated his surprise. "I wonder why?"

"Definitely a heat ray of some sort. Look at that!"

One of the rays had been jarred out of alignment for some undiscernible cause, and its line of radiation intersected a brook of sparkling pure ammonia—which promptly boiled furiously.

Three turned to ZZ One. "Make a note of this, One, will you?"

"Sure!" It was to ZZ One that the routine secretarial work fell and his method of taking a note was to make a mental addition to the accurate memory scroll within him. He had already gathered the hour by hour record of every important instrument on board ship during the trip to Jupiter. He added agreeably, "What reason shall I put for the reaction? The human masters would probably enjoy knowing."

"No reason. Or better," Three corrected himself, "no apparent reason. You might say the maximum temperature of the ray was about plus thirty, Centigrade."

Two interrupted. "Shall we try communicating?"

"It would be a waste of time," said Three. "There can't be more than a very few Jovians who know the radio-click code that's been developed between Jupiter and Ganymede. They'll have to send for one, and when he comes, he'll establish contact soon enough. Meanwhile, let's watch them. I don't understand their actions, I tell you frankly."

Nor did understanding come immediately. Heat radiation ceased, and other instruments were brought to the forefront and put into play. Several capsules fell at the feet of the watching robots, dropping rapidly and forcefully under Jupiter's gravity. They popped open and a blue liquid exuded, forming pools which proceeded to shrink rapidly by evaporation.

The nightmare wind whipped the vapors away, and where those vapors went, Jovians scrambled out of the way. One was too slow, threshed about wildly, and became very limp and still.

ZZ Two bent, dabbed a finger in one of the pools and stared at the dripping liquid. "I think this is oxygen," he said.

"Oxygen, all right," agreed Three. "This becomes stranger and stranger. It must certainly be a dangerous practice, for I would say that oxygen is poisonous to the creatures. One of them died!"

There was a pause, and then ZZ One, whose greater simplicity led at times to an increased directness of thought, said heavily, "It might be that these strange creatures in a rather childish way are attempting to destroy us."

And Two, struck by the suggestion, answered, "You know, Three, I think you're right!"

There had been a slight lull in Jovian activity and now a new structure was brought up. It possessed a slender rod that pointed skyward through the impenetrable Jovian murk. It stood with a rigidity in that starkly incredible wind that plainly indicated remarkable structural strength. From its tip came a cracking and then a flash that lit up the depths of the atmosphere into a gray fog.

For a moment the robots were bathed in clinging radiance and then Three said thoughtfully, "High-tension electricity! Quite respectable power, too. One, I think you're right. After all, the human masters have told us that these creatures seek to destroy all humanity. And organisms possessing such insane viciousness as to harbor a thought of harm against a human being"—his voice trembled at the thought—"would scarcely scruple at attempting to destroy us."

"It's a shame to have such distorted minds," said ZZ One. "Poor fellows!"

"I find it a very saddening thought," admitted Two. "Let's go back to the ship. We've seen enough for now."

They did so, and settled down to wait. As ZZ Three said, Jupiter was a roomy planet, and it might take time for Jovian transportation to bring a radio code expert to the ship. However, patience is a cheap commodity to robots.

As a matter of fact, Jupiter turned on its axis three times, according to chronometer, before the expert arrived. The rising and setting of the sun made no difference, of course, to the dead darkness at the bottom of three thousand miles of liquid-dense gas, so that one could not speak of day and night. But then, neither Jovian nor robot saw by visible light radiation and so that didn't matter.

Through this thirty-hour interval, the surrounding Jovians continued their attack with a patience and persevering relentlessness concerning which robot ZZ One made a good many mental notes. The ship was assaulted by as many varieties of forces as there were hours, and the robots observed every attack attentively, analyzing such weapons as they recognized. They by no means recognized all.

But the human masters had built well. The ship and the robots had taken fifteen years to construct, and their essentials could be expressed in a single phrase—raw strength. The attack spent itself uselessly and neither ship nor robot seemed the worse for it.

Three said, "This atmosphere handicaps them, I think. They can't use atomic disruptors, since they would only tear a hole in that soupy air and blow themselves up."

"They haven't used high explosives either," said Two, "which is well. They couldn't have hurt us, naturally, but it would have thrown us about a bit."

"High explosives are out of the question. You can't have an explosive without gas expansion, and gas just can't expand in this atmosphere."

"It's a very good atmosphere," muttered One. "I like it."

Which was natural, because he was built for it. The ZZ robots were the first robots ever turned out by the United States Robot and Mechanical Men Corp. that were not even faintly human in appearance. They were low and squat, with a center of gravity less than a foot above ground level. They had six legs apiece, stumpy and thick, designed to lift tons against two and a half times normal Earth gravity. Their reflexes were that many times Earth-normal speed, to make up for the gravity. And they were composed of a beryllium-iridium-bronze alloy that was proof against any known corrosive agent, also any known destructive agent short of a thousand-megatron atomic disruptor, under any conditions whatsoever.

To dispense with further description, they were indestructible, and so impressively powerful that they were the only robots ever built on whom the roboticists of the corporation had never quite had the nerve to pin a serial number nickname. One bright young fellow had suggested Sissy One, Two, and Three —but not in a very loud voice, and the suggestion was never repeated.

The last hours of the wait were spent in a puzzled discussion to find a possible description of a Jovian's appearance. ZZ One had made a note of their possession of tentacles and of their radial symmetry—and there he had stuck. Two and Three did their best, but couldn't help.

"You can't very well describe anything," Three declared finally, "without a standard of reference. These creatures are like nothing I know of—completely outside the positronic paths of my brain. It's like trying to describe gamma light to a robot unequipped for gamma ray reception."

It was just at that time that the weapon barrage ceased once more. The robots turned their attention to outside the ship.

A group of Jovians were advancing in curiously uneven fashion, but no amount of careful watching could determine the exact method of their locomotion. How they used their tentacles was uncertain. At times, the organisms took on a remarkable slithering motion, and then they moved at great speed, perhaps with the wind's help, for they were moving downwind.

The robots stepped out to meet the Jovians, who halted ten feet away. Both sides remained silent and motionless.

ZZ Two said, "They must be watching us, but I don't know how. Do either of you see any photo-sensitive organs?"

"I can't say," grunted Three in response. "I don't see anything about them that makes sense at all."

There was a sudden metallic clicking from among the Jovian group and ZZ One said delightedly, "It's the radio code. They've got the communications expert here."

It was, and they had! The complicated dot-dash system that over a period of twenty-five years had been laboriously developed by the beings of Jupiter and the Earthmen of Ganymede into a remarkably flexible means of communication was finally being put into practice at close range.

One Jovian remained in the forefront now, the others having fallen back. It was he that was speaking. The clicking said: "Where are you from?"

ZZ Three, as the most mentally advanced, naturally assumed spokesmanship for the robot group. "We are from Jupiter's satellite, Ganymede."

The Jovian continued: "What do you want?"

"Information. We have come to study your world and to bring back our findings. If we could have your cooperation—"

The Jovian clicking interrupted: "You must be destroyed!"

ZZ Three paused and said in a thoughtful aside to his two companions, "Exactly the attitude the human masters said they would take. They are very unusual."

Returning to his clicking, he asked simply, "Why?"

The Jovian evidently considered certain questions too obnoxious to be answered. He said, "If you leave within a single period of revolution, we will spare you—until such time as we emerge from our world to destroy the un-Jovian vermin of Ganymede."

"I would like to point out," said Three, "that we of Ganymede and the inner planets—"

The Jovian interrupted. "Our astronomy knows of the sun and of our four satellites. There are no inner planets."

Three conceded the point wearily. "We of Ganymede, then. We have no designs on Jupiter. We're prepared to offer friendship. For twenty-five years your people communicated freely with the human beings of Ganymede. Is there any reason to make sudden war upon the humans?"

"For twenty-five years," was the cold response, "we assumed the inhabitants of Ganymede to be Jovians. When we found out they were not, and that we had been treating lower animals on the scale of Jovian intelligences, we were bound to take steps to wipe out the dishonor."

Slowly and forcefully he finished. "We of Jupiter will suffer the existence of no vermin!"

The Jovian was backing away in some fashion, tacking against the wind, and the interview was evidently over.

The robots retreated inside the ship.

ZZ Two said, "It looks bad, doesn't it?" He continued thoughtfully, "It is as the human masters said. They possess an ultimately developed superiority complex, combined with an extreme intolerance for anyone or anything that disturbs that complex."

"The intolerance," observed Three, "is the natural consequence of the complex. The trouble is that their intolerance has teeth in it. They have weapons—and their science is great."

"I am not surprised now," burst out ZZ One, "that we were specifically instructed to disregard Jovian orders. They are horrible, intolerant, pseudo-superior beings!" He added emphatically, with robotical loyalty and faith, "No human master could ever be like that."

"That, though true, is beside the point," said Three. "The fact remains that the human masters are in terrible danger. This is a gigantic world and these Jovians are greater in numbers and resources by a hundred times or more than the humans of the entire Terrestrial Empire. If they can ever develop the force field to the point where they can use it as a spaceship hull—as the human masters have already done—they will overrun the system at will. The question remains as to how far they have advanced in that direction, what other weapons they have, what preparations they are making, and so on. To return with that information is our function, of course, and we had better decide on our next step."

"It may be difficult," said Two. "The Jovians won't help us." Which, at the moment, was rather an understatement.

Three thought a while. "It seems to me that we need only

wait," he observed. "They have tried to destroy us for thirty hours now and haven't succeeded. Certainly they have done their best. Now a superiority complex always involves the eternal necessity of saving face, and the ultimatum given us proves it in this case. They would never allow us to leave if they could destroy us. But if we don't leave then, rather than admit they cannot force us away, they will surely pretend that they are willing, for their own purposes, to have us stay."

Once again, they waited. The day passed. The weapon barrage did not resume. The robots did not leave. The bluff was called. And now the robots faced the Jovian radio code expert once again.

If the ZZ models had been equipped with a sense of humor, they would have enjoyed themselves immensely. As it was, they felt merely a solemn sense of satisfaction.

The Jovian said, "It has been our decision that you will be allowed to remain for a very short time, so that you may see our power for yourself. You shall then return to Ganymede to inform your companion vermin of the disastrous end to which they will unfailingly come within a solar revolution."

ZZ One made a mental note that a Jovian revolution took twelve Earthly years.

Three replied casually, "Thank you. May we accompany you to the nearest town? There are many things we would like to learn." He added as an afterthought, "Our ship is not to be touched, of course."

He said this as a request, not as a threat, for no ZZ model was ever pugnacious. All capacity for even the slightest annoyance had been carefully barred in their construction. With robots as vastly powerful as the ZZ's, unfailing good temper was essential for safety during the years of testing on Earth.

The Jovian said, "We are not interested in your verminous ship. No Jovian will pollute himself by approaching it. You may accompany us, but you must on no account approach closer than ten feet to any Jovian, or you will be instantly destroyed."

"Stuck up, aren't they?" observed Two in a genial whisper, as they plowed into the wind.

The town was a port on the shores of an incredible ammonia lake. The eternal wind whipped furious, frothy waves that shot across the liquid surface at the hectic rate enforced by the gravity. The port itself was neither large nor impressive and it seemed fairly evident that most of the construction was underground.

"What is the population of this place?" asked Three.

The Jovian replied: "It is a small town of ten million."

"I see. Make a note of that, One."

ZZ One did so mechanically, and then turned once more to the lake, at which he had been staring in fascination. He pulled at Three's elbow. "Say, do you suppose they have fish here?"

"What difference does it make?"

"I think we ought to know. The human masters ordered us to find out everything we could." Of the robots, One was the simplest and consequently, the one who took orders in the most literal fashion.

Two said, "Let One go and look if he likes. It won't do any harm if we let the kid have his fun."

"All right. There's no real objection if he doesn't waste his time. Fish isn't what we came for—but go ahead, One."

ZZ One made off in great excitement and slogged rapidly down the beach, plunging into the ammonia with a splash. The Jovians watched attentively. They had understood none of the previous conversation, of course.

The radio code expert clicked out, "It is apparent that your companion has decided to abandon life in despair at our greatness."

Three said in surprise, "Nothing of the sort. He wants to investigate the living organisms, if any, that live in the ammonia." He added apologetically, "Our friend is very curious at times, and he isn't quite as bright as we are, though that is only his misfortune. We understand that and try to humor him whenever we can."

There was a long pause, and the Jovian observed, "He will drown."

Three replied casually, "No danger of that. We don't drown. May we enter the town as soon as he returns?"

At that moment there was a spurt of liquid several hundred feet out in the lake. It sprayed upward wildly and then hurtled down in a wind-driven mist. Another spurt and another, then a wild white foaming that formed a trail toward shore, gradually quieting as it approached.

The two robots watched this in amazement and the utter lack of motion on the part of the Jovians indicated that they were watching as well.

Then the head of ZZ One broke the surface and he made his slow way out onto dry land. But something followed him! Some organism of gigantic size, that seemed nothing but fangs, claws, and spines. Then they saw that it wasn't following him under its own power, but was being dragged across the beach by ZZ One. There was a significant flabbiness about it.

ZZ One approached rather timidly and took communication into his own hands. He tapped out a message to the Jovian in agitated fashion. "I am very sorry this happened, but the thing attacked me. I was merely taking notes on it. It is not a valuable creature, I hope."

He was not answered immediately, for at the first appearance of the monster, there had been a wild break in the Jovian ranks. These reformed slowly, and cautious observation having proven the creature to be indeed dead, order was restored. Some of the bolder were curiously prodding the body.

ZZ Three said humbly, "I hope you will pardon our friend. He is sometimes clumsy. We have absolutely no intention of harming any Jovian creature."

"He attacked me," explained One. "He bit at me without provocation. See!" And he displayed a two-foot fang that ended in a jagged break. "He broke it on my shoulder and almost left a scratch. I just slapped it a bit to send it away—and it died. I'm sorry!"

The Jovian finally spoke and his code-clicking was a rather stuttery affair. "It is a wild creature, rarely found so close to shore, but the lake is deep just here."

Three said, still anxiously, "If you can use it for food, we are only too glad—"

"No. We can get food for ourselves without the help of verm —without the help of others. Eat it yourselves."

At that ZZ One heaved the creature up and back into the sea, with an easy motion of one arm. Three said casually, "Thank you for your kind offer, but we have no use for food. We don't eat, of course."

Escorted by two hundred or so armed Jovians, the robots passed down a series of ramps into the underground city. If, above the surface, the city had looked small and unimpressive, then from beneath, it took on the appearance of a vast megalopolis.

They were ushered into ground-cars that were operated by remote control—for no honest, self-respecting Jovian would risk his superiority by placing himself in the same car with vermin—and driven at frightful speed to the center of the town. They saw enough to decide that it extended fifty miles from end to end and reached downward into Jupiter's crust at least eight miles.

ZZ Two did not sound happy as he said, "If this is a sample of Jovian development then we shall not have a hopeful report to bring back to the human masters. After all, we landed on the vast surface of Jupiter at random, with the chances a thousand to one against coming near any really concentrated center of population. This must be, as the code expert says, a mere town."

"Ten million Jovians," said Three, abstractedly. "Total population must be in the trillions, which is high, very high, even for Jupiter. They probably have a completely urban civilization, which means that their scientific development must be tremendous. If they have force fields—"

Three had no neck, for in the interest of strength the heads of the ZZ models were riveted firmly onto the torso with the delicate positronic brains protected by three separate layers of inch-thick iridium alloy. But if he had had one, he would have shaken his head dolefully.

They had stopped now in a cleared space. Everywhere about them they could see avenues and structures crowded with Jovians, as curious as any Terrestrial crowd would have been in similar circumstances.

The code expert approached. "It is time now for me to retire until the next period of activity. We have gone so far as to arrange quarters for you at great inconvenience to ourselves for, of course, the structure will have to be pulled down and rebuilt afterwards. Nevertheless, you will be allowed to sleep for a space."

ZZ Three waved an arm in deprecation and tapped out, "We thank you but you must not trouble yourself. We don't mind remaining right here. If you want to sleep and rest, by all means do. We'll wait for you. As for us," casually, "we don't sleep."

The Jovian said nothing, though if it had had a face, the expression upon it might have been interesting. It left, and the robots remained in the car, with squads of well-armed Jovians, frequently replaced, surrounding them as guards.

It was hours before the ranks of those guards parted to allow the code expert to return. Along with him were other Jovians, whom he introduced.

"There are with me two officials of the central government who have graciously consented to speak with you."

One of the officials evidently knew the code, for his clicking interrupted the code expert sharply. He addressed the robots. "Vermin! Emerge from the ground-car that we may look at you."

The robots were only too willing to comply, so while Three and Two vaulted over the right side of the car, ZZ One dashed through the left side. The word through is used advisedly, for since he neglected to work the mechanism that lowered a section of side so that one might exit, he carried that side, plus two wheels and an axle, along with him. The car collapsed, and ZZ One stood staring at the ruins in embarrassed silence.

At last he clicked out gently, "I'm very sorry. I hope it wasn't an expensive car."

ZZ Two added apologetically, "Our companion is often clumsy. You must excuse him," and ZZ Three made a half-hearted attempt to put the car back together again.

ZZ One made another effort to excuse himself. "The material of the car was rather flimsy. You see?" He lifted a square-yard sheet of three-inch-thick, metal-hard plastic in both hands and exerted a bit of pressure. The sheet promptly snapped in two. "I should have made allowances," he admitted.

The Jovian government official said in slightly less sharp fashion, "The car would have had to be destroyed anyway, since being polluted by your presence." He paused, then: "Creatures! We Jovians lack vulgar curiosity concerning lower animals, but our scientists seek facts."

"We're right with you," replied Three, cheerfully, "so do we."

The Jovian ignored him. "You lack the mass-sensitive organ, apparently. How is it that you are aware of distant objects?"

Three grew interested. "Do you mean your people are directly sensitive to mass?"

"I am not here to answer your questions—your impudent questions—about us."

"I take it then that objects of low specific mass would be transparent to you, even in the absence of radiation." He turned to Two. "That's how they see. Their atmosphere is as transparent as space to them."

The Jovian clicking began once more, "You will answer my first question immediately, or my patience will end and I will order you destroyed."

Three said at once, "We are energy-sensitive, Jovian. We can adjust ourselves to the entire electromagnetic scale at will. At present, our long-distance sight is due to radio-wave radiation that we emit ourselves, and at close range, we see by—" He paused, and said to Two, "There isn't any code word for gamma ray, is there?"

"Not that I know of," Two answered.

Three continued to the Jovian: "At close range we see by other radiation for which there is no code word."

390 · ISAAC ASIMOV

"Of what is your body composed?" demanded the Jovian.

Two whispered, "He probably asks that because his mass-sensitivity can't penetrate past our skin. High density, you know. Ought we to tell him?"

Three replied uncertainly, "Our human masters didn't particularly say we were to keep anything secret." In radio code, to the Jovian, he said, "We are mostly iridium. For the rest copper, tin, a little beryllium, and a scattering of other substances."

The Jovians fell back and by the obscure writhing of various portions of their thoroughly indescribable bodies gave the impression that they were in animated conversation, although they made no sound.

And then the official returned. "Beings of Ganymede! It has been decided to show you through some of our factories that we may exhibit a tiny part of our great achievements. We will then allow you to return so that you may spread despair among the other verm—the other beings of the outer world."

Three said to Two, "Note the effect of their psychology. They must hammer home their superiority. It's still a matter of saving face." And in radio code, "We thank you for the opportunity."

But the face-saving was efficient, as the robots realized soon enough. The demonstration became a tour, and the tour a Grand Exhibition. The Jovians displayed everything, explained everything, answered all questions eagerly, and ZZ One made hundreds of despairing notes.

The war-potential of that single so-called unimportant town was greater by several times than that of all Ganymede. Ten more such towns would out-produce all the Terrestrial Empire. Yet ten more such towns would not be the fingernail fragment of the strength all Jupiter must be able to exert.

Three turned as One nudged him. "What is it?"

ZZ One said seriously, "If they have force fields, the human masters are lost, aren't they?"

"I'm afraid so. Why do you ask?"

"Because the Jovians aren't showing us through the right wing of this factory. It might be that force fields are being developed there. They would be wanting to keep it secret if they were. We'd better find out. It's the main point, you know."

Three regarded One somberly. "Perhaps you're right. It's no use ignoring anything."

They were in a huge steel mill now, watching hundred-foot beams of ammonia-resistant silicon-steel alloy being turned out twenty to the second. Three asked quietly, "What does that wing contain?"

The government official inquired of those in charge of the factory and explained: "That is the section of great heat. Various processes require huge temperatures which life cannot bear, and they must all be handled indirectly."

He led the way to a partition from which heat could be felt to radiate, and indicated a small, round area of transparent material. It was one of a row of such, through which the foggy red light of lines of glowing forges could be made out through the soupy atmosphere.

ZZ One fastened a look of suspicion on the Jovian and clicked out, "Would it be all right if I went in and looked around? I am very interested in this."

Three said, "You're being childish, One. They're telling the truth. Oh, well, nose around if you must. But don't take too long; we've got to move on."

The Jovian said, "You have no understanding of the heat involved. You will die."

"Oh no!" explained One casually. "Heat doesn't bother us."

There was a Jovian conference, and then a scene of scurrying confusion as the life of the factory was geared to this unusual emergency. Screens of heat-absorbent material were set up, and then a door dropped open, a door that had never before budged while the forges were working. ZZ One entered and the door closed behind him. Jovian officials crowded to the transparent areas to watch.

ZZ One walked to the nearest forge and tapped the outside.

Since he was too short to see into it comfortably, he tipped the forge until the molten metal licked at the lip of the container. He peered at it curiously, then dipped his hand in and stirred it awhile to test the consistency. Having done this, he withdrew his hand, shook off some of the fiery metallic droplets and wiped the rest on one of his six thighs. Slowly, he went down the line of forges, then signified his desire to leave.

The Jovians retired to a great distance when he came out the door and played a stream of ammonia on him, which hissed, bubbled and steamed until he was brought to bearable temperature once more.

ZZ One ignored the ammonia shower and said, "They were telling the truth. No force fields!"

Three began, "You see—" but One interrupted impatiently: "But there's no use delaying. The human masters instructed us to find out everything and that's that."

He turned to the Jovian and clicked out, without the slightest hesitation, "Listen, has Jovian science developed force fields?"

Bluntness was, of course, one of the natural consequences of One's more poorly developed mental powers. Two and Three knew that, so they refrained from expressing disapproval of the remark.

The Jovian official relaxed slowly from his strangely stiffened attitude, which had somehow given the impression that he had been staring stupidly at One's hand—the one he had dipped into the molten metal.

The Jovian said slowly, "Force fields? That, then, is your main object of curiosity?"

"Yes," said One, with emphasis.

There was a sudden and patent gain in confidence on the Jovian's part, for the clicking grew sharper. "Then come, vermin!"

Whereupon Three said to Two, "We're vermin again, I see—which sounds as if there's bad news ahead." And Two gloomily agreed.

It was to the very edge of the city that they were now led—
to the portion which on Earth would have been termed the
suburbs—and into one of a series of closely integrated structures, which might have corresponded vaguely to a Terrestrial
university.

There were no explanations, however, and none were asked
for. The Jovian official led the way rapidly, and the robots followed with the grim conviction that the worst was just about to
happen.

It was ZZ One who stopped before an opened wall-section
after the rest had passed on. "What's this?" he wanted to know.

The room was equipped with narrow, low benches, along
which Jovians manipulated rows of strange devices, of which
strong inch-long electro-magnets formed the principal feature.

"What's this?" asked One again.

The Jovian turned back and exhibited impatience. "This is a
students' biological laboratory. There's nothing there to interest you."

"But what are they doing?"

"They are studying microscopic life. Haven't you ever seen
a microscope before?"

Three interrupted in explanation. "He has, but not that type.
Our microscopes are meant for energy-sensitive organs and
work by refraction of radiant energy. Your microscopes evidently work on a mass-expansion basis. Rather ingenious."

ZZ One said, "Would it be all right if I inspected some of your
specimens?"

"Of what use will that be? You cannot use our microscopes
because of your sensory limitations and it will simply force us
to discard such specimens as you approach for no decent reason."

"But I don't need a microscope," explained One, with surprise. "I can easily adjust myself for microscopic vision."

He strode to the nearest bench, while the students in the
room crowded to the corner in an attempt to avoid contamina-
tion. ZZ One shoved a microscope aside, and inspected the slide

carefully. He backed away puzzled; then tried another, a third, a fourth.

He came back and addressed the Jovian. "Those are supposed to be alive, aren't they? I mean, those little worm-things."

The Jovian said, "Certainly."

"That's strange! When I look at them—they die!"

Three explained sharply, and said to his two companions, "We've forgotten our gamma-ray radiation. Let's get out of here, One, or we'll kill every bit of microscopic life in the room."

He turned to the Jovian. "I'm afraid that our presence is fatal to weaker forms of life. We had better leave. We hope the specimens are not too difficult to replace. And, while we're about it, you had better not stay too near us, or our radiation may affect you adversely. You feel all right so far, don't you?" he asked.

The Jovian led the way onward in proud silence, but it was to be noticed that thereafter he doubled the distance he had hitherto kept between himself and them.

Nothing more was said until the robots found themselves in a vast room. In the very center of it huge ingots of metal rested unsupported in mid-air—or, rather, supported by nothing visible—against the mighty Jovian gravity.

The Jovian clicked, "There is your force field in ultimate form, as recently perfected. Within that bubble is a vacuum, so that it is supporting the full weight of our atmosphere plus an amount of metal equivalent to two large spaceships. What do you say to that?"

"That space travel now becomes a possibility for you," said Three.

"Definitely. No metal or plastic has the strength to hold our atmosphere against a vacuum; but a force field can—and a force field bubble will be our spaceship! Within the year, we will be turning them out by the hundreds of thousands. Then we will swarm down upon Ganymede to destroy the verminous so-called intelligences that attempt to dispute our dominion of the universe."

"The human beings of Ganymede have never attempted—" began Three, in mild expostulation.

"Silence!" snapped the Jovian. "Return now and tell them what you've seen. Their own feeble force fields—such as the one your ship is equipped with—will not stand against us, for our smallest ship will be a hundred times the size and power of yours."

Three said, "Then there's nothing more to do and we will return, as you say, with the information. If you could lead us back to our ship, we'll say good-by. And by the way, just as a matter for the record, there's something you don't understand. The humans of Ganymede have force fields, of course, but our particular ship isn't equipped with one. We don't need any."

The robot turned away and motioned his companions to follow. For a moment they did not speak, then ZZ One muttered dejectedly, "Can't we try to destroy this place?"

"It won't help," said Three. "They'd get us by weight of numbers. It's no use. In an earthly decade, the human masters will be finished. It is impossible to stand against Jupiter. There's just too damn much of it. As long as they were tied to the surface, the humans were safe. But now that they have force fields . . . All we can do is to bring the news. By the preparation of hiding places, some few may survive for a short while."

The city was behind them. They were out on the open plain by the lake with their ship a dark spot on the horizon when the Jovian spoke suddenly:

"Creatures, you say you have no force field?"

Three replied without interest, "We don't need one."

"How then does your ship stand the vacuum of space without exploding because of the atmospheric pressure within?" And he moved a tentacle as if in mute gesture at the Jovian atmosphere that was weighing down upon them with a force of twenty million pounds to the square inch.

"Well," explained Three, "that's simple. Our ship isn't airtight. Pressures equalize within and without."

"Even in space? A vacuum in your ship? You lie!"

"You're welcome to inspect our ship. It has no force field and it isn't airtight. What's marvelous about that? We don't breathe. Our energy is through direct atomic power. The presence or absence of air pressure makes little difference to us and we're quite at home in a vacuum."

"But absolute zero!"

"It doesn't matter. We regulate our own heat. We're not interested in outside temperatures." He paused. "Well, we can make our own way back to the ship. Good-by. We'll give the humans of Ganymede your message—war to the end!"

But the Jovian said, "Wait! I'll be back." He turned and went toward the city.

The robots stared, and then waited in silence.

It was three hours before he returned and when he did, it was in breathless haste. He stopped within the usual ten feet of the robots, but then began inching his way forward in a curious groveling fashion. He did not speak until his rubbery gray skin was almost touching them, and then the radio code sounded, subdued and respectful.

"Honored sirs, I have been in communication with the head of our central government, who is now aware of all the facts, and I can assure you that Jupiter desires only peace."

"I beg your pardon," said Three, blankly.

The Jovian drove on hastily. "We are ready to resume communication with Ganymede and will gladly promise to make no attempt to venture out into space. Our force field will be used only on the Jovian surface."

"But—" Three began.

"Our government will be glad to receive any other representatives our honorable human brothers of Ganymede would care to send. If your honors will now condescend to swear peace—" A scaly tentacle swung out towards them, and Three, quite dazed, grasped it. Two and One did likewise as two more were extended to them.

The Jovian said solemnly, "There is then eternal peace between Jupiter and Ganymede."

The spaceship which leaked like a sieve was out in space again. The pressure and temperature were once more at zero, and the robots watched the huge but steadily shrinking globe that was Jupiter.

"They're definitely sincere," said ZZ Two, "and it's very gratifying, this complete about-face, but I don't get it."

"It is my idea," observed ZZ One, "that the Jovians came to their senses just in time and realized the incredible evil involved in the thought of harm to a human master. That would be only natural."

ZZ Three sighed and said, "Look, friends, it's all a matter of psychology. Those Jovians had a superiority complex a mile thick and when they couldn't destroy us, they were bound to save face. All their exhibitions, all their explanations, were simply a form of braggadocio, designed to impress us into the proper state of humiliation before their power and superiority."

"I see all that," interrupted Two, "but—"

Three went on: "But it worked the wrong way. All they did was to prove to themselves that we were stronger, that we didn't drown, that we didn't eat or sleep, that molten metal didn't hurt us. Even our very presence was fatal to Jovian life. Their last trump was the force field. But when they found out that *we* didn't need them at all, and could live in a vacuum at absolute zero, they broke." He paused, and added philosophically, "When a superiority complex like that breaks, it breaks all the way."

The other two considered that, and then Two said, "But it still doesn't make sense. Why should they care what we can or can't do? We're only robots. We're not the ones they have to fight."

"And that's the whole point, Two," said Three, softly. "It's only after we left Jupiter that I thought of it. Do you know that through an oversight, quite unintentionally, we neglected to tell them we were only robots?"

"They never asked us," said One.

"Exactly. So they thought we were human beings and that all the other human beings were like us!"

He looked once more at Jupiter, thoughtfully. "No wonder they decided to quit!"

THE TWONKY

Henry Kuttner

The entrance of the United States into World War II caused important changes in science fiction, particularly for John W. Campbell and *Astounding*. Not only were Heinlein, de Camp and Asimov suddenly busy with war research, but L. Ron Hubbard, then one of *Astounding's* top authors, was on active duty in the Navy (he was wounded in action early in the war, but recovered and returned to duty), and regular *Astounding* artists Hubert Rogers and Charles Schneeman were involved in war work.

Campbell admitted in mid-1942 that "temporarily, *Astounding* and *Unknown* have slumped a little in story quality. . . . To replace half a dozen second- or third-rate writers isn't so hard; to find enough new, top-rank authors capable of real production as well as real quality is something else again." But he was optimistic about the future, for he was already nurturing several new writers he felt would make their marks: he named Hal Clement, Will Stewart and Lewis Padgett.

Campbell was fudging here. Clement was indeed a new author who would contribute memorable fiction to *Astounding* in years to come, but "Will Stewart" was a pen name for longtime favorite Jack Williamson, and "Lewis Padgett" was either Henry Kuttner or C. L. Moore or often both.

Kuttner and Moore had each begun writing for *Weird Tales* and gradually switched to the science fiction magazines, which offered more numerous markets. Both corresponded with H. P. Lovecraft, and in 1936 Lovecraft sent some books to Kuttner, asking him to forward them to Moore when he'd read them. Kuttner admired Moore's writing, so he sent a note with the books. But since he didn't know she was a woman, he addressed it to *Mr.* C. L. Moore (and received a reply from Miss Catherine Moore). They began to correspond, Kuttner visited her in Indianapolis several times, and he persuaded her to collaborate on a story with him, sending the manuscript back and forth in the mails. They were satisfied with the result, and after their marriage in 1940 they wrote virtually everything together.

"We just traded typewriters," Moore recalls. "When one got stuck the other took over with a minimum of rewriting." A typical anecdote about their collaboration methods is that of the time Kuttner fell asleep from exhaustion while writing a story, and woke to find the completed manuscript on his desk. Moore had finished it while he slept. "We sincerely loved each other's writing and enjoyed tremendously what came out of the other guy's typewriter," she says.

Such an easy blending of talents between married writers is more rare than one might expect. Leigh Brackett and Edmond Hamilton worked on each other's stories only occasionally, probably because they had very different writing methods. Brackett once showed Hamilton the opening chapters of a novel on which they'd planned to collaborate; he loved them, and asked where the story was going from there. She confessed she had no idea. "You don't *know!*" he cried. "This is the so-and-so bleep adjective-deleted way to write a story I ever heard of!" Hamilton himself always wrote the last line of each story before he'd write the first one.

The Kuttner-Moore collaborative team was the most successful in science fiction, but it took years for them to get together. She was an attractive, popular brunette who lived in Indianapolis; he was short, unhandsome and quiet, and he lived in Los Angeles. But he frequently traveled to and from New York City, where his mother lived, and he'd always stop en route to visit her. Eventually she decided that the grim space heroes of her stories "would have been very boring to be married to," and found that Kuttner's quietness covered both a disciplined strength and an antic sense of humor. "He was the funniest person in the entire world! . . . any wild thing was bound to happen at any time!"

Kuttner was equally taken with her, though perhaps less extravagant in his comments to others. Edmond Hamilton met Kuttner in

1940 and, hearing that Kuttner knew Catherine Moore, he exclaimed, "C. L. Moore is one of my idols! What is she like?" Kuttner murmured, "She is very nice." A week later Hamilton heard that they'd been married.

The ceremony took place in New York City on June 7, 1940, with Kuttner's drinking companion Virgil Finlay as best man. Kuttner had moved to New York to establish closer contacts with the editors who bought his stories, though he detested the city. He'd once written to his agent, Julius Schwartz, "I can get the same effect as I do in New York by crawling into the dirtiest corner of the garage and screaming at the top of my voice, blowing the auto horn, and energetically sniffing the exhaust."

After the attack on Pearl Harbor, Kuttner, then twenty-seven, entered the Army Medical Department and was stationed at Fort Monmouth, New Jersey; Catherine lived nearby in Red Bank. They continued to write voluminously, under their own bylines and, eventually, nearly twenty pen names. "Lewis Padgett" was one of them, and it was under this name that "The Twonky" first appeared in *Astounding* for September 1942. (Lewis was the maiden name of Kuttner's mother, Padgett that of Moore's grandmother.)

Fritz Leiber recalls that the Kuttners invented personalities for all their pen names. "Lewis Padgett was a retired accountant who liked to water the lawn of an evening and then mosey down to the corner drugstore to pick up a quart of ice cream and whose wife collected recipes to surprise her bridge club." Moore adds that Padgett wore high stiff collars and looked very much like President Woodrow Wilson; one of the ways his wife surprised her bridge friends was by making whiskey sours and putting bananas in them.

It's difficult to figure out which of the Kuttners wrote any given story (she says, "We shifted off—one time *I* was Padgett, the next time Hank was!"), but "The Twonky" has always been credited to Henry Kuttner. Ray Bradbury remembers that Kuttner gave him a copy of the manuscript while he was writing it; it struck Bradbury immediately as a "very special" story, and it's proven to be one of Kuttner's most successful ones. In 1953 it was made into a movie starring Hans Conried.

You'll see a reference in the second line of the story to workmen being lost to the draft; this line has been omitted whenever the story was reprinted in one of Kuttner's collections, because it dates the story, but for our purposes it's a useful reminder that there was a war on when "The Twonky" was written.

Long before the United States entered World War II, science fiction writers were clearly aware of war clouds on the horizon. In 1936, S. Fowler Wright published a novel called *Prelude in Prague* which predicted with surprising accuracy the military strategy by which Hitler would overrun Czechoslovakia; the book was translated into a dozen European languages and angered the Nazis so much that they banned *all* of Wright's novels when they occupied France.

Japanese militarism too was noticed by science fiction writers. In a January 1940 magazine, Oscar J. Friend published a story about a world war in which Americans and "Japs" fought for possession of the Panama Canal. In the same year both Donald A. Wollheim and Eando Binder predicted a war with Japan that began with a Japanese surprise attack, though their details weren't as accurate as Wright's had been. Wollheim set his story in 1953, and Binder had the Japanese attacking through Mexico.

But it was Hitler's Germany that concerned most Americans during 1940 and 1941. There was so much suspicion of Nazi spies in this country that Robert Moore Williams wrote a story in which an alien scout visiting Earth was mistaken for a German "fifth columnist." Americans didn't like the Nazis' idea that they could create a superior "Aryan" race, either. A story by P. F. Costello had the Germans sending two soldiers to the future via time machine to bring back legions of their "super race" to help them fight the war—but the soldiers found that the world the Nazis were creating was populated only by savages, who quickly slaughtered them.

It wasn't until the attack on Pearl Harbor that real hatred for the Japanese began to show up in science fiction magazines, typified in editorials by John Campbell and Raymond Palmer. Campbell remarked caustically that "the Japs decided the world was too tame, too boring, and decided to try national hara-kiri." Palmer was similarly tart: "Japan has a reproduction rate of sufficient speed to double the population each succeeding generation. Well, we might admit that that provides them with a problem—but we'll tell the world Pearl Harbor was the wrong way to solve it. Or maybe it was right at that—considering what we intend to do to 'em as soon as we get a few things ready!"

Thereafter, sf's references to both the Germans and the Japanese became openly insulting. A story by Nelson S. Bond called Hitler "the chief germ in Germany" and referred to "his yellow-skinned and -spined allies, the Japs." Another Bond story, one concerning time travel into the past, had a character remarking, "That sounds like a swell idea. Go back and push a little paperhanger named Adolph Schicklgruber under a Munich street-car, huh? I'd gladly volunteer for the job." Murray Leinster wrote a story involving a Japanese fleet that was lured into a trap and sunk; the author remarked, "Finer navigation, perhaps, would have warned its crews, but a racial inferiority complex does not lead to discretion."

The publishers of *Amazing Stories* and *Fantastic Adventures* were Jewish and strongly anti-Nazi; as early as 1940, William B. Ziff printed a two-page statement in *Amazing* warning the United States that it "must arm to the teeth to discourage attack from abroad," and Palmer later said he had orders to buy anti-Axis stories. As a result, *Amazing* and *Fantastic Adventures* featured more war-related stories than any other science fiction magazines; but all the magazines published such stories, and hatred for the Germans and Japanese was common.

(A notable exception was "Nerves," in which Lester del Rey, outraged by the U.S.'s Nisei concentration camps, deliberately included a Japanese as one of his most sympathetic characters. Despite John Campbell's anti-Japanese editorializing, del Rey says "he not only recognized my intent but went along with it wholeheartedly.")

This was the climate in which Henry Kuttner wrote "The Twonky," and though the reference to the draft is the only direct evidence of war-consciousness in the story, in a larger sense it was a comment on the perils of dictatorship. A hundred stories by writers who defined the menace purely by references to the Germans and Japanese have become almost-quaint period pieces today, but "The

Twonky" still stands as a disturbing warning against regimentation. Kuttner managed to see to the heart of the danger: dictatorship isn't a matter of nationalities or even politics, but of human nature.

REFERENCES:

"Viewpoints." *Astonishing Stories,* October 1942.

Fantasy Fiction Field, May 17, 1941.

John W. Campbell, Jr., in "The Readers Always Write." *Spaceways,* July 1942.

"In Times to Come" by John W. Campbell, Jr. *Astounding Science-Fiction,* June 1942.

"The Campbell Era" by Jack Williamson. *Algol,* Summer 1975.

"The Secret Lives of Henry Kuttner" by Sam Moskowitz. *Amazing Stories,* October 1962.

"C. L. Moore Talks to *Chacal.*" *Chacal,* Winter 1976.

"C. L. Moore: Catherine the Great" by Sam Moskowitz. *Amazing Stories,* August 1962.

"An Interview with Leigh Brackett and Edmond Hamilton" by David Truesdale with Paul McGuire. *Tangent,* Summer 1976.

Afterword by Edmond Hamilton. *The Best of Edmond Hamilton.* Del Rey Books, 1977.

"The Many Faces of Henry Kuttner" by Fritz Leiber. *Henry Kuttner: A Memorial Symposium.* Sevagram Enterprises, 1958.

"Henry Kuttner: A Neglected Master" by Ray Bradbury. *The Best of Henry Kuttner.* Ballantine Books, 1975.

Science Fiction in the Cinema by John Baxter. A. S. Barnes, 1970.

"S. Fowler Wright: SF's Devil's Disciple" by Sam Moskowitz. *Amazing Stories,* February 1965.

Fantasy Fiction Field, June 14, 1941.

"Mind Over Matter" by Oscar J. Friend. *Startling Stories,* January 1940.

"Castaway" by Donald A. Wollheim. *Super Science Stories,* May 1940.

"Adam Link Fights a War" by Eando Binder. *Amazing Stories,* December 1940.

"Who Was Thomas Morrow?" by Robert Moore Williams. *Thrilling Wonder Stories,* April 1941.

"Flame for the Future" by P. F. Costello. *Amazing Stories,* October 1941.

"In Times to Come" by John W. Campbell, Jr. *Astounding Science-Fiction,* March 1942.

"The Observatory" by Raymond A. Palmer. *Amazing Stories,* August 1942.

"Horsesense Hank Does His Bit" by Nelson S. Bond. *Amazing Stories,* May 1942.

"Horsesense Hank in the Parallel Worlds" by Nelson S. Bond. *Amazing Stories,* August 1942.

"Four Little Ships" by Murray Leinster. *Astounding Science-Fiction,* November 1942.

"AMERICA Must Prepare NOW!" by William B. Ziff. *Amazing Stories,* October 1940.

Letter from Raymond A. Palmer, August 1975.

Early del Rey by Lester del Rey. Doubleday, 1975.

* * *

The turnover at Mideastern Radio was so great that Mickey Lloyd couldn't keep track of his men. It wasn't only the draft; employees kept quitting and going elsewhere, at a higher salary. So when the big-headed little man in overalls wandered vaguely out of a storeroom, Lloyd took one look at the brown dungaree suit—company provided—and said mildly, "The whistle blew half an hour ago. Hop to work."

"Work-k-k?" The man seemed to have trouble with the word.

Drunk? Lloyd, in his capacity as foreman, couldn't permit that. He flipped away his cigarette, walked forward, and sniffed. No, it wasn't liquor. He peered at the badge on the man's overalls.

"Two-oh-four, m-mm. Are you new here?"

"New. Huh?" The man rubbed a rising bump on his forehead. He was an odd-looking little chap, bald as a vacuum tube, with a pinched, pallid face and tiny eyes that held dazed wonder.

"Come on, Joe. Wake up!" Lloyd was beginning to sound impatient. "You work here, don't you?"

"Joe," said the man thoughtfully. "Work. Yes, I work. I make them." His words ran together oddly, as though he had a cleft palate.

With another glance at the badge, Lloyd gripped Joe's arm

and ran him through the assembly room. "Here's your place. Hop to it. Know what to do?"

The other drew his scrawny body erect. "I am—expert," he remarked. "Make them better than Ponthwank."

"O. K.," Lloyd said. "Make 'em, then." And he went away.

The man called Joe hesitated, nursing the bruise on his head. The overalls caught his attention, and he examined them wonderingly. Where—oh, yes. They had been hanging in the room from which he had first emerged. His own garments had, naturally, dissipated during the trip—what trip?

...the something ... when it slowed down and stopped. How odd this huge, machine-filled barn looked! It struck no chord of remembrance.

Amnesia, that was it. He was a worker. He made things. As for the unfamiliarity of his surroundings, that meant nothing. He was still dazed. The clouds would lift from his mind presently. They were beginning to do that already.

Work. Joe scuttled around the room, trying to goad his faulty memory. Men in overalls were doing things. Simple, obvious things. But how childish—how elemental! Perhaps this was a kindergarten.

After a while Joe went out into a stock room and examined some finished models of combination radio-phonographs. So that was it. Awkward and clumsy, but it wasn't his place to say so. No. His job was to make Twonkies.

Twonkies? The name jolted his memory again. Of course he knew how to make Twonkies. He'd made them all his life—had been specially trained for the job. Now they were using a different model of Twonky, but what the hell! Child's play for a clever workman.

Joe went back into the shop and found a vacant bench. He began to build a Twonky. Occasionally he slipped off and stole the material he needed. Once, when he couldn't locate any tungsten, he hastily built a small gadget and made it.

His bench was in a distant corner, badly lighted, though it seemed quite bright to Joe's eyes. Nobody noticed the console that was swiftly growing to completion there. Joe worked very,

very fast. He ignored the noon whistle, and, at quitting time, his task was finished. It could, perhaps, stand another coat of paint —it lacked the Shimmertone of a standard Twonky. But none of the others had Shimmertone. Joe sighed, crawled under the bench, looked in vain for a relaxopad, and went to sleep on the floor.

A few hours later he woke up. The factory changed. Maybe— Joe's mind felt funny. Sleep had cleared away the mists of amnesia, if such it had been, but he still felt dazed.

Muttering under his breath, he sent the Twonky into the stock room and compared it with the others. Superficially it was identical with a console radio-phonograph combination of the latest model. Following the pattern of the others, Joe had camouflaged and disguised the various organs and reactors.

He went back into the shop. Then the last of the mists cleared from his mind. Joe's shoulders jerked convulsively.

"Great Snell!" he gasped. "So that was it! I ran into a temporal snag!"

With a startled glance around, he fled to the storeroom from which he had first emerged. The overalls he took off and returned to their hook. After that, Joe went over to a corner, felt around in the air, nodded with satisfaction, and seated himself on nothing, three feet above the floor. Then Joe vanished.

"Time," said Kerry Westerfield, "is curved. Eventually it gets back to the same place where it started. That's duplication." He put his feet up on a conveniently outjutting rock of the chimney and stretched luxuriously. From the kitchen Martha made clinking noises with bottles and glasses.

"Yesterday at this time I had a Martini," Kerry said. "The time curve indicates that I should have another one now. Are you listening, angel?"

"I'm pouring," said the angel distantly.

"You get my point, then. Here's another. Time describes a spiral instead of a circle. If you call the first cycle *a*, the second one's *a plus 1*—see? Which means a double Martini tonight."

"I know where that would end," Martha remarked, coming

into the spacious, oak-raftered living room. She was a small, dark-haired woman with a singularly pretty face and a figure to match. Her tiny gingham apron looked slightly absurd in combination with slacks and silk blouse. "And they don't make infinity-proof gin. Here's your Martini." She did things with the shaker and manipulated glasses.

"Stir slowly," Kerry cautioned. "Never shake. Ah—that's it." He accepted the drink and eyed it appreciatively. Black hair, sprinkled with gray, gleamed in the lamplight as he sipped the Martini. "Good. Very good."

Martha drank slowly and eyed her husband. A nice guy, Kerry Westerfield. He was forty-odd, pleasantly ugly, with a wide mouth and an occasional sardonic gleam in his gray eyes, as he contemplated life. They had been married for twelve years, and liked it.

From outside, the late faint glow of sunset came through the windows, picking out the console cabinet that stood against the wall by the door. Kerry peered at it with appreciation.

"A pretty penny," he remarked. "Still—"

"What? Oh. The men had a tough time getting it up the stairs. Why don't you try it, Kerry?"

"Didn't you?"

"The old one was complicated enough," Martha said, in a baffled manner. "Gadgets. They confuse me. I was brought up on an Edison. You wound it up with a crank, and strange noises came out of a horn. That I could understand. But now—you push a button, and extraordinary things happen. Electric eyes, tone selections, records that get played on both sides, to the accompaniment of weird groanings and clickings from inside the console—probably you understand those things. I don't even want to. Whenever I play a Crosby record in a super-dooper like that, Bing seems embarrassed."

Kerry ate his olive. "I'm going to play some Debussy." He nodded toward a table. "There's a new Crosby record for you. The latest."

Martha wriggled happily. "Can I, maybe, huh?"

"Uh-huh."

"But you'll have to show me how."

"Simple enough," said Kerry, beaming at the console. "Those babies are pretty good, you know. They do everything but think."

"I wish it'd wash the dishes," Martha remarked. She set down her glass, got up, and vanished into the kitchen.

Kerry snapped on a lamp nearby and went over to examine the new radio, Mideastern's latest model, with all the new improvements. It had been expensive—but what the hell? He could afford it. And the old one had been pretty well shot.

It was not, he saw, plugged in. Nor were there any wires in evidence—not even a ground. Something new, perhaps. Built-in antenna *and* ground. Kerry crouched down, looked for a socket, and plugged the cord into it.

That done, he opened the doors and eyed the dials with every appearance of satisfaction. A beam of bluish light shot out and hit him in the eyes. From the depths of the console a faint, thoughtful clicking proceeded. Abruptly it stopped. Kerry blinked, fiddled with dials and switches, and bit at a fingernail.

The radio said, in a distant voice, "Psychology pattern checked and recorded."

"Eh?" Kerry twirled a dial. "Wonder what that was? Amateur station—no, they're off the air. Hm-m-m." He shrugged and went over to a chair beside the shelves of albums. His gaze ran swiftly over the titles and composers' names. Where was the "Swan of Tuolema"? There it was, next to "Finlandia," for no apparent reason. Kerry took down the album and opened it in his lap. With his free hand he extracted a cigarette from his pocket, put it between his lips, and fumbled for the matches on the table beside him. The first match he lit went out.

He tossed it into the fireplace and was about to reach for another when a faint noise caught his attention. The radio was walking across the room toward him. A whiplike tendril flicked out from somewhere, picked up a match, scratched it beneath the table top—as Kerry had done—and held the flame to the man's cigarette.

Automatic reflexes took over. Kerry sucked in his breath, and exploded in smoky, racking coughs. He bent double, gasping and momentarily blind.

When he could see again, the radio was back in its accustomed place.

Kerry caught his lower lip between his teeth. "Martha," he called.

"Soup's on," her voice said.

Kerry didn't answer. He stood up, went over to the radio, and looked at it hesitantly. The electric cord had been pulled out of its socket. Kerry gingerly replaced it.

He crouched to examine the console's legs. They looked like finely finished wood. His exploratory hand told him nothing. Wood—hard and brittle.

How in hell—

"Dinner!" Martha called.

Kerry threw his cigarette into the fireplace and slowly walked out of the room. His wife, setting a gravy boat in place, stared at him.

"How many Martinis did you have?"

"Just one," Kerry said in a vague way. "I must have dozed off for a minute. Yeah. I must have."

"Well, fall to," Martha commanded. "This is the last chance you'll have to make a pig of yourself on my dumplings, for a week, anyway."

Kerry absently felt for his wallet, took out an envelope, and tossed it toward his wife. "Here's your ticket, angel. Don't lose it."

"Oh? I rate a compartment!" Martha thrust the pasteboard back into its envelope and gurgled happily. "You're a pal. Sure you can get along without me?"

"Huh? Hm-m-m—I think so." Kerry salted his avocado. He shook himself and seemed to come out of a slight daze. "Sure, I'll be all right. You trot off to Denver and help Carol have her baby. It's all in the family."

"We-ell, my only sister—" Martha grinned. "You know how

she and Bill are. Quite nuts. They'll need a steadying hand just now."

There was no reply. Kerry was brooding over a forkful of avocado. He muttered something about the Venerable Bede.

"What about him?"

"Lecture tomorrow. Every term we bog down on the Bede, for some strange reason. Ah, well."

"Got your lecture ready?"

Kerry nodded. "Sure." For eight years he had taught at the University, and he certainly should know the schedule by this time!

Later, over coffee and cigarettes, Martha glanced at her wrist watch. "Nearly train time. I'd better finish packing. The dishes—"

"I'll do 'em." Kerry wandered after his wife into the bedroom and made motions of futile helpfulness. After a while, he carried the bags down to the car. Martha joined him, and they headed for the depot.

The train was on time. Half an hour after it had pulled out, Kerry drove the car back into the garage, let himself into the house and yawned mightily. He was tired. Well, the dishes, and then beer and a book in bed.

With a puzzled look at the radio, he entered the kitchen and did things with water and soap chips. The hall phone rang. Kerry wiped his hands on a dish towel and answered it.

It was Mike Fitzgerald, who taught psychology at the University.

"Hiya, Fitz."

"Hiya. Martha gone?"

"Yeah. I just drove her to the train."

"Feel like talking, then? I've got some pretty good Scotch. Why not run over and gab a while?"

"Like to," Kerry said, yawning again, "but I'm dead. Tomorrow's a big day. Rain check?"

"Sure. I just finished correcting papers, and felt the need of sharpening my mind. What's the matter?"

"Nothing. Wait a minute." Kerry put down the phone and looked over his shoulder, scowling. Noises were coming from the kitchen. What the hell!

He went along the hall and stopped in the doorway, motionless and staring. The radio was washing the dishes.

After a while he returned to the phone. Fitzgerald said, "Something?"

"My new radio," Kerry told him carefully. "It's washing the dishes."

Fitz didn't answer for a moment. His laugh was a bit hesitant. "Oh?"

"I'll call you back," Kerry said, and hung up. He stood motionless for a while, chewing his lip. Then he walked back to the kitchen and paused to watch.

The radio's back was toward him. Several limber tentacles were manipulating the dishes, expertly sousing them in hot, soapy water, scrubbing them with the little mop, dipping them into the rinse water, and then stacking them neatly in the metal rack. Those whip-lashes were the only sign of unusual activity. The legs were apparently solid.

"Hey!" Kerry said.

There was no response.

He sidled around till he could examine the radio more closely. The tentacles emerged from a slot under one of the dials. The electric cord was dangling. No juice, then. But what—

Kerry stepped back and fumbled out a cigarette. Instantly the radio turned, took a match from its container on the stove, and walked forward. Kerry blinked, studying the legs. They couldn't be wood. They were bending as the . . . the thing moved, elastic as rubber. The radio had a peculiar sidling motion unlike anything else on earth.

It lit Kerry's cigarette and went back to the sink, where it resumed the dishwashing.

Kerry phoned Fitzgerald again. "I wasn't kidding. I'm having hallucinations or something. That damned radio just lit a cigarette for me."

"Wait a minute—" Fitzgerald's voice sounded undecided. "This is a gag—eh?"

"No. And I don't think it's a hallucination, either. It's up your alley. Can you run over and test my knee-jerks?"

"All right," Fitz said. "Give me ten minutes. Have a drink ready."

He hung up, and Kerry, laying the phone back into its cradle, turned to see the radio walking out of the kitchen toward the living room. Its square, boxlike contour was subtly horrifying, like some bizarre sort of hobgoblin. Kerry shivered.

He followed the radio, to find it in its former place, motionless and impassive. He opened the doors, examining the turntable, the phonograph arm, and the other buttons and gadgets. There was nothing apparently unusual. Again he touched the legs. They were not wood, after all. Some plastic, which seemed quite hard. Or—maybe they were wood, after all. It was difficult to make certain, without damaging the finish. Kerry felt a natural reluctance to use a knife on his new console.

He tried the radio, getting local stations without trouble. The tone was good—unusually good, he thought. The phonograph—

He picked up Halvorsen's "Entrance of the Boyards" at random and slipped it into place, closing the lid. No sound emerged. Investigation proved that the needle was moving rhythmically along the groove, but without audible result. Well?

Kerry removed the record as the doorbell rang. It was Fitzgerald, a gangling, saturnine man with a leathery, wrinkled face and a tousled mop of dull-gray hair. He extended a large, bony hand.

"Where's my drink?"

" 'Lo, Fitz. Come in the kitchen. I'll mix. Highball?"

"Highball."

"O. K." Kerry led the way. "Don't drink it just yet, though. I want to show you my new combination."

"The one that washes dishes?" Fitzgerald asked. "What else does it do?"

Kerry gave the other a glass. "It won't play records."

"Oh, well. A minor matter, if it'll do the housework. Let's take a look at it." Fitzgerald went into the living room, selected "Afternoon of a Faun," and approached the radio. "It isn't plugged in."

"That doesn't matter a bit," Kerry said wildly.

"Batteries?" Fitzgerald slipped the record in place and adjusted the switches. "Ten inch—there. Now we'll see." He beamed triumphantly at Kerry. "Well? It's playing now."

It was.

Kerry said, "Try that Halvorsen piece. Here." He handed the disk to Fitzgerald, who pushed the reject switch and watched the lever arm lift.

But this time the phonograph refused to play. It didn't like "Entrance of the Boyards."

"That's funny," Fitzgerald grunted. "Probably the trouble's with the record. Let's try another."

There was no trouble with "Daphnis and Chloe." But the radio silently rejected the composer's "Bolero."

Kerry sat down and pointed to a nearby chair. "That doesn't prove anything. Come over here and watch. Don't drink anything yet. You, uh, you feel perfectly normal?"

"Sure. Well?"

Kerry took out a cigarette. The console walked across the room, picking up a match book on the way, and politely held the flame. Then it went back to its place against the wall.

Fitzgerald didn't say anything. After a while he took a cigarette from his pocket and waited. Nothing happened.

"So?" Kerry asked.

"A robot. That's the only possible answer. Where in the name of Petrarch did you get it?"

"You don't seem much surprised."

"I am, though. But I've seen robots before—Westinghouse tried it, you know. Only this—" Fitzgerald tapped his teeth with a nail. "Who made it?"

"How the devil should I know?" Kerry demanded. "The radio people, I suppose."

Fitzgerald narrowed his eyes. "Wait a minute. I don't quite understand—"

"There's nothing to understand. I bought this combination a few days ago. Turned in the old one. It was delivered this afternoon, and—" Kerry explained what had happened.

"You mean you didn't know it was a robot?"

"Exactly. I bought it as a radio. And ... and ... the damn thing seems almost alive to me."

"Nope." Fitzgerald shook his head, rose, and inspected the console carefully. "It's a new kind of robot. At least—" He hesitated. "What else is there to think? I suggest you get in touch with the Mideastern people tomorrow and check up."

"Let's open the cabinet and look inside," Kerry suggested.

Fitzgerald was willing, but the experiment proved impossible. The presumably wooden panels weren't screwed into place, and there was no apparent way of opening the console. Kerry found a screwdriver and applied it, gingerly at first, then with a sort of repressed fury. He could neither pry free a panel nor even scratch the dark, smooth finish of the cabinet.

"Damn!" he said finally. "Well, your guess is as good as mine. It's a robot. Only I didn't know they could make 'em like this. And why in a radio?"

"Don't ask me," Fitzgerald shrugged. "Check up tomorrow. That's the first step. Naturally I'm pretty baffled. If a new sort of specialized robot has been invented, why put it in a console? And what makes those legs move? There aren't any casters."

"I've been wondering about that, too."

"When it moves, the legs look—rubbery. But they're not. They're hard as ... as hardwood. Or plastic.

"I'm afraid of the thing," Kerry said.

"Want to stay at my place tonight?"

"N-no. No. I guess not. The—robot—can't hurt me."

"I don't think it wants to. It's been helping you, hasn't it?"

"Yeah," Kerry said, and went off to mix another drink.

The rest of the conversation was inconclusive. Fitzgerald, several hours later, went home rather worried. He wasn't as casual as he had pretended, for the sake of Kerry's nerves. The

impingement of something so entirely unexpected on normal
life was subtly frightening. And yet, as he had said, the robot
didn't seem menacing—

Kerry went to bed, with a new detective mystery. The radio
followed him into the bedroom and gently took the book out of
his hand. Kerry instinctively snatched for it.

"Hey!" he said. "What the devil—"

The radio went back into the living room. Kerry followed, in
time to see the book replaced on the shelf. After a bit Kerry
retreated, locking his door, and slept uneasily till dawn.

In dressing gown and slippers, he stumbled out to stare at the
console. It was back in its former place, looking as though it had
never moved. Kerry, rather white around the gills, made breakfast.

He was allowed only one cup of coffee. The radio appeared,
reprovingly took the second cup from his hand, and emptied it
into the sink.

That was quite enough for Kerry Westerfield. He found his
hat and topcoat and almost ran out of the house. He had a horrid
feeling that the radio might follow him, but it didn't, luckily for
his sanity. He was beginning to be worried.

During the morning he found time to telephone Mideastern.
The salesman knew nothing. It was a standard model combination—the latest. If it wasn't giving satisfaction, of course, he'd
be glad to—

"It's O. K.," Kerry said. "But who made the thing? That's
what I want to find out."

"One moment, sir." There was a delay. "It came from Mr.
Lloyd's department. One of our foremen."

"Let me speak to him, please."

But Lloyd wasn't very helpful. After much thought, he
remembered that the combination had been placed in the stock
room without a serial number. It had been added later.

"But who *made* it?"

"I just don't know. I can find out for you, I guess. Suppose I
ring you back."

"Don't forget," Kerry said, and went back to his class. The lecture on the Venerable Bede wasn't too successful.

At lunch he saw Fitzgerald, who seemed relieved when Kerry came over to his table. "Find out any more about your pet robot?" the psychology professor demanded.

No one else was within hearing. With a sigh Kerry sat down and lit a cigarette. "Not a thing. It's a pleasure to be able to do this myself." He drew smoke into his lungs. "I phoned the company."

"And?"

"They don't know anything. Except that it didn't have a serial number."

"That may be significant," Fitzgerald said.

Kerry told the other about the incidents of the book and the coffee, and Fitzgerald squinted thoughtfully at his milk. "I've given you some psych tests. Too much stimulation isn't good for you."

"A detective yarn!"

"Carrying it a bit to extremes, I'll admit. But I can understand *why* the robot acted that way—though I dunno how it managed it." He hesitated. "Without intelligence, that is."

"Intelligence?" Kerry licked his lips. "I'm not so sure that it's just a machine. And I'm not crazy."

"No, you're not. But you say the robot was in the front room. How could it tell what you were reading?"

"Short of X-ray vision and superfast scanning and assimilative powers, I can't imagine. Perhaps it doesn't want me to read anything."

"You've said something," Fitzgerald grunted. "Know much about theoretical—machines—of that type?"

"Robots?"

"Purely theoretical. Your brain's a colloid, you know. Compact, complicated—but slow. Suppose you work out a gadget with a multimillion radioatom unit embedded in an insulating material—the result is a brain, Kerry. A brain with a tremendous number of units interacting at light-velocity speeds. A radio tube adjusts current flow when it's operating at forty million separate signals a second. And—theoretically—a radioatomic brain of the type I've mentioned could include perception, recognition, consideration, reaction and adjustment in a hundred-thousandth of a second."

"Theory."

"I've thought so. But I'd like to find out where your radio came from."

A page came over. "Telephone call for Mr. Westerfield."

Kerry excused himself and left. When he returned, there was a puzzled frown knitting his dark brows. Fitzgerald looked at him inquiringly.

"Guy named Lloyd, at the Mideastern plant. I was talking to him about the radio."

"Any luck?"

Kerry shook his head. "No. Well, not much. He didn't know who had built the thing."

"But it was built in the plant?"

"Yes. About two weeks ago—but there's no record of who worked on it. Lloyd seemed to think that was very, very funny. If a radio's built in the plant, they *know* who put it together."

"So?"

"So nothing. I asked him how to open the cabinet, and he said it was easy. Just unscrew the panel in back."

"There aren't any screws," Fitzgerald said.

"I know."

They looked at one another.

Fitzgerald said, "I'd give fifty bucks to find out whether that robot was really built only two weeks ago."

"Why?"

"Because a radioatomic brain would need training. Even in such matters as the lighting of a cigarette."

"It saw me light one."

"And followed the example. The dish-washing—hm-m-m. Induction, I suppose. If that gadget has been trained, it's a robot. If it hasn't—" Fitzgerald stopped.

Kerry blinked. "Yes?"

"I don't know what the devil it is. It bears the same relation to a robot that we bear to *eohippus*. One thing I do know, Kerry; it's very probable that no scientist today has the knowledge it would take to make a . . . a thing like that."

"You're arguing in circles," Kerry said. "It *was* made."

"Uh-huh. But how—when—and by whom? That's what's got me worried."

"Well, I've a class in five minutes. Why not come over tonight?"

"Can't. I'm lecturing at the Hall. I'll phone you after, though."

With a nod Kerry went out, trying to dismiss the matter from his mind. He succeeded pretty well. But dining alone in a restaurant that night, he began to feel a general unwillingness to go home. A hobgoblin was waiting for him.

"Brandy," he told the waiter. "Make it double."

Two hours later a taxi let Kerry out at his door. He was remarkably drunk. Things swam before his eyes. He walked unsteadily toward the porch, mounted the steps with exaggerated care, and let himself into the house.

He switched on a lamp.

The radio came forward to meet him. Tentacles, thin, but strong as metal, coiled gently around his body, holding him motionless. A pang of violent fear struck through Kerry. He struggled desperately and tried to yell, but his throat was dry.

From the radio panel a beam of yellow light shot out, blinding the man. It swung down, aimed at his chest. Abruptly a queer taste was perceptible under Kerry's tongue.

After a minute or so, the ray clicked out, the tentacles flashed back out of sight, and the console returned to its corner. Kerry staggered weakly to a chair and relaxed, gulping.

He was sober. Which was quite impossible. Fourteen brandies infiltrate a definite amount of alcohol into the system. One can't wave a magic wand and instantly reach a state of sobriety. Yet that was exactly what had happened.

The—robot—was trying to be helpful. Only Kerry would have preferred to remain drunk.

He got up gingerly and sidled past the radio to the bookshelf.

One eye on the combination, he took down the detective novel he had tried to read on the preceding night. As he had expected, the radio took it from his hand and replaced it on the shelf. Kerry, remembering Fitzgerald's words, glanced at his watch. Reaction time, four seconds.

He took down a Chaucer and waited, but the radio didn't stir. However, when Kerry found a history volume, it was gently removed from his fingers. Reaction time, six seconds.

Kerry located a history twice as thick.

Reaction time, ten seconds.

Uh-huh. So the robot did read the books. That meant X-ray vision and superswift reactions. Jumping Jehoshaphat!

Kerry tested more books, wondering what the criterion was. "Alice in Wonderland" was snatched from his hand; Millay's poems were not. He made a list, with two columns, for future reference.

The robot, then, was not merely a servant. It was a censor. But what was the standard of comparison?

After a while he remembered his lecture tomorrow, and thumbed through his notes. Several points needed verification. Rather hesitantly he located the necessary reference book—and the robot took it away from him.

"Wait a minute," Kerry said. "I *need* that." He tried to pull the volume out of the tentacle's grasp, without success. The console paid no attention. It calmly replaced the book on its shelf.

Kerry stood biting his lip. This was a bit too much. The damned robot was a monitor. He sidled toward the book, snatched it, and was out in the hall before the radio could move.

The thing was coming after him. He could hear the soft padding of its . . . its feet. Kerry scurried into the bedroom and locked the door. He waited, heart thumping, as the knob was tried gently.

A wire-thin cilia crept through the crack of the door and fumbled with the key. Kerry suddenly jumped forward and shoved the auxiliary bolt into position. But that didn't help, either. The robot's precision tools—the specialized antenna—slid it back; and then the console opened the door, walked into the room, and came toward Kerry.

He felt a touch of panic. With a little gasp he threw the book at the thing, and it caught it deftly. Apparently that was all that was wanted, for the radio turned and went out, rocking awkwardly on its rubbery legs, carrying the forbidden volume. Kerry cursed quietly.

The phone rang. It was Fitzgerald.

"Well? How'd you make out?"

"Have you got a copy of Cassen's 'Social Literature of the Ages'?"

"I don't think so—no. Why?"

"I'll get it in the University library tomorrow, then." Kerry explained what had happened. Fitzgerald whistled softly.

"Interfering, is it? Hm-m-m. I wonder—"

"I'm afraid of the thing."

"I don't think it means you any harm. You say it sobered you up?"

"Yeah. With a light ray. That isn't very logical."

"It might be. The vibrationary equivalent of thiamin chloride."

"Light?"

"There's vitamin content in sunlight, you know. That isn't the important point. It's censoring your reading—and apparently it reads the books, with superfast reactions. That gadget, whatever it is, isn't merely a robot."

"You're telling me," Kerry said grimly. "It's a Hitler."

Fitzgerald didn't laugh. Rather soberly, he suggested, "Suppose you spend the night at my place?"

"No," Kerry said, his voice stubborn. "No so-and-so radio's going to chase me out of my house. I'll take an ax to the thing first."

"We-ell—you know what you're doing, I suppose. Phone me if . . . if anything happens."

"O. K.," Kerry said, and hung up. He went into the living

room and eyed the radio coldly. What the devil was it—and what was it trying to do? Certainly it wasn't merely a robot. Equally certainly, it wasn't alive, in the sense that a colloid brain is alive.

Lips thinned, he went over and fiddled with the dials and switches. A swing band's throbbing, erratic tempo came from the console. He tried the short-wave band—nothing unusual there. So?

So nothing. There was no answer.

After a while he went to bed.

At luncheon the next day he brought Cassen's "Social Literature" to show Fitzgerald.

"What about it?"

"Look here." Kerry flipped the pages and indicated a passage. "Does this mean anything to you?"

Fitzgerald read it. "Yeah. The point seems to be that individualism is necessary for the production of literature. Right?"

Kerry looked at him. "I don't know."

"Eh?"

"My mind goes funny."

Fitzgerald rumpled his gray hair, narrowing his eyes and watching the other man intently. "Come again. I don't quite—"

With angry patience, Kerry said, "This morning I went into the library and looked up this reference. I read it all right. But it didn't mean anything to me. Just words. Know how it is when you're fagged out and have been reading a lot? You'll run into a sentence with a lot of subjunctive clauses, and it doesn't percolate. Well, it was like that."

"Read it now," Fitzgerald said quietly, thrusting the book across the table.

Kerry obeyed, looking up with a wry smile. "No good."

"Read it aloud. I'll go over it with you, step by step."

But that didn't help. Kerry seemed utterly unable to assimilate the sense of the passage.

"Semantic block, maybe," Fitzgerald said, scratching his ear. "Is this the first time it's happened?"

"Yes . . . no. I don't know."

"Got any classes this afternoon? Good. Let's run over to your place."

Kerry thrust away his plate. "All right. I'm not hungry. Whenever you're ready—"

Half an hour later they were looking at the radio. It seemed quite harmless. Fitzgerald wasted some time trying to pry a panel off, but finally gave it up as a bad job. He found pencil and paper, seated himself opposite Kerry, and began to ask questions.

At one point he paused. "You didn't mention that before."

"Forgot it, I guess."

Fitzgerald tapped his teeth with the pencil. "Hm-m-m. The first time the radio acted up—"

"It hit me in the eye with a blue light—"

"Not that. I mean—what it said."

Kerry blinked. "What *it* said?" He hesitated. " 'Psychology pattern checked and noted,' or something like that. I thought I'd tuned in on some station and got part of a quiz program or something. You mean—"

"Were the words easy to understand? Good English?"

"No, now that I remember it," Kerry scowled. "They were slurred quite a lot. Vowels stressed."

"Uh-huh. Well, let's get on." They tried a word-association test.

Finally Fitzgerald leaned back, frowning. "I want to check this stuff with the last tests I gave you a few months ago. It looks funny to me—damned funny. I'd feel a lot better if I knew exactly what memory was. We've done considerable work on memonics—artificial memory. Still, it may not be that at all."

"Eh?"

"That—machine. Either it's got an artificial memory, has been highly trained, or else it's adjusted to a different *milieu* and culture. It has affected you—quite a lot."

Kerry licked dry lips. "How?"

"Implanted blocks in your mind. I haven't correlated them

yet. When I do, we may be able to figure out some sort of answer. No, that thing isn't a robot. It's a lot more than that."

Kerry took out a cigarette; the console walked across the room and lit it for him. The two men watched with a faint shrinking horror.

"You'd better stay with me tonight," Fitzgerald suggested.

"No," Kerry said. He shivered.

The next day Fitzgerald looked for Kerry at lunch, but the younger man did not appear. He telephoned the house, and Martha answered the call.

"Hel*lo!* When did you get back?"

"Hello, Fitz. About an hour ago. My sister went ahead and had her baby without me—so I came back." She stopped, and Fitzgerald was alarmed at her tone.

"Where's Kerry?"

"He's here. Can you come over, Fitz? I'm worried."

"What's the matter with him?"

"I . . . I don't know. Come right away."

"O. K.," Fitzgerald said, and hung up, biting his lips. He was worried. When, a short while later, he rang the Westerfield bell, he discovered that his nerves were badly out of control. But sight of Martha reassured him.

He followed her into the living room. Fitzgerald's glance went at once to the console, which was unchanged; and then to Kerry, seated motionless by a window. Kerry's face had a blank, dazed look. His pupils were dilated, and he seemed to recognize Fitzgerald only slowly.

"Hello, Fitz," he said.

"How do you feel?"

Martha broke in. "Fitz, what's wrong? Is he sick? Shall I call the doctor?"

Fitzgerald sat down. "Have you noticed anything funny about that radio?"

"No. Why?"

"Then listen." He told the whole story, watching incredulity struggle with reluctant belief on Martha's face. Presently she said, "I can't quite—"

"If Kerry takes out a cigarette, the thing will light it for him. Want to see how it works?"

"N-no. Yes. I suppose so." Martha's eyes were wide.

Fitzgerald gave Kerry a cigarette. The expected happened.

Martha didn't say a word. When the console had returned to its place, she shivered and went over to Kerry. He looked at her vaguely.

"He needs a doctor, Fitz."

"Yes." Fitzgerald didn't mention that a doctor might be quite useless.

"What is that thing?"

"It's more than a robot. And it's been readjusting Kerry. I told you what's happened. When I checked Kerry's psychology patterns, I found that they'd altered. He's lost most of his initiative."

"Nobody on earth could have made that—"

Fitzgerald scowled. "I thought of that. It seems to be the product of a well-developed culture, quite different from ours. Martian, perhaps. It's such a specialized thing that it naturally fits into a complicated culture. But I *do not* understand why it looks exactly like a Mideastern console radio."

Martha touched Kerry's hand. "Camouflage?"

"But why? You were one of my best pupils in psych, Martha. Look at this logically. Imagine a civilization where a gadget like that has its place. Use inductive reasoning."

"I'm trying to. I can't think very well. Fitz, I'm worried about Kerry."

"I'm all right," Kerry said.

Fitzgerald put his fingertips together. "It isn't a radio so much as a monitor. In this other civilization, perhaps every man has one, or maybe only a few—the ones who need it. It keeps them in line."

"By destroying initiative?"

Fitzgerald made a helpless gesture. "I don't know! It worked

426 · HENRY KUTTNER

that way in Kerry's case. In others—I don't know."

Martha stood up. "I don't think we should talk any more. Kerry needs a doctor. After that we can decide upon that." She pointed to the console.

Fitzgerald said, "It'd be rather a shame to wreck it, but—" His look was significant.

The console moved. It came out from its corner with a sidling, rocking gait and walked toward Fitzgerald. As he sprang up, the whiplike tentacles flashed out and seized him. A pale ray shone into the man's eyes.

Almost instantly it vanished; the tentacles withdrew, and the radio returned to its place. Fitzgerald stood motionless. Martha was on her feet, one hand at her mouth.

"Fitz!" Her voice shook.

He hesitated. "Yes? What's the matter?"

"Are you hurt? What did it do to you?"

Fitzgerald frowned a little. "Eh? Hurt? I don't—"

"The radio. What did it do?"

He looked toward the console. "Something wrong with it? Afraid I'm not much of a repair man, Martha."

"Fitz." She came forward and gripped his arm. "Listen to me." Quick words spilled from her mouth. The radio. Kerry. Their discussion—

Fitzgerald looked at her blankly, as though he didn't quite understand. "I guess I'm stupid today. I can't quite understand what you're talking about."

"The radio—you know! You said it changed Kerry—" Martha paused, staring at the man.

Fitzgerald was definitely puzzled. Martha was acting strangely. Queer! He'd always considered her a pretty level-headed girl. But now she was talking nonsense. At least, he couldn't figure out the meaning of her words—there was no sense to them.

And why was she talking about the radio? Wasn't it satisfactory? Kerry had said it was a good buy, with a fine tone and the latest gadgets in it. Fitzgerald wondered, for a fleeting second, if Martha had gone crazy.

In any case, he was late for his class. He said so. Martha didn't try to stop him when he went out. She was pale as chalk.

Kerry took out a cigarette. The radio walked over and held a match.

"*Kerry!*"

"Yes, Martha?" His voice was dead.

She stared at the ... the radio. Mars? Another world—another civilization? What was it? What did it want? *What was it trying to do?*

Martha let herself out of the house and went to the garage. When she returned, a small hatchet was gripped tightly in her hand.

Kerry watched. He saw Martha walk over to the radio and lift the hatchet. Then a beam of light shot out, and Martha vanished. A little dust floated up in the afternoon sunlight.

"Destruction of life-form threatening attack," the radio said, slurring the words together.

Kerry's brain turned over. He felt sick, dazed and horribly empty. Martha—

His mind—churned. Instinct and emotion fought with something that smothered them. Abruptly the dams crumbled, and the blocks were gone, the barriers down. Kerry cried out hoarsely, inarticulately, and sprang to his feet.

"*Martha!*" he yelled.

She was gone. Kerry looked around. Where—

What had happened? He couldn't remember.

He sat down in the chair again, rubbing his forehead. His free hand brought up a cigarette, an automatic reaction that brought instant response. The radio walked forward and held a lighted match ready.

Kerry made a choking, sick sound and flung himself out of the chair. He remembered now. He picked up the hatchet and sprang toward the console, teeth bared in a mirthless rictus.

Again the light beam flashed out.

Kerry vanished. The hatchet thudded onto the carpet.

The radio walked back to its place and stood motionless once

428 · HENRY KUTTNER

more. A faint clicking proceeded from its radioatomic brain.

"Subject basically unsuitable," it said, after a moment. "Elimination has been necessary." *Click!* "Preparation for next subject completed."

Click.

"We'll take it," the boy said.

"You won't be making a mistake," smiled the rental agent. "It's quiet, isolated, and the price is quite reasonable."

"Not so very," the girl put in. "But it *is* just what we've been looking for."

The agent shrugged. "Of course an unfurnished place would run less. But—"

"We haven't been married long enough to get any furniture," the boy grinned. He put an arm around his wife. "Like it, hon?"

"Hm-m-m. Who lived here before?"

The agent scratched his cheek. "Let's see. Some people named Westerfield, I think. It was given to me for listing just about a week ago. Nice place. If I didn't own my own house, I'd jump at it myself."

"Nice radio," the boy said. "Late model, isn't it?" He went over to examine the console.

"Come along," the girl urged. "Let's look at the kitchen again."

"O. K., hon."

They went out of the room. From the hall came the sound of the agent's smooth voice, growing fainter. Warm afternoon sunlight slanted through the windows.

For a moment there was silence. Then—

Click!

STORM WARNING

Donald A. Wollheim

By the end of 1942, science fiction's Golden Age was losing some of its luster because the war had taken away many of the young writers whose innovations had brought excitement to the field. But new talents were coming forth to fill the gap: Kuttner and Moore were at the forefront with their work in *Astounding,* and there were also signs of wonders to come in other magazines, primarily those edited by Robert W. Lowndes, Frederik Pohl and Donald A. Wollheim. In magazines with such esthetic titles as *Stirring Science Stories, Astonishing Stories* and *Future Fantasy combined with Science Fiction,* they published the first stories of Ray Bradbury, Wilson Tucker, C. M. Kornbluth, James Blish, Richard Wilson, Damon Knight—and the work of Lowndes, Pohl and Wollheim themselves.

Wollheim wasn't actually a "new" writer then; he'd published his first story as long ago as 1933, when *Wonder Stories* printed "The Man from Ariel," Wollheim's first story, written when he was nineteen or twenty. *Wonder,* however, neglected to pay Wollheim for the story despite repeated reminders; eventually Wollheim began writing to other authors whose stories had been published in the magazine, and discovered several who hadn't been paid—including one writer who wasn't even aware that his story had been published. Wollheim and three others hired a lawyer and sued the publisher, Hugo Gernsback; the result was a settlement out of court by which Gernsback paid the four authors the grand sum of seventy-five dollars, in installments, of which the lawyer collected ten dollars.

In 1935, Wollheim wrote another story and submitted it to *Wonder* under a pen name, using a friend's address; he wanted to find out if Gernsback would publish that one too without paying for it, and Gernsback did.

(The 1930s are frequently referred to in science fiction history as a time when the magazines paid "half a cent a word, on lawsuit." *Wonder Stories* was not the only offender.)

Wollheim, the son of a doctor, had been an avid reader of science fiction since 1927, when, on the last day before graduation from grammar school—"that slack day when one still reports to school, but lessons are over and pupils sit around a classroom killing a couple of hours until allowed to go home"—another student handed him a copy of *Amazing Stories.* "I think you'll like this," said his classmate, and he was certainly right; for years thereafter Wollheim read nothing but science fiction, except for schoolwork. Once he had "sold" his first story he realized that "science fiction was not to be just a reading hobby but also a life interest."

He became involved in the science fiction fan clubs of the 1930s and took part in early experiments with rockets; in September 1935 he assisted William Sykora in an attempt to deliver mail via rocket. "The rocket flew up about a couple hundred feet and then blew up, scattering letters in all directions, and also putting a hunk of steel through the arm of one little boy, a bystander," he told Damon Knight. "Will was arrested because of that and charged with manufacturing and transporting explosives in New York City without a license; he was duly fined."

A prolific contributor to sf fan magazines, Wollheim soon began to proselytize for Communism, whose ideas attracted so many of the intellectuals of the late Depression years; he wrote that "science fiction followers should actively work for the realization of the scientific socialist world-state as the only genuine justification for their activities and existence." By 1940, he had switched his interest to Technocracy, but this didn't last either. Currently he describes himself as "a disillusioned idealist, a latter-day cynic," adding, however, that "I have continued to retain my faith in humanity and in the future."

His friends of this period, who called themselves "Futurians," were all interested to varying degrees in political applications of sf's utopian visions. Richard Wilson attended some "Communist front" meetings, but he came from a Republican family and felt that the socialist cause "had nothing to do with me"; Frederik Pohl went to a meeting of the Flatbush Young Communist League and joined so that he could edit their mimeographed newsletter, since "that was my main interest—putting out fan magazines." Damon Knight, who moved to New York City in 1941, remembers the Futurians as young Bohemians with a great interest in avoiding work, so they usually stayed out of any activist political parties. "They showed their solidarity, however, by going to Russian movies occasionally and by listening intently to Shostakovich."

The one Futurian who seemed most committed to Communism was John B. Michel, who published a score of mediocre sf stories under pen names. It was Michel, in a story about a scientist seeking a loan to finance a new invention, who wrote the following description of a town banker: "He blinked his small piggish eyes rapidly and fiddled with the gold watch chain strung from the pockets of his vest."

The Futurians lived in various communal apartments and wrote reams of science fiction. (Damon Knight counts 129 Futurian-written stories by the end of 1942.) Many or most of these were published under pen names, often because they were collaborations between housemates. One of the pen names used was "Ivar Towers," which was taken from their name for one of the Futurian apartments, "The Ivory Tower."

In 1941, they formed "The Cabal," a group of writers who met once a week to read and criticize each other's latest stories. "Politeness was observed mostly in the breach," remembers Lowndes; ". . . stories which the Cabal unanimously agreed were ready for submission were turned over to me [as the Futurians' literary agent]. Considering all the circumstances . . . Cabal stories did not do too badly."

These circumstances included the fact that three of the Futurians were editors of science fiction magazines. Virtually all of the Futurians' stories were published by Pohl, Lowndes or Wollheim. Despite the number of inner- or outer-circle Futurians who went on to become accomplished writers, only Wollheim managed to sell any stories (two) to John Campbell. (Pohl sold two stories to Campbell, but they were rewrites of stories by a physicist friend, Milton Rothman.)

The least likely "failure" among the Futurians was Cyril M. Kornbluth, who wrote such famous fantasy stories as "Thirteen O'Clock" and "The Words of Guru" and became, under nine pen names, the most prolific and popular of the Futurian writers—yet he was unable to sell to Campbell during this period. He was still in his teens, cocky and precocious; there was a story in his family about the time a stranger cooed over him in his baby carriage and he remarked, "Madam, I am not the child you think me." He displayed the same aggressiveness when Pohl took him to meet Campbell. He was deliberately rude throughout the interview, explaining later, "I wanted to make sure he remembered me." Presumably Campbell did.

If Kornbluth was the *enfant terrible* of the Futurians, Wollheim was their Wise Old Man. He was in his late twenties, a veteran of ten years in science fiction and the editor of *Stirring Science Stories* and *Cosmic Stories.* Though these had been launched on a shoestring and paid no money for stories, Wollheim managed to make them superior to most of the paying magazines. (Knight still feels he was "a brilliant magazine editor.") Wollheim also stood out as an author, selling about forty stories during this period under his own name and half a dozen pen names.

"Storm Warning" originally appeared under the name "Millard Verne Gordon"—the pseudonym Wollheim had used in 1935 to test *Wonder Stories'* payment policy after his lawsuit against the magazine. It was published in *Future Fantasy and Science Fiction,* October 1942, edited by Robert W. Lowndes.

Wollheim says he wrote the story while in the grip of admiration for George R. Stewart's novel *Storm*—"an instance of imitation being the sincerest form of flattery." But the story has more of Wollheim than Stewart in it, displaying a strongly science fictional view of what would otherwise be a commonplace occurrence. "I have a very critical attitude toward reality," says Wollheim. "I am not sure anyone really knows what it is." In "Storm Warning" he presented an eerie reality in matter-of-fact prose that made it seem strangely believable.

Wollheim is seldom remembered as a writer, not only because he published so many of his stories under pen names but also because of his remarkable career as editor of Ace Books and, currently, his own imprint, DAW Books. But "Storm Warning" stands as evidence that he could have become equally famous as an author.

REFERENCES:

The Futurians by Damon Knight. Thomas Y. Crowell, 1977.
The Immortal Storm by Sam Moskowitz. The Atlanta Science Fiction Organization Press, 1954.
All Our Yesterdays by Harry Warner. Advent:Publishers, 1969.
The Universe Makers by Donald A. Wollheim. Harper & Row, 1971.
Donald A. Wollheim in *Novae Terrae,* January 1938.
Donald A. Wollheim in *Fantasy Digest,* March-April 1940.
"When Half-Worlds Meet" by "Hugh Raymond" (John B. Michel). *Cosmic Stories,* July 1941.
"Knight Piece" by Damon Knight. *Hell's Cartographers.* Weidenfeld and Nicolson, 1975.
"It Is Written . . ." by Robert A. W. Lowndes. *Magazine of Horror,* September 1968.
The Early Pohl by Frederik Pohl. Doubleday, 1976.
Letter from Donald A. Wollheim, April 11, 1975.
Letter from Damon Knight, April 7, 1976.
Two Dozen Dragon Eggs by Donald A. Wollheim. Powell Publications, 1969.

* * *

We had no indication of the odd business that was going to happen. The boys at the Weather Bureau still think they had all the fun. They think that being out in it wasn't as good as sitting in the station watching it all come about. Only there's some things they'll never understand about the weather, some things I think Ed and I alone will know. We were in the middle of it all.

We were riding out of Rock Springs at sunrise on a three-day leave but the Chief Meteorologist had asked us to take the night shift until then. It was just as well for the Bureau was on the edge of the desert and we had our duffel and horses tethered outside. The meteor fall of two days before came as a marvelous excuse to go out into the bad lands of the Great Divide Basin. I've always liked to ride out in the glorious wide empty Wyoming land and any excuse to spend three days out there was good.

Free also from the routine and monotony of the Weather Bureau as well. Of course I like the work, but still the open air and the open spaces must be bred in the blood of all of us born and raised out there in the West. I know it's tame and civilized today but even so, to jog along with a haphazard sort of prospector's aim was really fine.

Aim was of course to try and locate fragments of the big meteor that landed out there two nights before. Lots of people had seen it, myself for one, because I happened to be out on the roof taking readings. There had been a brilliant streak of blue-white across the northern sky and a sharp flash way off like an explosion. I understand that folks in Superior claim to have felt a jolt as if something big had smashed up out there in the trackless dust and dunes between Mud Lake, Morrow Creek and the town. That's quite a lot of empty territory and Ed and I had about as much chance of finding the meteor as the well-known needle in the haystack. But it was a swell excuse.

"Cold Front coming down from Saskatchewan," the Chief said as he came in and looked over our charts. We were getting ready to leave. "Unusual for this time of year."

I nodded, unworried. We had the mountains between us and any cold wave from that direction. We wouldn't freeze at night even if the cold got down as far as Casper, which would be highly unlikely. The Chief was bending low over the map tracing out the various lows and highs. He frowned a bit when he came to a new little low I had traced in from the first reports of that day.

"An unreported low turning up just off Washington State.

That's really odd. Since when are storms originating so close?"

"Coming east too and growing, according to Seattle's wire," said Ed. The Chief sat down and stared at the map.

"I don't like it, it's all out of wack," he said. Then he stood up and held out his hand to me.

"Well, good-bye boys and have a good time. If you find that meteor, bring me back a chunk too."

"Sure will," I said and we shook hands and yelled at the other boys and went out.

The first rays of the sun were just coming up as we left. Outwards we jogged easily, the town and civilization fell behind rapidly and we went on into the golden glow of the Sweetwater basin.

We made good time that day though we didn't hurry. We kept up a nice steady trot, resting now and then. We didn't talk much for we were too busy just breathing in the clean open air and enjoying the sensation of freedom. An occasional desert toad or the flash of a disturbed snake were the only signs of life we saw and the multiform shapes of the cactus and sage our only garden. It was enough.

Towards evening at the bureau, the Chief first noted the slight growth of the Southern Warm Front. A report from Utah set him buzzing. The Cold Front had now reached the borders of Wyoming and was still moving on. The baby storm that was born where it had no right to be born was still growing and now occupied a large area over Oregon and Idaho. The Chief was heard to remark that the conjunction of things seemed to place southwest Wyoming as a possible center of lots of wild weather. He started worrying a bit about us too.

We didn't worry. We didn't have any real indications but our weather men's senses acted aright. We felt a sort of odd expectancy in the air as we camped. Nothing definite, a sort of extra stillness in the air as if forces were pressing from all sides, forces that were still far away and still vague.

We spoke a bit around the fire about the storm that the Chief had noted when we left. Ed thought it would fizzle out. I think

I had a feeling then that it wasn't just a short-lived freak. I think I had an idea we might see something of it.

Next morning there was just the faintest trace of extra chill in the air. I'm used to Wyoming mornings and I know just how cold it ought to be at sunrise and how hot. This morning it was just the slightest bit colder.

"That Canadian Cold Front must have reaached the other side of the mountains," I said, waving towards the great rampart of the Rockies to the East. "We're probably feeling the only tendril of it to get over."

"That's sort of odd," Ed said. "There shouldn't be any getting over at all. It must be a very powerful front."

I nodded and wondered what the boys in the bureau were getting on it. Probably snowfall in the northern part of the state. If I had known what the Chief knew that morning, I might have started back in a hurry. But neither of us did and I guess we saw something that no one else has as a result.

For at the bureau, the Chief knew that morning that we were in for some extraordinary weather. He predicted for the Rock Springs paper the wildest storm ever. You see the Southern Warm Front had definitely gotten a salient through by that time. It was already giving Salt Lake City one of the hottest days on record and what was more the warm wave was coming our way steadily.

The next thing was that storm from the west. It was growing smaller and tighter again and had passed over Idaho Falls two hours ago raging and squawling. It was heading in our direction like an arrow from a bow.

And finally the Cold Front had done the impossible. It was beginning to sweep over the heights and to swoop down into the Divide basin, heading straight for the Warm Front coming north.

And there was Ed and I with a premonition and nothing more. We were riding along right into the conflux of the whole mess and we were looking for meteors. We were looking for what we expected to be some big craters or pock marks in the ground and a bunch of pitted iron rocks scattered around a vicinity of several miles.

Towards ten that morning we came over a slight rise and dipped down into a bowl-shaped region. I stopped and stared around. Ed wheeled and came back.

"What's up?" he asked.

"Notice anything funny in the air?" I asked and gave a deep sniff.

Ed drew in some sharp breaths and stared around.

"Sort of odd," he finally admitted. "Nothing I can place but it's sort of odd."

"Yes," I answered. "Odd is the word. I can't place anything wrong but it seems to smell differently than the air did a few minutes ago." I stared around and wrinkled my brow.

"I think I know now," I finally said. "The temperature's changed somewhat. It's warmer."

Ed frowned. "Colder, I'd say."

I became puzzled. I waved my hands through the air a bit. "I think you're right, I must be wrong. Now it feels a bit colder."

Ed walked his horse a bit. I started slowly after him.

"Y'know," I finally said, "I think I've got it. It's colder but it *smells* like warm air. I don't know if you can quite understand what I'm driving at. It smells as if the temperature should be steaming yet actually it's sort of chilly. It doesn't smell natural."

Ed nodded. He was puzzled and so was I. There was something wrong here. Something that got on our nerves.

Far ahead I saw something sparkle. I stared as we rode and then mentioned it to Ed. He looked too.

There was something, no, several things far off at the edge of the bowl near the next rise that glistened. They looked like bits of glass.

"The meteor, maybe?" queried Ed. I shrugged. We rode steadily on in that direction.

"Say something smells funny here," Ed remarked, stopping again.

I came up next to him. He was right. The sense of strangeness in the air had increased the nearer we got to the glistening things. It was still the same—warm-cold. There was something else again. Something like vegetation in the air. Like something growing only there still wasn't any more growth than the usual cacti and sage. It smelled differently from any other growing things and yet it smelled like vegetation.

It was unearthly that air. I can't describe it any other way. It was unearthly. Plant smells that couldn't come from any plant or forest I ever encountered, a cold warmness unlike anything that meteorology records.

Yet it wasn't bad, it wasn't frightening. It was just peculiar. It was mystifying.

We could see the sparkling things now. They were like bubbles of glass. Big iridescent glassy balls lying like some giant child's marbles on the desert.

We knew then that, if they were the meteors, they were like none that had ever been recorded before. We knew we had made a find that would go on record and yet we weren't elated. We were ill at ease. It was the funny weather that did it.

I noticed then for the first time that there were black clouds beginning to show far in the west. It was the first wave of the storm.

We rode nearer the strange bubbles. We would see them clearly now. They seemed cracked a bit as if they had broken. One had a gaping hole in its side. It must have been hollow, just a glassy shell.

Ed and I stopped short at the same time. Or rather our horses did. We were willing too but our mounts got the idea just as quickly. It was the smell.

There was a new odor in the air. A sudden one. It had just that instant wafted itself across our nostrils. It was at first repelling. That's why we stopped. But sniffing it a bit took a little of the repulsion away. It wasn't so very awful.

In fact it wasn't actually bad. It was hard to describe. Not exactly like anything I've ever smelled before. Vaguely it was acrid and vaguely it was dry. Mostly I would say that it smelled like a curious mixture of burning rubber and zinc ointment.

It grew stronger as we sat there and then it began to die away a bit as a slight breeze moved it on. We both got the impression at the same time that it had come from the broken glass bubbles.

We rode on cautiously.

"Maybe the meteors landed in an alkali pool and there's been some chemical reaction going on," I opined to Ed. "Could be," he said and we rode nearer.

The black clouds were piling up now in the west and a faint breeze began to stir. Ed and I dismounted to look into the odd meteors.

"Looks like we better get under cover till it blows over," he remarked.

"We've got a few minutes, I think," I replied. "Besides by the rise right here is just about the best cover around."

Back at the Weather Station, the temperature was rising steadily and the Chief was getting everything battened down. The storm was coming next and meeting the thin edge of the Warm Front wedge which was now passing Rock Springs would create havoc. Then the cold wave might get that far because it was over the divide and heading for the other two. In a few minutes all hell would break lose. The Chief wondered where we were.

We were looking into the hole in the nearest bubble. The things, they must have been the meteors we were looking for, were about twelve feet in diameter and pretty nearly perfect spheres. They were thick shelled and smooth and very glassy and iridescent and like mother-of-pearl on the inside. They were quite hollow and we couldn't figure out what they were made of and what they could be. Nothing I had read or learned could explain the things. That they were meteoric in origin I was sure because there was the evidence of the scattered ground and broken rocks about to show the impact. Yet they must have been terrifically strong or something because, save for the few cracks and the hole in one, they were intact.

Inside they stank of that rubber-zinc smell. It was powerful. Very powerful.

The stink had obviously come from the bubbles—there was no pool around.

It suddenly occurred to me that we had breathed air of some other world. For if these things were meteoric and the smell had come from the inside, then it was no air of Earth that smelled like burning rubber and zinc ointment. It was the air of somewhere, I don't know where, somewhere out among the endless reaches of the stars. *Somewhere out there*, out beyond the sun.

Another thought occurred to me.

"Do you think these things could have carried some creatures?" I asked. Ed stared at me awhile, bit his lip, looked slowly around. He shrugged his shoulders without saying anything.

"The oddness of the air," I went on, "maybe it was like the air of some other world. Maybe they were trying to make our own air more breathable to them?"

Ed didn't answer that one either. It didn't require any. And he didn't ask me who I meant by "they."

"And what makes the stink?" Ed finally commented. This time I shrugged.

Around us the smell waxed and waned. As if breezes were playing with a stream of noxious vapor. And yet, I suddenly realized, no breezes were blowing. The air was quite still. But still the smell grew stronger at one moment and weaker at another.

It was as if some creature were moving silently about leaving no trace of itself save its scent.

"Look!" said Ed suddenly. He pointed to the west. I looked and stared at the sky. The whole west was a mass of seething dark clouds. But it was a curiously arrested mass. There was a sharply defined edge to the area—an edge of blue against which the black clouds piled in vain and we could see lightnings crackle and flash in the storm. Yet no wind reached us and no thunder and the sky was serene and blue overhead.

It looked as if the storm had come up against a solid obstacle beyond which it could go no further. But there was no such obstacle visible.

As a meteorologist I knew that meant there must be a powerful opposing bank of air shielding us. We could not see it for air is invisible but it must be there straining against the cloud bank.

I noticed now that a pressure was growing in my ears. Something was concentrating around this area. We were in for it if the forces of the air ever broke through.

The stink welled up powerfully suddenly. More so than it had before. It seemed to pass by us and through us and around us. Then again it was gone. It almost vanished from everything. We could detect but the faintest traces of it after that passage.

Ed and I rode out to an outcropping of rock. We dismounted. We got well under the rock and we waited. It wouldn't be long before the protecting air bank gave way.

To the south now storm clouds materialized and then finally to the east and north. As I learned later the cold wave had eddied around us and met the Equatorial Front at last and now we were huddled with some inexplicable globes from unknown space and a bunch of strange stinks and atmosphere, ringed around by a seething raging sea of storm. And yet above, the sky was still blue and clear.

We were in the midst of a dead center, in the midst of an inexplicable high pressure area, most of whose air did not originate on Earth and the powers of the Earth's atmosphere were hurling themselves against us from every direction.

I saw that the area of clear was slowly but surely contracting. A lancing freezing breeze suddenly enveloped us. A breakthrough from the north. But it seemed to become curiously blunted and broken up by countless thrusts of the oddly reeking air. I realized as the jet of cold air reached my lungs how different the atmosphere was in this pocket from that we are accustomed to breathe. It was truly alien.

And yet always this strange air seemed to resist the advances of the normal. Another slight breeze, this one wet and warm, came in from the south and again a whirl of the rubbery-odored wind dispersed it.

Then there came an intolerable moment. A moment of terrific compression and rise and the black storm clouds tore through in wild streaks overhead and spiderwebbed the sky rapidly into total darkness. The area of peace became narrow, restricted, enclosed by walls of lightning-shot storm.

I got an odd impression then. That we were embattled. That the forces of nature were determined to annihilate and utterly rip apart our little region of invading alien air, that the meteor gases were determined to resist to the last, determined to keep their curious *stinks* intact!

The lightning flashed and flashed. Endless giant bolts, yet always outside our region. And we heard them only when a lance of cold or hot storm pierced through to us. The alien air clearly would not transmit the sounds, it was standing rigid against the interrupting vibrations!

Ed and I have conferred since then. We both agree that we had the same impressions. That a genuine life and death fight was going on. That that pocket of other-worldly air seemed to be consciously fighting to keep itself from being absorbed by the storm, from being diffused to total destruction so that no atom of the unearthly gases could exist save as incredibly rare elements in the total atmosphere of the Earth. It seemed to be trying to maintain its entirety, its identity.

It was in that last period that Ed and I saw the inexplicable things. We saw the things that don't make sense. For we saw part of the clear area suddenly contract as if some of the defending force had been withdrawn and we saw suddenly one of the glass globes, one of the least cracked, whirl up from the ground and rush into the storm, rush straight up!

It was moving through the clear air without any visible propulsion. We thought then that perhaps a jet of the storm had pierced through to carry it up as a ball will ride on a jet of water. But no, for the globe hurled itself into the storm, contrary to the direction of the winds, against the forces of the storm.

The globe was trying to break through the ceiling of black to the clear air above. But the constant lightnings that flickered around it kept it in our sight. Again and again it darted against the mass of clouds and was hurled wildly and furiously about. For a moment we thought it would force its way out of our sight and then there was a sudden flash and a sharp snap that even we heard and a few fragments of glassy stuff came falling down.

I realized suddenly that the storm had actually abated its fury while this strange thing was going on. As if the very elements themselves watched the outcome of the ball's flight. And now the storm raged in again with renewed vigor as if triumphant.

The area was definitely being forced back. Soon not more than twenty yards separated us from the front and we could hear the dull endless rumbling of the thunder. The stink was back again and all around us. Tiny trickles of cold wet air broke through now and then but were still being lost in the smell.

Then came the last moment. A sort of terrible crescendo in the storm and the stink finally broke for good. I saw it and what I saw is inexplicable save for a very fantastic hypothesis which I believe only because I must.

And after that revealing moment the last shreds of the stellar air broke for good. For only a brief instant more the storm raged, an instant in which for the first and last time Ed and I got soaked and hurled around by the wind and rain and the horses almost broke their tether. Then it was over.

The dark clouds lifted rapidly. In a few minutes they had incredibly thinned out, there was a slight rain, and by the time ten more minutes had passed, the sun was shining, the sky was blue and things were almost dry. On the northern horizon faint shreds of cloud lingered but that was all.

Of the meteor globes only a few shards and splinters remained.

I've talked the matter over, as I said, and there is no really acceptable answer to the whole curious business. We know that we don't really know very much about things. As a meteorologist I can tell you that. Why we've been discussing the weather

from caveman days and yet it was not more than twenty years
ago that the theory of weather fronts was formulated which first
allowed really decent predictions. And the theory of fronts,
which is what we modern weather people use, has lots of imperfections in it. For instance we still don't know anything about
the why of things. Why does a storm form at all? We know how
it grows, sure, but why did it start and how?

We don't know. We don't know very much at all. We breathe
this air and it was only in the last century that we first began
to find out how many different elements and gases made it up
and we don't know for sure yet.

I think it's possible that living things may exist that are made
of gas only. We're protoplasm, you know, but do you know that
we're not solid matter—we're liquid? Protoplasm is liquid.
Flesh is liquid arranged in suspension in cells of dead substances. And most of us is water and water is the origin of all life.
And water is composed of two common gases, hydrogen and
oxygen. And those gases are found everywhere in the universe,
astronomers say.

So I say that if the elements of our life can be boiled down to
gases, then why can't gases combine as gases and still have the
elements of life? Water is always present in the atmosphere as
vapor, then why not a life as a sort of water vapor variant?

I think it makes sense. I think it might smell odd if we accidentally inhaled such a vapor life. Because we could inhale it
like we do water vapor. It might smell, say for example, like
burning rubber and zinc ointment.

Because in that last moment when the storm was at its height
and the area of unearthly air was compressed to its smallest I
noticed that at one point a definite outline could be seen against
the black clouds and the blue-white glare of the lightning. A
section of the smelly air had been sort of trapped and pinned
off from the main section. And it had a definite shape under that
terrible storm pressure.

I can't say what it was like because it wasn't exactly like
anything save maybe a great amoeba being pushed down

against the ground. There were lots of arms and stubby wiggly things sticking out and the main mass was squashy and thick. And it flowed along the ground sort of like a snail. It seemed to be writhing and trying to slither away and spread out.

It couldn't because the storm was hammering at it. And I definitely saw a big black mass, round like a fist, hammer at one section of the thing's base as it tried to spread out.

Then the storm smashed down hard on the odd outline and it squashed out flat and was gone.

I imagine there were others and I think that when they aren't being compressed they could have spread out naturally about a hundred yards along the ground and upwards. And I think we have things like that only of Earthly origin right in the atmosphere now. And I don't think that our breathing and walking and living right through them means a thing to them at all. But they objected to the invaders from space. They smelled differently, they were different, they must have come from a different sort of planet, a planet cooler than ours with deserts and vegetation different from our own. And they would have tried to remake our atmosphere into one of their own. And our native air-dwellers stopped them.

That's what I think.